"*If* you thought the true gothic novel died with the nineteenth century, this will change your mind. [*The Shadow of the Wind*] is the real deal, a novel full of cheesy splendor and creaking trapdoors, a novel where even the subplots have subplots. . . . This is one gorgeous read." —Stephen King

"*Gabriel* García Márquez meets Umberto Eco meets Jorge Luis Borges for a sprawling magic show, exasperatingly tricky, and mostly wonderful by the Spanish novelist Carlos Ruiz Zafón. . . . His novel eddies in currents of passion, revenge, and mysteries whose layers peel away onionlike yet persist in growing back. At times these mysteries take on the aspect of the supernatural. The figures appear beleaguered by ghosts until these give way to something even more frightening: the creak of real floors undermined by real rot and the inexorability of human destinies grimmer than any ghostly one could be. . . . [W]e are taken on a wild ride that executes its hairpin bends with breathtaking lurches." —*The New York Times Book Review*

"*Once* again I have encountered a book that proves how wonderful it is to become immersed in a rich, long novel . . . This novel has it all: seduction, danger, revenge, and a mystery that the author teases with mastery. Zafón has outdone even the mighty Charles Dickens." —*The Philadelphia Inquirer*

"What is outstanding is the metaphysical concept of books that assume a life of their own . . . even the plot and characters of Carax's fictitious work are interwoven into this meticulously crafted mosaic." —*Library Journal*

"*The Shadow of the Wind* is a dazzling novel about the power that one book can exert over the right reader, a remarkable debut from a young Spanish writer. . . . [It] is one of those lovely books, like A. S. Byatt's *Possession*, that celebrates the strong bond between reader and book, while showing us how elusive the truth of literature can be. Read it and be lost in the shadowy world of Julián Carax and his devotees; you'll be thinking what book you might save for posterity one day." —*The Times-Picayune*

"Part detective story, part boy's adventure, part romance, fantasy, and gothic horror, the intricate plot is urged on by extravagant foreshadowing and nail-nibbling tension. This is rich, lavish storytelling, very much in the tradition of Ross King's *Ex Libris*." —*Booklist*

"The plot is labyrinthine, the characters and coincidences Dickensian, the whole echoing with literary flourishes and references. It's a bit like A. S. Byatt's *Possession* and Arturo Pérez-Reverte's *The Club Dumas*, with touches of Jorge Luis Borges, Umberto Eco, Ross King, Charles Palliser, and Gabriel García Márquez. Bibliophiles will feast on its riches." —*Orlando Sentinel*

"Zafón takes readers on an obsessive journey into a dark world, revealing the stories behind one boy's curiosity and the strange, brutal truth that comes with it." —*The Good Book Guide*, named as Editor's Choice

"A potent mix: a coming-of-age story set in Barcelona's post-war years, an edge of fantasy, a tragic love story, and a labyrinth of mystery surrounding a writer whose work has been systematically destroyed." —Benedicte Page, *Bookseller*

"For the bibliophiles there can be few more enticing-sounding places than the 'Cemetery of Forgotten Books.'. . . *The Shadow of the Wind* has been a publishing phenomenon in Spain and throughout Europe. It is safe to assume that the English translation of the book will also become a bestseller and there can be no doubt that it deserves to do so. Combining all the best elements of crime fiction with an investigation of the power of literature to shape our lives and imaginations, it is one of the most original and compelling stories of the past decade."

— *Waterstone's Quarterly*

"Before everything else, Carlos Ruiz Zafón's European bestseller is a book about a mysterious book and its even more mysterious author. Try to imagine a blend of Grand Guignol thriller, historical fiction, occasional farce, existential mystery, and passionate love story; then double it. If that's too hard to do, let me put it another way: if you love A. S. Byatt's *Possession*, García Márquez's *One Hundred Years of Solitude*, the short stories of Borges, Umberto Eco's *The Name of the Rose*, Arturo Pérez-Reverte's *The Club Dumas*, or Paul Auster's New York trilogy, not to mention Victor Hugo's *Hunchback of Notre Dame* and William Hjortsberg's *Falling Angel*, then you will love *The Shadow of the Wind*. . . . [A]nyone who enjoys novels that are scary, erotic, touching, tragic, and thrilling should rush right out to the nearest bookstore and pick up *The Shadow of the Wind*. Really, you should."

— Michael Dirda, *The Washington Post*

ABOUT THE AUTHOR

CARLOS RUIZ ZAFÓN, author of *The Shadow of the Wind* and *The Angel's Game*, among other novels, is one of the world's most read and best-loved writers. His work has been translated into more than forty languages and published around the world, garnering numerous international prizes and reaching millions of readers. He divides his time between Barcelona and Los Angeles.

LUCIA GRAVES is the author and translator of many works and has overseen Spanish-language editions of the poetry of her father, Robert Graves.

The
Shadow
of the Wind

CARLOS RUIZ ZAFÓN

Translated by Lucia Graves

PENGUIN BOOKS

PENGUIN BOOKS

Published by the Penguin Group

Penguin Group (USA) Inc., 375 Hudson Street, New York, New York 10014, U.S.A.
Penguin Group (Canada), 90 Eglinton Avenue East, Suite 700, Toronto,
Ontario, Canada M4P 2Y3 (a division of Pearson Penguin Canada Inc.)
Penguin Books Ltd, 80 Strand, London WC2R 0RL, England
Penguin Ireland, 25 St Stephen's Green, Dublin 2, Ireland (a division of Penguin Books Ltd)
Penguin Group (Australia), 250 Camberwell Road, Camberwell,
Victoria 3124, Australia (a division of Pearson Australia Group Pty Ltd)
Penguin Books India Pvt Ltd, 11 Community Centre, Panchsheel Park, New Delhi – 110 017, India
Penguin Group (NZ), 67 Apollo Drive, Rosedale, North Shore 0632, New Zealand
(a division of Pearson New Zealand Ltd)
Penguin Books (South Africa) (Pty) Ltd, 24 Sturdee Avenue,
Rosebank, Johannesburg 2196, South Africa

Penguin Books Ltd, Registered Offices: 80 Strand, London WC2R 0RL, England

Originally published in Spanish as *La Sombra del Viento* by Editorial Planeta, S.A., Barcelona
First published in the United States of America by The Penguin Press,
a member of Penguin Group (USA) Inc. 2004
Published in Penguin Books 2005

This publication has been translated with aid from the General Department for Books,
Archives and Libraries of the Spanish Ministry of Education, Culture and Sports.

25 27 29 30 28 26 24

Copyright © Carlos Ruiz Zafón, 2001
Translation copyright © Lucia Graves, 2004
All rights reserved

PUBLISHER'S NOTE
This is a work of fiction. Names, characters, places, and incidents either are the product
of the author's imagination or are used fictitiously, and any resemblance to actual persons,
living or dead, business establishments, events, or locales is entirely coincidental.

THE LIBRARY OF CONGRESS HAS CATALOGED THE HARDCOVER EDITION AS FOLLOWS:
Ruiz Zafón, Carlos, 1964–
[La Sombra del viento. English]
The shadow of the wind / Carlos Ruiz Zafón ; translated by Lucia Graves.
p.   cm.
ISBN 1-59420-010-6 (hc.)
ISBN 978-0-14-303490-2 (pbk.)
I. Graves, Lucia. II. Title.
PQ6668.U49S6613   2004
863'.64—d22   2003062376

Printed in the United States of America
Designed by Stephanie Huntwork

For Joan Ramon Planas, who deserves better

The

Cemetery of

Forgotten Books

I STILL REMEMBER THE DAY MY FATHER TOOK ME TO THE CEMETERY OF Forgotten Books for the first time. It was the early summer of 1945, and we walked through the streets of a Barcelona trapped beneath ashen skies as dawn poured over Rambla de Santa Mónica in a wreath of liquid copper.

"Daniel, you mustn't tell anyone what you're about to see today," my father warned. "Not even your friend Tomás. No one."

"Not even Mommy?"

My father sighed, hiding behind the sad smile that followed him like a shadow through life.

"Of course you can tell her," he answered, heavyhearted. "We keep no secrets from her. You can tell her everything."

Shortly after the Civil War, an outbreak of cholera had taken my mother away. We buried her in Montjuïc on my fourth birthday. I can only recall that it rained all day and all night, and that when I asked my father whether heaven was crying, he couldn't bring himself to reply. Six years later my mother's absence remained in the air around us, a deafening silence that I had not yet learned to stifle with words. My father and I lived in a modest apartment on Calle Santa Ana, a stone's throw from the church square. The apartment was directly above the bookshop, a legacy from my grandfather that specialized in rare collectors' editions and secondhand books—an enchanted bazaar, which my father hoped would one day be mine. I was raised among books, making invisible friends in pages that seemed cast from dust and whose smell I carry on my hands to this day. As a child I learned to fall asleep talking to my mother in the darkness of my bedroom, telling her about the day's events, my adventures at school, and the things I had been taught. I couldn't hear her voice or feel her touch, but her radiance and her warmth haunted every corner of our home, and I believed, with the innocence of those who can still count their age on their ten fingers, that if I closed my eyes and spoke to her, she would be able to hear me wherever she was. Sometimes my father would listen to me from the dining room, crying in silence.

On that June morning, I woke up screaming at first light. My heart was pounding in my chest as if it feared that my soul wanted to carve its way out and run off down the stairs. My father hurried into my room and held me in his arms, trying to calm me.

"I can't remember her face. I can't remember Mommy's face," I muttered, breathless.

My father held me tight.

"Don't worry, Daniel. I'll remember for both of us."

We looked at each other in the half-light, searching for words that didn't exist. For the first time, I realized my father was growing old. He stood up and drew the curtains to let in the pale glint of dawn.

"Come, Daniel, get dressed. I want to show you something," he said.

"Now? At five o'clock in the morning?"

"Some things can only be seen in the shadows," my father said, flashing a mysterious smile probably borrowed from the pages of one of his worn Alexandre Dumas romances.

Night watchmen still lingered in the misty streets when we stepped out of the front door. The lamps along the Ramblas sketched an avenue of vapor that faded as the city began to awake. When we reached Calle Arco del Teatro, we continued through its arch toward the Raval quarter, entering a vault of blue haze. I followed my father through that narrow lane, more of a scar than a street, until the gleam of the Ramblas faded behind us. The brightness of dawn filtered down from balconies and cornices in streaks of slanting light that dissolved before touching the ground. At last my father stopped in front of a large door of carved wood, blackened by time and humidity. Before us loomed what to my eyes seemed the carcass of a palace, a place of echoes and shadows.

"Daniel, you mustn't tell anyone what you're about to see today. Not even your friend Tomás. No one."

A smallish man with vulturine features framed by thick gray hair opened the door. His impenetrable aquiline gaze rested on mine.

"Good morning, Isaac. This is my son, Daniel," my father announced. "Soon he'll be eleven, and one day the shop will be his. It's time he knew this place."

The man called Isaac nodded and invited us in. A blue-tinted gloom obscured the sinuous contours of a marble staircase and a gallery of frescoes peopled with angels and fabulous creatures. We followed our host through a palatial corridor and arrived at a sprawling round hall, a virtual basilica of shadows spiraling up under a high glass dome, its dimness pierced by shafts of light that stabbed from above. A labyrinth of passageways and crammed bookshelves rose from base to pinnacle like a beehive woven with tunnels, steps, platforms, and bridges that presaged an immense library of seemingly impossible geometry. I looked at my father, stunned. He smiled at me and winked.

"Welcome to the Cemetery of Forgotten Books, Daniel."

I could make out about a dozen human figures scattered among the library's corridors and platforms. Some of them turned to greet me from afar, and I recognized the faces of various colleagues of my father's, fellows of the secondhand-booksellers' guild. To my ten-year-old eyes, they looked like a brotherhood of alchemists in furtive study. My father knelt next to me and, with his eyes fixed on mine, addressed me in the hushed voice he reserved for promises and secrets.

"This is a place of mystery, Daniel, a sanctuary. Every book, every volume you see here, has a soul. The soul of the person who wrote it and of those who read it and lived and dreamed with it. Every time a book changes hands, every time someone runs his eyes down its pages, its spirit grows and strengthens. This place was already ancient when my father brought me here for the first time, many years ago. Perhaps as old as the city itself. Nobody knows for certain how long it has existed, or who created it. I will tell you what my father told me, though. When a library disappears, or a bookshop closes down, when a book is consigned to oblivion, those of us who know this place, its guardians, make sure that it gets here. In this place, books no longer remembered by anyone, books that are lost in time, live forever, waiting for the day when they will reach a new reader's hands. In the shop we buy and sell them, but in truth books have no owner. Every book you see here has been somebody's best friend. Now they have only us, Daniel. Do you think you'll be able to keep such a secret?"

My gaze was lost in the immensity of the place and its sorcery of light. I nodded, and my father smiled.

"And do you know the best thing about it?" he asked.

I shook my head.

"According to tradition, the first time someone visits this place, he must choose a book, whichever he wants, and adopt it, making sure that it will never disappear, that it will always stay alive. It's a very important promise. For life," explained my father. "Today it's your turn."

For almost half an hour, I wandered within the winding labyrinth, breathing in the smell of old paper and dust. I let my hand brush across the avenues of exposed spines, musing over what my choice would be. Among the titles faded by age, I distinguished words in familiar languages and others I couldn't identify. I roamed through galleries filled with hundreds, thousands of volumes. After a while it occurred to me that between the covers of each of those books lay a boundless universe waiting to be discovered, while beyond those walls, in the outside world, people allowed life to pass by in afternoons of football and radio soaps, content to do little more than gaze at their navels. It might have been that notion, or just chance, or its more flamboyant relative, destiny, but at that precise moment I knew I had already chosen the book I was going to adopt, or that was going to adopt me. It stood out timidly on one corner of a shelf, bound in wine-colored leather. The gold letters of its title gleamed in the light bleeding from the dome above. I drew near and caressed them with the tips of my fingers, reading to myself.

THE SHADOW OF THE WIND
JULIÁN CARAX

I had never heard of the title or the author, but I didn't care. The decision had been taken. I pulled the volume down with great care and leafed through the pages, letting them flutter. Once liberated from its prison on the shelf, the book shed a cloud of golden dust. Pleased with my choice, I tucked it under my arm and retraced my steps through the labyrinth with a smile on my lips. Perhaps the bewitching atmosphere of the place had got the better of me, but I felt sure that *The Shadow of the Wind* had been waiting for me there for years, probably since before I was born.

THAT AFTERNOON, BACK IN THE APARTMENT ON CALLE SANTA ANA, I barricaded myself in my room to read the first few lines. Before I knew what was happening, I had fallen right into it. The novel told the story of a man in search of his real father, whom he never knew and whose existence was only revealed to him by his mother on her deathbed. The story of that quest became a ghostly odyssey in which the protagonist struggled to recover his lost youth, and in which the shadow of a cursed love slowly surfaced to haunt him until his last breath. As it unfolded, the structure of the story began to remind me of one of those Russian dolls that contain innumerable ever-smaller dolls within. Step by step the narrative split into a thousand stories, as if it had entered a gallery of mirrors, its identity fragmented into endless reflections. The minutes and hours glided by as in a dream. When the cathedral bells tolled midnight, I barely heard them. Under the warm light cast by the reading lamp, I was plunged into a new world of images and sensations, peopled by characters who seemed as real to me as my room. Page after page I let the spell of the story and its world take me over, until the breath of dawn touched my window and my tired eyes slid over the last page. I lay in the bluish half-light with the book on my chest and listened to the murmur of the sleeping city. My eyes began to close, but I resisted. I did not want to lose the story's spell or bid farewell to its characters yet.

Once, in my father's bookshop, I heard a regular customer say that few things leave a deeper mark on a reader than the first book that finds its way into his heart. Those first images, the echo of words we think we have left behind, accompany us throughout our lives and sculpt a palace in our memory to which, sooner or later—no matter how many books we read, how many worlds we discover, or how much we learn or forget—we will return. For me those enchanted pages will always be the ones I found among the passageways of the Cemetery of Forgotten Books.

Days
of Ashes

1945–1949

A SECRET'S WORTH DEPENDS ON THE PEOPLE FROM WHOM IT MUST be kept. My first thought on waking was to tell my best friend about the Cemetery of Forgotten Books. Tomás Aguilar was a classmate who devoted his free time and his talent to the invention of wonderfully ingenious contraptions of dubious practicality, like the aerostatic dart or the dynamo spinning top. I pictured us both, equipped with flashlights and compasses, uncovering the mysteries of those bibliographic catacombs. Who better than Tomás to share my secret? Then, remembering my promise, I decided that circumstances advised me to adopt what in detective novels is termed a different modus operandi. At noon I approached my father to quiz him about the book and about Julián Carax—both world famous, I assumed. My plan was to get my hands on his complete works and read them all by the end of the week. To my surprise, I discovered that my father, a natural-born librarian and a walking lexicon of publishers' catalogs and oddities, had never heard of The Shadow of the Wind or Julián Carax. Intrigued, he examined the printing history on the back of the title page for clues.

"It says here that this copy is part of an edition of twenty-five hundred printed in Barcelona by Cabestany Editores, in June 1936."

"Do you know the publishing house?"

"It closed down years ago. But, wait, this is not the original. The first edition came out in November 1935 but was printed in Paris. . . . Published by Galiano & Neuval. Doesn't ring a bell."

"So is this a translation?"

"It doesn't say so. From what I can see, the text must be the original one."

"A book in Spanish, first published in France?"

"It's not that unusual, not in times like these," my father put in. "Perhaps Barceló can help us. . . ."

Gustavo Barceló was an old colleague of my father's who now owned a cavernous establishment on Calle Fernando with a commanding position in the city's secondhand-book trade. Perpetually affixed to his mouth was an unlit pipe that impregnated his person with the aroma of a Persian market. He liked to describe himself as the last romantic, and he was not above claiming that a remote line in his ancestry led directly to Lord Byron himself. As if to prove this connection, Barceló fashioned his wardrobe in the style of a nineteenth-century dandy. His casual attire consisted of a cravat, white patent leather shoes, and a plain glass monocle that, according to malicious gossip, he did not remove even in the intimacy of the lavatory. Flights of fancy aside, the most significant relative in his lineage was his begetter, an industrialist who had become fabulously wealthy by questionable means at the end of the nineteenth century. According to my father, Gustavo Barceló was, technically speaking, loaded, and his palatial bookshop was more of a passion than a business. He loved books unreservedly, and—although he denied this categorically—if someone stepped into his bookshop and fell in love with a tome he could not afford, Barceló would lower its price, or even give it away, if he felt that the buyer was a serious reader and not an accidental browser. Barceló also boasted an elephantine memory allied to a pedantry that matched his demeanor and the sonority of his voice. If anyone knew about odd books, it was he. That afternoon, after closing the shop, my father suggested that we stroll along to the Els Quatre Gats, a café on Calle Montsió, where Barceló and his bibliophile knights of the round table gathered to discuss the finer points of decadent poets, dead languages, and neglected, moth-ridden master-pieces.

ELS QUATRE GATS WAS JUST A FIVE-MINUTE WALK FROM OUR HOUSE AND one of my favorite haunts. My parents had met there in 1932, and I attributed my one-way ticket into this world in part to the old café's charms. Stone dragons guarded a lamplit façade anchored in shadows. Inside, voices seemed shaded by the echoes of other times. Accountants, dreamers, and would-be geniuses shared tables with the specters of Pablo Picasso, Isaac Albéniz, Federico García Lorca, and Salvador Dalí. There any poor devil could pass for a historical figure for the price of a small coffee.

"Sempere, old man," proclaimed Barceló when he saw my father come in. "Hail the prodigal son. To what do we owe the honor?"

"You owe the honor to my son, Daniel, Don Gustavo. He's just made a discovery."

"Well, then, pray come and sit down with us, for we must celebrate this ephemeral event," he announced.

"Ephemeral?" I whispered to my father.

"Barceló can express himself only in frilly words," my father whispered back. "Don't say anything, or he'll get carried away."

The lesser members of the coterie made room for us in their circle, and Barceló, who enjoyed flaunting his generosity in public, insisted on treating us.

"How old is the lad?" inquired Barceló, inspecting me out of the corner of his eye.

"Almost eleven," I announced.

Barceló flashed a sly smile.

"In other words, ten. Don't add on any years, you rascal. Life will see to that without your help."

A few of his chums grumbled in assent. Barceló signaled to a waiter of such remarkable decrepitude that he looked as if he should be declared a national landmark.

"A cognac for my friend Sempere, from the good bottle, and a cinnamon milk shake for the young one——he's a growing boy. Ah, and bring us some bits of ham, but spare us the delicacies you brought us earlier, eh? If we fancy rubber, we'll call for Pirelli tires."

The waiter nodded and left, dragging his feet.

"I hate to bring up the subject," Barceló said, "but how can there be jobs? In this country nobody ever retires, not even after they're dead. Just look at El Cid. I tell you, we're a hopeless case."

He sucked on his cold pipe, eyes already scanning the book in my hands. Despite his pretentious façade and his verbosity, Barceló could smell good prey the way a wolf scents blood.

"Let me see," he said, feigning disinterest. "What have we here?"

I glanced at my father. He nodded approvingly. Without further ado, I handed Barceló the book. The bookseller greeted it with expert hands. His pianist's fingers quickly explored its texture, consistency, and condition. He located the page with the publication and printer's notices and studied it with Holmesian flair. The rest watched in silence, as if awaiting a miracle, or permission to breathe again.

"Carax. Interesting," he murmured in an inscrutable tone.

I held out my hand to recover the book. Barceló arched his eyebrows but gave it back with an icy smile.

"Where did you find it, young man?"

"It's a secret," I answered, knowing that my father would be smiling to himself. Barceló frowned and looked at my father. "Sempere, my dearest old friend, because it's you and because of the high esteem I hold you in, and in honor of the long and profound friendship that unites us like brothers, let's call it at forty duros, end of story."

"You'll have to discuss that with my son," my father pointed out. "The book is his."

Barceló granted me a wolfish smile. "What do you say, laddie? Forty duros isn't bad for a first sale. . . . Sempere, this boy of yours will make a name for himself in the business."

The choir cheered his remark. Barceló gave me a triumphant look and pulled out his leather wallet. He ceremoniously counted out two hundred pesetas, which in those days was quite a fortune, and handed them to me. But I just shook my head. Barceló scowled.

"Dear boy, greed is most certainly an ugly, not to say mortal, sin. Be sensible. Call me crazy, but I'll raise that to sixty duros, and you can open a retirement fund. At your age you must start thinking of the future."

I shook my head again. Barceló shot a poisonous look at my father through his monocle.

"Don't look at me," said my father. "I'm only here as an escort."

Barceló sighed and peered at me closely.

"Let's see, junior. *What* is it you want?"

"What I want is to know who Julián Carax is and where I can find other books he's written."

Barceló chuckled and pocketed his wallet, reconsidering his adversary.

"Goodness, a scholar. Sempere, what do you feed the boy?"

The bookseller leaned toward me confidentially, and for a second I thought he betrayed a look of respect that had not been there a few moments earlier.

"We'll make a deal," he said. "Tomorrow, Sunday, in the afternoon, drop by the Ateneo library and ask for me. Bring your precious find with you so that I can examine it properly, and I'll tell you what I know about Julián Carax. Quid pro quo."

"Quid pro what?"

"Latin, young man. There's no such thing as dead languages, only dormant minds. Paraphrasing, it means that you can't get something for nothing, but since I like you, I'm going to do you a favor."

The man's oratory could kill flies in midair, but I suspected that if I wanted to find out anything about Julián Carax, I'd be well advised to stay on good terms with him. I proffered my most saintly smile in delight at his Latin outpourings.

"Remember, tomorrow, in the Ateneo," pronounced the bookseller. "But bring the book, or there's no deal."

"Fine."

Our conversation slowly merged into the murmuring of the other members of the coffee set. The discussion turned to some documents found in the basement of El Escorial that hinted at the possibility that Don Miguel de Cervantes had in fact been the nom de plume of a large, hairy lady of letters from Toledo. Barceló seemed distracted, not tempted to claim a share in the debate. He remained quiet, observing me from his fake monocle with a masked smile. Or perhaps he was only looking at the book I held in my hands.

· 2 ·

T HAT SUNDAY, CLOUDS SPILLED DOWN FROM THE SKY AND swamped the streets with a hot mist that made the thermometers on the walls perspire. Halfway through the afternoon, the temperature was already grazing the nineties as I set off toward Calle Canuda for my appointment with Barceló, carrying my book under my arm, beads of sweat on my forehead. The Ateneo was—and remains—one of the many places in Barcelona where the nineteenth century has not yet been served its eviction notice. A grand stone staircase led up from a palatial courtyard to a ghostly network of passageways and reading rooms. There, inventions such as the telephone, the wristwatch, and haste seemed futuristic anachronisms. The porter, or perhaps it was a statue in uniform, barely noticed my arrival. I glided up to the first floor, blessing the blades of a fan that swirled above the sleepy readers, melting like ice cubes over their books.

Don Gustavo's profile was outlined against the windows of a gallery that overlooked the building's interior garden. Despite the almost tropical atmosphere, he sported his customary foppish attire, his monocle shining in the dark like a coin at the bottom of a well. Next to him was a figure swathed in a white alpaca dress who looked to me like an angel.

When Barceló heard my footsteps, he half closed his eyes and signaled for me to come nearer. "Daniel, isn't it?" asked the bookseller. "Did you bring the book?"

I nodded on both counts and accepted the chair Barceló offered me next to him and his mysterious companion. For a while the bookseller only smiled placidly, taking no notice of my presence. I soon abandoned all hope of being introduced to the lady in white, whoever she might be. Barceló behaved as if she wasn't there and neither of us could see her. I cast a sidelong glance at her, afraid of meeting her eyes, which stared vacantly into the distance. The skin on her face and arms was pale, almost translucent. Her features were sharp, sketched with firm strokes and framed by a black head of hair that shone like damp stone. I figured she must be, at most, twenty, but there was something about her manner that made me think she could be ageless. She seemed trapped in that state of perpetual youth reserved for mannequins in shop windows. I was trying to catch any sign of a pulse under her swan's neck when I realized that Barceló was staring at me.

"So are you going to tell me where you found the book?" he asked.

"I would, but I promised my father I would keep the secret," I explained.

"I see. Sempere and his mysteries," said Barceló. "I think I can guess where. You've hit the jackpot, son. That's what I call finding a needle in a field of lilies. May I have a look?"

I handed him the book, and Barceló took it with infinite care. "You've read it, I suppose."

"Yes, sir."

"I envy you. I've always thought that the best time to read Carax is when one still has a young heart and a blank soul. Did you know this was the last novel he wrote?"

I shook my head.

"Do you know how many copies like this one there are in the market, Daniel?"

"Thousands, I suppose."

"None," Barceló specified. "Only yours. The rest were burned."

"Burned?"

For an answer Barceló only smiled enigmatically while he leafed through the book, stroking the paper as if it were a rare silk. The lady in white turned slowly. Her lips formed a timid and trembling smile. Her eyes groped the void, pupils white as marble. I gulped. She was blind.

"You don't know my niece Clara, do you?" asked Barceló.

I could only shake my head, unable to take my eyes off the woman with the china doll's complexion and white eyes, the saddest eyes I have ever seen.

"Actually, the expert on Julián Carax is Clara, which is why I brought her along," said Barceló. "Come to think of it, I'll retire to another room, if you don't mind, to inspect this tome while you get to know each other. Is that all right?"

I looked at him aghast. The scoundrel gave me a little pat on the back and left with my book under his arm.

"You've impressed him, you know," said the voice behind me.

I turned to discover the faint smile of the bookseller's niece. Her voice was pure crystal, transparent and so fragile I feared that her words would break if I interrupted them.

"My uncle said he offered you a good sum of money for the Carax book, but you refused it," Clara added. "You have earned his respect."

"All evidence to the contrary." I sighed.

I noticed that when she smiled, Clara leaned her head slightly to one side and her fingers played with a ring that looked like a wreath of sapphires.

"How old are you?" she asked.

"Almost eleven," I replied. "How old are you, Miss Clara?"

Clara laughed at my cheeky innocence.

"Almost twice your age, but even so, there's no need to call me Miss Clara."

"You seem younger, miss," I remarked, hoping that this would prove a good way out of my indiscretion.

"I'll trust you, then, because I don't know what I look like," she answered. "But if I seem younger to you, all the more reason to drop the 'miss.'"

"Whatever you say, Miss Clara."

I observed her hands spread like wings on her lap, the suggestion of her fragile waist under the alpaca folds, the shape of her shoulders, the extreme paleness of her neck, the line of her lips, which I would have given my soul to stroke with the tips of my fingers. Never before had I had a chance to examine a woman so closely and with such precision, yet without the danger of meeting her eyes.

"What are you looking at?" asked Clara, not without a pinch of malice.

"Your uncle says you're an expert on Julián Carax, miss," I improvised. My mouth felt dry.

"My uncle would say anything if that bought him a few minutes alone with a book that fascinates him," explained Clara. "But you must be wondering how someone who is blind can be a book expert."

"The thought had not crossed my mind."

"For someone who is almost eleven, you're not a bad liar. Be careful, or you'll end up like my uncle."

Fearful of making yet another faux pas, I decided to remain silent. I just sat gawking at her, imbibing her presence.

"Here, come, get closer," Clara said.

"Pardon me?"

"Come closer, don't be afraid. I won't bite you."

I left my chair and went over to where she was sitting. The bookseller's niece raised her right hand, trying to find me. Without quite knowing what to do, I, too, stretched out my hand, toward hers. She took it in her left hand and, without saying anything, offered me her right hand. Instinctively I understood what she was asking me to do, and guided her to my face. Her touch was both firm and delicate. Her fingers ran over my cheeks and cheekbones. I stood there motionless, hardly daring to breathe, while Clara read my features with her hands. While she did, she smiled to herself, and I noticed a slight movement of her lips, like a voiceless murmuring. I felt the brush of her hands on my forehead, on my hair and eyelids. She paused on my lips, following their shape with her forefinger and ring finger. Her fingers smelled of cinnamon. I swallowed, feeling my pulse race, and gave silent thanks there were no eyewitnesses to my blushing, which could have set a cigar alight a foot away.

· 3 ·

THAT AFTERNOON OF MIST AND DRIZZLE, CLARA BARCELÓ STOLE my heart, my breath, and my sleep. In the haunted shade of the Ateneo, her hands wrote a curse on my skin that wasn't to be broken for years. While I stared, enraptured, she explained how she, too, had stumbled on the work of Julián Carax by chance in a village in Provence. Her father, a prominent lawyer linked to the Catalan president's cabinet, had had the foresight to send his wife and daughter to the other side of the border at the start of the Civil War. Some considered his fear exaggerated, and maintained that nothing could possibly happen in Barcelona. In Spain, both the cradle and pinnacle of Christian civilization, barbarism was for anarchists— those people who rode bicycles and wore darned socks—and surely they wouldn't get very far. But Clara's father believed that nations never see themselves clearly in the mirror, much less when war preys on their minds. He had a good understanding of history and knew that the future could be read much more clearly in the streets, factories, and barracks than in the morning press. For months he wrote a letter to his wife and daughter once a week. At first he did it from his office on Calle Diputación, but later his letters had no return address. In the end he wrote secretly, from a cell in Montjuïc Castle, into which no one saw him go and from which, like countless others, he would never come out.

. . .

CLARA'S MOTHER READ THE LETTERS ALOUD, BARELY ABLE TO HOLD back her tears and skipping paragraphs that her daughter sensed without needing to hear them. Later, as her mother slept, Clara would convince her cousin Claudette to reread her father's letters from start to finish. That is how Clara read, with borrowed eyes. Nobody ever saw her shed a tear, not even when the letters from the lawyer stopped coming, not even when news of the war made them all fear the worst.

"My father knew from the start what was going to happen," Clara explained. "He stayed close to his friends because he felt it was his duty. What killed him was his loyalty to people who, when their time came, betrayed him. Never trust anyone, Daniel, especially the people you admire. Those are the ones who will make you suffer the worst blows."

Clara spoke these words with a hardness that seemed grown out of years of secret brooding. I gladly lost myself in her porcelain gaze and listened to her talk about things that at the time I could not possibly understand. She described people, scenes, and objects she had never seen with the detail and precision of a Flemish master. Her words evoked textures and echoes, the color of voices, the rhythm of footsteps. She explained how, during her years of exile in France, she and her cousin Claudette had shared a private tutor. He was a man in his fifties, a bit of a tippler, who affected literary airs and boasted of being able to recite Virgil's *Aeneid* in Latin without an accent. The girls had nicknamed him "Monsieur Roquefort" by virtue of the peculiar aroma he exuded, despite the baths of eau de cologne in which he marinated his Rabelaisian anatomy. Notwithstanding his peculiarities (notably his firm and militant conviction that blood sausages and other pork delicacies provided a miracle cure for bad circulation and gout), Monsieur Roquefort was a man of refined taste. Since his youth he had traveled to Paris once a month to spice up his cultural savoir faire with the latest literary novelties, visit museums, and, rumor had it, allow himself a night out in the arms of a nymphet he had christened "Madame Bovary," even though her name was Hortense and she limited her reading to twenty-franc notes. In the course of these educational escapades, Monsieur Roquefort frequently visited a secondhand bookstall positioned outside Notre-Dame. It was there, by chance, one afternoon in 1929, that he came across a novel by an unknown author, someone called Julián Carax. Always open to the *nouveau*, Monsieur Roquefort bought the book on a whim. The title seemed suggestive, and he was in the habit of reading something light on his train journey home. It was called *The Red House,* and on the back cover there was a blurred picture of the author, perhaps a photograph or a charcoal sketch. According to the biographical notes, Monsieur Julián Carax was twenty-seven, born with the century in Barcelona, and currently living in Paris; he wrote in French and worked at night as a professional pianist in a hostess bar. The blurb, written in the pompous, moldy style of the age, proclaimed that this was a first work of dazzling courage, the mark of a protean and trailblazing talent, and a sign of hope for the future of all of European letters. In spite of such solemn claims, the synopsis that followed suggested that the story contained some vaguely sinister elements slowly marinated in saucy melodrama, which, to the eyes of Monsieur Roquefort, was always a plus: after the classics what he most enjoyed were tales of crime, boudoir intrigue, and questionable conduct.

The Red House TELLS THE STORY OF A MYSTERIOUS, TORMENTED individual who breaks into toy shops and museums to steal dolls and puppets. Once they are in his power, he pulls out their eyes and takes them back to his lugubrious abode, a ghostly old conservatory lingering on the misty banks of the Seine. One fateful night he breaks into a sumptuous mansion on Avenue Foch determined to plunder the private collection of dolls belonging to a tycoon who, predictably, had grown insanely rich through devious means during the industrial revolution. As he is about to leave with his loot, our *voleur* is surprised by the tycoon's daughter, a young lady of Parisian high society named Giselle, exquisitely well read and highly refined but cursed with a morbid nature and naturally doomed to fall madly in love with the intruder. As the meandering saga continues through tumultuous incidents in dimly lit settings, the heroine begins to unravel the mystery that drives the enigmatic protagonist (whose name, of course, is never revealed) to blind the dolls, and as she does so, she discovers a horrible secret about her own father and his collection of china figures. At last the tale sinks into a tragic, darkly perfumed gothic denouement.

Monsieur Roquefort had literary pretensions himself and was the owner of a vast collection of letters of rejection signed by every self-respecting Parisian publisher, in response to the books of verse and prose he sent them so relentlessly. Thus he was able to identify the novel's publishing house as a second-rate firm, known, if anything, for its books on cookery, sewing, and other lesser handicrafts. The owner of the bookstall told him that when the novel had appeared, it had merited but two scant reviews from provincial dailies, strategically placed next to the obituary notices. The critics had a field day writing Carax off in a few lines, advising him not to leave his employment as a pianist, as it was obvious that he was not going to hit the right note in literature. Monsieur Roquefort, whose heart and pocket softened when faced with lost causes, decided to invest half a franc on the book by the unknown Carax and at the same time took away an exquisite edition of the great master Gustave Flaubert, whose unrecognized successor he considered himself to be.

The train to Lyons was packed, and Monsieur Roquefort was obliged to share his second-class compartment with a couple of nuns who had given him disapproving looks from the moment they left the Gare d'Austerlitz, mumbling under their breath. Faced with such scrutiny, the teacher decided to extract the novel from his briefcase and barricade himself behind its pages. Much to his surprise, hundreds of kilometers later, he discovered he had quite forgotten about the sisters, the rocking of the train, and the dark landscape sliding past the windows like a nightmare scene from the Lumière brothers. He read all night, unaware of the nuns' snoring or of the stations that flashed by in the fog. At daybreak, as he turned the last page, Monsieur Roquefort realized that his eyes were tearing up and his heart was poisoned with envy and amazement.

THAT MONDAY, MONSIEUR ROQUEFORT CALLED THE PUBLISHER IN Paris to request information on Julián Carax. After much insistence a telephonist with an asthmatic voice and a virulent disposition replied that Carax had no known address and that, anyhow, he no longer had dealings with the firm. She added that, since its publication, *The Red House* had sold exactly seventy-seven copies, most of which had presumably been acquired by young ladies of easy virtue and other regulars of the club where the author churned out nocturnes and polonaises for a few coins. The remaining copies had been returned and pulped for printing missals, fines, and lottery tickets.

The mysterious author's wretched luck won Monsieur Roquefort's sympathy, and during the following ten years, on each of his visits to Paris, he would scour the secondhand bookshops in search of other works by Julián Carax. He never found a single one. Almost nobody had heard of Carax, and those for whom the name rang a bell knew very little. Some swore he had brought out other books, always with small publishers, and with ridiculous print runs. Those books, if they really existed, were impossible to find. One bookseller claimed he had once had a book by Julián Carax in his hands. It was called *The Cathedral Thief,* but this was a long time ago, and besides, he wasn't quite sure. At the end of 1935, news reached Monsieur Roquefort that a new novel by Julián Carax, *The Shadow of the Wind,* had been published by a small firm in Paris. He wrote to the publisher asking whether he could buy a few copies but never got an answer. The following year, in the spring of 1936, his old friend at the bookstall by the Seine asked him whether he was still interested in Carax. Monsieur Roquefort assured him that he never gave up. It was now a question of stubbornness: if the world was determined to bury Carax, he wasn't going to go along. His friend then explained that some weeks earlier a rumor about Carax had been doing the rounds. It seemed that at last his fortunes had improved. He was going to marry a lady of good social standing and, after a few years' silence, had published a novel that, for the first time, had earned him a good review in none less than *Le Monde*. But just when it seemed that his luck was about to change, the bookseller went on, Carax had been involved in a duel in Père Lachaise cemetery. The circumstances surrounding this event were unclear. All the bookseller knew was that the duel had taken place at dawn on the day Carax was due to be married, and that the bridegroom had never made it to the church.

There was an opinion to match every taste: some maintained he had died in the duel and his body had been left abandoned in an unmarked grave; others, more optimistic, preferred to believe that Carax was tangled up in some shady affair that had forced him to abandon his fiancée at the altar, flee from Paris, and return to Barcelona. The nameless grave could never be found, and shortly afterward a new version of the facts began to circulate: Julián Carax, who had been plagued by misfortune, had died in his native city in the most dire straits. The girls in the brothel where he played the piano had organized a collection to pay for a decent burial, but when the money order reached Barcelona, the body had already been buried in a common grave, along with beggars and people with no name who turned up floating in the harbor waters or died of cold at the entrance to the subway.

IF ONLY BECAUSE HE LIKED TO OPPOSE GENERAL VIEWS, MONSIEUR Roquefort did not forget Carax. Eleven years after his discovery of *The Red House,* he decided to lend the novel to his two pupils, hoping that perhaps that strange book might encourage them to acquire the reading habit. Clara and Claudette were by then teenagers with hormones coursing through their veins, obsessed by the world winking at them from beyond the windows of the study. Despite the tutor's best efforts, the girls had until then proved immune to the charms of the classics, Aesop's fables, or the immortal verse of Dante Alighieri. Fearing that his contract might be terminated if Clara's mother discovered that he was forming them into two illiterate, featherbrained young women, Monsieur Roquefort presented them with Carax's novel dressed up as a love story, which was at least half true.

· 4 ·

N EVER BEFORE HAD I FELT TRAPPED, SEDUCED, AND CAUGHT UP in a story," Clara explained, "the way I did with that book. Until then, reading was just a duty, a sort of fine one had to pay teachers and tutors without quite knowing why. I had never known the pleasure of reading, of exploring the recesses of the soul, of letting myself be carried away by imagination, beauty, and the mystery of fiction and language. For me all those things were born with that novel. Have you ever kissed a girl, Daniel?"

My brain seized up; my saliva turned to sawdust.

"Well, you're still very young. But it's that same feeling, that first-time spark that you never forget. This is a world of shadows, Daniel, and magic is a rare asset. That book taught me that by reading, I could live more intensely. It could give me back the sight I had lost. For that reason alone, a book that didn't matter to anyone changed my life."

By then I was hopelessly dumbstruck, at the mercy of this creature whose words and charms I had neither means nor desire to resist. I wished that she would never stop speaking, that her voice would wrap itself around me forever, and that her uncle would never return to break the spell of that moment that belonged only to me.

"For years I looked for other books by Julián Carax," Clara went on. "I asked in libraries, in bookshops, in schools. Always in vain. No one had ever heard of him or of his books. I couldn't understand it. Later on, Monsieur Roquefort heard a rumor, a strange story about someone who went around libraries and bookshops looking for works by Julián Carax. If he found any, he would buy them, steal them, or get them by some other means, after which he would immediately set fire to them. Nobody knew who he was or why he did it. Another mystery to add to Carax's own enigma. In time, my mother decided she wanted to return to Spain. She was ill, and Barcelona had always been her home. I was secretly hoping to make some discovery about Carax here, since, after all, Barcelona was the city in which he was born and from which he had disappeared at the start of the war. But even with the help of my uncle, all I could find were dead ends. As for my mother, much the same thing happened with her own search. The Barcelona she encountered on her return was not the place she had left behind. She discovered a city of shadows, one no longer inhabited by my father, although every corner was haunted by his memory. As if all that misery were not enough, she insisted on hiring someone to find out exactly what had happened to him. After months of investigation, all the detective was able to recover was a broken wristwatch and the name of the man who had killed my father in the moat of Montjuïc Castle. His name was Fumero, Javier Fumero. We were told that this individual—and he wasn't the only one—had started off as a hired gunman with the FAI anarchist syndicate and had then flirted with the communists and the fascists, tricking them all, selling his services to the highest bidder. After the fall of Barcelona, he had gone over to the winning side and joined the police force. Now he is a famous bemedaled inspector. Nobody remembers my father. Not surprisingly, my mother faded away within a few months. The doctors said it was her heart, and I think that for once they were right. When she died, I went to live with my uncle Gustavo, the sole relative of my mother's left in Barcelona. I adored him, because he always gave me books when he came to visit us. He has been my only family and my best friend through all these years. Even if he seems a little arrogant at times, he has a good heart, bless him. Every night, without fail, even if he's dropping with sleep, he'll read to me for a while."

"I could read to you, if you like, Miss Clara," I suggested courteously, instantly regretting my audacity, for I was convinced that for Clara my company could only be a nuisance, if not a joke.

"Thanks, Daniel," she answered. "I'd love that."

"Whenever you wish."

She nodded slowly, looking for me with her smile.

"Unfortunately, I no longer have that copy of *The Red House*," she said. "Monsieur Roquefort refused to part with it. I could try to tell you the story, but it would be like describing a cathedral by saying it's a pile of stones ending in a spire."

"I'm sure you'd tell it much better than that," I spluttered.

Women have an infallible instinct for knowing when a man has fallen madly in love with them, especially when the male in question is both a complete dunce and a minor. I fulfilled all the requirements for Clara Barceló to send me packing, but I preferred to think that her blindness afforded me a margin for error and that my crime—my complete and pathetic devotion to a woman twice my age, my intelligence, and my height—would remain in the dark. I wondered what on earth she saw in me that could make her want to befriend me, other than a pale reflection of herself, an echo of solitude and loss. In my schoolboy reveries, we were always two fugitives riding on the spine of a book, eager to escape into worlds of fiction and secondhand dreams.

WHEN BARCELÓ RETURNED WEARING A FELINE SMILE, TWO HOURS HAD passed. To me they had seemed like two minutes. The bookseller handed me the book and winked.

"Have a good look at it, little dumpling. I don't want you coming back to me saying I've switched it, eh?"

"I trust you," I said.

"Stuff and nonsense. The last guy who said that to me (a tourist who was convinced that Hemingway had invented the *fabada* stew during the San Fermín bull run) bought a copy of *Hamlet* signed by Shakespeare in ballpoint, imagine that. So keep your eyes peeled. In the book business, you can't even trust the index."

It was getting dark when we stepped out into Calle Canuda. A fresh breeze combed the city, and Barceló removed his coat and put it over Clara's shoulders. Seeing no better opportunity, I tentatively let slip that if they thought it was all right, I could drop by their home the following day to read a few chapters of *The Shadow of the Wind* to Clara. Barceló looked at me out of the corner of his eye and gave a hollow laugh.

"Boy, you're getting ahead of yourself!" he muttered, although his tone implied consent.

"Well, if that's not convenient, perhaps another day or . . ."

"It's up to Clara," said the bookseller. "We've already got seven cats and two cockatoos. One more creature won't make much difference."

"I'll see you tomorrow, then, around seven," concluded Clara. "Do you know the address?"

· 5 ·

THERE WAS A TIME, IN MY CHILDHOOD, WHEN, PERHAPS BECAUSE I
had been raised among books and booksellers, I dreamed of becom-
ing a novelist. The root of my literary ambitions, apart from the marvelous
simplicity with which one sees things at the age of five, lay in a prodigious
piece of craftsmanship and precision that was exhibited in a fountain-pen
shop on Calle Anselmo Clavé, just behind the Military Government build-
ing. The object of my devotion, a plush black pen, adorned with heaven
knows how many refinements and flourishes, presided over the shop win-
dow as if it were the crown jewels. A baroque fantasy magnificently
wrought in silver and gold that shone like the lighthouse at Alexandria, the
nib was a wonder in its own right. When my father and I went out for a
walk, I wouldn't stop pestering him until he took me to see the pen. My fa-
ther declared that it must be, at the very least, the pen of an emperor. I was
secretly convinced that with such a marvel one would be able to write any-
thing, from novels to encyclopedias, and letters whose supernatural power
would surpass any postal limitations—a letter written with that pen would
reach the most remote corners of the world, even that unknowable place to
which my father said my mother had gone and from where she would never
return.

One day we decided to go into the shop and inquire about the blessed artifact. It turned out to be the queen of all fountain pens, a Montblanc Meinsterstück in a numbered series, that had once belonged, or so the shop attendant assured us, to Victor Hugo himself. From that gold nib, we were informed, had sprung the manuscript of *Les Misérables*.

"Just as Vichy Catalán water springs from the source at Caldas," the clerk swore.

He told us he had bought it personally from a most serious collector from Paris, and that he had assured himself of the item's authenticity.

"And what is the price of this fountain of marvels, if you don't mind telling me?" my father asked.

The very mention of the sum drew the color from his face, but I had already fallen under the pen's spell. The clerk, who seemed to think we understood physics, began to assail us with incomprehensible gibberish about the alloys of precious metals, enamels from the Far East, and a revolutionary theory on pistons and communicating chambers, all of which was part of the Teutonic science underpinning the glorious stroke of that champion of scrivening technology. I have to say in his favor that, despite the fact that we must have looked like two poor devils, the clerk allowed us to handle the pen as much as we liked, filled it with ink for us, and offered me a piece of parchment so that I could write my name on it and thus commence my literary career in the footsteps of Victor Hugo. Then, after the clerk had polished it with a cloth to restore its shiny splendor, it was returned to its throne.

"Perhaps another day," mumbled my father.

Once we were out in the street again, he told me in a subdued voice that we couldn't afford the asking price. The bookshop provided just enough to keep us afloat and send me to a decent school. The great Victor Hugo's Montblanc pen would have to wait. I didn't say anything, but my father must have noticed my disappointment.

"I tell you what we'll do," he proposed. "When you're old enough to start writing, we'll come back and buy it."

"What if someone buys it first?"

"No one is going to take this one, you can be quite sure. And if not, we can ask Don Federico to make us one. That man has the hands of a master."

Don Federico was the neighborhood watchmaker, an occasional customer at the bookshop, and probably the most polite and courteous man in the whole of the Northern Hemisphere. His reputation as a craftsman preceded him from the Ribera quarter to the Ninot Market. Another reputation haunted him as well, this one of a less salubrious nature, related to his erotic leanings toward muscular young men from the more virile ranks of the proletariat, and to a certain penchant for dressing up like the music-hall star Estrellita Castro.

"What if Don Federico is no good at fancy-pen stuff?" I asked, unaware that to less innocent ears, the phrase might have had a salacious echo.

My father arched an eyebrow, fearing perhaps that some foul rumors might have sullied my innocence.

"Don Federico is very knowledgeable about all things German and could make a Volkswagen if he put his mind to it. Besides, I'd like to find out whether fountain pens existed in Victor Hugo's day. There are a lot of con artists about."

My father's zeal for historical fact checking left me cold. I believed obstinately in the pen's illustrious past, even though I didn't think it was such a bad idea for Don Federico to make me a substitute. There would be time enough to reach the heights of Victor Hugo. To my consolation, and true to my father's predictions, the Montblanc pen remained for years in that shop window, which we visited religiously every Saturday morning.

"It's still there," I would say, astounded.

"It's waiting for you," my father would say. "It knows that one day it will be yours and that you'll write a masterpiece with it."

"I want to write a letter. To Mommy. So that she doesn't feel lonely."

My father regarded me. "Your mother isn't lonely, Daniel. She's with God. And with us, even if we can't see her."

This very same theory had been formulated for me in school by Father Vicente, a veteran Jesuit, expert at expounding on all the mysteries of the universe—from the gramophone to a toothache—quoting the Gospel According to Matthew. Yet on my father's lips, the words sounded hollow.

"And what does God want her for?"

"I don't know. If one day we see Him, we'll ask Him."

Eventually I discarded the idea of the celestial letter and concluded that, while I was at it, I might as well begin with the masterpiece—that would be more practical. In the absence of the pen, my father lent me a Staedler pencil, a number two, with which I scribbled in a notebook. Unsurprisingly, my story told of an extraordinary fountain pen, remarkably similar to the one in the shop, though enchanted. To be more precise, the pen was possessed by the tortured soul of its previous owner, a novelist who had died of hunger and cold. When the pen fell into the hands of an apprentice, it insisted on reproducing on paper the author's last work, which he had not been able to finish in his lifetime. I don't remember where I got that idea from, but I never again had another one like it. My attempts to re-create the novel on the pages of my notebook turned out to be disastrous. My syntax was plagued by an anemic creativity, and my metaphorical flights reminded me of the advertisements for fizzy footbaths that I used to read in tram stops. I blamed the pencil and longed for the pen, which was bound to turn me into a master writer.

My father followed my tortuous progress with a mixture of pride and concern.

"How's your story going, Daniel?"

"I don't know. I suppose if I had the pen, everything would be different."

My father told me that sort of reasoning could only have occurred to a budding author. "Just keep going, and before you've finished your first work, I'll buy it for you."

"Do you promise?"

He always answered with a smile. Luckily for my father, my literary dreams soon dwindled and were minced into mere oratory. What contributed to this was the discovery of mechanical toys and all sorts of tin gadgets you could find in the bric-a-brac stalls of the Encantes Market at prices that were better suited to our finances. Childhood devotions make unfaithful and fickle lovers, and soon I had eyes only for Meccanos and windup boats. I stopped asking my father to take me to see Victor Hugo's pen, and he didn't mention it again. That world seemed to have vanished, but for a long time the image I had of my father, which I still preserve today, was that of a thin man wearing an old suit that was too large for him and a secondhand hat he had bought on Calle Condal for seven pesetas, a man who could not afford to buy his son a wretched pen that was useless but seemed to mean everything to him.

When I returned from Clara and the Ateneo that night, my father was waiting for me in the dining room, wearing his usual expression of defeat and anxiety.

"I was beginning to think you'd got lost somewhere," he said. "Tomás Aguilar phoned. He said you'd arranged to meet. Did you forget?"

"It's Barceló. When he starts talking there's no stopping him," I replied, nodding as I spoke. "I didn't know how to shake him off."

"He's a good man, but he does go on. You must be hungry. Merceditas brought down some of the soup she made for her mother. That girl is an angel."

We sat down at the table to savor Merceditas's offering. She was the daughter of the lady on the third floor, and everyone had her down to become a nun and a saint, although more than once I'd seen her with an able-handed sailor who sometimes walked her back to the door. She always drowned him with kisses.

"You look pensive tonight," said my father, trying to make conversation.

"It must be this humidity, it dilates the brain. That's what Barceló says."

"It must be something else. Is anything worrying you, Daniel?"

"No. Just thinking."

"What about?"

"The war."

My father nodded gloomily and quietly sipped his soup. He was a very private person, and, although he lived in the past, he hardly ever mentioned it. I had grown up convinced that the slow procession of the postwar years, a world of stillness, poverty, and hidden resentment, was as natural as tap water, that the mute sadness that seeped from the walls of the wounded city was the real face of its soul. One of the pitfalls of childhood is that one doesn't have to understand something to feel it. By the time the mind is able to comprehend what has happened, the wounds of the heart are already too deep. That evening in early summer, as I walked back through the somber, treacherous twilight of Barcelona, I could not blot out Clara's story about her father's disappearance. In my world death was like a nameless and incomprehensible hand, a door-to-door salesman who took away mothers, beggars, or ninety-year-old neighbors, like a hellish lottery. But I couldn't absorb the idea that death could actually walk by my side, with a human face and a heart that was poisoned with hatred, that death could be dressed in a uniform or a raincoat, queue up at a cinema, laugh in bars, or take his children out for a walk to Ciudadela Park in the morning, and then, in the afternoon, make someone disappear in the dungeons of Montjuïc Castle or in a common grave with no name or ceremony. Going over all this in my mind, it occurred to me that perhaps the papier-mâché world that I accepted as real was only a stage setting. Much like the arrival of Spanish trains, in those stolen years you never knew when the end of childhood was due.

We shared the soup, a broth made from leftovers with bits of bread in it, surrounded by the sticky droning of radio soaps that filtered out through open windows into the church square.

"So tell me. How did things go with Gustavo today?"

"I met his niece, Clara."

"The blind girl? I hear she's a real beauty."

"I don't know. I don't notice things like that."

"You'd better not."

"I told them I might go by their house tomorrow, after school, to read to her for a while—as she's so lonely. If you'll let me."

My father looked at me askance, as if he were wondering whether he was growing old prematurely or whether I was growing up too quickly. I decided to change the subject, and the only one I could find was the one that was consuming me.

"Is it true that during the war people were taken to Montjuïc Castle and were never seen again?"

My father finished his spoonful of soup unperturbed and looked closely at me, his brief smile slipping away from his lips.

"Who told you that? Barceló?"

"No. Tomás Aguilar. He sometimes tells stories at school."

My father nodded slowly.

"When there's a war, things happen that are very hard to explain,

Daniel. Often even I don't know what they really mean. Sometimes it's best to leave things alone."

He sighed and sipped his soup with no appetite. I watched him without saying a word.

"Before your mother died, she made me promise that I would never talk to you about the war, that I wouldn't let you remember any of what happened."

I didn't know how to answer. My father half closed his eyes, as if he were searching for something in the air—looks, silences, or perhaps my mother, to corroborate what he had just said.

"Sometimes I think I've been wrong to listen to her. I don't know."

"It doesn't matter, Dad. . . ."

"No, it does matter, Daniel. Nothing is ever the same after a war. And yes, it's true that lots of people who went into that castle never came out."

Our eyes met briefly. After a while my father got up and took refuge in his bedroom. I cleared the plates, placed them in the small marble kitchen sink, and washed them up. When I returned to the sitting room, I turned off the light and sat in my father's old armchair. The breeze from the street made the curtains flutter. I was not sleepy, nor did I feel like trying to sleep. I went over to the balcony and looked out far enough to see the hazy glow shed by the streetlamps in Puerta del Ángel. A motionless figure stood out in a patch of shadow on the cobbled street. The flickering amber glow of a cigarette was reflected in his eyes. He wore dark clothes, with one hand buried in the pocket of his jacket, the other holding the cigarette that wove a web of blue smoke around his profile. He observed me silently, his face obscured by the street lighting behind him. He remained there for almost a minute smoking nonchalantly, his eyes fixed on mine. Then, when the cathedral bells struck midnight, the figure gave a faint nod of the head, followed, I sensed, by a smile that I could not see. I wanted to return the greeting but was paralyzed. The figure turned, and I saw the man walking away, with a slight limp. Any other night I would barely have noticed the presence of that stranger, but as soon as I'd lost sight of him in the mist, I felt a cold sweat on my forehead and found it hard to breathe. I had read an identical description of that scene in *The Shadow of the Wind*. In the story the protagonist would go out onto the balcony every night at midnight and discover that a stranger was watching him from the shadows, smoking nonchalantly. The stranger's face was always veiled by darkness, and only his eyes could be guessed at in the night, burning like hot coals. The stranger would remain there, his right hand buried in the pocket of his black jacket, and then he would go away, limping. In the scene I had just witnessed, that stranger could have been any person of the night, a figure with no face and no name. In Carax's novel, that figure was the devil.

· 6 ·

A DEEP, DREAMLESS SLEEP AND THE PROSPECT OF SEEING CLARA again that afternoon persuaded me that the vision had been pure coincidence. Perhaps that unexpected and feverish outbreak of imagination was just a side effect of the growth spurt I'd been waiting for, an event that all the women in the building said would turn me into a man, if not of stature, at least of a certain height. At seven on the dot, dressed in my Sunday best and smelling strongly of the Varón Dandy eau de cologne I had borrowed from my father, I turned up at the house of Gustavo Barceló ready to make my début as personal reader and living-room pest. The bookseller and his niece shared a palatial apartment in Plaza Real. A uniformed maid, wearing a white cap and the expressionless look of a soldier, opened the door for me with theatrical servility.

"You must be Master Daniel," she said. "I'm Bernarda, at your service."

Bernarda affected a ceremonial tone that could not conceal a Cáceres accent thick enough to spread on toast. With pomp and solemnity, she led me through the Barceló residence. The apartment, which was on the first floor, circled the building and formed a ring of galleries, sitting rooms, and passageways that to me, used as I was to our modest family home on Calle Santa Ana, seemed like a miniature of the Escorial palace. It was obvious that, as well as books, incunabula, and all manner of arcane bibliography, Don Gustavo also collected statues, paintings, and altarpieces, not to mention abundant fauna and flora. I followed Bernarda through a gallery that was full to overflowing with foliage and tropical species. A golden, dusky light filtered through the glass panes of the gallery and the languid tones from a piano hovered in the air. Bernarda fought her way through the jungle brandishing her docker's arms as if they were machetes. I followed her closely, examining the surroundings and noticing the presence of half a dozen cats and a couple of cockatoos (of a violent color and encyclopedic size) which, the maid explained, Barceló had christened Ortega and Gasset, respectively. Clara was waiting for me in a sitting room on the other side of this forest, overlooking the square. Draped in a diaphanous turquoise-blue cotton dress, the object of my confused desire was playing the piano beneath the weak light that came through the rose window. Clara played badly, with no sense of rhythm and mistaking half the notes, but to me her serenade was liquid heaven. I saw her sitting up straight at the keyboard, with a half smile and her head tilted to one side, and she seemed like a celestial vision. I was about to clear my throat to indicate my presence, but the whiff of cologne betrayed me. Clara suddenly stopped her playing, and an embarrassed smile lit up her face.

"For a moment I thought you were my uncle," she said. "He has forbidden me to play Mompou, because he says that what I do with him is a sacrilege."

The only Mompou I knew was a gaunt priest with a tendency to flatulence who taught us physics and chemistry at school. The association of ideas seemed to me both grotesque and downright improbable.

"Well, I think you play beautifully."

"No I don't. My uncle is a real music enthusiast, and he's even hired a music teacher to mend my ways—a young composer who shows a lot of promise called Adrián Neri. He's studied in Paris and Vienna. You've got to meet him. He's writing a symphony that is going to have its premiere with the Barcelona City Orchestra—his uncle sits on the management board. He's a genius."

"The uncle or the nephew?"

"Don't be wicked, Daniel. I'm sure you'll really fall for Adrián."

More likely he'll fall on me like a grand piano plummeting down from the seventh floor, I thought.

"Would you like a snack?" Clara offered. "Bernarda makes the most breathtaking cinnamon sponge cakes."

We took our afternoon snack like royalty, wolfing down everything the maid put before us. I had no idea about the protocol for this unfamiliar occasion and was not sure how to behave. Clara, who always seemed to know what I was thinking, suggested that I read from *The Shadow of the Wind* whenever I liked and that, while we were at it, I might as well start at the beginning. And so, trying to sound like one of those pompous voices on Radio Nacional that recited patriotic vignettes after the midday Angelus, I threw myself into revisiting the text of the novel. My voice, rather stiff at first, slowly became more relaxed, and soon I forgot myself and was submerged once more in the narrative, discovering cadences and turns of phrase that flowed like musical motifs, riddles made of timbre and pauses I had not noticed during my first reading. New details, strands of images, and fantasy appeared between the lines and new shapes revealed themselves, as in the structure of a building looked at from different angles. I read for about an hour, getting through five chapters, until my throat felt dry and half a dozen clocks chimed throughout the apartment, reminding me that it was getting late. I closed the book and observed that Clara was smiling at me calmly.

"It reminds me a bit of *The Red House,*" she said. "But this story seems less somber."

"Don't you believe it," I said. "This is just the beginning. Later on, things get complicated."

"You have to go, don't you?" Clara asked.

"I'm afraid so. It's not that I want to, but . . ."

"If you have nothing else to do, you could come back tomorrow," she suggested. "But I don't want to take advantage of you. . . ."

"Six o'clock?" I offered. "That way we'll have more time."

That meeting in the music room of the Plaza Real apartment was the first of many more throughout the summer of 1945 and the years to follow. Soon my visits to the Barcelós became almost daily, except for Tuesdays and Thursdays, when Clara had music lessons with Adrián Neri. I spent long hours there, and in time I memorized every room, every passageway, and every plant in Don Gustavo's forest. *The Shadow of the Wind* lasted us about a fortnight, but we had no trouble in finding successors with which to fill our reading hours. Barceló owned a fabulous library, and, for want of more Julián Carax titles, we ambled through dozens of minor classics and major bagatelles. Some afternoons we barely read, and spent our time just talking or even going out for a walk around the square or as far as the cathedral. Clara loved to sit and listen to the murmuring of people in the cloister and guess at the echoes of footsteps in the stone alleyways. She would ask me to describe the façades, the people, the cars, the shops, the lampposts and shop windows that we passed on our way. Often she would take my arm and I would guide her through our own private Barcelona, one that only she and I could see. We always ended up in a dairy shop on Calle Petritxol, sharing a bowl of whipped cream or a cup of hot chocolate with sponge fingers. Sometimes people would look at us askance, and more than one know-it-all waiter referred to her as "your older sister," but I paid no attention to their taunts and insinuations. Other times, I don't know whether out of malice or morbidity, Clara confided in me, telling me far-fetched secrets that I was not sure how to take. One of her favorite topics concerned a stranger, a person who sometimes came up to her when she was alone on the street and spoke to her in a hoarse voice. This mysterious person, who never mentioned his name, asked her questions about Don Gustavo and even about me. Once he had stroked her throat. Such stories tormented me mercilessly. Another time Clara told me she had begged the supposed stranger to let her read his face with her hands. He did not reply, which she took as a yes. When she raised her hands to his face, he stopped her suddenly, but she still managed to feel what she thought was leather.

"As if he wore a leather mask," she said.

"You're making that up, Clara."

Clara would swear again and again that it was true, and I would give up, tortured by the image of that phantom who found pleasure in caressing her swan's neck——and heaven knows what else——while all I could do was long for it. Had I paused to reflect, I would have understood that my devotion to Clara brought me no more than suffering. Perhaps for that very reason, I adored her all the more, because of the eternal human stupidity of pursuing those who hurt us the most. During that bleak postwar summer, the only thing I feared was the arrival of the new school term, when I would no longer be able to spend all day with Clara.

BY DINT OF SEEING ME SO OFTEN AROUND THE HOUSE, BERNARDA, whose severe appearance concealed a doting maternal instinct, became fond of me and, in her own manner, decided to adopt me.

"You can tell this boy hasn't got a mother, sir," she would say to Barceló. "I feel so sorry for him, poor little mite."

Bernarda had arrived in Barcelona shortly after the war, fleeing from poverty and from a father who on a good day would beat her up and tell her she was stupid, ugly, and a slut, and on a bad one would corner her in the pigsty, drunk, and fondle her until she sobbed with terror—at which point he'd let her go, calling her prudish and stuck up, like her mother. Barceló had come across Bernarda by chance when she worked in a vegetable stall in the Borne Market and, following his instinct, had offered her a post in his household.

"Ours will be a brand-new *Pygmalion*," he announced. "You shall be my Eliza and I'll be your Professor Higgins."

Bernarda, whose literary appetite was more than satisfied with the church newsletter, looked at him out of the corner of her eye.

"One might be poor and ignorant, but very decent, too," she said.

Barceló was not exactly George Bernard Shaw, but even if he had not managed to endow his pupil with the eloquence and spirit of a salon dame, his efforts had refined Bernarda and taught her the manners and speech of a provincial maid. She was twenty-eight, but I always thought she carried ten more years on her back, even if they showed only in her eyes. She was a serial churchgoer with an ecstatic devotion to Our Lady of Lourdes. Every morning she went to the eight o'clock service at the basilica of Santa María del Mar, and she confessed no less than three times a week, four in warm weather. Don Gustavo, who was a confirmed agnostic (which Bernarda suspected might be a respiratory condition, like asthma, but afflicting only refined gentlemen), deemed it mathematically impossible that the maid should be able to sin sufficiently to keep up that schedule of confession and contrition.

"You're as good as gold, Bernarda," he would say indignantly. "These people who see sin everywhere are sick in their souls and, if you really press me, in their bowels. The endemic condition of the Iberian saint is chronic constipation."

Every time she heard such blasphemy, Bernarda would make the sign of the cross five times over. Later, at night, she would say a prayer for the tainted soul of Mr. Barceló, who had a good heart but whose brains had rotted away due to excessive reading, like that fellow Sancho Panza. Very occasionally Bernarda had boyfriends, who would beat her, take what little money she had stashed in a savings account, and sooner or later dump her. Every time one of these crises arose, Bernarda would lock herself up in her room for days, where she would cry an ocean and swear she was going to kill herself with rat poison or bleach. After exhausting all his persuasive tricks, Barceló would get truly frightened and call the locksmith to open the door. Then the family doctor would administer a sedative strong enough to calm a horse. When the poor thing woke up two days later, the bookseller would buy her roses, chocolates, and a new dress and would take her to the movies to see the latest from Cary Grant, who in her book was the handsomest man in recorded history.

"Did you know? They say Cary Grant is queer," she would murmur, stuffing herself with chocolates. "Is that possible?"

"Rubbish," Barceló would swear. "Dunces and blockheads live in a state of perpetual envy."

"You do speak well, sir. It shows that you've been to that Sorbet university."

"The Sorbonne," he would answer, gently correcting her.

It was very difficult not to love Bernarda. Without being asked, she would cook and sew for me. She would mend my clothes and my shoes, comb and cut my hair, buy me vitamins and toothpaste. Once she even gave me a small medal with a glass container full of holy water, which a sister of hers who lived in San Adrián del Besós had brought all the way from

Lourdes by bus. Sometimes, while she inspected my head in search of lice and other parasites, she would speak to me in a hushed voice.

"Miss Clara is the most wonderful person in the world, and may God strike me dead if it should ever enter my head to criticize her, but it's not right that you, Master Daniel, should become too obsessed with her, if you know what I mean."

"Don't worry, Bernarda, we're only friends."

"That's just what I say."

To illustrate her arguments, Bernarda would then bring up some story she had heard on the radio about a boy who had fallen in love with his teacher and on whom some sort of avenging spell had been cast. It made his hair and his teeth fall out, and his face and hands were covered with some incriminating fungus, a sort of leprosy of lust.

"Lust is a bad thing," Bernarda would conclude. "Take it from me."

Despite the jokes he made at my expense, Don Gustavo looked favorably on my devotion to Clara and my eager commitment to be her companion. I attributed his tolerance to the fact that he probably considered me harmless. From time to time, he would still let slip enticing offers to buy the Carax novel from me. He would tell me that he had mentioned the subject to colleagues in the antiquarian book trade, and they all agreed that a Carax could now be worth a fortune, especially in Paris. I always refused his offers, at which he would just smile shrewdly. He had given me a copy of the keys to the apartment so that I could come and go without having to worry about whether he or Bernarda were there to open the door. My father was another story. As the years went by, he had got over his instinctive reluctance to talk about any subject that truly worried him. One of the first consequences of that progress was that he began to show his obvious disapproval of my relationship with Clara.

"You ought to go out with friends your own age, like Tomás Aguilar, whom you seem to have forgotten, though he's a splendid boy, and not with a woman who is old enough to be married."

"What does it matter how old we each are if we're good friends?"

What hurt me most was the reference to Tomás, because it was true. I

hadn't gone out with him for months, whereas before we had been insepa-
rable. My father looked at me reprovingly.

"Daniel, you don't know anything about women, and this one is playing
with you like a cat with a canary."

"You're the one who doesn't know anything about women," I would re-
ply, offended. "And much less about Clara."

Our conversations on the subject rarely went any further than an ex-
change of reproaches and wounded looks. When I was not at school or with
Clara, I devoted my time to helping my father in the bookshop—tidying up
the storeroom in the back of the shop, delivering orders, running errands,
or even serving regular customers. My father complained that I didn't really
put my mind or my heart into the work. I, in turn, replied that I spent my
whole life working there and I couldn't see what he could possibly complain
about. Many nights, when sleep eluded me, I'd lie awake remembering the
intimacy, the small world we had shared during the years following my
mother's death, the years of Victor Hugo's pen and the tin trains. I recalled
them as years of peace and sadness, a world that was vanishing and that had
begun to evaporate on the dawn when my father took me to the Cemetery
of Forgotten Books. Time played on the opposite team. One day my father
discovered that I'd given Carax's book to Clara, and he rose in anger.

"You disappoint me, Daniel," he said. "When I took you to that secret
place, I told you that the book you chose was something special, that you
were going to adopt it and had to be responsible for it."

"I was ten at the time, Father, and that was a child's game."

My father looked at me as if I'd stabbed him.

"And now you're fourteen, and not only are you still a child, you're a
child who thinks he's a man. Life is going to deal you a great many blows,
Daniel. And very soon."

In those days I wanted to believe that my father was hurt because I spent
so much time with the Barcelós. The bookseller and his niece lived a life of
luxury that my father could barely dream of. I thought he resented the fact
that Don Gustavo's maid behaved as if she were my mother, and was of-
fended by my acceptance that someone could take on that role. Sometimes,

while I was in the back room wrapping up parcels or preparing an order, I would hear a customer joking with my father.

"What you need is a good woman, Sempere. These days there are plenty of good-looking widows around, in the prime of their life, if you see what I mean. A young lady would sort out your life, my friend, and take twenty years off you. What a good pair of breasts can't do . . ."

My father never responded to these insinuations, but I found them increasingly sensible. Once, at dinnertime, which had become a battleground of silences and stolen glances, I brought up the subject. I thought that if I were the one to suggest it, it would make things easier. My father was an attractive man, always clean and neat in appearance, and I knew for a fact that more than one lady in the neighborhood approved of him and would have welcomed more than reading suggestions from him.

"It's been very easy for you to find a substitute for your mother," he answered bitterly. "But for me there is no such person, and I have no interest at all in looking."

As time went by, the hints from my father and from Bernarda, and even Barceló's intimations, began to make an impression on me. Something inside me told me that I was entering a cul-de-sac, that I could not hope for Clara to see anything more in me than a boy ten years her junior. Every day it felt more difficult to be near her, to bear the touch of her hands, or to take her by the arm when we went out for a walk. There came a point when her mere proximity translated into an almost physical pain. Nobody was unaware of this fact, least of all Clara.

"Daniel, I think we need to talk," she would say. "I don't think I've behaved very well toward you—"

I never let her finish her sentences. I would leave the room with any old excuse and flee, unable to face the possibility that the fantasy world I had built around Clara might be dissolving. I could not know that my troubles had only just begun.

An
Empty Plate

1950

· 7 ·

ON MY SIXTEENTH BIRTHDAY, I SPAWNED THE MOST ILL-FATED idea that had ever occurred to me. Without consulting anybody, I decided to host a birthday party and invite Barceló, Bernarda, and Clara. In my father's estimation, the whole thing was a recipe for disaster.

"It's my birthday," I answered sharply. "I work for you all the other days of the year. For once, at least, you could try to please me."

"Suit yourself."

The preceding months had been the most bewildering in my strange friendship with Clara. I hardly ever read to her anymore. Clara would systematically avoid being left on her own with me. Whenever I called by her apartment, her uncle popped up, pretending to read a newspaper, or else Bernarda would materialize, bustling about in the background and casting sidelong glances. Other times the company would take the form of one or several of Clara's friends. I called them the "Sisterly Brigade." Always chaste and modest in appearance, they patrolled the area around Clara with a missal in one hand and a policeman's eye, making it abundantly clear that I was in the way and that my presence embarrassed Clara and the entire world. Worst of all, however, was Neri, the music teacher, whose wretched symphony remained unfinished. He was a smooth talker, a rich kid from the snobby uptown district of San Gervasio, who, despite the Mozartian airs he affected, reminded me more of a tango singer, slick with brilliantine. The only talent I recognized in him was a badly concealed mean streak. He would suck up to Don Gustavo with no dignity or decorum, and he flirted with Bernarda in the kitchen, making her laugh with his silly gifts of sugared almonds and his fondness for bottom pinching. In short, I hated his guts. The dislike was mutual. Neri would turn up with his scores and his arrogant manner, regarding me as if I were some undesirable little cabin boy and making all sorts of objections to my presence.

"Don't you have to go and do your homework, son?"

"And you, maestro, don't you have a symphony to finish?"

In the end they would all get the better of me and I would depart, crestfallen and defeated, wishing I had Don Gustavo's gift of the gab so that I could put the conceited so-and-so in his place.

ON MY BIRTHDAY MY FATHER WENT DOWN TO THE BAKERY ON THE corner and bought the finest cake he could find. He set the dinner table silently, bringing out the silver and the best dinner service. He lit a few candles and prepared a meal of what he thought were my favorite dishes. We didn't exchange a word all afternoon. In the evening he went into his room, slipped into his best suit, and came out again holding a packet wrapped in shiny cellophane paper, which he placed on the coffee table in the dining room. My present. He sat at the table, poured himself a glass of white wine, and waited. The invitation specified dinner would be served at eight-thirty. At nine-thirty we were still waiting. My father glanced at me sadly. Inside, I was boiling with rage.

"You must be pleased with yourself," I said. "Isn't this what you wanted?"

"No."

Half an hour later, Bernarda arrived. She bore a funereal expression and a message from Miss Clara, who wished me many happy returns but unfortunately would be unable to attend my birthday dinner. Mr. Barceló had been obliged to leave town on business for a few days, and she'd had to change her music lesson with Maestro Neri. Bernarda had come because it was her afternoon off.

"Clara can't come because she has a music lesson?" I asked, quite astounded.

Bernarda looked down. She was almost in tears when she handed me a small parcel containing her present and kissed me on both cheeks.

"If you don't like it, you can exchange it," she said.

I was left alone with my father, staring at the fine dinner service, the silver, and the candles that were quietly burning themselves out.

"I'm sorry, Daniel," said my father.

I nodded in silence, shrugging my shoulders.

"Aren't you even going to open your present?" he asked.

My only response was the slam of the front door as I left the apartment. I rushed furiously down the stairs, my eyes brimming with tears of rage as I stepped outside. The street was freezing, desolate, suffused in an eerie blue radiance. I felt as if my heart had been flayed open. Everything around me trembled. I walked off aimlessly, paying scant attention to a stranger who was observing me from Puerta del Ángel. He wore a dark suit, right hand buried in the pocket of his jacket, eyes like wisps of light in the glow of his cigarette. Limping slightly, he began to follow me.

I wandered through the streets for an hour or more, until I found myself at the base of the Columbus monument. Crossing over to the port, I sat on the stony steps that descended into the dark waters, next to the dock that sheltered the pleasure boats. Someone had chartered a night trip, and I could hear laughter and music wafting across from the procession of lights and reflections in the inner harbor. I remembered the days when my father would take me on that very same boat for a trip to the breakwater point. From there you could see the cemetery on the slopes of Montjuïc, the endless city of the dead. Sometimes I waved, thinking that my mother was still there and could see us going by. My father would also wave. It was years since we had boarded a pleasure boat, although I knew that sometimes he did the trip on his own.

"A good night for remorse, Daniel," came a voice from the shadows. "Cigarette?"

I jumped up with a start. A hand was offering me a cigarette out of the dark.

"Who are you?"

The stranger moved forward until he was on the very edge of darkness, his face still concealed. A puff of blue smoke rose from his cigarette. I immediately recognized the black suit and the hand hidden in the jacket pocket. His eyes shone like glass beads.

"A friend," he said. "Or that's what I aspire to be. A cigarette?"

"I don't smoke."

"Good for you. Unfortunately, I have nothing else to offer you, Daniel."

He had a rasping, wounded voice. He dragged his words out so that they sounded muffled and distant like the old 78s Barceló collected.

"How do you know my name?"

"I know a lot about you. Your name is the least of it."

"What else do you know?"

"I could embarrass you, but I don't have the time or the inclination. Just say that I know you have something that interests me. And I'm ready to pay you good money for it."

"I'm afraid you've mistaken me for someone else."

"No, I hardly think so. I tend to make other mistakes, but never when it comes to people. How much do you want for it?"

"For what?"

"For *The Shadow of the Wind*."

"What makes you think I have it?"

"That's beyond discussion, Daniel. It's just a question of price. I've known you have it for a long time. People talk. I listen."

"Well, you must have heard wrong. I don't have that book. And if I did, I wouldn't sell it."

"Your integrity is admirable, especially in these days of sycophants and ass lickers, but you don't have to pretend with me. Say how much. A thousand duros? Money means nothing to me. You set the price."

"I've already told you: it's not for sale, and I don't have it," I replied. "You've made a mistake, you see."

The stranger remained silent and motionless, enveloped in the blue smoke of a cigarette that never seemed to go out. I realized he didn't smell of tobacco, but of burned paper. Good paper, the sort used for books.

"Perhaps you're the one who's making a mistake now," he suggested.

"Are you threatening me?"

"Probably."

I gulped. Despite my bravado, the man frightened me out of my skin.

"May I ask why you are so interested?"

"That's my business."

"Mine, too, if you are threatening me about a book I don't have."

"I like you, Daniel. You've got guts, and you seem bright. A thousand duros? With that you could buy a huge amount of books. Good books, not that rubbish you guard with such zeal. Come on, a thousand duros and we'll remain friends."

"You and I are not friends."

"Yes we are, but you haven't yet realized it. I don't blame you, with so much on your mind. Your friend Clara, for instance. A woman like that . . . anyone could lose his senses."

The mention of Clara's name froze the blood in my veins. "What do you know about Clara?"

"I daresay I know more than you, and that you'd do best to forget her, although I know you won't. I too have been sixteen. . . ."

Suddenly a terrible certainty hit me. That man was the anonymous stranger who pestered Clara in the street. He was real. Clara had not lied. The man took a step forward. I moved back. I had never been so frightened in my life.

"Clara doesn't have the book; you should know that. Don't you ever dare touch her again."

"I'm not in the least bit interested in your friend, Daniel, and one day you'll share my feeling. What I want is the book. And I'd rather obtain it by fair means, without harming anyone. Do you understand?"

Unable to come up with anything better, I decided to lie through my teeth. "Someone called Adrián Neri has it. A musician. You may have heard of him."

"Doesn't ring a bell, and that's the worst thing one can say about a musician. Are you sure you haven't invented this Adrián Neri?"

"I wish I had."

"In that case, since you seem to be so close, maybe you could persuade him to return it to you. These things are easily solved between friends. Or would you rather I asked Clara?"

I shook my head. "I'll speak to Neri, but I don't think he'll give it back to me. Perhaps he doesn't even have it anymore. Anyhow, what do you want the book for? Don't tell me it's to read it."

"No. I know it by heart."

"Are you a collector?"

"Something like that."

"Do you have other books by Carax?"

"I've had them at some point. Julián Carax is my specialty, Daniel. I travel the world in search of his books."

"And what do you do with them if you don't read them?"

The stranger made a stifled, desperate sound. It took me a while to realize that he was laughing.

"The only thing that should be done with them, Daniel," he answered.

He pulled a box of matches out of his pocket. He took one and struck it. The flame showed his face for the first time. My blood froze. He had no nose, lips, or eyelids. His face was nothing but a mask of black scarred skin, consumed by fire. It was the same dead skin that Clara had touched.

"Burn them," he whispered, his voice and his eyes poisoned by hate.

A gust of air blew out the match he held in his fingers, and his face was once again hidden in darkness.

"We'll meet again, Daniel. I never forget a face, and I don't think you will either," he said calmly. "For your sake, and for the sake of your friend Clara, I hope you make the right decision. Sort this thing out with Mr. Neri—a rather pretentious name. I wouldn't trust him an inch."

With that, the stranger turned around and walked off toward the docks, a shape melting into the shadows, cocooned in his hollow laughter.

· 8 ·

A REEF OF CLOUDS AND LIGHTNING RACED ACROSS THE SKIES FROM the sea. I should have run to take shelter from the approaching downpour, but the man's words were beginning to sink in. My hands were shaking, and my mind wasn't far behind. I looked up and saw the storm spilling like rivers of blackened blood from between the clouds, blotting out the moon and covering the roofs and façades of the city in darkness. I tried to pick up the pace, but I was consumed with fear and walked with leaden feet and legs, chased by the rain. I took refuge under the canopy of a newspaper kiosk, trying to collect my thoughts and decide what to do next. A clap of thunder roared close by, and I felt the ground shake under my feet. A few seconds later, the weak current of the lighting system, which had defined the shapes of buildings and windows, faded away. On the flooding sidewalks, the streetlamps blinked, then went out like candles snuffed by the wind. There wasn't a soul to be seen in the streets, and the darkness of the blackout spread with a fetid smell that rose from the sewers. The night became opaque, impenetrable, as the rain folded the city in its shroud.

"A woman like that . . . anyone could lose his senses."

I started to run up the Ramblas with only one thought in mind: Clara.

Bernarda had said Barceló was away on business. It was her day off, and she usually spent the night with her aunt Reme and her cousins in the nearby town of San Adrián del Besós. That left Clara alone in the cavernous Plaza Real apartment and that faceless, menacing man unleashed in the storm with heaven knows what in mind. As I hurried under the downpour toward Plaza Real, all I could think was that I had placed Clara in danger by giving her Carax's book. When I reached the entrance to the square, I was soaked to the bone. I rushed to take shelter under the arches of Calle Fernando. I thought I saw shadowy forms creeping up behind me. Beggars. The front door was closed. I searched in my pockets for the keys Barceló had given me. One of the tramps came up, petitioning me to let him spend the night in the lobby. I closed the door before he'd had time to finish his sentence.

THE STAIRCASE WAS A WELL OF DARKNESS. FLASHES OF LIGHTNING BLED through the cracks in the front door, lighting up the outline of the steps for a second. I groped my way forward and found the first step by tripping over it. Holding on to the banister, I slowly ascended. Soon the steps gave way to a flat surface, and I realized I had reached the first-floor landing. I felt the marble walls, cold and hostile, and found the reliefs on the oak door and the aluminum doorknobs. After fumbling about for a bit, I managed to insert the key. When the door of the apartment opened, a streak of blue light blinded me for an instant and a gust of warm air graced my skin. Bernarda's room was in the back of the apartment, by the kitchen. I went there first, although I was sure the maid wasn't home. I rapped on the door with my knuckles and, as there was no answer, allowed myself to enter. It was a simple room, with a large bed, a cupboard with tinted mirrors, and a chest of drawers on which Bernarda had placed enough effigies and prints of saints and the Virgin Mary to start a holy order. I closed the door, and when I turned around, my heart almost stopped: a dozen scarlet eyes were advancing toward me from the end of the corridor. Barceló's cats knew me well and tolerated my presence. They surrounded me, meowing gently, but as soon as they realized that my drenched clothes did not give out the desired warmth, they abandoned me with indifference.

Clara's room was at the other end of the apartment, next to the library and the music room. The cats' invisible steps followed me through the passageway. In the flickering darkness of the storm, Barceló's residence seemed vast and sinister, altered from the place I had come to consider my second home. I reached the front of the apartment, where it faced the square. The conservatory opened before me, dense and impassable. I penetrated its jungle of leaves and branches. For a moment it occurred to me that if the faceless stranger had managed to sneak into the apartment, this was where he would probably choose to wait for me. I almost thought I could perceive the smell of burned paper he left in the air around him, but then I realized that what I had detected was only tobacco. A burst of panic needled me. Nobody in the household smoked, and Barceló's unlit pipe was purely ornamental.

When I reached the music room, the glow from a flash of lightning revealed spirals of smoke that drifted in the air like garlands of vapor. Next to the gallery, the piano keyboard displayed its endless grin. I crossed the music room and went over to the library door. It was closed. I opened it and was welcomed by the brightness from the glass-covered balcony that encircled Barceló's personal library. The walls, lined with packed bookshelves, formed an oval in whose center stood a reading table and two plush armchairs. I knew that Clara kept Carax's book in a glass cabinet by the arch of the balcony. I crept up to it. My plan, or my lack of it, was to lay my hands on the book, take it out of there, give it to that lunatic, and lose sight of him forever after. Nobody would notice the book's absence, except me.

Julián Carax's book was waiting for me, as it always did, its spine just visible at the end of a shelf. I took it in my hands and pressed it against my chest, as if embracing an old friend whom I was about to betray. Judas, I thought. I decided to leave the place without making Clara aware of my presence. I would take the book and disappear from Clara Barceló's life forever. Quietly, I stepped out of the library. The door of her bedroom was just visible at the end of the corridor. I pictured her lying on her bed, asleep. I imagined my fingers stroking her neck, exploring a body I had conjured up from my fantasies. I turned around, ready to throw away six years of daydreaming, but something halted my step before I reached the music room. A voice whistling behind me, behind a door. A deep voice that whispered and laughed. In Clara's room. I walked slowly up to the door. I put my fingers on the doorknob. My fingers trembled. I had arrived too late. I swallowed hard and opened the door.

· 9 ·

CLARA'S NAKED BODY LAY STRETCHED OUT ON WHITE SHEETS that shone like washed silk. Maestro Neri's hands slid over her lips, her neck, and her breasts. Her white eyes looked up to the ceiling, her eyelids shuddering as the music teacher charged at her, entering her body between her pale and trembling thighs. The same hands that had read my face six years earlier in the gloom of the Ateneo now clutched the maestro's sweat-glazed buttocks, the nails digging into them, as they guided him toward her with desperate, animal desire. I couldn't breathe. I must have stayed there, paralyzed, watching them for almost half a minute, until Neri's eyes, disbelieving at first, then aflame with anger, became aware of my presence. Still panting, astounded, he stopped. Clara grabbed him, not understanding, rubbing her body against his, licking his neck.

"What's the matter?" she moaned. "Why are you stopping?"

Adrián Neri's eyes burned with rage. "Nothing," he murmured. "I'll be right back."

Neri stood up and threw himself at me, clenching his fists. I didn't even see him coming. I couldn't take my eyes off Clara, wrapped in sweat, breathless, her ribs visible under her skin and her breasts quivering. The music teacher grabbed me by the neck and dragged me out of the bedroom. My feet were barely touching the floor, and however hard I tried, I was unable to escape Neri's grip, as he carried me like a bundle through the conservatory.

"I'm going to break your neck, you wretch," he muttered.

He hauled me toward the front door, opened it, and flung me with all his might onto the landing. Carax's book slipped out of my hands. He picked it up and threw it furiously at my face.

"If I ever see you around here again, or if I find out that you've gone up to Clara in the street, I swear I'll give you such a beating you'll end up in the hospital—and I don't give a shit how young you are," he said in a cold voice. "Understood?"

I got up with difficulty. In the struggle Neri had torn my jacket and my pride.

"How did you get in?"

I didn't answer. Neri sighed, shaking his head. "Come on," he barked, barely containing his fury. "Give me the keys."

"What keys?"

He punched me so hard I collapsed. When I got up, there was blood in my mouth and a ringing in my left ear that bored through my head like a policeman's whistle. I touched my face and felt the cut on my lips burning under my fingers. A bloodstained signet ring shone on the music teacher's finger.

"I said the keys."

"Piss off," I spit out.

I didn't see the next blow coming. I just felt as if a jackhammer had torn my stomach out. I folded up, like a broken puppet, unable to breathe, staggering back against the wall. Neri grabbed me by my hair and rummaged in my pockets until he found the keys. I slid down to the floor, holding my stomach, whimpering with agony and anger.

"Tell Clara that—"

He slammed the door in my face, leaving me in complete darkness. I groped around for the book. I found it and slid down the stairs with it, leaning against the walls, panting. I went outside spitting blood and gasping for breath. The biting cold and the wind tightened around my soaking clothes. The cut on my face was stinging.

"Are you all right?" asked a voice in the shadow.

It was the beggar I had refused to help a short time before. Feeling ashamed, I nodded, avoiding his eyes. I started to walk away.

"Wait a minute, at least until the rain eases off," the beggar suggested.

He took me by the arm and led me to a corner under the arches where he kept a bundle of possessions and a bag with old, dirty clothes.

"I have a bit of wine. It's not too bad. Drink a little. It will help you warm up. And disinfect that . . ."

I took a swig from the bottle he offered me. It tasted of diesel oil laced with vinegar, but its heat calmed my stomach and my nerves. A few drops sprinkled over my wound, and I saw stars in the blackest night of my life.

"Good, isn't it?" The beggar smiled. "Go on, have another shot. This stuff can raise a person back from the dead."

"No thanks. You have some," I mumbled.

The beggar had a long drink. I watched him closely. He looked like some gray government accountant who had been sleeping in the same suit for the last fifteen years. He stretched out his hand, and I shook it.

"Fermín Romero de Torres, currently unemployed. Pleased to meet you."

"Daniel Sempere, complete idiot. The pleasure is all mine."

"Don't sell yourself short. On nights like this, everything looks worse than it is. You'd never guess it, but I'm a born optimist. I have no doubt at all that the present regime's days are numbered. All intelligence points toward the Americans invading us any day now and setting Franco up with a peanut stand down in Melilla. Then my position, my reputation, and my lost honor will be restored."

"What did you work at?"

"Secret service. High espionage," said Fermín Romero de Torres. "Suffice it to say that I was President Maciá's man in Havana."

I nodded. Another madman. At night Barcelona gathered them in by the handful. And idiots like me, too.

"Listen, that cut doesn't look good to me. They've given you quite a tanning, eh?"

I touched my mouth with my fingers. It was still bleeding.

"Woman trouble?" he asked. "You could have saved yourself the effort.

Women in this country—and I've seen a bit of the world—are a sanctimonious, frigid lot. Believe me. I remember a little mulatto girl I left behind in Cuba. No comparison, eh? No comparison. The Caribbean female draws up to you with that island swing of hers and whispers '*Ay, papito,* gimme pleasure, gimme pleasure.' And a real man, with blood in his veins . . . well, what can I say?"

It seemed to me that Fermín Romero de Torres, or whatever his true name was, longed for lighthearted conversation almost as much as he longed for a hot bath, a plate of stew, and a clean change of clothes. I got him going for a while, as I waited for my pain to subside. It wasn't very difficult, because all the man needed was a nod at the right moment and someone who appeared to be listening. The beggar was about to recount the details of a bizarre plan for kidnapping Franco's wife when I saw that the rain had abated and the storm seemed to be slowly moving away toward the north.

"It's getting late," I mumbled, standing up.

Fermín Romero de Torres nodded with a sad look and helped me get up, making as if he were dusting down my drenched clothes.

"Some other day, then," he said in a resigned tone. "I'm afraid talking is my undoing. Once I start . . . Listen, this business about the kidnapping, it should go no further, understand?"

"Don't worry. I'm as silent as a grave. And thanks for the wine."

I set off toward the Ramblas. I stopped by the entrance to the square and turned to look at the Barcelós' apartment. The windows were still in darkness, weeping with rain. I wanted to hate Clara but was unable to. To truly hate is an art one learns with time.

I swore to myself that I would never see her again, that I wouldn't mention her name or remember the time I had wasted by her side. For some strange reason, I felt at peace. The anger that had driven me out of my home had gone. I was afraid it would return, and with renewed vigor, the following day. I was afraid that jealousy and shame would slowly consume me once all the pieces of my memory of that night fell into place. But dawn was still a few hours away, and there was one more thing I had to do before I could return home with a clean conscience.

. . .

CALLE ARCO DEL TEATRO WAS THERE WAITING FOR ME. A STREAM OF black water converged in the center of the narrow street and made its way, like a funeral procession, toward the heart of the Raval quarter. I recognized the old wooden door and the baroque façade to which my father had brought me that morning at dawn, six years before. I went up the steps and took shelter from the rain under the arched doorway. It reeked of urine and rotten wood. More than ever, the Cemetery of Forgotten Books smelled of death. I didn't recall that the door knocker was shaped as a demon's face. I took it by its horns and knocked three times. The cavernous echo dispersed within the building. After a while I knocked again, six knocks this time, each one louder than before, until my fist hurt. A few more minutes went by, and I began to fear that perhaps there was no longer anyone there. I crouched down against the door and took the Carax book from the inside pocket of my jacket. I opened it and reread that first sentence that had entranced me years before.

That summer it rained every day, and although many said it was God's wrath because the villagers had opened a casino next to the church, I knew that it was my fault, and mine alone, for I had learned to lie and my lips still retained the last words spoken by my mother on her deathbed: "I never loved the man I married but another, who, I was told, had been killed in the war; look for him and tell him my last thoughts were for him, for he is your real father."

I smiled, remembering that first night of feverish reading six years earlier. I closed the book and was about to knock one last time, but before my fingers touched the knocker, the large door opened far enough to reveal the profile of the keeper. He was carrying an oil lamp.

"Good evening," I mumbled. "Isaac, isn't it?"

The keeper observed me without blinking. The glow from the oil lamp sculpted his angular features in amber and scarlet hues, conferring on him a striking likeness to the little demon on the door knocker.

"You're Sempere junior," he muttered wearily.

"Your memory is excellent."

"And your sense of timing is lousy. Do you know what the time is?"

His sharp eyes had already detected the book under my jacket. Isaac stared at me questioningly. I took the book out and showed it to him.

"Carax," he said. "I'd say there are at most ten people in this town who know of him, or who have read this book."

"Well, one of them is intent on setting fire to it. I can't think of a better hiding place than this."

"This is a cemetery, not a safe."

"Exactly. What this book needs is to be buried where nobody can find it."

Isaac glanced suspiciously down the alleyway. He opened the door a few inches and beckoned me to slip inside. The dark, unfathomable vestibule smelled of wax and damp. An intermittent drip could be heard in the gloom. Isaac gave me the lamp to hold while he put his hand in his coat and pulled out a ring of keys that would have been the envy of any jailer. When, by some imponderable science, he found the right one, he inserted it into a bolt under a glass case full of relays and cogwheels, like a large music box. With a twist of his wrist, the mechanism clicked and levers and fulcrums slid in an amazing mechanical ballet until the large door was clamped by a circle of steel bars that locked into place in the stone wall.

"The Bank of Spain couldn't do better," I remarked, impressed. "It looks like something out of Jules Verne."

"Kafka," Isaac corrected, retrieving the oil lamp and starting off toward the depths of the building. "The day you come to realize that the book business is nothing but an empty plate and you decide you want to learn how to rob a bank, or how to set one up, which is much the same thing, come and see me and I'll teach you a few tricks about bolts."

I followed him through corridors that I still remembered, flanked with fading frescoes of angels and shadowlike creatures. Isaac held the lamp up high, casting a flickering bubble of red light. He limped slightly, and his frayed flannel coat looked like an undertaker's. It occurred to me that this man, somewhere between Charon and the librarian at Alexandria, seemed to belong in one of Julián Carax's novels.

"Do you know anything about Carax?" I asked.

Isaac stopped at the end of a gallery and looked at me with indifference. "Not much. Only what they told me."

"Who?"

"Someone who knew him well, or thought so at least."

My heart missed a beat. "When was that?"

"When I still had use for a comb. You must have been in swaddling clothes. And you don't seem to have come on much, quite frankly. Look at yourself: you're shaking."

"It's my wet clothes, and it's very cold in here."

"Is it? Well, next time pray send advance notice of your call, and I'll turn on the fancy central heating system to welcome you, little rosebud. Come on, follow me. My office is over there. There's a stove and something for you to wrap yourself in while we dry your clothes. And some Mercurochrome and peroxide wouldn't go amiss either. You look as if you've just been dropped from a police van."

"Don't bother, really."

"I'm not bothering. I'm doing it for me, not for you. Once you've passed through this door, you play by my rules. This cemetery admits only books. You might catch pneumonia, and I don't want to call the morgue. We'll see about the book later. In thirty-eight years, I have yet to see one that will run away."

"I can't tell you how grateful I am——"

"Then don't. If I've let you in, it's out of respect for your father. Otherwise I would have left you in the street. Now, do follow me. If you behave yourself, I might consider telling you what I know of your friend Julián Carax."

Out of the corner of my eye, when he thought I couldn't see him, I noticed that, despite himself, he was smiling mischievously. Isaac clearly seemed to relish the role of sinister watchdog. I also smiled to myself. There was no doubt in my mind about to whom the face on the door knocker belonged.

10

ISAAC THREW A COUPLE OF BLANKETS OVER MY SHOULDERS AND offered me a cup of some steaming concoction that smelled of hot chocolate and hotter liquor.

"You were saying about Carax . . ."

"There's not much to say. The first person I heard mention Carax was Toni Cabestany, the publisher. I'm talking about twenty years ago, when his firm was still in business. Whenever he returned from one of his scouting trips to London, Paris, or Vienna, Cabestany would drop by and we'd chat for a while. We were both widowers by then, and he would complain that we were now married to the books, I to the old ones and he to his ledgers. We were good friends. On one of his visits, he told me how, for a pittance, he'd just acquired the Spanish rights for the novels of Julián Carax, a young writer from Barcelona who lived in Paris. This must have been in 1928 or 1929. Seems that Carax worked nights as a pianist in some small-time brothel in Pigalle and wrote during the day in a shabby attic in Saint-Germain. Paris is the only city in the world where starving to death is still considered an art. Carax had published a couple of novels in France, which had turned out to be total flops. No one gave him the time of day in Paris, and Cabestany had always liked to buy cheap."

"So did Carax write in Spanish or in French?"

"Who knows? Probably both. His mother was French, a music teacher, I believe, and he'd lived in Paris since he was about nineteen or twenty. Cabestany told me that his manuscripts arrived in Spanish. Whether they were a translation or the original, he didn't care. His favorite language was money, the rest was neither here nor there. It occurred to Cabestany that perhaps, by a stroke of luck, he might place a few thousand copies in the Spanish market."

"Did he?"

Isaac frowned as he poured me a bit more of his restorative potion. "I think the one that sold most, *The Red House,* sold about ninety copies."

"But he continued to publish Carax's books, even though he was losing money," I pointed out.

"That's right. Beats me. Cabestany wasn't exactly a romantic. But I suppose everyone has his secrets. . . . Between 1928 and 1936, he published eight of Carax's novels. Anyway, where Cabestany really made his money was in catechisms and a series of cheap sentimental novels starring a provincial heroine called Violeta LaFleur. Those sold like candy in kiosks. My guess, or anybody's, is that he published Carax's novels because it tickled his fancy, or just to contradict Darwin."

"What happened to Mr. Cabestany?"

Isaac sighed, looking up. "Age—the price we all must pay. He got ill and had a few money problems. In 1936 his eldest son took over the firm, but he was the sort who can't even read the size of his underpants. The business collapsed in less than a year. Fortunately, Cabestany never saw what his heirs did with the fruit of his life's labors, or what the war did to his country. A stroke saw him off on All Souls' Night, with a Cuban cigar in his lips and a twenty-five-year-old on his lap. What a way to go. The son was another breed altogether. Arrogant as only idiots can be. His first grand idea was to try to sell the entire stock of the company backlist, his father's legacy, and turn it into pulp or something like that. A friend, another brat, with a house in Caldetas and an Italian sports car, had convinced him that photo romances and *Mein Kampf* were going to sell like hotcakes, and, as a result, there would be a huge demand for paper."

"Did he really do that?"

"He would have, but he ran out of time. Shortly after his taking over the firm, someone turned up at his office and made him a very generous offer. He wanted to buy the whole remaining stock of Julián Carax novels and was offering to pay three times their market value."

"Say no more. To burn them," I murmured.

Isaac smiled. He looked surprised. "Actually, yes. And here I was thinking you were a bit slow, what with so much asking and not knowing anything."

"Who was that man?"

"Someone called Aubert or Coubert, I can't quite remember."

"Laín Coubert?"

"Does that sound familiar?"

"It's the name of one of the characters in *The Shadow of the Wind,* the last of Carax's novels."

Isaac frowned. "A fictional character?"

"In the novel Laín Coubert is the name used by the devil."

"A bit theatrical, if you ask me. But whoever he was, at least he had a sense of humor," Isaac reckoned.

With the memory of that night's encounter still fresh in my mind, I could not see the humorous side of it, from any angle, but I saved my opinion for a more auspicious occasion.

"This person, Coubert, or whatever his name is—was his face burned, disfigured?"

Isaac looked at me with a smile that betrayed both enjoyment and concern. "I haven't the foggiest. The person who told me all this never actually got to see him, and only knew because Cabestany's son told his secretary the following day. He didn't mention anything about burned faces. Are you sure you haven't got this out of some radio show?"

I threw my head back, as if to make light of the subject. "How did the matter end? Did the publisher's son sell the books to Coubert?" I asked.

"The senseless dunce tried to be too clever by half. He asked for more money than Coubert was proposing, and Coubert withdrew his offer. A few days later, shortly after midnight, Cabestany's warehouse in Pueblo Nuevo burned down to its foundations. And for free."

An Empty Plate · 71

I sighed. "What happened to Carax's books, then? Were they all destroyed?"

"Nearly all. Luckily, when Cabestany's secretary heard about the offer, she had a premonition. On her own initiative, she went to the warehouse and took a copy of each of the Carax titles. She was the one who had corresponded with Carax, and over the years they had formed a friendship of sorts. Her name was Nuria, and I think she was the only person in the publishing house, and probably in all of Barcelona, who read Carax's novels. Nuria has a fondness for lost causes. When she was little, she would take in small animals she picked up in the street. In time she went on to adopt failed authors, maybe because her father wanted to be one and never made it."

"You seem to know her very well."

Isaac wore his devilish smile. "More than she thinks I do. She's my daughter."

Silence and doubt gnawed at me. The more I heard of the story, the more confused I felt. "Apparently, Carax returned to Barcelona in 1936. Some say he died here. Did he have any relatives left here? Someone who might know about him?"

Isaac sighed. "Goodness only knows. Carax's parents had been separated for some time, I believe. The mother had gone off to South America, where she remarried. I don't think he was on speaking terms with his father since he moved to Paris."

"Why was that?"

"I don't know. People tend to complicate their own lives, as if living weren't already complicated enough."

"Do you know whether Carax's father is still alive?"

"I hope so. He was younger than me, but I go out very little these days and I haven't read the obituary pages for years—acquaintances drop dead like flies, and, quite frankly, it puts the wind up you. By the way, Carax was his mother's surname. The father was called Fortuny. He had a hat shop on Ronda de San Antonio."

"Is it possible, then, do you think, that when he returned to Barcelona, Carax may have felt tempted to visit your daughter, Nuria, if they were friends, since he wasn't on good terms with his father?"

Isaac laughed bitterly. "I'm probably the last person who would know. After all, I'm her father. I know that once, in 1932 or 1933, Nuria went to Paris on business for Cabestany, and she stayed in Julián Carax's apartment for a couple of weeks. It was Cabestany who told me. According to my daughter, she stayed in a hotel. She was unmarried at the time, and I had an inkling that Carax was a bit smitten with her. My Nuria is the sort who breaks a man's heart by just walking into a shop."

"Do you mean they were lovers?"

"You like melodrama, eh? Look, I've never interfered in Nuria's private life, because mine isn't picture perfect either. If you ever have a daughter— a blessing I wouldn't wish on anyone, because it's Murphy's Law that sooner or later she will break your heart—anyhow, as I was saying, if you ever have a daughter, you'll begin, without realizing it, to divide men into two camps: those you suspect are sleeping with her and those you don't. Whoever says that's not true is lying through his teeth. I suspected that Carax was one of the first, so I didn't care whether he was a genius or a poor wretch. To me he was always a scoundrel."

"Perhaps you were mistaken."

"Don't be offended, but you're still very young and know as much about women as I do about baking marzipan pastries."

"No contest there," I agreed. "What happened to the books your daughter took from the warehouse?"

"They're here."

"Here?"

"Where do you think your book came from—the one you found on the day your father brought you to this place?"

"I don't understand."

"It's very simple. One night, some days after the fire in Cabestany's warehouse, my daughter, Nuria, turned up here. She looked nervous. She said that someone had been following her and she was afraid it was the man called Coubert, who was trying to get hold of the books to destroy them. Nuria said she had come to hide Carax's books. She went into the large hall and hid them in the maze of bookshelves, like buried treasure. I didn't ask her where she'd put them, nor did she tell me. Before she left, she said that as soon as she managed to find Carax, she'd come back for them. It seemed to me that she was still in love with him, but I didn't say anything. I asked her whether she'd seen him recently, whether she'd had any news. She said she hadn't heard from him for months, practically since he'd sent the final corrections for the manuscript of his last book. I can't say whether she was lying. What I do know is that after that day Nuria didn't hear from Carax again, and those books were left here, gathering dust."

"Do you think your daughter would be willing to talk to me about all this?"

"Could be, but I don't know whether she'd be able to tell you anything that yours truly hasn't told you already. Remember, all this happened a long time ago. The truth is that we don't get on as well as I'd like. We see each other once a month. We go out to lunch somewhere close by, and then she's off as quick as she came. I know that a few years ago she married a nice man, a journalist, a bit harebrained, I'd say, one of those people who are always getting into trouble over politics, but with a good heart. They had a civil wedding, with no guests. I found out a month later. She has never introduced me to her husband. Miquel, his name is. Or something like that. I don't suppose she's very proud of her father, and I don't blame her. Now she's a changed woman. Imagine, she even learned to knit, and I'm told she no longer dresses like Simone de Beauvoir. One of these days, I'll find out I'm a grandfather. For years she's been working at home as an Italian and French translator. I don't know where she got the talent from, quite frankly. Not from her father, that's for sure. Let me write down her address, though I'm not sure it's a very good idea to say I sent you."

Isaac scribbled something on the corner of an old newspaper and handed me the scrap of paper.

"I'm very grateful. You never know, maybe she'll remember something. . . ."

Isaac smiled with some sadness. "As a child she'd remember everything. Everything. Then children grow up, and you no longer know what they think or what they feel. And that's how it should be, I suppose. Don't tell Nuria what I've told you, will you? What's been said here tonight should go no further."

"Don't worry. Do you think she still thinks about Carax?"

Isaac gave a long sigh and lowered his eyes. "Heaven knows. I don't know whether she really loved him. These things remain locked inside, and now she's a married woman. When I was your age, I had a girlfriend, Teresita Boadas, her name was—she sewed aprons in the Santamaría textile factory, on Calle Comercio. She was sixteen, two years younger than me, and she was the first woman I ever fell for. Don't look at me like that. I know you youngsters think we old people have never fallen in love. Teresita's father had an ice cart in the Borne Market and had been born dumb. You can't imagine how scared I was the day I asked him for his daughter's hand and he spent five long minutes staring at me, without any apparent reaction, holding the ice pick in his hand. I'd been saving up for two years to buy Teresita a wedding ring when she fell ill. Something she'd caught in the workshop, she told me. Six months later she was dead of tuberculosis. I can still remember how the dumb man moaned the day we buried her in the Pueblo Nuevo cemetery."

Isaac fell into a deep silence. I didn't dare breathe. After a while he looked up and smiled.

"I'm speaking of fifty-five years ago, imagine! But if I must be frank, a day doesn't go by without me thinking of her, of the walks we used to take as far as the ruins of the 1888 Universal Exhibition, or of how she would laugh at me when I read her the poems I wrote in the back room of my uncle Leopoldo's grocery store. I even remember the face of a Gypsy woman who read our fortune on El Bogatell beach and told us we'd always be together. In her own way, she was right. What can I say? Well, yes, I think Nuria still remembers that man, even if she doesn't say so. And the truth is, I'll never forgive Carax for that. You're still very young, but I know how much these things hurt. If you want my opinion, Carax was a robber of hearts, and he took my daughter's to the grave or to hell. I'll only ask you one thing: if you see her and talk to her, let me know how she is. Find out whether she's happy. And whether she's forgiven her father."

SHORTLY BEFORE DAWN, WITH ONLY AN OIL LAMP TO LIGHT MY WAY, I went back into the Cemetery of Forgotten Books. As I did so, I imagined

Isaac's daughter wandering through the same dark and endless corridors with exactly the same determination as guided me that day: to save the book. I thought I remembered the route I'd followed the first time I visited that place with my father, but soon I realized that the folds of the labyrinth bent the passages into spirals that were impossible to recall. Three times I tried to follow a path I thought I had memorized, and three times the maze returned me to the same point. Isaac waited for me there, a wry smile on his face.

"Do you intend to come back for it one day?" he asked.

"Of course."

"In that case you might like to cheat a little."

"Cheat?"

"Young man, you're a bit slow on the uptake, aren't you? Remember the Minotaur."

It took me a few seconds to understand what he was suggesting. Isaac pulled an old penknife out of his pocket and handed it to me.

"Make a mark on every corner, a notch only you will recognize. It's old wood and so full of scratches and grooves that nobody will notice it, unless the person knows what he's looking for. . . ."

I followed his advice and once more penetrated the heart of the structure. Every time I changed direction, I stopped to mark the shelves with a C and an X on the side of the passage that I was intending to take. Twenty minutes later I had lost myself in the depths of the tower, and then, quite by chance, the place where I was going to bury the novel was revealed to me. To my right I noticed a row of volumes on the disentailment of church property penned by the distinguished Jovellanos. To my adolescent eyes, such a camouflage would have dissuaded even the craftiest mind. I took out a few tomes and inspected the second row that was concealed behind those walls of marble prose. Among little clouds of dust, various plays by Moratín and a brand-new *Curial e Güelfa* stood side by side with Spinoza's *Tractatus Theologico-Politicus*. As a coup de grâce, I resolved to confine the Carax book between the 1901 yearbook of judicial minutiae from the civil courts of Gerona and a collection of novels by Juan Valera. In order to make space, I decided to remove and take with me the book of Golden Age poetry that separated them, and in its place I slipped in *The Shadow of the Wind*. I took my leave of the novel with a wink and put the Jovellanos anthology back in its place, walling in the back row.

Without further ado I left the place, finding my route by the marks I had made on the way in. As I walked in the dark through the tunnels and tunnels of books, I could not help being overcome by a sense of sadness. I couldn't help thinking that if I, by pure chance, had found a whole universe in a single unknown book, buried in that endless necropolis, tens of thousands more would remain unexplored, forgotten forever. I felt myself surrounded by millions of abandoned pages, by worlds and souls without an owner sinking in an ocean of darkness, while the world that throbbed outside the library seemed to be losing its memory, day after day, unknowingly, feeling all the wiser the more it forgot.

DAWN WAS BREAKING WHEN I RETURNED TO THE APARTMENT ON CALLE Santa Ana. Opening the door quietly, I slipped in without switching on the light. From the entrance hall, I could see the dining room at the end of the corridor, the table still decked out for the party. The cake was there, untouched, and the dinner service still waited for the meal. I could make out the motionless silhouette of my father in the armchair, as he observed the scene from the window. He was awake and still wearing his best suit. Wreaths of smoke rose lazily from a cigarette he held between his index and ring fingers, as if it were a pen. I hadn't seen my father smoke for years.

"Good morning," he murmured, putting out the cigarette in an ashtray that was full of half-smoked butts.

I looked at him without knowing what to say. The light from behind him concealed his eyes.

"Clara phoned a few times last night, a couple of hours after you left," he said. "She sounded very worried. She left a message for you to call her, no matter what time it was."

"I don't intend to see or speak to Clara again," I said.

My father nodded but didn't reply. I fell into one of the dining-room chairs and stared at the floor.

"Aren't you going to tell me where you've been?"

"Just around."

"You've given me one hell of a fright."

There was no anger in his voice and hardly any reproach, just tiredness.

"I know. And I'm sorry," I answered.

"What have you done to your face?"

"I slipped in the rain and fell."

"That rain must have a good right hook. Put something on it."

"It's nothing. I don't even notice it," I lied. "What I need is to get some sleep. I can barely stand up."

"At least open your present before you go to bed," said my father.

He pointed to the packet wrapped in cellophane, which he had placed the night before on the coffee table. I hesitated for a moment. My father nodded. I took the packet and felt its weight. I handed it to my father without opening it.

"You'd better return it. I don't deserve any presents."

"Presents are made for the pleasure of who gives them, not for the merits of who receives them," said my father. "Besides, it can't be returned. Open it."

I undid the carefully wrapped package in the dim light of dawn. It contained a shiny carved wooden box, edged with gold rivets. Even before opening it, I was smiling. The sound of the clasp when it unlocked was exquisite, like the ticking of a watch. Inside, the case was lined with dark blue velvet. Victor Hugo's fabulous Montblanc Meinsterstück rested in the center. It was a dazzling sight. I took it and gazed at it by the light of the balcony. The gold clip of the pen top had an inscription.

DANIEL SEMPERE, 1950

I stared at my father, dumbfounded. I don't think I had ever seen him look as happy as he seemed to me at that moment. Without saying anything, he got up from his armchair and held me tight. I felt a lump in my throat and, lost for words, fell utterly silent.

True to

Character

1951–1953

11

T HAT YEAR AUTUMN BLANKETED BARCELONA WITH FALLEN LEAVES that rippled through the streets like silvery scales. The distant memory of the night of my sixteenth birthday had put a damper on my spirits, or perhaps life had decided to grant me a sabbatical from my melodramatic woes so that I could begin to grow up. I was surprised at how little I thought about Clara Barceló, or Julián Carax, or that faceless cipher who smelled of burned paper and claimed to be a character straight out of a book. By November, I had observed a month of sobriety, a month without going anywhere near Plaza Real to beg a glimpse of Clara through the window. The merit, I must confess, was not altogether mine. Business in the bookshop was picking up, and my father and I had more on our hands than we could juggle.

"At this rate we'll have to hire another person to help us find the orders," my father remarked. "What we'd really need is someone very special, half detective, half poet, someone who won't charge much or be afraid to tackle the impossible."

"I think I have the right candidate," I said.

I found Fermín Romero de Torres in his usual lodgings below the arches of Calle Fernando. The beggar was putting together the front page of the

Monday paper from bits he had rescued from a trash can. The lead story went on about the greatness of national public works as yet more proof of the glorious progress of the dictatorship's policies.

"Good God! Another dam!" I heard him cry. "These fascists will turn us all into a race of saints and frogs."

"Good morning," I said quietly. "Do you remember me?"

The beggar raised his head, and a wonderful smile suddenly lit up his face.

"Do mine eyes deceive me? How are things with you, my friend? You'll accept a swig of red wine, I hope?"

"It's on me today," I said. "Are you hungry?"

"Well, I wouldn't say no to a good plate of seafood, but I'll eat anything that's thrown at me."

On our way to the bookshop, Fermín Romero de Torres filled me in on all manner of escapades he had devised during the last weeks to avoid the Security Services, and in particular one Inspector Fumero, his nemesis, with whom he appeared to have a running battle.

"Fumero?" I asked. That was the name of the soldier who had murdered Clara Barceló's father in Montjuïc Castle at the outbreak of the war.

The little man nodded fearfully, turning pale. He looked famished and dirty, and he stank from months of living in the streets. The poor fellow had no idea where I was taking him, and I noticed a certain apprehension, a growing anxiety that he tried to disguise with incessant chatter. When we arrived at the shop, he gave me a troubled look.

"Please come in. This is my father's bookshop. I'd like to introduce you to him."

The beggar hunched himself up into a bundle of grime and nerves. "No, no, I wouldn't hear of it. I don't look presentable, and this is a classy establishment. I would embarrass you. . . ."

My father put his head around the door, glanced at the beggar, and then looked at me out of the corner of his eye.

"Dad, this is Fermín Romero de Torres."

"At your service," said the beggar, almost shaking.

My father smiled at him calmly and stretched out his hand. The beggar didn't dare take it, mortified by his appearance and the filth that covered his skin.

"Listen, I think it's best if I go away and leave you," he stammered.

My father took him gently by the arm. "Not at all; my son has told me you're going to have lunch with us."

The beggar looked at us amazed, terrified.

"Why don't you come up to our home and have a nice hot bath?" said my father. "Afterward, if that's all right, we could walk down to Can Solé for lunch."

Fermín Romero de Torres mumbled something unintelligible. Still smiling, my father led him toward the front door and practically had to drag him up the stairs to the apartment while I closed the shop. By dint of honeyed words and underhanded tactics, we managed to remove his rags and get him into the bath. With nothing on, he looked like a wartime photograph and trembled like a plucked chicken. Deep marks showed on his wrists and ankles, and his trunk and back were covered with terrible scars that were painful to see. My father and I exchanged horrified looks but made no comment.

The beggar allowed himself to be washed like a child, frightened and shivering. While I searched for clean clothes, I could hear my father's voice talking to him without pause. I found him a suit that my father no longer wore, an old shirt, and some underwear. From the pile of clothes the beggar had taken off, not even the shoes could be rescued. I chose a pair that my father seldom put on because they were too small for him. Then I wrapped the rags in newspaper, including a pair of trousers that were the color and consistency of smoked ham, and shoved them in the trash can. When I returned to the bathroom, my father was shaving Fermín in the bathtub. Pale and smelling of soap, he looked twenty years younger. From what I could see, the two had already struck up a friendship. It may have been the effects of the bath salts, but Fermín Romero de Torres was on overdrive.

"Believe me, Mr. Sempere, if fate hadn't led me into the world of international intrigue, what I would have gone for, what was closest to my heart, was humanities. As a child I felt the call of poetry and wanted to be a Sophocles or a Virgil, because tragedy and dead languages give me the goose pimples. But my father, God rest his soul, was a pigheaded man without much vision. He'd always wanted one of his children to join the Civil Guard, and none of my seven sisters would have qualified for that, despite the facial-hair problem that characterized all the women on my mother's side of the family. On his deathbed my father made me swear that if I didn't succeed in wearing the Civil Guard's three-cornered hat, at least I would become a civil servant and abandon all my literary ambitions. I'm rather old-fashioned, and I believe that a father, however dim-witted, should be obeyed, if you see what I mean. Even so, don't imagine that I set aside all intellectual pursuits during my years of adventure. I've read a great deal, and can recite some of the best fragments of *La Divina Commedia* from memory."

"Come on, boss, put these clothes on, if you don't mind; your erudition is beyond any doubt," I said, coming to my father's rescue.

When Fermín Romero de Torres came out of the bath, sparkling clean, his eyes beamed with gratitude. My father wrapped him up in a towel, and the beggar laughed from the sheer pleasure of feeling clean fabric brushing his skin. I helped him into his change of clothes, which proved about ten sizes too big. My father removed his belt and handed it to me to put around him.

"You look very dashing," said my father. "Doesn't he, Daniel?"

"Anyone might mistake you for a film star."

"Come off it. I'm not what I used to be. I lost my Herculean muscles in prison, and since then . . ."

"Well, I think you look like Charles Boyer, at least in build," objected my father. "Which reminds me: I wanted to propose something to you."

"For you, Mr. Sempere, I would kill, if I had to. Just say the name, and I'll get rid of the guy before he knows what's hit him."

"It won't come to that. What I wanted to offer you was a job in the bookshop. It consists of looking for rare books for our clients. It's almost like literary archaeology, and it would be just as important for you to know the classics as the basic black-market techniques. I can't pay you much at present, but you can eat at our table and, until we find you a good *pensión,* you can stay here with us, in the apartment, if that's all right with you."

The beggar looked at both of us, dumbfounded.

"What do you say?" asked my father. "Will you join the team?"

I thought he was going to say something, but at that moment Fermín Romero de Torres burst into tears.

WITH HIS FIRST WAGES, FERMÍN ROMERO DE TORRES BOUGHT HIMSELF A glamorous hat and a pair of galoshes and insisted on treating me and my father to a dish of bull's tail, which was served on Mondays in a restaurant a couple of blocks away from the Monumental bull ring. My father had found him a room in a *pensión* on Calle Joaquín Costa, where, thanks to the friendship between our neighbor Merceditas and the landlady, we were able to avoid filling in the guest form required by the police, thus removing Fermín Romero de Torres from under the nose of Inspector Fumero and his henchmen. Sometimes I thought about the terrible scars that covered his body and felt tempted to ask him about them, fearing that perhaps Inspector Fumero might have something to do with them. But there was a look in the eyes of that poor man that made me think it was better not to bring up the subject. Perhaps he would tell us one day, when he felt the time was right. Every morning, at seven on the dot, Fermín waited for us by the shop door with a smile on his face, neatly turned out and ready to work an unbroken twelve-hour shift, or even longer. He had discovered a passion for chocolate and Swiss rolls—which did not lessen his enthusiasm for the great names of Greek tragedy—and this meant he had put on a little weight. He shaved like a young swell, combed his hair back with brilliantine, and was growing a pencil mustache to look fashionable. Thirty days after emerging from our bathtub, the ex-beggar was unrecognizable. But despite his spectacular change, where Fermín Romero de Torres had really left us openmouthed was on the battlefield. His sleuthlike instincts, which I had attributed to delirious fantasies, proved surgically precise. He could solve the strangest requests in a matter of days, even hours. Was there no title he didn't know, and no stratagem for obtaining it at a good price that didn't occur to him? He could talk his way into the private libraries of duchesses on Avenida Pearson and horse-riding dilettantes, always adopting fictitious identities, and would depart with the said books as gifts or bought for a pittance.

The transformation from beggar into model citizen seemed miraculous, like one of those stories that priests from poor parishes loved to tell to illustrate the Lord's infinite mercy—stories that invariably sounded too good to be true, like the ads for hair-restorer lotions that were plastered over the trams.

Three and a half months after Fermín started work in the bookshop, the telephone in the apartment on Calle Santa Ana woke us up one Sunday at two o'clock in the morning. It was Fermín's landlady. In a voice choked with anxiety, she explained that Mr. Romero de Torres had locked himself in his room and was shouting like a madman, banging on the walls and swearing that if anyone dared come in, he would slit his own throat with a broken bottle.

"Don't call the police, please. We'll be right there."

Rushing out, we made our way toward Calle Joaquín Costa. It was a cold night, with icy wind and tar-black skies. We hurried past the two ancient hospices—Casa de la Misericordia and Casa de Piedad—ignoring looks and words from dark doorways smelling of charcoal. Soon we reached the corner of Calle Ferlandina. Joaquín Costa lay there, a gap in the rows of blackened beehives, blending into the darkness of the Raval quarter. The landlady's eldest son was waiting for us downstairs.

"Have you called the police?" asked my father.

"Not yet," answered the son.

We ran upstairs. The *pensión* was on the second floor, the staircase a spiral of grime scarcely visible in the ocher light shed by naked bulbs that hung limply from a bare wire. Doña Encarna, the landlady, the widow of a Civil Guard corporal, met us at the door wrapped in a light blue dressing gown, crowned with a matching set of curlers.

"Look here, Mr. Sempere, this is a decent house. I have more offers than I can take, and I don't need to put up with this kind of thing," she said as she guided us through a dark corridor that reeked of ammonia and damp.

"I understand," mumbled my father.

Fermín Romero de Torres's screams could be heard tearing at the walls at the end of the corridor. Several drawn and frightened faces peeped around half-open doors—boardinghouse faces fed on watery soup.

"And the rest of you, off to sleep, for fuck's sake! This isn't a variety show at the Molino!" cried Doña Encarna furiously.

We stopped in front of the door to Fermín's room. My father rapped gently with his knuckles.

"Fermín? Are you there? It's Sempere."

The howl that pierced the walls chilled me. Even Doña Encarna lost her matronly composure and put her hands on her heart, hidden under the many folds of her ample chest.

My father called again. "Fermín? Come on, open the door."

Fermín howled again, throwing himself against the walls, yelling obscenities at the top of his voice. My father sighed.

"Doña Encarna, do you have a key to this room?"

"Well, of course."

"Give it to me, please."

Doña Encarna hesitated. The other guests were peering into the corridor again, white with terror. Those shouts must have been heard from the army headquarters.

"And you, Daniel, run and find Dr. Baró. He lives very close, in number twelve, Riera Alta."

"Listen, wouldn't it be better to call a priest? He sounds to me as if he's possessed by the devil," suggested Doña Encarna.

"No. A doctor will do fine. Come on, Daniel. Run. And you, please give me that key."

Dr. Baró was a sleepless bachelor who spent his nights reading Zola and looking at 3-D pictures of young ladies in racy underwear to relieve his boredom. He was a regular customer at my father's bookshop, and, though he described himself as a second-rate quack, he had a better eye for reaching the right diagnosis than most of the smart doctors with elegant practices on Calle Muntaner. Many of his patients were old whores from the neighborhood or poor wretches who could barely afford to pay him, but he would see them all the same. I heard him say repeatedly that the world was God's chamber pot and that his sole remaining wish was for Barcelona's football team to win the league, once and for all, so that he could die in peace. He opened the door in his dressing gown, smelling of wine and flaunting an unlit cigarette between his lips.

"Daniel?"

"My father sent me. It's an emergency."

When we returned to the *pensión,* we found Doña Encarna sobbing with fear and the other guests turned the color of old candle wax. My father was holding Fermín Romero de Torres in his arms in a corner of the room. Fermín was naked, crying and shaking. The room was a wreck, the walls stained with something that could have been either blood or excrement—I couldn't tell. Dr. Baró quickly took in the situation and gestured to my father to lay Fermín on the bed. They were helped by Doña Encarna's son, a would-be boxer. Fermín moaned and thrashed about as if some vermin were devouring his insides.

"But for goodness' sake, what's the matter with this poor man? What's wrong with him?" groaned Doña Encarna from the door, shaking her head.

The doctor took his pulse, examined his pupils with a flashlight, and, without saying a word, proceeded to prepare an injection from a bottle he carried in his bag.

"Hold him down. This will make him sleep. Daniel, help us."

Between us four we managed to immobilize Fermín, who jerked violently when he felt the stab of the needle in his thigh. His muscles tensed like steel cables, but after a few seconds his eyes clouded over and his body went limp.

"Hey, be careful, that man's not very strong, and anything could kill him," said Doña Encarna.

"Don't worry. He's only asleep," said the doctor as he examined the scars that covered Fermín's starved body.

I saw him shake his head slowly. "Bastards," he mumbled.

"What are these scars from?" I asked. "Cuts?"

Dr. Baró shook his head again, without looking up. He found a blanket amid the wreckage and covered his patient with it. "Burns. This man has been tortured," he explained. "These marks are from a soldering iron."

Fermín slept for two days. When he awoke, he could not remember anything; he just thought he'd woken up in a dark cell, that was all. He felt so ashamed of his behavior that he went down on his knees to beg for Doña Encarna's forgiveness. He swore he would paint the *pensión* for her and, knowing she was very devout, promised she would have ten masses said for her in the Church of Belén.

"What you have to do is get better and not frighten me like that again. I'm too old for that sort of thing."

My father paid for the damages and begged Doña Encarna to give Fermín another chance. She gladly agreed. Most of her guests were dispossessed people who were alone in the world, like her. Once she had got over the fright, she felt an even greater affection for Fermín and made him promise her that he would take the tablets Dr. Baró had prescribed.

"For you, Doña Encarna, I'd swallow a brick if need be."

In time we all pretended we'd forgotten what had happened, but never again did I take the stories about Inspector Fumero lightly. After that incident we would take Fermín with us almost every Sunday for an afternoon snack at the Novedades Café, so as not to leave him on his own. Then we'd walk up to the Fémina Cinema, on the corner of Calle Diputación and Paseo de Gracia. One of the ushers was a friend of my father's, and he would let us sneak in through the fire exit on the ground floor during the newsreel, always when the Generalissimo was in the act of cutting the ribbon to inaugurate some new reservoir, which really got on Fermín's nerves.

"What a disgrace," he would say indignantly.

"Don't you like the cinema, Fermín?"

"Between you and me, this business of the seventh art leaves me cold. As far as I can see, it's only a way of feeding the mindless and making them even more stupid. Worse than football or bullfights. The cinema began as an invention for entertaining the illiterate masses. Fifty years on, it's much the same."

Fermín's attitude changed radically the day he discovered Carole Lombard.

"What breasts, Jesus, Mary, and Joseph, what breasts!" he exclaimed in the middle of the film, beside himself. "Those aren't tits, they're two schooners!"

"Shut up, you degenerate, or I'll call the manager," muttered a voice straight from the confessional, a few rows behind us. "People have no shame. What a country of pigs we live in."

"You'd better lower your voice, Fermín," I advised him.

Fermín Romero de Torres wasn't listening to me. He was lost in the gentle swell of that miraculous bosom, with an enraptured smile and unblinking eyes. Later, walking back along Paseo de Gracia, I noticed that our bibliographic detective was still in a trance.

"I think we're going to have to find you a woman," I said. "A woman will brighten up your life, you'll see."

Fermín sighed, his mind still dwelling on charms that seemed to overcome the laws of gravity.

"Do you speak from experience, Daniel?" he asked in all innocence.

I just smiled, knowing that my father was watching me.

After that day Fermín Romero de Torres took to going to the movies every Sunday. My father preferred to stay at home reading, but Fermín would not miss a single double feature. He'd buy a pile of chocolates and sit in row seventeen, where he would devour them while he waited for the appearance of that day's diva. As far as he was concerned, plot was superfluous, and he didn't stop talking until some well-endowed lady filled the screen.

"I've been thinking about what you said the other day, about finding a woman for me," said Fermín Romero de Torres. "Perhaps you're right. In the *pensión* there's a new lodger, an ex-seminarist from Seville with plenty of spirit, who brings in some impressive young ladies every now and then. I must say, the race has improved no end. I don't know how the lad manages it, because he's not much to look at; perhaps he renders them senseless with prayers. He's got the room next to mine, so I can hear everything, and, judging by the sound effects, the friar must be a real artist. Just shows what a uniform can do. Tell me, what sort of women do you like, Daniel?"

"I don't know much about them, honestly."

"Nobody knows much about women, not even Freud, not even women themselves. But it's like electricity: you don't have to know how it works to get a shock on the fingers. Come on, out with it. How do you like them? People might not agree with me, but I think a woman should have a feminine shape, something you can get your hands on. You, on the other hand, look like you might be partial to the skinny type, a point of view I fully respect, don't misunderstand me."

"Frankly, I don't have much experience with women. None, to be precise."

Fermín Romero de Torres looked at me carefully, intrigued by this revelation.

"I thought that what happened that night, you know, when you were beaten up . . ."

"If only everything hurt as little as a blow to the face . . ."

Fermín seemed to read my mind, and smiled supportively. "Don't let that upset you, then. With women the best part is the discovery. There's nothing like the first time, nothing. You don't know what life is until you undress a woman the first time. A button at a time, like peeling a hot sweet potato on a winter's night."

A few seconds later, Veronica Lake made her grand entrance onto the scene, and Fermín was transported to another plane. Taking advantage of a reel in which Miss Lake was absent, Fermín announced that he was going to pay a visit to the candy stand in the foyer to replenish his stocks. After months of starvation, my friend had lost all sense of proportion, but, due to his metabolism, he never quite lost that hungry, squalid postwar look. I was left alone, barely following the action on the screen. I would lie if I said I was thinking of Clara. I was thinking only of her body, trembling under the music teacher's charges, glistening with sweat and pleasure. My gaze left the screen, and only then did I notice a spectator who had just come in. I saw his silhouette moving to the center of the orchestra, six rows in front of me. He sat down. Cinemas are full of lonely people, I thought. Like me.

I tried to concentrate on picking up the thread of the story. The hero, a cynical but good-hearted detective, was telling a secondary character why women like Veronica Lake were the ruin of all sensible males and why all one could do was love them desperately and perish, betrayed by their double dealings. Fermín Romero de Torres, who was becoming an adept film scholar, called this genre "the praying mantis paradigm." According to him, its permutations were nothing but misogynist fantasies for constipated office clerks, for pious women shriveled with boredom who dreamed about turning to a life of vice and unbridled lechery. I smiled as I imagined the asides my friend the critic would have made had he not gone to his meeting with the candy stand. But the smile froze on my face. The spectator who sat six rows in front of me had turned around and was staring at me. The projector's misty beam bored through the darkness of the hall, a slim cloud of flickering light that revealed only outlines and blots of color. I recognized Coubert, the faceless man, immediately. His steely look, his shining eyes with no eyelids; his smile as he licked his nonexistent lips in the dark. I felt cold fingers gripping my heart. Two hundred violins broke out on-screen, there were shots and shouts, and the scene dissolved. For a moment the hall plunged into utter darkness, and I could only hear my own heartbeat hammering in my temples. Slowly a new scene glowed on the screen, replacing the darkness of the room with a haze of blue and purple. The man without a face had disappeared. I turned and caught a glimpse of a silhouette walking up the aisle and passing Fermín, who was returning from his gastronomic safari. He moved into the row, took his seat, and handed me a praline chocolate.

"Daniel, you're as white as a nun's buttock. Are you all right?" he asked, giving me a worried look.

A mysterious breath of air wafted through the hall.

"It smells odd," Fermín remarked. "Like a rancid fart, from a councilman or a lawyer."

"No. It smells of burned paper."

"Go on. Have a lemon Sugus candy—it cures everything."

"I don't feel like one."

"Keep it, then, you never know when a Sugus candy might get you out of a pickle."

I put the sweet in my jacket pocket and drifted through the rest of the film without paying any attention to Veronica Lake or to the victims of her fatal charms. Fermín Romero de Torres was engrossed in the show and the chocolates. When the lights went on at the end of the film, I felt myself to be waking from a bad dream and was tempted to imagine that the man in the theater had been a mere illusion, a trick of memory. But his brief glance in the dark had been enough to convey his message. He had not forgotten me, or our pact.

· 12 ·

THE FIRST EFFECT OF FERMÍN'S ARRIVAL SOON BECAME APPARENT: I discovered I had much more free time. When Fermín was not out hunting some exotic volume to satisfy a customer's request, he spent his time organizing stocks in the bookshop, dreaming up marketing strategies, polishing the shop sign and windows till they sparkled, or buffing up the spines of the books with a rag and a bit of alcohol. Given this windfall, I decided to devote my leisure time to a couple of pursuits I had lately put aside: attempting to unravel the Carax mystery and, above all, spending more time with my friend Tomás Aguilar, whom I greatly missed.

Tomás was a thoughtful, reserved boy whom other children feared because his vaguely thuggish features gave him a grave and threatening look. He had a wrestler's build, gladiator's shoulders, and a steely, penetrating gaze. We had met many years before in the course of a fistfight, during my first week at the Jesuit school on Calle Caspe. His father had come to pick him up after classes, accompanied by a conceited girl who turned out to be Tomás's sister. I had the brilliant idea of making some tasteless remark about her and before I could blink, Tomás had thrown himself on me and was showering me with a deluge of blows that left me smarting for a few weeks. Tomás was twice my size, strength, and ferocity. During our school-yard duel, surrounded by boys who were thirsty for a bloody fight, I lost a tooth but gained an improved sense of proportion. I refused to tell my father or the priests who had inflicted such a thundering beating on me. Neither did I volunteer the fact that the father of my adversary had watched the thumping with an expression of sheer pleasure, joining in the chorus with the other schoolchildren.

"It was my fault," I said, closing the subject.

Three weeks later Tomás came up to me during the break. I was paralyzed with fear. He is coming to finish me off, I thought. I began to stammer, but soon I understood that all he wanted to do was apologize for the thrashing, because he knew the fight had been uneven and unfair.

"I'm the one who should say I'm sorry, for picking on your sister," I said. "I would have done it the other day, but you did my mouth in before I could speak."

Tomás looked down, ashamed of himself. I gazed at that shy and quiet giant who wandered around the classrooms and school corridors like a lost soul. All the other children—me included—were scared stiff of him, and nobody spoke to him or dared look him in the eye. With his head down, almost shaking, he asked me whether I'd like to be his friend. I said I would. He held out his hand, and I shook it. His handshake hurt, but I didn't flinch. That afternoon he invited me to his house for an after-school snack and showed me his collection of strange gadgets made from bits of scrap metal, which he kept in his room.

"I made them," he explained proudly.

I was incapable of understanding how they worked or even what they were supposed to be, but I didn't say anything. I just nodded in admiration. It seemed to me that this oversize, solitary boy had constructed his own tin companions and that I was the first person he was introducing them to. It was his secret. I shared mine. I told him about my mother and how much I missed her. When my voice broke, Tomás hugged me, without saying a word. We were ten years old. From that day on, Tomás Aguilar became my best—and I his only—friend.

Despite his aggressive looks, Tomás was a peaceful and good-hearted person whose appearance discouraged confrontations. He stammered quite a bit, especially when he spoke to anyone who wasn't his mother, his sister, or me, which was hardly ever. He was fascinated by outlandish inventions and mechanical devices, and I soon discovered that he carried out autopsies on all manner of appliances, from gramophones to adding machines, in order to discover their secrets. When he wasn't with me or working for his father, Tomás spent most of his time secluded in his room, devising incomprehensible contraptions. His intelligence was matched by his lack of practicality. His interest in the real world centered on details such as the synchronicity of traffic lights on Gran Vía, the mysteries of the illuminated fountains of Montjuïc, or the clockwork souls of the automatons at the Tibidabo amusement park.

Every afternoon Tomás worked in his father's office, and sometimes, on his way out, he'd stop by the bookshop. My father always showed an interest in his inventions and gave him manuals on mechanics or biographies of engineers like Eiffel and Edison, whom Tomás idolized. As the years went by, Tomás became very attached to my father and spent ages trying to invent an automatic system with which to file his bibliographic index cards, using parts of an old electric fan. He had been working on the project for four years now, but my father still showed great enthusiasm for its progress, because he didn't want Tomás to lose heart.

When I first introduced Tomás to Fermín, I was concerned about how Fermín was going to react to my friend.

"You must be Daniel's inventor friend. It's a great pleasure to make your acquaintance. Fermín Romero de Torres, bibliographic adviser to the Sempere bookshop, at your service."

"Tomás Aguilar," stammered my friend, smiling and shaking Fermín's hand.

"Watch out, my friend, for what you have here isn't a hand, it's a hydraulic press. I need violinist's fingers for my work with the firm."

Tomás let go of his hand and apologized.

"So tell me, where do you stand on Fermat's theorem?" asked Fermín, rubbing his fingers.

After that they became engrossed in an unintelligible discussion about arcane mathematics, which was Dutch to me. From that day on, Fermín always addressed him with the formal *usted* or called him "doctor," and pretended not to notice the boy's stammer. As a way of repaying Fermín for his infinite patience, Tomás brought him boxes of Swiss chocolates stamped with photographs of impossibly blue lakes, cows parading along Technicolor-green fields, and camera-ready cuckoo clocks.

"Your friend Tomás is talented, but he lacks drive and could benefit from a more winning demeanor. It's the only way to get anywhere," Fermín said to me one day. "Alas, that's the scientist's mind for you. Just consider Albert Einstein. All those prodigious inventions, and the first one they find a practical application for is the atom bomb—without his permission. Tomás is going to have a hard time in academic circles with that boxer's face of his. In this world the only opinion that holds court is prejudice."

Driven by a wish to save Tomás from a life of penury and misunderstanding, Fermín had decided that he needed to develop my friend's latent conversational and social skills.

"Like the good ape he is, man is a social animal, characterized by cronyism, nepotism, corruption, and gossip. That's the intrinsic blueprint for our 'ethical behavior,'" he argued. "It's pure biology."

"Aren't you exaggerating?"

"Sometimes you're so naïve, Daniel."

Tomás had inherited his tough looks from his father, a prosperous property manager with an office on Calle Pelayo, close to the sumptuous El Siglo department store. Mr. Aguilar belonged to that race of privileged minds who are always right. A man of deep convictions, he believed, among other things, that his son was both fainthearted and mentally deficient. To compensate for these shameful traits, he employed all sorts of private tutors in the hope of improving his firstborn. "I want you to treat my son as if he were an imbecile, do you understand?" I would often hear him say. The teachers tried everything, even pleading, but Tomás was in the habit of addressing them only in Latin, a language he spoke with papal fluency and in which he did not stammer. Sooner or later they all resigned in despair, fearing he might be possessed: he might be spouting demonic instructions in Aramaic at them, for all they knew. Mr. Aguilar's only hope was that military service would make a man of him.

Tomás had a sister, Beatriz. I owed our friendship to her, because if I hadn't seen her that afternoon, long ago, holding on to her father's hand, waiting for the classes to end, and hadn't decided to make a joke in very bad taste at her expense, my friend would never have rained all those blows on me and I would never have had the courage to speak to him. Bea Aguilar was the very image of her mother and the apple of her father's eye. Red-headed and exquisitely pale, she always wore very expensive dresses made of silk or pure wool. She had a mannequin's waist and wandered around straight as a rod, playing the role of princess in her own fairy tale. Her eyes were a greeny blue, but she insisted on describing them as "emerald and sapphire." Despite her many years as a pupil at the strict Catholic school of the Teresian mothers, or perhaps for that very reason, when her father wasn't looking, Bea drank anise liqueur from a tall glass, wore nylon stockings from the elegant shop La Perla Gris, and dolled herself up like the screen goddesses who sent my friend Fermín into a trance. I couldn't stand the sight of her, and she repaid my open hostility with languid looks of disdain and indifference. Bea had a boyfriend who was doing his military service as a lieutenant in Murcia, a slick-haired member of the Falangist Party called Pablo Cascos Buendía. He belonged to an aristocratic family who owned a number of shipyards on the Galician *rías* and spent half his time on leave thanks to an uncle in the Military Government. Second Lieutenant Cascos Buendía wasted no opportunity to lecture people on the genetic and spiritual superiority of the Spanish people and the imminent decline of the Bolshevik empire.

"Marx is dead," he would say solemnly.

"He died in 1883, to be precise," I would answer.

"Zip it, bonehead, or I'll kick you all the way to the Rock of Gibraltar."

More than once I had caught Bea smiling to herself at the inanities that her boyfriend came out with. She would raise her eyes and watch me, with a look I couldn't fathom. I would smile back with the feeble civility of enemies held together by an indefinite truce but would look away quickly. I would have died before admitting it, but in my heart of hearts, I was afraid of her.

Aₜ the beginning of that year, Tomás and Fermín decided to pool their respective brains on a new project that, they predicted, would get us both out of being drafted. Fermín, in particular, did not share Mr. Aguilar's enthusiasm for the army experience.

"The only use for military service is that it reveals the number of morons in the population," he would remark. "And that can be discovered in the first two weeks; there's no need for two years. Army, Marriage, the Church, and Banking: the Four Horsemen of the Apocalypse. Yes, go on, laugh."

Fermín Romero de Torres's anarchist-libertarian leanings were to be shaken one October afternoon when, in a twist of fate, we had a visit from an old friend. My father had gone to Argentona, to price a book collection, and would not be back until the evening. I was left in charge of the counter while Fermín insisted on climbing up a ladder like a tightrope walker to tidy up the books on the top shelf, just inches from the ceiling. Shortly before closing time, when the sun had already set, Bernarda's profile appeared at the shop window. She was dressed in her Thursday clothes—Thursday was her day off—and she waved at me. My heart soared just to see her, and I signaled to her to come in.

"My goodness, how you've grown!" she said from the entrance. "I would hardly have recognized you . . . why, you're a man now!"

She embraced me, shedding a few tears and touching my head, shoulders, and face, as if to make sure I hadn't broken anything during her absence.

"You're really missed in the house, Master Daniel," she said, with downcast eyes.

"I've missed you, too, Bernarda. Come on, give me a kiss."

She kissed me shyly, and I planted a couple of noisy kisses on each cheek. She laughed. In her eyes I could see she was waiting for me to ask her about Clara, but I had decided not to.

"You're looking very pretty today, and very elegant. How come you've decided to pay us a visit?"

"The truth is, I've been wanting to come for a long time, but you know how things are, we're all busy, and, for all his learning, Mr. Barceló is as demanding as a child. You just have to rise above it and get on with things. But what brings me here today is that, well, tomorrow is my niece's birthday, the one from San Adrián, and I'd like to give her a present. I thought I could get her a good book, with a lot of writing and few pictures, but as I'm such a dimwit and don't understand—"

Before I could answer, a whole hardback set of the complete works of Blasco Ibáñez plummeted from on high, and the place shook with a ballistic roar. Bernarda and I looked up anxiously. Fermín was sliding down the ladder, like a trapeze artist, a secretive smile lighting up his face, his eyes filled with rapturous lust.

"Bernarda, this is—"

"Fermín Romero de Torres, bibliographic adviser for Sempere and Son, at your service, madam," Fermín proclaimed, taking Bernarda's hand and kissing it ceremoniously.

"You must be confused, I'm no madam—"

"Marquise, at the very least," interrupted Fermín. "I should know. I have stepped out with the finest ladies on Avenida Pearson. Allow me the honor of accompanying you to our classics section for children and young adults, where I notice that by good fortune we have an anthology of the best of Emilio Salgari and his epic tale of Sandokan."

"Oh dear, I don't know, I'm not sure about lives of saints. The girl's father used to be very left wing, you know. . . ."

"Say no more, for here I have none other than Jules Verne's *The Mysterious Island,* a tale of high adventure and great educational content, because of all the science."

"If you think so . . ."

I followed them quietly, noticing how Fermín was drooling over Bernarda and how she seemed overwhelmed by the attentions showered upon her by the little man with scruffy looks and the tongue of a barker. He was devouring her with his eyes as greedily as if she were a piece of chocolate.

"What about you, Master Daniel? What do you think?"

"Fermín Romero de Torres is the resident expert here. You can trust him."

"Well, then, I'll take the one about the island, if you'd be kind enough to wrap it for me. What do I owe you?"

"It's on the house," I said.

"No it isn't, I won't hear of it."

"If you'll allow me, madam, it's on me, Fermín Romero de Torres. You'd make me the happiest man in Barcelona."

Bernarda looked at us both. She was speechless.

"Listen, I'm paying for what I buy, and this is a present I want to give my niece—"

"Well, then, perhaps you'll allow me, in exchange, to invite you to an afternoon tea," Fermín quickly interjected, smoothing down his hair.

"Go on, Bernarda," I encouraged her. "You'll enjoy yourself. Look, while I wrap this up, Fermín can go and get his jacket."

Fermín hurried off to the back room to comb his hair, splash on some cologne, and put on his jacket. I slipped him a few duros from the till.

"Where shall I take her?" he whispered to me, as nervous as a child.

"I'd take her to Els Quatre Gats," I said. "I know for a fact that it's a lucky place for romance."

I handed Bernarda the packet and winked at her.

"What do I owe you then, Master Daniel?"

"I'm not sure. I'll let you know. The book didn't have a price on it, and I have to ask my father," I lied.

I watched them leave arm in arm and disappear down Calle Santa Ana, hoping there was somebody on duty up in heaven who, for once, would grant the couple a lucky break. I hung the CLOSED notice in the shop window. I had just gone into the back room for a moment to look through my father's order book when I heard the tinkle of the doorbell. I thought Fermín must have forgotten something, or perhaps my father was back from his day trip.

"Hello?"

A few seconds passed, and no answer came. I continued to leaf through the order book.

I heard slow footsteps in the shop.

"Fermín? Father?"

No answer. I thought I heard a stifled laugh, and I shut the order book. Perhaps some client had ignored the CLOSED sign. I was about to go and serve whoever it was when I heard the sound of several books falling from the shelves. I swallowed. Grabbing hold of a letter opener, I slowly moved toward the door of the back room. I didn't dare call out a second time. Soon I heard the steps again, walking away. The doorbell sounded, and I felt a draft of air from the street. I peered into the shop. There was no one there. I ran to the front door and double-locked it, then took a deep breath, feeling ridiculous and cowardly. I was returning to the back room when I noticed a piece of paper on the counter. As I got closer, I realized it was a photograph, an old studio picture of the sort that were printed on thick cardboard. The edges were burned, and the smoky image seemed to have charcoal finger marks over it. I examined it under the lamp. The photograph showed a young couple smiling at the camera. He didn't look much older than seventeen or eighteen, with light-colored hair and delicate, aristocratic features. She may have been a bit younger than him, one or two years at the most. She had pale skin and a finely chiseled face framed by short black hair. She looked intoxicated with happiness. The man had his arm around her waist, and she seemed to be whispering something to him in a teasing way. The image conveyed a warmth that drew a smile from me, as if I had recognized two old friends in those strangers. Behind them I could make out an ornate shop window, full of old-fashioned hats. I concentrated on the couple. From their clothes I could guess that the picture was at least twenty-five or thirty years old. It was an image full of light and hope, rich with the promise that exists only in the eyes of the young. Fire had destroyed almost all of the area surrounding the photograph, but one could still discern a stern face behind the old-style counter, a suggestion of a ghostly figure behind the letters engraved on the glass.

Sons of Antonio Fortuny
Established in 1888

The night I returned to the Cemetery of Forgotten Books, Isaac had told me that Carax used his mother's surname, not his father's, which was Fortuny. Carax's father had a hat shop on Ronda de San Antonio. I looked again at the portrait of that couple and knew for sure that the young man was Julián Carax, smiling at me from the past, unable to see the flames that were closing in on him.

City

of Shadows

1954

· *14* ·

THE FOLLOWING MORNING FERMÍN CAME TO WORK BORNE ON the wings of Cupid, smiling and whistling boleros. In any other circumstances, I would have inquired about his outing with Bernarda, but that day I was not in the mood for his poetic outbursts. My father had arranged to have an order of books delivered to Professor Javier Velázquez at eleven o'clock in his study at the university. The very mention of the professor made Fermín wince, so I offered to take the books myself.

"That sorry specimen is both pedantic and corrupt. A fascist buttock polisher," Fermín declared, raising his fist and striking the pose he reserved for his avenging moods. "With the pitiful excuse of his professorship and final exams, he would even have it off with Gertrude Stein, given the chance."

"Calm down, Fermín. Velázquez pays well, always in advance, and besides, he recommends us to everyone," my father said.

"That's money stained with the blood of innocent virgins," Fermín protested. "For the life of God, I hereby swear that I have never lain with an underage woman, and not for lack of inclination or opportunities. Bear in mind that what you see today is but a shadow of my former self, but there was a time when I cut as dashing a figure as they come. Yet even then, just to be on the safe side, or if I sensed that a girl might be overly flighty, I would not proceed without seeing some form of identification or, failing that, a written paternal authorization. One has to maintain certain moral standards."

My father rolled his eyes. "It's pointless to argue with you, Fermín."

"Well, if I'm right, I'm right."

Sensing a debate brewing, I picked up the parcel, which I had prepared the night before—a couple of Rilkes and an apocryphal essay attributed to a disciple of Darwin claiming Spaniards came from a more evolved simian ancestor than their French neighbors. As the door closed behind me, Fermín and my father were deep in argument about ethics.

It was a magnificent day; the skies were electric blue, and a crystal breeze carried the cool scent of autumn and the sea. I will always prefer Barcelona in October. It is when the spirit of the city seems to stroll most proudly through the streets, and you feel all the wiser after drinking water from the old fountain of Canaletas—which, at this time of year only, doesn't taste of chlorine. I was walking along briskly, dodging bootblacks, pen pushers returning from their midmorning coffee, lottery vendors, and a whole ballet of street sweepers who seemed to be polishing the streets with paintbrushes, unhurriedly and with a pointillist's strokes. Barcelona was already beginning to fill up with cars in those days, and when I reached the traffic lights at the crossing with Calle Balmes, I noticed a brigade of gray office clerks in gray raincoats staring as hungrily at a bloodred Studebaker sedan as they would ogle a music-hall siren in a negligee. I went on up Balmes toward Gran Vía, negotiating traffic lights, cars, and even motorcycles with sidecars. In a shop window, I saw a Philips poster announcing the arrival of a new messiah, the TV set. Some predicted that this peculiar contraption was going to change our lives forever and turn us all into creatures of the future, like the Americans. Fermín Romero de Torres, always up to date on state-of-art technology, had already prophesied a grimmer outcome.

"Television, my dear Daniel, is the Antichrist, and I can assure you that after only three or four generations, people will no longer even know how to fart on their own and humans will return to living in caves, to medieval savagery, and to the general state of imbecility that slugs overcame back in the Pleistocene era. Our world will not die as a result of the bomb, as the papers say, it will die of laughter, of banality, of making a joke of everything, and a lousy joke at that."

Professor Velázquez's office was on the second floor of the Literature Faculty, in Plaza Universidad, at the end of a gallery paved with hypnotic chessboard tiling and awash in powdery light that spilled down onto the southern cloister. I found the professor at the door of a lecture room, pretending to be listening to a female student while considering her spectacular figure. She wore a dark red suit that drew attention to her waistline and revealed classically proportioned calves covered in fine nylon stockings. Professor Velázquez enjoyed a reputation as a Don Juan, and there were those who considered that the sentimental education of a respectable young lady was never complete without a proverbial weekend in some small hotel on the Sitges promenade, reciting Alexandrines tête-à-tête with the distinguished academic.

My commercial instincts advised me against interrupting his conversation, so I decided to kill time by conjuring up an X ray of the pupil. Perhaps the brisk walk had raised my spirits, or perhaps it was just my age, not to mention the fact that I spent more time among muses that were trapped in the pages of old books than in the company of girls of flesh and bone—who always seemed to me beings of a far lower order than Clara Barceló. Whatever the reason, as I cataloged each and every detail of her enticing and exquisitely clad anatomy—which I could see only from the back, but which in my mind I had already visualized in its full glory—I felt a vaguely wolfish shiver run down my spine.

"Why, here's Daniel," cried Professor Velázquez. "Thank goodness it's you, not that madman who came last time, the one with the bullfighter's name. He seemed drunk to me, or else eminently certifiable. He had the nerve to ask me whether I knew the etymology of the word 'prick,' in a sarcastic tone that was quite out of place."

"It's just that the doctor has him under some really strong medication. Something to do with his liver."

"No doubt because he's smashed all day," said Velázquez. "If I were you,

I'd call the police. I bet you he has a file. And God, how his feet stank—there are lots of shitty leftists on the loose who haven't seen a bathtub since the Republic fell."

I was about to come up with some other plausible excuse for Fermín when the student who had been talking to Professor Velázquez turned around, and it was as if the world had stopped spinning. She smiled at me, and my ears went up in flames.

"Hello, Daniel," said Beatriz Aguilar.

I nodded at her, tongue-tied. I realized I'd been drooling over my best friend's sister, Bea. The one woman I was completely terrified of.

"Oh, so you know each other?" asked Velázquez, intrigued.

"Daniel is an old friend of the family," Bea explained. "And the only one who ever had the courage to tell me to my face that I'm stuck up and vain."

Velázquez looked at me with astonishment.

"That was years ago," I explained. "And I didn't mean it."

"Well, I'm still waiting for an apology."

Velázquez laughed heartily and took the parcel from my hands.

"I think I'm in the way here," he said, opening it. "Ah, wonderful. Listen, Daniel, tell your father I'm looking for a book called *Moorslayer: Early Reminiscences of the Generalissimo in the Moroccan War* by Francisco Franco Bahamonde, with a prologue and notes by Pemán."

"Consider it done. We'll let you know in a couple of weeks."

"I take your word for it, and now I'll be off. Thirty-two blank minds await me."

Professor Velázquez winked at me and disappeared into the lecture room. I didn't know where to look.

"Listen Bea, about that insult, I promise I—"

"I was only teasing you, Daniel. I know that was kid stuff, and besides, Tomás gave you a good enough beating."

"It still hurts."

Bea's smile looked like a peace offering, or at least an offer of a truce.

"Besides, you were right, I'm a bit stuck up and sometimes a little vain," she said. "You don't like me much, do you, Daniel?"

The question took me completely by surprise. Disarmed, I realized how easily you can lose all animosity toward someone you've deemed your enemy as soon as that person stops behaving as such.

"No, that's not true."

"Tomás says it's not that you don't like me, it's that you can't stand my father and you make me pay for it, because you don't dare face up to him. I don't blame you. No one dares cross my father."

I felt the blood drain from my cheeks, but after a few seconds I found myself smiling and nodding. "Anyone would say Tomás knows me better than I do myself."

"I wouldn't put it past him. My brother knows us all inside out, only he never says anything. But if he ever decides to open his mouth, the whole world will collapse. He's very fond of you, you know."

I raised my shoulders and looked down.

"He's always talking about you, and about your father and the bookshop, and this friend you have working with you. Tomás says he's a genius waiting to be discovered. Sometimes it's as if he considers you his real family, instead of the one he has at home."

My eyes met hers: hard, frank, fearless. I did not know what to say, so I just smiled. I felt she was ensnaring me with her honesty, and I looked down at the courtyard.

"I didn't know you studied here."

"It's my first year."

"Literature?"

"My father thinks science is not for the weaker sex."

"Of course. Too many numbers."

"I don't care, because what I like is reading. Besides, you meet interesting people here."

"Like Professor Velázquez?"

Bea gave me a wry smile. "I might be in my first year, but I know enough to see them coming, Daniel. Especially men of his sort."

I wondered what sort I was.

"Besides, Professor Velázquez is a good friend of my father's. They both belong to the Society for the Protection and Promotion of Spanish Operetta."

I tried to look impressed. "A noble calling. And how's your boyfriend, Lieutenant Cascos Buendía?"

Her smile left her. "Pablo will be here on leave in three weeks."

"You must be happy."

"Very. He's a great guy, though I can imagine what you must think of him."

I doubt it, I thought. Bea watched me, looking slightly tense. I was about to change the subject, but my tongue got ahead of me.

"Tomás says you're getting married and you're going off to live in El Ferrol."

She nodded without blinking. "As soon as Pablo finishes his military service."

"You must be feeling impatient," I said, sensing a spiteful note in my voice, an insolent tone that came from God knows where.

"I don't mind, really. His family has properties out there, a couple of shipyards, and Pablo is going to be in charge of one of them. He has a great talent for leadership."

"It shows."

Bea forced a smile. "Besides, I've seen quite enough of Barcelona, after all these years. . . ." Her eyes looked tired and sad.

"I hear El Ferrol is a fascinating place. Full of life. And the seafood is supposed to be fabulous, especially the spider crabs."

Bea sighed, shaking her head. She looked as if she wanted to cry with anger but was too proud. Instead she laughed calmly.

"After ten years you still enjoy insulting me, don't you, Daniel? Go on, then, don't hold back. It's my fault for thinking that perhaps we could be friends, or pretend to be, but I suppose I'm not as good as my brother. I'm sorry I've wasted your time."

She turned around and started walking down the corridor that led to the library. I saw her move away along the black and white tiles, her shadow cutting through the curtains of light that fell from the gallery windows.

"Bea, wait."

I cursed myself and ran after her. I stopped her halfway down the corridor, grabbing her by the arm. She threw me a burning look.

"I'm sorry. But you're wrong: it's not your fault, it's mine. I'm the one who isn't as good as your brother. And if I've insulted you, it's because I'm jealous of that idiot boyfriend of yours and because I'm angry to think that someone like you would follow him to El Ferrol. It might as well be the Congo."

"Daniel . . ."

"You're wrong about me, because we can be friends if you let me try, now that you know how worthless I am. And you're wrong about Barcelona, too, because you may think you've seen everything, but I can guarantee that's not true. If you'll allow me, I can prove it to you."

I saw a smile light up and a slow, silent tear fall down her cheek.

"You'd better be right," she said. "Because if you're not, I'll tell my brother, and he'll pull your head off like a stopper."

I held out my hand to her. "That sounds fair. Friends?"

She offered me hers.

"What time do you finish your classes on Friday?" I asked.

She hesitated for a moment. "At five."

"I'll be waiting for you in the cloister at five o'clock sharp. And before dark I'll prove to you that there's something in Barcelona you haven't seen yet, and that you can't go off to El Ferrol with that idiot whom I don't believe you love, because if you go, the memory of this city will pursue you and you'll die of sadness."

"You seem very sure of yourself, Daniel."

I, who was never even sure what the time was, nodded with the conviction of the ignorant. I stood there watching her walk away down that endless corridor until her silhouette blended with the darkness. I asked myself what on earth I had done.

· *15* ·

T HE FORTUNY HAT SHOP, OR WHAT WAS LEFT OF IT, LANGUISHED AT the foot of a narrow, miserable-looking building blackened by soot on Ronda de San Antonio next to Plaza de Goya. One could still read the letters engraved on the filthy window, and a sign in the shape of a bowler hat still hung above the shop front, promising designs made to measure and the latest novelties from Paris. The door was secured with a padlock that had seen at least a decade of undisturbed service. I pressed my forehead against the glass pane, trying to peek into the murky interior.

"If you've come about the rental, you're late," spit a voice behind my back. "The administrator has already left."

The woman who was speaking to me must have been about sixty and wore the national costume of all pious widows. A couple of rollers stuck out under the pink scarf that covered her hair, and her padded slippers matched her flesh-colored knee-highs. I assumed she was the caretaker of the building.

"Is the shop for rent?"

"Isn't that why you've come?"

"Not really, but you never know, I might be interested."

The caretaker frowned, debating whether to grant me the benefit of the doubt. I slipped on my trademark angelic smile.

"How long has the shop been closed?"

"For a good twelve years, since the old man died."

"Mr. Fortuny? Did you know him?"

"I've been here for forty-eight years, young man."

"So perhaps you also knew Mr. Fortuny's son."

"Julián? Well, of course."

I took the burned photograph out of my pocket and showed it to her. "Do you think you'd be able to tell me whether the young man in the photograph is Julián Carax?"

The caretaker looked at me rather suspiciously. She took the photograph and stared at it.

"Do you recognize him?"

"Carax was his mother's maiden name," the caretaker explained in a disapproving tone. "This is Julián, yes. I remember him being very fair, but here, in the photograph, his hair looks darker."

"Could you tell me who the girl is?"

"And who is asking?"

"I'm sorry, my name is Daniel Sempere. I'm trying to find out about Mr. Carax, about Julián."

"Julián went to Paris, 'round about 1918 or 1919. His father wanted to shove him in the army, you see. I think the mother took him with her so that he could escape from all that, poor kid. Mr. Fortuny was left alone, in the attic apartment."

"Do you know when Julián returned to Barcelona?"

The caretaker looked at me but didn't speak for a while.

"Don't you know? Julián died that same year in Paris."

"Excuse me?"

"I said Julián passed away. In Paris. Soon after he got there. He would have done better joining the army."

"May I ask you how you know that?"

"How do you think? Because his father told me."

I nodded slowly. "I see. Did he say what he died of?"

"Quite frankly, the old man never gave me any details. Once, not long after Julián left, a letter arrived for him, and when I mentioned it to his father, he told me his son had died and if anything else came for him, I should throw it away. Why are you looking at me like that?"

"Mr. Fortuny lied to you. Julián didn't die in 1919."

"Say that again?"

"Julián lived in Paris until at least 1935, and then he returned to Barcelona."

The caretaker's face lit up. "So Julián is here, in Barcelona? Where?"

I nodded again, hoping that by doing so she would be encouraged to tell me more.

"Holy Mary . . . what wonderful news. Well, if he's still alive, that is. He was such a sweet child, a bit strange and given to daydreaming, that's true, but there was something about him that won you over. He wouldn't have been much good as a soldier, you could tell that a mile off. My Isabelita really liked him. Imagine, for a time I even thought they'd end up getting married. Kid stuff . . . May I see that photograph again?"

I handed the photo back to her. The caretaker gazed at it as if it were a lucky charm, a return ticket to her youth. "It's strange, you know, it's as if he were here right now . . . and that mean old bastard saying he was dead. I must say, I wonder why God sends some people into this world. And what happened to Julián in Paris? I'm sure he got rich. I always thought Julián would be wealthy one day."

"Not exactly. He became a writer."

"He wrote stories?"

"Something like that."

"For the radio? Oh, how lovely. Well, it doesn't surprise me, you know. As a child he used to tell stories to the kids in the neighborhood. In the summer sometimes my Isabelita and her cousins would go up to the roof terrace at night and listen to him. They said he never told the same story twice. But it's true that they were all about dead people and ghosts. As I say, he was a bit of an odd child. Although, with a father like that, the odd thing was that he wasn't completely nuts. I'm not surprised that his wife left him in the end, because he really was nasty. Listen: I never meddle in people's affairs, everything's fine by me, but that man wasn't a good person. In a block of apartments, nothing's secret in the end. He beat her, you know? You always heard screams coming from their apartment, and more than once the police had to come around. I can understand that sometimes a husband has to beat his wife to get her to respect him, I'm not saying they shouldn't; there's a lot of tarts about, and young girls are not brought up the way they used to be. But this one, well, he liked to beat her for the hell of it, if you see what I mean. The only friend that poor woman had was a young girl, Viçenteta, who lived in four-two. Sometimes the poor woman would take shelter in Viçenteta's apartment, to get away from her husband's beatings. And she told her things. . . ."

"What sort of things?"

The caretaker took on a confidential manner, raising an eyebrow and glancing sideways right and left. "Like the kid wasn't the hatter's."

"Julián? Do you mean to say Julián wasn't Mr. Fortuny's son?"

"That's what the Frenchwoman told Viçenteta, I don't know whether out of spite or heaven knows why. The girl told me years later, when they didn't live here anymore."

"So who was Julián's real father?"

"The Frenchwoman never said. Perhaps she didn't even know. You know what foreigners are like."

"And do you think that's why her husband beat her?"

"Goodness knows. Three times they had to take her to the hospital, do you hear? Three times. And the swine had the nerve to tell everyone that she was the one to blame, that she was a drunk and was always falling about the house from drinking so much. But I don't believe that. He quarreled with all the neighbors. Once he even went to the police to report my late husband, God rest his soul, for stealing from his shop. As far as he was concerned, anyone from the south was a layabout and a thief, the pig."

"Did you say you recognized the girl who is next to Julián in the photograph?"

The caretaker concentrated on the image once again. "Never seen her before. Very pretty."

"From the picture it looks like they were a couple," I suggested, trying to jog her memory.

She handed it back to me, shaking her head. "I don't know anything about photographs. As far as I know, Julián never had a girlfriend, but I imagine that if he did, he wouldn't have told me. It was hard enough to find out that my Isabelita had got involved with that fellow. . . . You young people never say anything. And us old folks don't know how to stop talking."

"Do you remember his friends, anyone special who came around here?"

The caretaker shrugged her shoulders. "Well, it was such a long time ago. Besides, in the last years Julián was hardly ever here, you see. He'd made a friend at school, a boy from a very good family, the Aldayas—now, that's saying something. Nobody talks about them now, but in those days it was like mentioning the royal family. Lots of money. I know because sometimes they would send a car to fetch Julián. You should have seen that car. Not even Franco would have one like it. With a chauffeur, and all shiny. My Paco, who knew about cars, told me it was a *rolsroi,* or something like that. Fit for an emperor."

"Do you remember the name of that friend?"

"Listen: with a surname like Aldaya, there's no need for first names, if you see what I mean. I also remember another boy, a bit of a scatterbrain, called Miquel. I think he was also a classmate. But don't ask me for his surname or what he looked like."

We seemed to have reached a dead end, and I feared that the caretaker would start losing interest. I decided to follow a hunch. "Is anyone living in the Fortuny apartment now?"

"No. The old man died without leaving a will, and his wife, as far as I know, is still in Buenos Aires and didn't even come back for the funeral. Can't blame her."

"Why Buenos Aires?"

"Because she couldn't find anywhere farther away, I guess. She left everything in the hands of a lawyer, a very strange man. I've never seen him, but my daughter Isabelita, who lives on the fifth floor, right underneath, says that sometimes, since he has the key, he comes at night and spends hours walking around the apartment and then leaves. Once she said that she could even hear what sounded like women's high heels. What can I say . . . ?"

"Maybe they were stilts," I suggested.

She looked at me blankly. Obviously this was a serious subject for the caretaker.

"And nobody else has visited the apartment in all these years?"

"Once this very creepy individual came along, one of those people who never stop smiling, a giggler, but you could see him coming a mile off. He said he was in the Crime Squad. He wanted to see the apartment."

"Did he say why?"

The caretaker shook her head.

"Do you remember his name?"

"Inspector something or other. I didn't even believe he was a policeman. The whole thing stank, do you know what I mean? It smelled of something personal. I sent him packing and told him I didn't have the keys to the apartment and if he wanted anything, he should call the lawyer. He said he'd come back, but I haven't seen him around here anymore. Good riddance."

"You wouldn't by any chance have the name and address of the lawyer, would you?"

"You ought to ask the administrator of this building, Mr. Molins. His office is quite close, number twenty-eight, Floridablanca, first floor. Tell him I sent you—Señora Aurora, at your service."

"I'm really grateful. So, tell me, Doña Aurora, is the Fortuny apartment empty, then?"

"No, not empty, because nobody has taken anything from there in all these years since the old man died. Sometimes it even smells. I'd say there are rats in the apartment, mark my words."

"Do you think it would be possible to have a look? We might find something that tells us what really happened to Julián. . . ."

"Oh no, I can't do that. You must talk to Mr. Molins, he's the one in charge."

I smiled at her mischievously. "But you must have a master key, I imagine. Even if you told that guy you didn't . . . Don't tell me you're not dying to see what's in there."

Doña Aurora looked at me out of the corner of her eye.

"You're a devil."

THE DOOR GAVE WAY LIKE A TOMBSTONE, WITH A SUDDEN GROAN, exhaling dank, foul-smelling air from within. I pushed the front door inward, discovering a corridor that sank into darkness. The place was stuffy and reeked of damp. Spiraling threads of grime and dust hung from the ceiling like white hair. The broken floor tiles were covered by what looked like a layer of ash. I noticed what appeared to be footprints making their way into the apartment.

"Holy Mother of God!" mumbled the caretaker. "There's more shit here than on the floor of a henhouse."

"If you'd rather, I'll go in on my own," I said.

"That's exactly what you'd like. Come on, you go ahead, I'll follow."

We closed the door behind us and waited by the entrance for a moment until our eyes became accustomed to the dark. I could hear the nervous breathing of the caretaker and noticed the sour smell of her sweat. I felt like a tomb robber, whose soul is poisoned by greed and desire.

"Hey, what's that noise?" asked the caretaker in an anxious tone. Something fluttered in the dark, disturbed by our presence. I thought I glimpsed a pale shape flickering about at the end of the corridor.

"Pigeons," I said. "They must have got in through a broken window and made a nest here."

"Those ugly birds give me the creeps," said the caretaker. "And they shit like there's no tomorrow."

"Relax, Doña Aurora, they only attack when they're hungry."

We ventured in a few steps till we reached the end of the corridor, where a dining room opened onto the balcony. Just visible was a shabby table covered with a tattered tablecloth that looked more like a shroud. Four chairs held a wake, together with a couple of grimy glass cabinets that guarded the tableware: an assortment of glasses and a tea set. In a corner stood the old upright piano that had belonged to Carax's mother. The keys were dark with dirt, and the joins could hardly be seen under the film of dust. An armchair with a long, threadbare cover was slowly disintegrating next to the balcony. Beside it was a coffee table on which rested a pair of reading glasses and a Bible bound in pale leather and edged with gold, of the sort that used to be given as presents for a child's first communion. It still had its bookmark, a piece of scarlet string.

"Look, that chair is where the old man was found dead. The doctor said he'd been there for two days. How sad to go like that, like a dog, all alone. Not that he didn't have it coming, but even so . . ."

I went up to the chair where Mr. Fortuny had died. Next to the Bible was a small box containing black-and-white photographs, old studio portraits. I knelt down to examine them, almost afraid to touch them. I felt I was profaning the memories of a poor old man, but my curiosity got the better of me. The first print showed a young couple with a boy who could not have been more than four years old. I recognized him by his eyes.

"Look, there they are. Mr. Fortuny as a young man, and her . . ."

"Didn't Julián have any brothers or sisters?"

The caretaker shrugged her shoulders and let out a sigh. "I heard rumors that she miscarried once because of the beatings her husband gave her, but I don't know. People love to gossip, don't they? But not me. All I know is that once Julián told the kids in the building that he had a sister only he could see. He said she came out of mirrors as if she were made of thin air and that she lived with Satan himself in a palace at the bottom of a lake. My Isabelita had nightmares for a whole month. That child could be really morbid at times."

I glanced at the kitchen. There was a broken pane in a small window overlooking an inner courtyard, and you could hear the nervous and hostile flapping of the pigeons' wings on the other side.

"Do all the apartments have the same layout?" I asked.

"The ones that look onto the street do. But this one is an attic, so it's a bit different. There's the kitchen and a laundry room that overlooks the inside yard. Down this corridor there are three bedrooms, and a bathroom at the end. Properly decorated, they can look very nice, believe me. This one is similar to my Isabelita's apartment—but of course right now it looks like a tomb."

"Do you know which Julián's room was?"

"The first door is the master bedroom. The second is a smaller room. It was probably that one, I'd say."

I went down the corridor. The paint on the walls was falling off in shreds. At the end of the passage, the bathroom door was ajar. A face seemed to stare at me from the mirror. It could have been mine, or perhaps the face of the sister who lived there. As I got closer, it withdrew into darkness. I tried to open the second door.

"It's locked," I said.

The caretaker looked at me in astonishment. "These doors don't have locks," she said.

"This one does."

"Then the old man must have had it put in, because all the other apartments . . ."

I looked down and noticed that the footprints in the dust led up to the locked door. "Someone's been in this room," I said. "Recently."

"Don't scare me," said the caretaker.

I went up to the other door. It didn't have a lock. It opened with a rusty groan when I touched it. In the middle stood an old four-poster bed, unmade. The sheets had turned yellowish, like winding sheets, and a crucifix presided over the bed. The room also contained a chest of drawers with a small mirror on it, a basin, a pitcher, and a chair. A wardrobe, its door ajar, stood against the wall. I went around the bed to a bedside table with a glass top, under which lay photographs of ancestors, funeral cards, and lottery tickets. On the table were a carved wooden music box and a pocketwatch, frozen forever at twenty past five. I tried to wind up the music box, but the melody got stuck after six notes. When I opened the drawer of the bedside table, I found an empty spectacle case, a nail clipper, a hip flask, and a medal of the Virgin of Lourdes. Nothing else.

"There must be a key to that room somewhere," I said.

"The administrator must have it. Look, I think it's best we leave."

Suddenly I looked down at the music box. I lifted the cover and there, blocking the mechanism, I found a gold key. I took it out, and the music box resumed its tinkling. I recognized a tune by Ravel.

"This must be the key." I smiled at the caretaker.

"Listen, if the room was locked, there must be a reason. Even if it's just out of respect for the memory of—"

"If you'd rather, you can wait for me down in your apartment, Doña Aurora."

"You're a devil. Go on. Open up if you must."

· 16 ·

A BREATH OF COLD AIR WHISTLED THROUGH THE HOLE IN THE lock, licking at my fingers while I inserted the key. The lock that Mr. Fortuny had fitted in the door of his son's unoccupied room was three times the size of the one on the front door. Doña Aurora looked at me apprehensively, as if we were about to open a Pandora's box.

"Is this room on the front of the house?" I asked.

The caretaker shook her head. "It has a small window, for ventilation. It looks out over the yard."

I pushed the door inward. An impenetrable well of darkness opened up before us. The meager light from behind crept ahead, barely able to scratch at the shadows. The window overlooking the yard was covered with pages of yellowed newspaper. I tore them off, and a needle of hazy light bored through the darkness.

"Jesus, Mary, and Joseph," murmured the caretaker.

The room was infested with crucifixes. They hung from the ceiling, dangling from the ends of strings, and they covered the walls, hooked on nails. There were dozens of them. You could sense them in every corner, carved with a knife on the wooden furniture, scratched on the floor tiles, painted red on the mirrors. The footprints that had led us to the doorway could now be traced in the dust around the naked bed, just a skeleton of wires and worm-eaten wood. At one end of the room, under the window, stood a closed rolltop desk, crowned by a trio of metal crucifixes. I opened it with care. There was no dust in the joins of the wooden slats, from which I inferred that the desk had been opened quite recently. It had six drawers. The locks had been forced open. I inspected them one by one. Empty.

I knelt down by the desk and fingered the scratches that covered the wood, imagining Julián Carax's hands making those doodles, hieroglyphics whose meaning had been obscured by time. In the desk, I noticed a pile of notebooks and a vase filled with pencils and pens. I took one of the notebooks and glanced at it. Drawings and single words. Mathematical exercises. Unconnected phrases, quotes from books. Unfinished poems. All the notebooks looked the same. Some drawings were repeated page after page, with slight variations. I was struck by the figure of a man who seemed to be made of flames. Another might have been an angel or a reptile coiled around a cross. Rough sketches hinted at a fantastic rambling house, woven with towers and cathedral-like arches. The strokes were confident and showed a certain facility. Young Carax appeared to be a draftsman of some promise, but none of the drawings were more than rough sketches.

I was about to put the last notebook back in its place without looking at it when something slipped out from its pages and fell at my feet. It was a photograph in which I recognized the same girl who appeared in the other picture—the one taken at the foot of that building. The girl was posed in a luxurious garden, and beyond the treetops, just visible, was the shape of the house I had seen sketched in the drawings of the adolescent Carax. I recognized it immediately. It was the villa called "The White Friar," on Avenida del Tibidabo. On the back of the photograph was an inscription that simply said:

Penélope, who loves you

I put it in my pocket, closed the desk, and smiled at the caretaker.

"Seen enough?" she asked, anxious to leave the place.

"Almost," I replied. "Before, you said that soon after Julián left for Paris, a letter came for him, but his father told you to throw it away. . . ."

The caretaker hesitated for a moment, and then she nodded. "I put the letter in the drawer of the cabinet in the entrance hall, in case the French-woman should come back one day. It must still be there."

We went down to the cabinet and opened the top drawer. An ocher-colored envelope lay on top of a collection of stopped watches, buttons, and coins that had ceased being legal tender twenty years ago. I picked up the envelope and examined it.

"Did you read it?"

"What do you take me for?"

"I meant no offense. It would have been quite natural, under the circumstances, if you thought that Julián was dead. . . ."

The caretaker shrugged, looked down, and started walking toward the door. I took advantage of that moment to put the letter in the inside pocket of my jacket.

"Look, I don't want you to get the wrong impression," said the care-taker.

"Of course not. What did the letter say?"

"It was a love letter. Like the stories on the radio, only sadder, you know, because it sounded as if it was really true. Believe me, I felt like crying when I read it."

"You're all heart, Doña Aurora."

"And you're a devil."

THAT SAME AFTERNOON, AFTER SAYING GOOD-BYE TO DOÑA AURORA and promising that I would keep her up to date with my investigations on Julián Carax, I went along to see the administrator of the block of apart-ments. Mr. Molins had seen better days and now moldered away in a filthy first-floor office on Calle Floridablanca. Still, Molins was a cheerful and self-satisfied individual. His mouth was glued to a half-smoked cigar that seemed to grow out of his mustache. It was hard to tell whether he was asleep or awake, because he breathed like most people snore. His hair was greasy and flattened over his forehead, and he had mischievous piggy eyes. His suit wouldn't have fetched more than ten pesetas in the Encantes Flea Market, but he made up for it with a gaudy tie of tropical colors. Judging by the appearance of the office, not much was managed anymore, except the bugs and cobwebs of a forgotten Barcelona.

"We're in the middle of refurbishment," he said apologetically.

To break the ice, I let drop the name of Doña Aurora, as if I were referring to some old friend of the family.

"When she was young, she was a real looker" was Molins's comment. "With age she's gone on the heavier side, but then I'm not what I used to be either. You may not believe this, but when I was your age, I was an Adonis. Girls would go on their knees to beg for a quickie, or to have my babies. Alas, the twentieth century is for shit. What can I do for you, young man?"

I presented him with a more or less plausible story about a supposed distant relationship with the Fortunys. After five minutes' chatter, Molins dragged himself to his filing cabinet and gave me the address of the lawyer who dealt with matters related to Sophie Carax, Julián's mother.

"Let me see . . . José María Requejo. Fifty-nine, Calle León XIII. But we send the mail twice a year to a PO box in the main post office, on Vía Layetana."

"Do you know Mr. Requejo?"

"I've spoken to his secretary occasionally on the telephone. The fact is that all business with him is done by mail, and my secretary deals with that. And today she's at the hairdresser's. Lawyers don't have time for face-to-face dealings anymore. There are no gentlemen left in the profession."

There didn't seem to be any reliable addresses left either. A quick glance at the street guide on the manager's desk confirmed what I suspected: the address of the supposed lawyer, Mr. Requejo, didn't exist. I told Mr. Molins, who took the news in as if it were a joke.

"Well, I'll be dammed!" he said laughing. "What did I say? Crooks."

The manager lay back in his chair and made another of his snoring noises.

"Would you happen to have the number of that PO box?"

"According to the index card it's 2837, although I can't read my secretary's numbers. As I'm sure you know, women are no good at math. What they're good for is—"

"May I see the card?"

"Sure. Help yourself."

He handed me the index card, and I looked at it. The numbers were perfectly legible. The PO box was 2321. It horrified me to think of the accounting that must have gone on in that office.

"Did you have much contact with Mr. Fortuny during his lifetime?" I asked.

"So-so. Quite the ascetic type. I remember that when I found out that the Frenchwoman had left him, I invited him to go whoring with a few mates of mine, nearby, in a fabulous establishment I know next to La Paloma dance hall. Just to cheer him up, eh? That's all. And you know what? He would not talk to me, even greet me in the street anymore, as if I were invisible. What do you make of that?"

"I'm in shock. What else can you tell me about the Fortuny family? Do you remember them well?"

"Those were different times," he murmured nostalgically. "The fact is that I already knew Grandfather Fortuny, the one who started the hat shop. About the son, there isn't much to tell. Now, the wife, she was spectacular. What a woman. And decent, eh? Despite all the rumors and gossip . . ."

"Like the one about Julián's not being the legitimate son of Mr. Fortuny?"

"And where did you hear that?"

"As I said, I'm part of the family. Everything gets out."

"None of that was ever proved."

"But it was talked about," I said encouragingly.

"People talk too much. Humans aren't descended from monkeys. They come from parrots."

"And what did people say?"

"Don't you feel like a little glass of rum? It's Cuban, like all the good stuff that kills you."

"No thanks, but I'll keep you company. In the meantime, you can tell me . . ."

Antoni Fortuny, whom everyone called the hatter, met Sophie Carax in 1899 by the steps of Barcelona Cathedral. He was returning from making a vow to Saint Eustace— for of all the saints, Saint Eustace was considered the most diligent and the least fussy when it came to granting miracles to do with love. Antoni Fortuny, who was already over thirty and a confirmed bachelor, was looking for a wife, and wanted her right away. Sophie was a French girl who lived in a boardinghouse for young ladies on Calle Riera Alta and gave private music and piano lessons to the offspring of the most privileged families in Barcelona. She had no family or capital to rely on, only her youth and what musical education she had received from her father—the pianist at a Nîmes theater—before he died of tuberculosis in 1886. Antoni Fortuny, on the contrary, was a man on the road to prosperity. He had recently inherited his father's business, a hat shop of some repute on Ronda de San Antonio, where he had learned the trade that he dreamed of one day teaching his own son. He found Sophie Carax fragile, beautiful, young, docile, and fertile. Saint Eustace had obliged. After four months of insistent courting, Sophie accepted Antoni's marriage proposal. Mr. Molins, who had been a friend of Fortuny the elder, warned Antoni that he was marrying a stranger. He said that Sophie seemed like a nice girl, but perhaps this marriage was a bit too convenient for her, and he should wait a year at least. . . . Antoni Fortuny replied that he already knew everything he needed to about his future wife. The rest did not interest him. They were married at the Basílica del Pino and spent their three-day honeymoon in a spa in the nearby seaside resort of Mongat. The morning before they left, the hatter asked Mr. Molins, in confidence, to be initiated into the mysteries of the bedroom. Molins sarcastically told him to ask his wife. The newlyweds returned to Barcelona after only two days. The neighbors said Sophie was crying when she came into the building. Years later Viçenteta swore that Sophie had told her the following: that the hatter had not laid a finger on her and that when she had tried to seduce him, he had called her a whore and told her he was disgusted by the obscenity of what she was proposing. Six months later Sophie announced to her husband that she was with child. By another man.

Antoni Fortuny had seen his own father hit his mother on countless occasions and did what he thought was the right thing to do. He stopped only when he feared that one more blow would kill her. Despite the beating, Sophie refused to reveal the identity of the child's father. Applying his own logic to the matter, Antoni Fortuny decided that it must be the devil, for that child was the child of sin, and sin had only one father: the One. Convinced in this manner that sin had sneaked into his home and also between his wife's thighs, the hatter took to hanging crucifixes everywhere: on the walls, on the doors of all the rooms, and on the ceiling. When Sophie discovered him scattering crosses in the bedroom to which she had been confined, she grew afraid and, with tears in her eyes, asked him whether he had gone mad. Blind with rage, he turned around and hit her. "A whore like the rest," he spit as he threw her out onto the landing, after flaying her with blows from his belt. The following day, when Antoni Fortuny opened the door of his apartment to go down to the hat shop, Sophie was still there, covered in dried blood and shivering with cold. The doctors never managed to fix the fractures on her right hand completely. Sophie Carax would never be able to play the piano again, but she would give birth to a boy, whom she would name Julián after the father she had lost when she was still too young—as happens with all good things in life. Fortuny considered throwing her out of his home but thought the scandal would not be good for business. Nobody would buy hats from a man known to be a cuckold—the two didn't go together. From then on, Sophie was assigned a dark, cold room at the back of the apartment.

It was there she gave birth to her son with the help of two neighbors. Antoni did not return home until three days later. "This is the son God has given you," Sophie announced. "If you want to punish anyone, punish me, but not an innocent creature. The boy needs a home and a father. My sins are not his. I beg you to take pity on us."

The first months were difficult for both of them. Antoni Fortuny had downgraded his wife to the rank of servant. They no longer shared a bed or table and rarely exchanged any words except to resolve some domestic matter. Once a month, usually coinciding with the full moon, Antoni Fortuny showed up in Sophie's bedroom at dawn and, without a word, charged at his former wife with vigor but little skill. Making the most of these rare and aggressive moments of intimacy, Sophie tried to win him over by whispering words of love and caressing him. But the hatter was not a man for frivolities, and the eagerness of desire evaporated in a matter of minutes, or even seconds. These assaults brought no children. After a few years, Antoni Fortuny stopped visiting Sophie's chamber for good and took up the habit of reading the Gospels until the small hours, seeking in them a solace for his torment.

With the help of the Gospels, the hatter made an effort to kindle some affection for the child with deep eyes who loved making a joke of everything and inventing shadows where there were none. Despite his efforts, Antoni Fortuny was unable to feel as if little Julián were his own flesh and blood, nor did he recognize any aspect of himself in him. The boy, for his part, did not seem very interested either in hats or in the teachings of the catechism. During the Christmas season he would amuse himself by changing the positions of the small figures in the Nativity scene and devising plots in which Baby Jesus had been kidnapped by the three magi from the East, with wicked intentions. He soon became obsessed with drawing angels with wolf's teeth and inventing stories about hooded spirits that came out of walls and ate people's ideas while they slept. In time the hatter lost all hope of being able to set this boy on the right path. The child was not a Fortuny and never would be. Julián maintained that he was bored in school and came home with his notebooks full of drawings of monstrous beings, winged serpents, and buildings that were alive, walked, and devoured the unsuspecting. By then it was quite clear that fantasy and invention interested him far more than the daily reality around him. Of all the disappointments amassed during his lifetime, none hurt Antoni Fortuny more than that son whom the devil had sent to mock him.

At the age of ten, Julián announced that he wanted to be a painter, like Velázquez. He dreamed of embarking on canvases that the great master had been unable to paint during his life because, Julián argued, he'd been obliged to paint so many time-consuming portraits of mentally retarded royals. To make matters worse, Sophie, perhaps to relieve her loneliness and remember her father, decided to give him piano lessons. Julián, who loved music, art, and all matters that were not practical in the world of men, soon learned the rudiments of harmony and concluded that he preferred to invent his own compositions rather than follow the music-book scores. At that time Antoni Fortuny still suspected that part of the boy's mental deficiencies were due to his diet, which was far too influenced by his mother's French cooking. It was a well-known fact that the richness of buttery foods led to moral ruin and confusion of the intellect. He forbade Sophie to cook with butter ever again. The results were not entirely as he had anticipated.

At twelve Julián began to lose his feverish interest in painting and in Velázquez, but the hatter's initial hopes did not last long. Julián was abandoning his canvas dreams for a far more pernicious vice. He had discovered the library on Calle del Carmen and devoted any time he was allowed off from the hat shop to visiting the sanctuary of books and devouring volumes of fiction, poetry, and history. The day before his thirteenth birthday, he announced that he wanted to be someone called Robert Louis Stevenson, evidently a foreigner. The hatter remarked that with luck he'd become a quarry worker. At that point he became convinced that his son was nothing but an idiot.

At night Antoni Fortuny often writhed in his bed with anger and frustration, unable to get any sleep. At the bottom of his heart, he loved that child, he told himself. And although she didn't deserve it, he also loved the slut who had betrayed him from the very first day. He loved her with all his soul, but in his own way, which was the correct way. All he asked God was to show him how the three of them could be happy, preferably also in his own way. He begged the Lord to send him a signal, a whisper, a crumb of His presence. God, in His infinite wisdom, and perhaps overwhelmed by the avalanche of requests from so many tormented souls, did not answer. While Antoni Fortuny was engulfed by remorse and suspicions, on the other side of the wall Sophie slowly faded away, her life shipwrecked on a sea of disappointment, isolation, and guilt. She did not love the man she served, but she felt she belonged to him, and the possibility of leaving him and taking her son with her to some other place seemed inconceivable. She remembered Julián's real father with bitterness, and eventually grew to hate him and everything he stood for. In her desperation she began to shout back at Antoni Fortuny. Insults and sharp recriminations flew around the apartment like knives, stabbing anyone who dared get in their way, usually Julián. Later the hatter never remembered exactly why he had beaten his wife. He remembered only the anger and the shame. He would then swear to himself that this would never happen again, that, if necessary, he would give himself up to the authorities and get himself locked up in prison.

Antoni Fortuny was sure that, with God's help, he would end up being a better man than his own father. But sooner or later, his fists would once more meet Sophie's tender flesh, and in time Fortuny felt that if he could not possess her as a husband, he would do so as a tyrant. In this manner, secretly, the Fortuny family let the years go by, silencing their hearts and their souls to the point where, from so much keeping quiet, they forgot the words with which to express their real feelings and became strangers living under the same roof, like so many other families in the vast city.

It was past two-thirty when I returned to the bookshop. As I walked in, Fermín gave me a sarcastic look from the top of a ladder, where he was polishing up a collection of the *Episodios Nacionales* by the famous Don Benito.

"Who is this I see before me? We thought you must have set off to the New World by now, Daniel."

"I got delayed on the way. Where's my father?"

"Since you didn't turn up, he went off to deliver the rest of the orders. He asked me to tell you that this afternoon he was going to Tiana to value a private library belonging to a widow. Your father's a wolf in sheep's clothing. He said not to wait for him to close the shop."

"Was he annoyed?"

Fermín shook his head, coming down the stepladder with feline nimbleness.

"Not at all. Your father is a saint. Besides, he was very happy to see you're dating a young lady."

"What?"

Fermín winked at me and smacked his lips.

"Oh, you little devil, you were hiding your light under a bushel! And what a girl, eh? Good enough to stop traffic. And such class. You can tell she's been to good schools, although she has fire in her eyes. . . . If Bernarda hadn't stolen my heart, and I haven't yet told you all about our outing—there were sparks coming out of those eyes, I tell you, sparks, it was like a bonfire on Midsummer Night—"

"Fermín," I interrupted. "What the hell are you talking about?"

"About your fiancée."

"I don't have a fiancée, Fermín."

"Well, these days you young people call them anything, sugar pie, or—"

"Fermín, will you please start again. What are you talking about?"

Fermín Romero de Torres looked at me disconcertedly.

"Let me see. This afternoon, about an hour or an hour and a half ago, a gorgeous young lady came by and asked for you. Your father and yours truly were on the premises, and I can assure you without a shadow of doubt that the girl was no apparition. I could even describe her smell. Lavender, only sweeter. Like a little sugar bun just out of the oven."

"Did little sugar bun say she was my fiancée, by any chance?"

"Well, not in so many words, but she gave a sort of quick smile, if you see what I mean, and said that she would see you on Friday afternoon. All we did was put two and two together."

"Bea . . ." I mumbled.

"Ergo, she exists," said Fermín with relief.

"Yes, but she's not my girlfriend."

"Well, I don't know what you're waiting for, then."

"She's Tomás Aguilar's sister."

"Your friend the inventor?"

I nodded.

"All the more reason. Even if she were the pope's niece, she's a bombshell. If I were you, I'd be on the ready."

"Bea already has a fiancé. A lieutenant doing his military service."

Fermín sighed with irritation. "Ah, the army, blight and refuge for the basest simian instincts. All the better, because this way you can cuckold him without feeling guilty."

"You're delirious, Fermín. Bea's getting married when the lieutenant finishes his service."

Fermín gave me a sneaky smile. "Funny you should say that, because I have a feeling she's not. I don't think this pumpkin is going to be tying the knot anytime soon."

"What do you know?"

"About women and other worldly matters, considerably more than you. As Freud tells us, women want the opposite of what they think or say they want, which, when you consider it, is not so bad, because men, as is more than evident, respond, contrariwise, to the dictates of their genital and digestive organs."

"Stop lecturing me, Fermín, I can see what you're getting at. If you have anything to say, say it."

"Right, then, in a nutshell: this one hasn't a single bone of obedient-little-wife material in her heavenly body."

"Hasn't she? Then what kind of bone does your expertise detect in her?"

Fermín came closer, adopting a confidential tone. "The passionate kind," he said, raising his eyebrows with an air of mystery. "And you can be sure I mean that as a compliment."

As usual, Fermín was right. Feeling defeated, I decided that attack was the best form of defense. "Speaking of passion, tell me about Bernarda. Was there or was there not a kiss?"

"Don't insult me, Daniel. Let me remind you that you are talking to a professional in the craft of seduction, and this business of kissing is for amateurs and little old men in slippers. Real women are won over bit by bit. It's all a question of psychology, like a good *faena* in the bullring."

"In other words, she gave you the brush-off."

"The woman is yet to be born who is capable of giving Fermín Romero de Torres the brush-off. The trouble is that man, going back to Freud—and excuse the metaphor—heats up like a lightbulb: red hot in the twinkling of an eye and cold again in a flash. The female, on the other hand—and this is pure science—heats up like an iron, if you see what I mean. Slowly, over a low heat, like a tasty stew. But then, once she has heated up, there's no stopping her. Like the steel furnaces in Vizcaya."

I weighed up Fermín's thermodynamic theories. "Is that what you're doing with Bernarda? Heating up the iron?"

Fermín winked at me. "That woman is a volcano on the point of eruption, with a libido of igneous magma yet the heart of an angel," he said, licking his lips. "If I had to establish a true parallel, she reminds me of my succulent mulatto girl in Havana, who was very devout and always worshiped her saints. But since, deep down, I'm an old-fashioned gent who doesn't like to take advantage of women, I contented myself with a chaste kiss on the cheek. I'm not in a hurry, you see? All good things must wait. There are yokels out there who think that if they touch a woman's behind and she doesn't complain, they've hooked her. Amateurs. The female heart is a labyrinth of subtleties, too challenging for the uncouth mind of the male racketeer. If you really want to possess a woman, you must think like her, and the first thing to do is to win over her soul. The rest, that sweet, soft wrapping that steals away your senses and your virtue, is a bonus."

I clapped solemnly at his discourse. "You're a poet, Fermín."

"No, I'm with Ortega and I'm a pragmatist. Poetry lies, in its adorable wicked way, and what I say is truer than a slice of bread and tomato. That's just what the master said: show me a Don Juan and I'll show you a loser in disguise. What I aim for is permanence, durability. Bear witness that I will make Bernarda, if not an honest woman, because that she already is, at least a happy one."

I smiled as I nodded. His enthusiasm was contagious, and his diction beyond improvement. "Take good care of her, Fermín. Do it for me. Bernarda has a heart of gold, and she has already suffered too many disappointments."

"Do you think I can't see that? It's written all over her, like a stamp from the society of war widows. Trust me: I wrote the book on taking shit from everybody and his mother. I'm going to make this woman blissfully happy even if it's the last thing I ever do in this world."

"Do I have your word?"

He stretched out his hand with the composure of a Knight Templar. I shook it.

"Yes, the word of Fermín Romero de Torres."

BUSINESS WAS SLOW IN THE SHOP THAT AFTERNOON, WITH BARELY A couple of browsers. In view of the situation, I suggested Fermín take the rest of the day off.

"Go on, go and find Bernarda and take her to the cinema or go window shopping with her on Calle Puertaferrissa, walking arm in arm, she loves that."

Fermín did not hesitate to take me up on my offer and rushed off to smarten himself up in the back room, where he always kept a change of clothes and all kinds of eau de colognes and ointments in a toilet bag that would have been the envy of Veronica Lake. When he emerged, he looked like a screen idol, only fifty pounds lighter. He wore a suit that had belonged to my father and a felt hat that was a couple of sizes too large, a problem he solved by placing balls of newspaper under the crown.

"By the way, Fermín. Before you go . . . I wanted to ask you a favor."

"Say no more. You give the order, I'm already on it."

"I'm going to ask you to keep this between us, okay? Not a word to my father."

He beamed. "Ah, you rascal. Something to do with that girl, eh?"

"No. This is a matter of high intrigue. Your department."

"Well, I also know a lot about girls. I'm telling you this because if you ever have a technical query, you know who to ask. Privacy assured. I'm like a doctor when it comes to such matters. No need to be prudish."

"I'll bear that in mind. Right now what I would like to know is who owns a PO box in the main post office, on Vía Layetana. Number 2321. And, if possible, who collects the mail that goes there. Do you think you'll be able to lend me a hand?"

Fermín wrote down the number with a ballpoint on his instep, under his sock.

"Piece of cake. All official institutions find me irresistible. Give me a few days and I'll have a full report ready for you."

"We agreed not to say a word of this to my father?"

"Don't worry. I'll be like the Sphinx."

"I'm very grateful. Now, go on, off with you, and have a good time."

I said good-bye with a military salute and watched him leave looking as debonair as a cock on his way to the henhouse.

He couldn't have been gone for more than five minutes when I heard the tinkle of the doorbell and lifted my head from the columns of numbers and crossings-out. A man had just come in, hidden behind a gray raincoat and a felt hat. He sported a pencil mustache and had glassy blue eyes. He smiled like a salesman, a forced smile. I was sorry Fermín was not there, because he was an expert at seeing off travelers selling camphor and other junk whenever they slipped into the bookshop. The visitor offered me his greasy grin, casually picking up a book from a pile that stood by the entrance waiting to be sorted and priced. Everything about him communicated disdain for all he saw. You're not even going to sell me a "good afternoon," I thought.

"A lot of words, eh?" he said.

"It's a book; they usually have quite a few words. Anything I can do for you, sir?"

The man put the book back on the pile, nodding indifferently and ignoring my question. "I say reading is for people who have a lot of time and nothing to do. Like women. Those of us who have to work don't have time for make-believe. We're too busy earning a living. Don't you agree?"

"It's an opinion. Were you looking for anything in particular?"

"It's not an opinion. It's a fact. That's what's wrong with this country:

people don't want to work. There are a lot of layabouts around. Don't you agree?"

"I don't know, sir. Perhaps. Here, as you can see, we only sell books."

The man came up to the counter, his eyes darting around the shop, settling occasionally on mine. His appearance and manner seemed vaguely familiar, though I couldn't say why. Something about him reminded me of one of those figures from old-fashioned playing cards or the sort used by fortune-tellers, a print straight from the pages of an incunabulum: his presence was both funereal and incandescent, like a curse dressed in Sunday best.

"If you'll tell me what I can do for you . . ."

"It's really me who was coming to do you a service. Are you the owner of this establishment?"

"No. The owner is my father."

"And the name is?"

"My name or my father's?"

The man proffered a sarcastic smile. A giggler, I thought.

"I take it that the sign saying Sempere and Son applies to both of you, then?"

"That's very perceptive of you. May I ask the reason for your visit, if you are not interested in a book?"

"The reason for my visit, which is a courtesy call, is to warn you. It has come to my attention that you're doing business with undesirable characters, in particular inverts and criminals."

I stared at him in astonishment. "Excuse me?"

The man fixed me with his eyes. "I'm talking about pansies and thieves. Don't tell me you don't know what I'm talking about."

"I'm afraid I haven't the faintest idea, nor am I remotely interested in listening to you any longer."

The man nodded in an unfriendly and truculent manner. "You'll just have to endure me, then. I suppose you're aware of citizen Federico Flaviá's activities."

"Don Federico is the neighborhood's watchmaker, an excellent person. I very much doubt that he's a criminal."

"I was talking about pansies. I have proof that this old queen frequents your shop, I imagine to buy little romantic novels and pornography."

"And may I ask you what business this is of yours?"

His answer was to pull out his wallet and place it open on the counter. I recognized a grimy police ID with his picture on it, looking a bit younger. I read up to where it said "Chief Inspector Francisco Javier Fumero."

"Speak to me with respect, boy, or I'll raise hell, and you and your father will be in deep trouble for selling communist rubbish. Do you hear?"

I wanted to reply, but the words had frozen on my lips.

"Still, this pansy isn't what brought me here today. Sooner or later he'll end up in the police station, like all the rest of his persuasion, and I'll make sure he's given a lesson. What worries me is that, according to my information, you're employing a common thief, an undesirable individual of the worst sort."

"I don't know who you're talking about, Inspector."

Fumero gave his servile, sticky giggle.

"God only knows what name he's using now. Years ago he called himself Wilfredo Camagüey, the Mambo King, and said he was an expert in voodoo, dance teacher to the Bourbon royal heir, and Mata Hari's lover. Other times he takes the names of ambassadors, variety artists, or bullfighters. We've lost count by now."

"I'm afraid I'm unable to help you. I don't know anyone called Wilfredo Camagüey."

"I'm sure you don't, but you know whom I'm referring to, don't you?"

"No."

Fumero laughed again, that forced, affected laugh that seemed to sum him up like the blurb on a book jacket. "You like to make things difficult, don't you? Look, I've come here as a friend, to warn you that whoever takes on someone as undesirable as this ends up with his fingers scorched, and you're treating me like a liar."

"Not at all. I appreciate your visit and your warning, but I can assure you that there hasn't—"

"Don't give me that crap, because if I damn well feel like it, I'll beat the shit out of you and lock you up in the cooler, is that clear? But today I'm in a good mood, so I'm going to leave you with just a warning. It's up to you to choose your company. If you like pansies and thieves, you must be a bit of both yourself. Things have to be clear where I'm concerned. Either you're with me or you're against me. That's life. That simple. So what is it going to be?"

I didn't say anything. Fumero nodded, letting go another giggle.

"Very good, Mr. Sempere. It's your call. Not a very good beginning for us. If you want problems, you'll get them. Life isn't like novels, you know. In life you have to take sides. And it's clear which side you've chosen. The side taken by idiots, the losing side."

"I'm going to ask you to leave, please."

He walked off toward the door, followed by his sibylline laugh. "We'll meet again. And tell your friend that Inspector Fumero is keeping an eye on him and sends him his best regards."

The call from the inspector and the echo of his words ruined my afternoon. After a quarter of an hour of running to and fro behind the counter, my stomach tightening into a knot, I decided to close the bookshop before the usual time and go out for a walk. I wandered about aimlessly, unable to rid my mind of the insinuations and threats made by that sinister thug. I wondered whether I should alert my father and Fermín about the visit, but I imagined that would have been precisely Fumero's intention: to sow doubt, anguish, fear, and uncertainty among us. I decided not to play his game. On the other hand, his suggestions about Fermín's past alarmed me. I felt ashamed of myself on discovering that for a moment I had given credit to the policeman's words. In the end, after much consideration, I decided to banish the entire episode to the back of my mind.

On my way home, I passed the watchmaker's shop. Don Federico greeted me from behind the counter, beckoning me to come in. The watchmaker was an affable, cheerful character who never forgot anyone's birthday, the sort of person you could always go to with a dilemma, knowing that he would find a solution. I couldn't help shivering at the thought that he was on Inspector Fumero's blacklist, and wondered whether I should warn him, although I could not imagine how, without getting caught up in matters that were none of my business. Feeling more confused than ever, I went into his shop and smiled at him.

"How are you, Daniel? What's that face for?"

"Bad day," I said. "How's everything, Don Federico?"

"Smooth as silk. They don't make watches like they used to anymore, so I've got plenty of work. If things go on like this, I'm going to have to hire an assistant. Your friend the inventor, would he be interested? He must be good at this sort of thing."

It didn't take much to imagine what Tomás's reactionary father would think of his son accepting a job in the establishment of the neighborhood's official fairy queen. "I'll let him know."

"By the way, Daniel, I've got the alarm clock your father brought around two weeks ago. I don't know what he did to it, but he'd be better off buying a new one than having it fixed."

I remembered that sometimes, on suffocating summer nights, my father would sleep out on the balcony.

"It probably fell onto the street," I said.

"That explains it. Ask him to let me know what to do about it. I can get a Radiant for him at a very good price. Look, take this one with you if you like, and let him try it out. If he likes it, he can pay for it later. If not, just bring it back."

"Thank you very much, Don Federico."

The watchmaker began to wrap up the monstrosity in question.

"The latest technology," he said with pleasure. "By the way, I loved the book Fermín sold me the other day. It was by this fellow Graham Greene. That Fermín was a tremendous hire."

I nodded. "Yes, he's worth twice his weight in gold."

"I've noticed he never wears a watch. Tell him to come by the shop and we'll sort something out."

"I will. Thank you, Don Federico."

When he handed me the alarm clock, the watchmaker observed me closely and arched his eyebrows. "Are you sure there's nothing the matter, Daniel? Just a bad day?"

I nodded again and smiled. "There's nothing the matter, Don Federico. Take care."

"You too, Daniel."

When I got home, I found my father asleep on the sofa, the newspaper on his chest. I left the alarm clock on the table with a note saying "Don Federico says dump the old one" and slipped quietly into my room. I lay down on my bed in the dark and fell asleep thinking about the inspector, Fermín, and the watchmaker. When I woke up again, it was already two o'clock in the morning. I peered into the corridor and saw that my father had retired to his bedroom with the new alarm clock. The apartment was full of shadows, and the world seemed a gloomier and more sinister place than it had been only the night before. I realized that, in fact, I had never quite believed that Inspector Fumero existed. I went into the kitchen, poured myself a glass of cold milk, and wondered whether Fermín would be all right in his *pensión*.

On my way back to my room, I tried to banish the image of the policeman from my mind. I tried to get back to sleep but realized that it was impossible. I turned on the light and decided to examine the envelope addressed to Julián Carax that I had stolen from Doña Aurora that morning and which was still in the pocket of my jacket. I placed it on my desk, under the beam of the reading lamp. It was a parchmentlike envelope, with yellowing serrated borders and clayish to the touch. The postmark, just a shadow, said "18 October 1919." The wax seal had come unstuck, probably thanks to Doña Aurora's good offices. In its place was a reddish stain, like a trace of lipstick that had kissed the fold of the envelope on which the return address was written.

Penélope Aldaya
Avenida del Tibidabo, 32, Barcelona

I opened the envelope and pulled out the letter, an ocher-colored sheet neatly folded in two. The handwriting, in blue ink, glided nervously across the page, paling slowly until it regained intensity every few words. Everything on that page spoke of another time: the strokes that depended on the ink pot, the words scratched on the thick paper by the tip of the nib, the rugged feel of the paper. I spread the letter out on the desk and read it, breathless.

Dear Julián:

This morning I found out through Jorge that you did in fact leave Barcelona to go in pursuit of your dreams. I always feared that those dreams would never allow you to be mine, or anyone else's. I would have liked to see you one last time, to be able to look into your eyes and tell you things that I don't know how to say in a letter. Nothing came out the way we had planned. I know you too well, and I know you won't write to me, that you won't even send me your address, that you will want to be another person. I know you will hate me for not having been there as I had promised. That you will think I failed you. That I didn't have the courage.

I have imagined you so many times, alone on that train, convinced that I had betrayed you. Many times I tried to find you through Miquel, but he told me that you didn't want to have anything more to do with me. What lies did they tell you, Julián? What did they say about me? Why did you believe them?

Now I know I have already lost you. I have lost everything. Even so, I can't let you go forever and allow you to forget me without letting you know that I don't bear you any grudge, that I knew it from the start, I knew that I was going to lose you and that you would never see in me what I see in you. I want you to know that I loved you from the very first day and that I still love you, now more than ever, even if you don't want me to.

I am writing to you in secret, without anyone knowing. Jorge has sworn that if he sees you again, he'll kill you. I'm not allowed to go out of the house anymore, I can't even look out of the window. I don't think they'll ever forgive me. Someone I trust has promised to mail this letter to you. I won't mention the name so as not to compromise the person in question. I don't know whether my words will reach you. But if they do, and should you decide to return to fetch me here, I know you will find the way to do it. As I write, I imagine you in that train, full of dreams and with your soul broken by betrayal, fleeing from us all and from yourself. There are so many things I cannot tell you, Julián. Things we never knew and it's better you should never know.

All I wish is for you to be happy, Julián, that everything you aspire to achieve may come true and that, although you may forget me in the course of time, one day you may finally understand how much I loved you.

Always,
Penélope

· 17 ·

THE WORDS OF PENÉLOPE ALDAYA, WHICH I READ AND REREAD
that night until I knew them by heart, brushed aside all the bitterness
Inspector Fumero's visit had left in me. At dawn, after spending the night
wide awake, engrossed in that letter and the voice I sensed behind the
words, I left the house. I dressed quietly and left a note for my father on
the hall cabinet saying I had a few errands to run and would be in the book-
shop by nine-thirty. When I stepped out of the main door, the bluish shad-
ows of early morning still darkened the puddles left in the street by the
night's drizzle. I buttoned up my jacket and set off briskly toward Plaza de
Cataluña. The stairs up from the subway station gave off a swirl of warm air.
At the ticket office of the Ferrocarriles Catalanes, I bought a third-class fare
to Tibidabo station. I made the journey in a carriage full of office workers,
maids, and day laborers carrying sandwiches the size of bricks wrapped in
newspaper. Taking refuge in the darkness of the tunnels, I rested my head
against the window, while the train journeyed through the bowels of the
city to the foot of Mount Tibidabo, which presides over Barcelona. When I
reemerged into the streets, it seemed as if I were discovering another place.
Dawn was breaking, and a purple blade of light cut through the clouds,
spraying its hue over the fronts of mansions and stately homes that bordered
Avenida del Tibidabo. A blue tram was crawling lazily uphill in the mist. I

ran after it and managed to clamber onto the back platform as the conductor looked on disapprovingly. The wooden carriage was almost empty. Two friars and a lady in mourning with ashen skin swayed, half asleep, to the rocking of the carriage.

"I'm going only as far as number thirty-two," I told the conductor, offering him my best smile.

"I don't care if you're going to Cape Horn," he replied with indifference. "Even Christ's soldiers here have paid for their tickets. Either you fork out or you walk out. And I'm not charging you for the rhyme."

Clad in sandals and the austere brown sackcloth cloaks of the Franciscan order, the friars nodded, showing their two pink tickets to prove the conductor's point.

"I'll get off, then," I said. "Because I haven't any small change."

"As you wish. But wait for the next stop. I don't want any accidents on my shift."

The tram climbed almost at walking pace, hugging the shade of the trees and peeping over the walls and gardens of castlelike mansions that I imagined filled with statues, fountains, stables, and secret chapels. I looked out from one side of the platform and noticed the White Friar villa, silhouetted between the trees. As the train approached the corner with Calle Román Macaya, it slowed down until it almost came to a halt. The driver rang his bell, and the conductor threw me a sharp look. "Go on, smartie. Off you get, number thirty-two is just there."

I got off and heard the clattering of the blue tram as it disappeared into the mist. The Aldaya residence was on the opposite side of the street from The White Friar, guarded by a large wrought-iron gate woven with ivy and dead leaves. Set in the iron bars, barely visible, was a small door, firmly locked. Above the gate, knotted into the shape of black iron snakes, was the number 32. I tried to peer into the property from there but could make out only the angles and arches of a dark tower. A trail of rust bled from the keyhole in the door. I knelt down and tried to get a better view of the courtyard from that position. All I could see was a tangle of weeds and the outline of what seemed to be a fountain or a pond from which an outstretched hand emerged, pointing up to the sky. It took me a few moments to realize that it was a stone hand and that there were other limbs and shapes I could not quite make out submerged in the fountain. Farther away, veiled by the weeds, I caught sight of a marble staircase, broken and covered in rubble and fallen leaves. The glory and fortune of the Aldayas had faded a long time ago. The place was a graveyard.

I walked back a few steps and then turned the corner to have a look at the south wing of the house. From here you could get a better view of one of the mansion's towers. At that moment I noticed a human figure at the edge of my vision, an emaciated man in blue overalls, who brandished a large broom with which he was attacking the dead leaves on the pavement. He regarded me with some suspicion, and I imagined he must be the care-taker of one of the neighboring properties. I smiled as only someone who has spent many hours behind a counter can do.

"Good morning," I intoned cordially. "Do you know whether the Al-dayas' house has been closed for long?"

He stared at me as if I had inquired about the sex of angels. The little man touched his chin with yellowed fingers that betrayed a weakness for cheap unfiltered Celtas. I regretted not having a packet on me with which to win him over. I rummaged in the pocket of my jacket to see what offer-ing I could come up with.

"At least twenty or twenty-five years, and let's hope it continues that way," said the caretaker in that flat, resigned tone of people beaten into ser-vility.

"Have you been here long?"

The man nodded. "Yours truly has been employed here with the Mira-vells since 1920."

"You wouldn't have any idea what happened to the Aldaya family, would you?"

"Well, as you know, they lost everything at the time of the Republic," he said. "He who makes trouble . . . What little I know is what I've heard in the home of the Miravells, who used to be friends of the Aldayas. I think the eldest son, Jorge, went abroad, to Argentina. It seems they had factories there. Very rich people. They always fall on their feet. You wouldn't have a cigarette, by any chance?"

"I'm sorry, but I can offer you a Sugus candy—it's a known fact that they have as much nicotine in them as a Montecristo cigar, as well as bucketloads of vitamins."

The caretaker frowned in disbelief, but he accepted. I offered him the lemon Sugus candy Fermín had given me an eternity ago, which I'd found in my pocket, hidden in a fold of the lining. I hoped it would not be rancid.

"It's good," ruled the caretaker, sucking at the rubbery sweet.

"You're chewing the pride of the national sweets industry. The Generalissimo swallows them by the handful, like sugared almonds. And tell me, did you ever hear any mention of the Aldayas' daughter, Penélope?"

The caretaker leaned on his broom in the manner of Rodin's *Thinker*.

"I think you must be mistaken. The Aldayas didn't have any daughters. They were all boys."

"Are you sure? I know that a young girl called Penélope Aldaya lived in this house around the year 1919. She was probably Jorge's sister."

"That might be, but as I said, I've been here only since 1920."

"What about the property? Who owns it now?"

"As far as I know, it's still for sale, though they were talking about knocking it down to build a school. That's the best thing they could do, frankly. Tear it down to its foundations."

"What makes you say that?"

The caretaker gave me a guarded look. When he smiled, I noticed he was missing at least four upper teeth. "Those people, the Aldayas. They were a shady lot, if you listen to what they say."

"I'm afraid I don't. What do they say about them?"

"You know. The noises and all that. Personally, I don't believe in that kind of stuff, don't get me wrong, but they say that more than one person has soiled his pants in there."

"Don't tell me the house is haunted," I said, suppressing a smile.

"You can laugh. But where there's smoke . . ."

"Have you seen anything?"

"Not exactly, no. But I've heard."

"Heard? What?"

"Well, one night, years ago, when I accompanied Master Joanet. Only because he insisted, you know? I didn't want to have anything to do with that place. . . . As I was saying, I heard something strange there. A sort of sobbing."

The caretaker produced his own version of the noise to which he was referring. It sounded like someone with consumption humming a litany of folk songs.

"It must have been the wind," I suggested.

"It must have, but I was scared shitless. Hey, you wouldn't have another one of those sweets, would you?"

"Please accept a throat lozenge. They tone you up after a sweet."

"Come on, then," agreed the caretaker, putting out his hand to collect it.

I gave him the whole box. The strong taste of licorice seemed to loosen his tongue regarding the extraordinary tale of the Aldaya mansion.

"Between you and me, it's some story. Once, Joanet, the son of Mr. Miravell, a huge guy, twice your size (he's on the national handball team, that should give you some idea) . . . Anyhow, some mates of young Joanet had heard stories about the Aldaya house, and they roped him in. And he roped *me* in, asking me to go with him—all that bragging, and he didn't dare go on his own. Rich kids, what do you expect? He was determined to go in there at night, to show off in front of his girlfriend, and he nearly pisses himself. I mean, now you're looking at it in the daylight, but at night the place looks quite different. Anyway, Joanet says he went up to the second floor (I refused to go in, of course—it can't be lawful, even if the house has been abandoned for at least ten years), and he says there was something there. He thought he heard a sort of voice in one of the rooms, but when he tried to go in, the door shut in his face. What do you think of that?"

"I think it was a draft," I said.

"Or something else," the caretaker pointed out, lowering his voice. "The other day it was on the radio: the universe is full of mysteries. Imagine, they think they've found the Holy Shroud, the real one, bang in downtown Toledo. It had been sewn to a cinema screen, to hide it from the Muslims. Apparently they wanted to use it so they could say Jesus Christ was a black man. What do you make of that?"

"I am speechless."

"Exactly. Mysteries galore. They should knock that building down and throw lime over the ground."

I thanked him for the information and was about to turn down the avenue when I looked up and saw Tibidabo Mountain awakening behind the clouds of gauze. Suddenly I felt like taking the funicular up the hill to visit the old amusement park crowning its top and wander among its merry-go-rounds and the eerie automaton halls, but I had promised to be back in the bookshop on time.

As I returned to the station, I pictured Julián Carax walking down that same road, gazing at those same solemn façades that had hardly changed since then, perhaps even waiting to board the blue tram that tiptoed up to heaven. When I reached the foot of the avenue, I took out the photograph of Penélope Aldaya smiling in the courtyard of the family mansion. Her eyes spoke of an untroubled soul and an undisclosed future. "Penélope, who loves you."

I imagined Julián Carax at my age, holding that image in his hands, perhaps in the shade of the same tree that now sheltered me. I could almost see him smiling confidently, contemplating a future as wide and luminous as that avenue, and for a moment I thought there were no more ghosts there than those of absence and loss, and that the light that smiled on me was borrowed light, real only as long as I could hold it in my eyes, second by second.

· 18 ·

WHEN I GOT BACK HOME, I REALIZED THAT FERMÍN OR MY father had already opened the bookshop. I went up to the apartment for a moment to have a quick bite. My father had left some toast and jam and a thermos of strong coffee on the dining-room table for me. I polished it all off and was down again in ten minutes, reborn. I entered the bookshop through the door in the back room that adjoined the entrance hall of the building and went straight to my closet. I put on the blue apron I usually wore to protect my clothes from the dust on boxes and shelves. At the bottom of the cupboard, I kept an old tin cookie box, a treasure chest of sorts. There I stored a menagerie of useless bits of junk that I couldn't bring myself to throw away: watches and fountain pens damaged beyond repair, old coins, marbles, wartime bullet cases I'd found in Laberinto Park, and fading postcards of Barcelona from the turn of the century. Still floating among all those bits and pieces was the old scrap of newspaper on which Isaac Monfort had written down his daughter Nuria's address, the night I went to the Cemetery of Forgotten Books to hide *The Shadow of the Wind*. I examined it in the dusty light that filtered between shelves and piled-up boxes, then closed the tin box and put the address in my wallet. Having resolved to occupy both mind and hands with the most trivial job that I could find, I walked into the shop.

"Good morning," I announced.

Fermín was classifying the contents of various parcels that had arrived from a collector in Salamanca, and my father was struggling to decipher a German catalog of Lutheran apocrypha.

"And may God grant us an even better afternoon," sang Fermín—a veiled reference, no doubt, to my meeting with Bea.

I didn't grant him the pleasure of an answer. Instead I turned to the inevitable monthly chore of getting the account book up to date, checking receipts and order forms, collections and payments. The sound of the radio orchestrated our serene monotony, treating us to a selection of hit songs by the celebrated crooner Antonio Machín, quite fashionable at the time. Caribbean rhythms tended to get on my father's nerves, but he tolerated the tropical soundscape because the tunes reminded Fermín of his beloved Cuba. The scene was repeated every week: my father pretended not to hear, and Fermín would abandon himself to a vague wiggling in time to the *danzón,* punctuating the commercial breaks with anecdotes about his adventures in Havana. The shop door was ajar, and a sweet aroma of fresh bread and coffee wafted through, lifting our spirits. After a while our neighbor Merceditas, who was on her way back from doing her shopping in Boquería Market, stopped by the shop window and peered around the door.

"Good morning, Mr. Sempere," she sang.

My father blushed and smiled at her. I had the feeling that he liked Merceditas, but his monkish manners confined him to an impregnable silence. Fermín ogled her out of the corner of his eye, keeping the tempo with his gentle hip swaying and licking his lips as if a Swiss roll had just walked in through the door. Merceditas opened a paper bag and gave us three shiny apples. I imagined she still fancied the idea of working in the bookshop and made little effort to hide her dislike for Fermín, the usurper.

"Aren't they beautiful? I saw them and said to myself, these are for the Semperes," she said in an affected tone. "I know you intellectuals like apples, like that Isaac of the gravity thing, you know."

"Isaac Newton, pumpkin," Fermín specified.

Merceditas looked angrily at him. "Hello, Mr. Smartmouth. You can be grateful that I've brought one for you, too, and not a sour grapefruit, which is what you deserve."

"But, woman, coming from your nubile hands, this offering, this fleshy fruit of the original sin, ignites my—"

"Fermín, please," interrupted my father.

"Yes, Mr. Sempere," said Fermín obediently, beating a retreat.

Merceditas was on the point of shooting something back at Fermín when we heard an uproar in the street. We all fell silent, listening expectantly. We could hear indignant cries outside, followed by a surge of murmuring. Merceditas carefully put her head around the door. We saw a number of shopkeepers walk by looking uncomfortable and swearing under their breath. Soon Don Anacleto Olmo appeared—a resident of our block and unofficial spokesman for the Royal Academy of Language in the neighborhood. Don Anacleto was a high-school teacher with a degree in Spanish literature and a handful of other subjects, and he shared an apartment on the first floor with seven cats. When he was not teaching, he moonlighted as a blurb writer for a prestigious publishing firm, and it was rumored that he also composed erotic verse that he published under the saucy alias of "Humberto Peacock." While among friends Don Anacleto was an unassuming, genial fellow, in public he felt obliged to act the part of declamatory poet, and the affected purple prose of his speech had won him the nickname of "the Victorian."

That morning the teacher's face was pink with distress, and his hands, in which he held his ivory cane, were almost shaking. All four of us stared at him.

"Don Anacleto, what's the matter?" asked my father.

"Franco has died, please say he has," prompted Fermín.

"Shut up, you beast," Merceditas cut in. "Let the doctor talk."

Don Anacleto took a deep breath, regained his composure, and, with his customary majesty, unfolded his account of what had happened.

"Dear friends, life is the stuff of drama, and even the noblest of the Lord's creatures can taste the bitterness of destiny's capricious and obstinate ways. Last night, in the small hours, while the city enjoyed the well-deserved sleep of all hardworking people, Don Federico Flaviá i Pujades, a well-loved neighbor who has so greatly contributed to this community's enrichment and solace in his role as watchmaker, only three doors down from this bookshop, was arrested by the State Police."

I felt my heart sink.

"Jesus, Mary, and Joseph!" remarked Merceditas.

Fermín puffed with disappointment, for it was clear that the dictator remained in perfect health.

Well on his way now, Don Anacleto took a deep breath and prepared to go on.

"According to a reliable account revealed to me by sources close to Police Headquarters, last night, shortly after midnight, two bemedaled undercover members of the Crime Squad caught Don Federico clad in the lush, licentious costume of a diva and singing risqué variety songs on the stage of some dive in Calle Escudillers, where he was allegedly entertaining an audience mostly made up of brainwise meagerly endowed members of the public. These godforsaken creatures, who had eloped that same afternoon from the sheltering premises of a hospice belonging to a religious order, had pulled down their trousers in the frenzy of the show and were dancing about with no restraint, clapping their hands, with their privates in full bloom and their mouths drooling."

Merceditas made the sign of the cross, alarmed by the salacious turn the events were taking.

"On learning of what had transpired, the pious mothers of some of those poor souls made a formal complaint on the grounds of public scandal and affront to the most basic code of morality. The press, nefarious vulture that feeds on misfortune and dishonor, did not take long to pick up the scent of carrion. Thanks to the wretched offices of a professional informer, not forty minutes had elapsed since the arrival of the two members of the police when Kiko Calabuig appeared on the scene. Calabuig, ace reporter for the muckraking daily *El Caso,* was determined to uncover whatever deplorable vignettes were necessary and to leave no shady stone unturned to spice up his lurid report in time for today's edition. Needless to say, the spectacle that took place in those premises is described with tabloid viciousness as Dantesque and horrifying, in twenty-four-point headlines."

"This can't be right," said my father. "I thought Don Federico had learned his lesson."

Don Anacleto gave a priestly nod. "Yes, but don't forget the old sayings

'The leopard cannot change his spots' and 'Man cannot live by bromide alone. . . .' And you still haven't heard the worst."

"Then, please, sire, could you get to the frigging point? Because with all this metaphorical spin and flourish, I'm beginning to feel a fiery bowel movement at the gates," Fermín protested.

"Pay no attention to this animal. I love the way you speak. It's like the voice on the newsreel, Dr. Anacleto," interposed Merceditas.

"Thank you, child, but I'm only a humble teacher. So, back to what I was saying, without further delay, preambles, or frills. It seems that the watchmaker, who at the time of his arrest was going by the nom de guerre of 'Lady of the Curls,' had already been arrested under similar circumstances on a couple of occasions—which were registered in the annals of crime by the guardians of law and order."

"Criminals with a badge, you mean," Fermín spit out.

"I don't get involved in politics. But I can tell you that, after knocking poor Don Federico off the stage with a well-aimed bottle, the two officers led him to the police station on Vía Layetana. With a bit of luck, and under different circumstances, things would just have ended up with some joke cracking and perhaps a couple of slaps in the face and other minor humiliations, but, by great misfortune, it so happened that the noted Inspector Fumero was on duty last night."

"Fumero," muttered Fermín. The very mention of his nemesis made him shudder.

"The one and only. As I was saying, the champion of urban safety, who had just returned from a triumphant raid on an illegal betting and beetle-racing establishment on Calle Vigatans, was informed about what had happened by the anguished mother of one of the missing boys and the alleged mastermind behind the escapade, Pepet Guardiola. At that the famous inspector, who, it appears, had knocked back some twelve double shots of brandy since suppertime, decided to intervene in the matter. After examining the aggravating factors at hand, Fumero proceeded to inform the sergeant on duty that so much *faggotry* (and I cite the word in its starkest literal sense, despite the presence of a young lady, for its documentary relevance to the events in question) required a lesson, and that what the watch-maker—that is to say, our Don Federico Flaviá i Pujades—needed, for his own good and that of the immortal souls of the Mongoloid kids, whose presence was incidental but a deciding factor in the case, was to spend the night in a common cell, down in the lower basement of the institution, in the company of a select group of thugs. As you probably know, this cell is famous in the criminal world for its inhospitable and precarious sanitary conditions, and the inclusion of an ordinary citizen in the list of guests is always cause for celebration, for it adds spice and novelty to the monotony of prison life."

Having reached this point, Don Anacleto proceeded to sketch a brief but endearing portrait of the victim, whom, of course, we all knew well.

"I don't need to remind you that Mr. Flaviá i Pujades has been blessed with a fragile and delicate personality, all goodness of heart and Christian charity. If a fly finds its way into his shop, instead of smashing it with a slipper, he'll open the door and windows wide so that the insect, one of God's creatures, is swept back by the draft into the ecosystem. I know that Don Federico is a man of faith, always very devout and involved in parish activities, but all his life he has had to live with a hidden compulsion, which, on very rare occasions, has got the better of him, sending him off into the streets dolled up as a tart. His ability to mend anything from wristwatches to sewing machines is legendary, and as a person he is well loved by every one of us who knew him and frequented his establishment, even by those who did not approve of his occasional night escapades sporting a wig, a comb, and a flamenco dress."

"You speak of him as if he were dead," ventured Fermín with dismay.

"Not dead, thank God."

I heaved a sigh of relief. Don Federico lived with his deaf octogenarian mother, known in the neighborhood as "La Pepita," who was famous for letting off hurricane-force wind capable of stunning the sparrows on her balcony and sending them spiraling down to the ground.

"Little did Pepita imagine that her Federico," continued the high-school teacher, "had spent the night in a filthy cell, where a whole band of pimps and roughnecks had handled him like a party whore, only to give him the beating of his life when they had tired of his lean flesh, while the rest of the inmates sang in chorus, 'Pansy, pansy, eat shit, you old dandy!'"

A deadly silence came over us. Merceditas sobbed. Fermín tried to comfort her with a tender embrace, but she jumped to one side.

· 19 ·

Imagine the scene," Don Anacleto concluded to everyone's dismay.

The epilogue to the story did nothing to raise our hopes. Halfway through the morning, a gray police van had dumped Don Federico on his doorstep. He was covered in blood, his dress was in shreds, and he had lost his wig and his collection of fine costume jewelry. He had been urinated on, and his face was full of cuts and bruises. The baker's son had discovered him huddled in the doorframe, shaking and crying like a baby.

"It's not fair, no, sir," argued Merceditas, positioned by the door of the bookshop, far from Fermín's wandering hands. "Poor thing, he has a heart of gold, and he always minds his own business. So he likes dressing up as a Gypsy and singing in front of people? Who cares? People are evil."

"Not evil," Fermín objected. "Moronic, which isn't quite the same thing. Evil presupposes a moral decision, intention, and some forethought. A moron or a lout, however, doesn't stop to think or reason. He acts on instinct, like a stable animal, convinced that he's doing good, that he's always right, and sanctimoniously proud to go around fucking up, if you'll excuse the French, anyone he perceives to be different from himself, be it because of skin color, creed, language, nationality, or, as in the case of Don Federico, his leisure habits. What the world needs is more thoroughly evil people and fewer borderline pigheads."

"Don't talk nonsense. What we need is a bit more Christian charity and less spitefulness. We're a disgraceful lot," Merceditas cut in. "Everybody goes to mass, but nobody pays attention to the words of Our Lord Jesus Christ."

"Merceditas, let's not mention the missal industry. That's part of the problem, not the solution."

"There goes the atheist again. And what has the clergy done to you, may I ask?"

"Come on, don't quarrel now," interrupted my father. "And you, Fermín, go and see about Don Federico, find out whether he needs anything, whether he wants someone to go to the pharmacy for him or have something bought at the market."

"Yes, Mr. Sempere. Right away. Oratory is my undoing, as you know."

"Your undoing is the shamelessness and the irreverence you carry around with you," said Merceditas. "Blasphemer. You ought to have your soul cleaned out with hydrochloric acid."

"Look here, Merceditas, just because I know you're a good person (though a bit narrow-minded and as ignorant as a brick), and because right now we're facing a social emergency in the neighborhood, in the face of which one must prioritize one's efforts, I will refrain from clarifying a few cardinal points for you—"

"Fermín!" cried my father.

Fermín closed his mouth and rushed out of the shop. Merceditas watched him with disapproval.

"That man is going to get you into trouble one of these days, mark my words. He's an anarchist, a Mason, or a Jew at the very least. With that great big nose of his—"

"Pay no attention to him. He likes to be contradictory."

Merceditas looked annoyed and shook her head. "Well, I'll leave you now. Some of us have more than one job to do, and time is short. Good morning."

We all nodded politely and watched her walk away, straight-backed, taking it out on the street with her high heels. My father drew a deep breath, as if wanting to inhale the peace that had just been recovered. Don Anacleto sagged next to him, having finally descended from his flights of rhetoric. His face was pale, and a sad autumnal look had flooded his eyes. "This country has gone to the dogs," he said.

"Come now, Don Anacleto, cheer up. Things have always been like this, here and everywhere else. The trouble is, there are some low moments, and when those strike close to home, everything looks blacker. You'll see how Don Federico overcomes this. He's stronger than we all think."

The teacher was mumbling under his breath. "It's like the tide, you see?" he said, beside himself. "The savagery, I mean. It goes away, and you feel safe, but it always returns, it always returns . . . and it chokes us. I see it every day at school. My God . . . Apes, that's what we get in the classrooms. Darwin was a dreamer, I can assure you. No evolution or anything of the sort. For every one who can reason, I have to battle with nine orangutans."

We could only nod meekly. Dr. Anacleto raised a hand to say good-bye and left, his head bowed. He appeared five years older than when he came in. My father sighed. We looked at each other briefly, not knowing what to say. I wondered whether I should tell him about Inspector Fumero's visit to the bookshop. This has been a warning, I thought. A caution. Fumero had used poor Don Federico as a telegram.

"Is anything the matter, Daniel? You're pale."

I sighed and looked down. I started to tell him about the incident with Inspector Fumero the other afternoon and his threats. My father listened, containing the anger that the burning in his eyes betrayed.

"It's my fault," I said. "I should have said something. . . ."

My father shook his head. "No. You couldn't have known, Daniel."

"But—"

"Don't even think about it. And not a word to Fermín. God knows how he would react if he knew the man was after him again."

"But we have to do something."

"Make sure he doesn't get into trouble."

I nodded, not very convinced, and began to continue the work Fermín had started while my father returned to his correspondence. Between paragraphs my father would look over at me. I pretended not to notice.

"How did it go with Professor Velázquez yesterday? Everything all right?" he asked, eager to change the subject.

"Yes. He was pleased with the books. He mentioned that he was looking for a book of Franco's letters."

"The *Moorslayer* book. But it's apocryphal . . . a joke by Madariaga. What did you say to him?"

"That we were on the case and would give him some news in two weeks' time at the latest."

"Well done. We'll put Fermín on the case and charge Velázquez a fortune."

I nodded. We continued going through the motions of our routine. My father was still looking at me. Here we go, I thought.

"Yesterday a very nice girl came by the shop. Fermín says she's Tomás Aguilar's sister?"

"Yes."

My father nodded, considering the coincidence with an expression of mild surprise. He granted me a moment's peace before he charged at me again, this time adopted the look of someone who has just remembered something.

"By the way, Daniel, we're not going to be very busy today, and, well, maybe you'd like to take some time off to do your own thing. Besides, I think you've been working too hard lately."

"I'm fine, thanks."

"I was even considering leaving Fermín here and going along to the Liceo Opera House with Barceló. This afternoon they're performing *Tannhäuser,* and he's invited me, as he has a few seats reserved in the stalls." My father pretended to be reading his letters. He was a dreadful actor.

"Since when do you like Wagner?"

He shrugged his shoulders. "Never look a gift horse in the mouth. . . . Besides, with Barceló it makes no difference what it is, because he spends the whole show commenting on the performance and criticizing the wardrobe and the tempo. He often asks after you. Perhaps you should go around to see him at the shop one day."

"One of these days."

"Right, then, if you agree, let's leave Fermín in charge today and we'll go out and enjoy ourselves a bit. It's about time. And if you need any money . . ."

"Dad. Bea is not my girlfriend."

"Who said anything about girlfriends? That's settled, then. It's up to you. If you need any money, take it from the till, but leave a note so Fermín doesn't get a fright when he closes at the end of the day."

Having said that, he feigned absentmindedness and wandered into the back room, smiling from ear to ear. I looked at my watch. It was ten-thirty in the morning. I had arranged to meet Bea at five in the university cloister, and, to my dismay, the day was turning out to be longer than *The Brothers Karamazov.*

Fermín soon returned from the watchmaker's home and informed us that a commando team of women from the neighborhood had set up a permanent guard to attend to poor Don Federico, whom the doctor had diagnosed as having three broken ribs, a large number of bruises, and an uncommonly severe rectal tear.

"Did you have to buy anything?" asked my father.

"They had enough medicines and ointments to open a pharmacy, so I took the liberty of buying him some flowers, a bottle of cologne, and three jars of peach juice—Don Federico's favorite."

"You did the right thing. Let me know what I owe you," said my father. "And how did you find him?"

"Beaten to a pulp, quite frankly. Just to see him huddled up in his bed like a ball of wool, moaning that he wanted to die, I was filled with murderous intentions, believe me. I feel like showing up at the offices of the Crime Squad and bumping off half a dozen pricks with a blunderbuss, beginning with that burst boil, Fumero."

"Fermín, let's have some peace and quiet. I strictly forbid you to do anything of the sort."

"Whatever you say, Mr. Sempere."

"And how has Pepita taken it?"

"With exemplary courage. The neighbors have doped her with shots of brandy, and when I saw her, she had collapsed onto the sofa and was snoring like a boar and letting off farts that pierced bullet holes through the upholstery."

"True to character. Fermín, I'm going to ask you to look after the shop today; I'm going around to Don Federico's for a while. Later I've arranged to meet Barceló. And Daniel has things to do."

I raised my eyes just in time to catch Fermín and my father exchanging meaningful looks.

"What a couple of matchmakers," I said. They were still laughing at me when I walked out through the door.

A COLD, SLASHING BREEZE SWEPT THE STREETS, SCATTERING STRIPS OF mist in its path. The steely sun snatched copper reflections from the roofs and belfries of the Gothic quarter. There were still some hours to go until my appointment with Bea in the university cloister, so I decided to try my luck and call on Nuria Monfort, hoping she was still living at the address provided by her father some time ago.

Plaza de San Felipe Neri is like a small air shaft in the maze of streets that crisscross the Gothic quarter, hidden behind the old Roman walls. The holes left by machine-gun fire during the war pockmark the church walls. That morning a group of children played soldiers, oblivious to the memory of the stones. A young woman, her hair streaked with silver, watched them from the bench where she sat with an open book on her lap and an absent smile. The address showed that Nuria Monfort lived in a building by the entrance to the square. The year of its construction was still visible on the blackened stone arch that crowned the front door: 1801. Once I was in the hallway, there was just enough light to make out the shadowy chamber from which a staircase twisted upward in an erratic spiral. I inspected the beehive of brass letterboxes. The names of the tenants appeared on pieces of yellowed cardboard inserted in slots, as was common in those days.

Miquel Moliner / Nuria Monfort

3—2

I went up slowly, almost fearing that the building would collapse if I were to tread firmly on those tiny dollhouse steps. There were two doors on every landing, with no number or sign. When I reached the third floor, I chose one at random and rapped on it with my knuckles. The staircase smelled of damp, of old stone, and of clay. I rapped a few times but got no answer. I decided to try my luck with the other door. I knocked with my fist three times. Inside the apartment I could hear a radio blaring the pious daily broadcast of *Moments for Reflection with Father Martín Calzado*.

The door was opened by a woman in a padded turquoise-blue checked dressing gown, slippers, and a helmet of curlers. In that dim light, she looked like a deep-sea diver. Behind her the velvety voice of Father Martín Calzado was devoting some words to the sponsors of the program, a brand of beauty products called Aurorín, much favored by pilgrims to the sanctuary of Lourdes and with miraculous properties when it came to pustules and warts.

"Good afternoon. I'm looking for Señora Monfort."

"Nurieta? You've got the wrong door, young man. It's the one opposite."

"I'm so sorry. It's just that I knocked and there was no answer."

"You're not a debt collector, are you?" asked the neighbor suddenly, suspicious from experience.

"No. Señora Monfort's father sent me."

"Ah, all right. Nurieta must be down below, reading. Didn't you see her when you came up?"

When I got to the bottom of the stairs, I saw that the woman with the silvery hair and the book in her hands was still fixed on her bench in the square. I observed her carefully. Nuria Monfort was a beautiful woman, with the sort of features that graced fashion magazines or studio portraits, but a woman whose youth seemed to be ebbing away through her eyes. There was something of her father in her slightness of build. I imagined she must be in her early forties, judging from the gray hair and the lines that aged her face. In a low light, she would have seemed ten years younger.

"Señora Monfort?"

She looked at me as though waking up from a trance, without seeing me.

"My name is Daniel. Your father gave me your address some time ago. He said you might be able to talk to me about Julián Carax."

When she heard those words, her dreamy look left her. I had a feeling that mentioning her father had not been a good idea.

"What is it you want?" she asked suspiciously.

I felt that if I didn't gain her trust at that very moment, I would have blown my one chance. The only card I could play was to tell the truth.

"Please let me explain. About eight years ago, almost by chance, I found a novel by Julián Carax in the Cemetery of Forgotten Books. You had hidden it there to save it from being destroyed by a man who calls himself Laín Coubert," I said.

She stared at me, without moving, as if she were afraid that the world around her was going to fall apart.

"I'll only take a few minutes of your time," I added. "I promise."

She nodded, with a look of resignation. "How's my father?" she asked, avoiding my eyes.

"He's well. He's aged a little. And he misses you a lot."

Nuria Monfort let out a sigh I couldn't decipher. "You'd better come up to the apartment. I don't want to talk about this on the street."

· 20 ·

Nuria Monfort lived adrift in shadows. A narrow corridor led to a dining room that also served as kitchen, library, and office. On the way I noticed a modest bedroom, with no windows. That was all, other than a tiny bathroom with no shower or tub out of which all kinds of odors emanated, from smells of cooking from the bar below to a musty stench of pipes and drains that dated from the turn of the century. The entire apartment was sunk in perpetual gloom, like a block of darkness propped up between peeling walls. It smelled of black tobacco, cold, and absence. Nuria Monfort observed me while I pretended not to notice the precarious condition of her home.

"I go down to the street because there's hardly any light in the apartment," she said. "My husband has promised to give me a reading lamp when he comes back."

"Is your husband away?"

"Miquel is in prison."

"I'm sorry, I didn't know. . . ."

"You couldn't have known. I'm not ashamed of telling you, because he isn't a criminal. This last time they took him away for printing leaflets for the metalworkers' union. That was two years ago. The neighbors think he's in America, traveling. My father doesn't know either, and I wouldn't like him to find out."

"Don't worry. He won't find out through me," I said.

A tense silence wove itself around us, and I imagined she was considering whether I was a spy sent by Isaac.

"It must be hard to run a house on one's own," I said stupidly, just to fill the void.

"It's not easy. I get what money I can from translations, but with a husband in prison, that's not nearly enough. The lawyers have bled me dry, and I'm up to my neck in debts. Translating is almost as badly paid as writing."

She looked at me as if she was expecting an answer. I just smiled meekly. "You translate books?"

"Not anymore. Now I've started to translate forms, contracts, and customs documents—that pays much better. You get only a pittance for translating literature, though a bit more than for writing it, it's true. The residents' association has already tried to throw me out a couple of times. The least of their worries is that I'm behind with the maintenance fees. You can imagine, a woman who speaks foreign languages and wears trousers. . . . More than one neighbor has accused me of running a house of ill repute in this apartment. I should be so lucky. . . ."

I hoped the darkness would hide my blushes.

"I'm sorry. I don't know why I'm telling you all this. I'm embarrassing you."

"It's my fault. I asked."

She laughed nervously. She had around her a burning aura of loneliness.

"You remind me a bit of Julián," she said suddenly. "The way you look, and your gestures. He used to do what you are doing now. He would stare at you without saying a word, and you wouldn't know what he was thinking, and so, like an idiot, you'd tell him things it would have been better to keep to yourself. . . . Can I offer you anything? A cup of coffee maybe?"

"Nothing, thanks. I don't want to trouble you."

"It's no trouble. I was about to make one for myself."

Something told me that that cup of coffee was all she was having for lunch. I refused again and watched her walk over to a corner of the dining room where there was a small electric stove.

"Make yourself comfortable," she said, her back to me.

I looked around and asked myself how. Nuria Monfort's office consisted of a desk that took up the corner next to the balcony, an Underwood typewriter with an oil lamp beside it, and a shelf full of dictionaries and manuals. There were no family photos, but the wall by the desk was covered with postcards, all of them pictures of a bridge I remembered seeing somewhere but couldn't pinpoint—perhaps Paris or Rome. Beneath this display the desk showcased an almost obsessive neatness and order. The pencils were sharpened and perfectly lined up. The papers and folders were arranged and placed in three symmetrical rows. When I turned around, I realized that Nuria Monfort was gazing at me from the entrance to the corridor. She regarded me in silence, the way one looks at strangers on the street or in the subway. She lit a cigarette and stayed where she was, her face masked by spirals of blue smoke. I suddenly thought that, despite herself, Nuria Monfort exuded a certain air of the femme fatale, like those women in the movies who dazzled Fermín when they materialized out of the mist of a Berlin station, enveloped in halos of improbable light, the sort of beautiful women whose own appearance bored them.

"There's not much to tell," she began. "I met Julián over twenty years ago, in Paris. At that time I was working for Cabestany, the publishing house. Mr. Cabestany had acquired the rights to Julián's novels for peanuts. At first I worked in the accounts department, but when Mr. Cabestany found out that I spoke French, Italian, and a little German, he moved me to the purchasing department, and I became his personal secretary. One of my jobs was to correspond with foreign authors and publishers with whom our firm had business, and that's how I came into contact with Julián Carax."

"Your father told me you two were good friends."

"My father probably told you we had a fling or something along those lines, right? According to him, I run after any pair of pants, like a bitch in heat."

That woman's frankness and her brazen manner left me speechless. I took too long to come up with an acceptable reply. By then Nuria Monfort was smiling to herself and shaking her head.

"Pay no attention to him. My father got that idea from a trip to Paris I once had to make, back in 1933, to resolve some matters between Mr. Cabestany and Gallimard. I spent a week in the city and stayed in Julián's apartment for the simple reason that Mr. Cabestany preferred to save on hotel expenses. Very romantic, as you can see. Until then my relationship with Julián Carax had been conducted strictly by letter, normally dealing with copyright, proofs, or editorial matters. What I knew about him, or imagined, had come from reading the manuscripts he sent us."

"Did he tell you anything about his life in Paris?"

"No. Julián didn't like talking about his books or about himself. I didn't think he was happy in Paris. Though he gave the impression that he was one of those people who cannot be happy anywhere. The truth is, I never got to know him well. He wouldn't let you. He was a very private person, and sometimes it seemed to me that he was no longer interested in the world or in people. Mr. Cabestany thought he was shy and perhaps a bit crazy, but I got the feeling that Julián was living in the past, locked in his memories. Julián lived within himself, for his books and inside them—a comfortable prison of his own design."

"You say this as if you envied him."

"There are worse prisons than words, Daniel."

I nodded, not quite sure what she meant.

"Did Julián ever talk about those memories, about his years in Barcelona?"

"Very little. During the week I was staying with him in Paris, he told me a bit about his family. His mother was French, a music teacher. His father had a hat shop or something like that. I know he was a very religious man, and very strict."

"Did Julián explain to you what sort of a relationship he had with him?"

"I know they didn't get on at all. It was something that went back a long time. In fact, the reason Julián went to Paris was to avoid being put into the army by his father. His mother had promised him she would take him as far away as possible from that man, rather than let that happen."

"That man was his father, after all."

Nuria Monfort smiled. It was just a hint of a smile and her eyes shone weary and sad.

"Even if he was, he never behaved like one, and Julián never considered him as such. Once he confessed to me that before getting married, his mother had had an affair with a stranger whose name she never revealed to him. That man was Julián's real father."

"It sounds like the beginning of *The Shadow of the Wind*. Do you think he told you the truth?"

Nuria Monfort nodded. "Julián told me he had grown up watching how the hatter—that's what he called him—insulted and beat his mother. Then he would go into Julián's room and tell him he was the son of sin, that he had inherited his mother's weak and despicable personality and would be miserable all his life, a failure at whatever he tried to do. . . ."

"Did Julián feel resentful toward his father?"

"Time is a great healer. I never felt that Julián hated him. Perhaps that would have been better. I got the impression that he lost all respect for the hatter as a result of all those scenes. Julián spoke about all that as if it didn't matter to him, as if it were part of a past he had left behind, but these things are never forgotten. The words with which a child's heart is poisoned, through malice or through ignorance, remain branded in his memory, and sooner or later they burn his soul."

I wondered whether she was talking from experience, and the image of my friend Tomás Aguilar came to my mind, listening stoically to the diatribes of his haughty father.

"How old was Julián when his father started speaking to him like that?"

"About eight or ten, I imagine."

I sighed.

"As soon as he was old enough to join the army, his mother took him to Paris. I don't think they even said good-bye. The hatter could never accept that his family had abandoned him."

"Did you ever hear Julián mention a girl called Penélope?"

"Penélope? I don't think so. I'd remember."

"She was a girlfriend of his, from the time when he still lived in Barcelona."

I pulled out the photograph of Carax and Penélope Aldaya and handed it to her. I noticed how a smile lit up her face when she saw an adolescent Julián Carax. Nostalgia and loss were consuming her.

"He looks so young here. . . . Is this the Penélope you mentioned?"

I nodded.

"Very good-looking. Julián always managed to be surrounded by pretty women."

Like you, I thought. "Do you know whether he had lots . . . ?"

That smile again, at my expense. "Girlfriends? Lovers? I don't know. To tell you the truth, I never heard him speak about any woman in his life. Once, just to needle him, I asked him. You must know that he earned his living playing the piano in a hostess bar. I asked him whether he wasn't tempted, surrounded all day by beauties of easy virtue. He didn't find the joke funny. He replied that he had no right to love anyone, that he deserved to be alone."

"Did he say why?"

"Julián never said why."

"Even so, in the end, shortly before returning to Barcelona in 1936, Julián Carax was going to get married."

"So they said."

"Do you doubt it?"

She looked skeptical as she shrugged her shoulders. "As I said, in all the years we knew each other, Julián never mentioned any woman in particular, and even less one he was going to marry. The story about his supposed marriage reached me later. Neuval, Carax's last publisher, told Cabestany that the fiancée was a woman twenty years older than Julián, a rich widow in poor health. According to Neuval, she had been more or less supporting him for years. The doctors gave her six months to live, a year at the most. Neuval said she wanted to marry Julián so that he could inherit from her."

"But the marriage ceremony never took place."

"If there ever was such a plan, or such a widow."

"From what I know, Carax was involved in a duel, on the dawn of the very day he was due to be married. Do you know who with, or why?"

"Neuval supposed it was someone connected to the widow. A grasping distant relative who didn't want to see the inheritance fall into the hands of some upstart. Neuval published mostly penny dreadfuls, and I think the genre had gone to his head."

"I see you don't really believe the story of the wedding and the duel."

"No. I never believed it."

"What do you think happened, then? Why did Carax return to Barcelona?"

She smiled sadly. "I've been asking myself this question for seventeen years."

Nuria Monfort lit another cigarette. She offered me one. I was tempted to accept but refused.

"But you must have some theory?" I suggested.

"All I know is that in the summer of 1936, shortly after the outbreak of the war, an employee at the municipal morgue phoned our firm to say they had received the body of Julián Carax three days earlier. They'd found him dead in an alleyway of the Raval quarter, dressed in rags and with a bullet through his heart. He had a book on him, a copy of *The Shadow of the Wind,* and his passport. The stamp showed he'd crossed the French border a month before. Where he had been during that time, nobody knew. The police contacted his father, but he refused to take responsibility for the body, alleging that he didn't have a son. After two days without anyone's claiming the corpse, he was buried in a common grave in Montjuïc Cemetery. I couldn't even take him flowers, because nobody could tell me where he'd been buried. It was the employee of the morgue—who had kept the book found in Julián's jacket—who had the idea of phoning Cabestany's publishing house a couple of days later. That is how I found out what had happened. I couldn't understand it. If Julián had anyone left in Barcelona to whom he could turn, it was me or, at a pinch, Mr. Cabestany. We were his only friends, but he never told us he'd returned. We only knew he'd come back to Barcelona after he died. . . ."

"Were you able to find out anything else after getting the news?"

"No. Those were the first months of the war, and Julián was not the only one to disappear without a trace. Nobody talks about it anymore, but there are lots of nameless graves, like Julián's. Asking was like banging your head against a brick wall. With the help of Mr. Cabestany, who by then was very ill, I made a complaint to the police and pulled all the strings I could. All I got out of it was a visit from a young inspector, an arrogant, sinister sort, who told me it would be a good idea not to ask any more questions and to concentrate my efforts on having a more positive attitude, because the country was in full cry, on a crusade. Those were his words. His name was Fumero, that's all I remember. It seems that now he's quite an important man. He's often mentioned in the papers. Maybe you've heard of him."

I swallowed. "Vaguely."

"I heard nothing more about Julián until someone got in touch with the publishers and said he was interested in acquiring all the copies of Carax's novels that were left in the warehouse."

"Laín Coubert."

Nuria Monfort nodded.

"Have you any idea who that man was?"

"I have an inkling, but I'm not sure. In March 1936—I remember the date because at the time we were preparing *The Shadow of the Wind* for press—someone called the publishers to ask for his address. He said he was an old friend and he wanted to visit Julián in Paris. Give him a surprise. They put him onto me, and I said I wasn't authorized to give out that information."

"Did he say who he was?"

"Someone called Jorge."

"Jorge Aldaya?"

"It might have been. Julián had mentioned him on more than one occasion. I think they had been together at San Gabriel's School, and sometimes Julián referred to him as if he'd been his best friend."

"Did you know that Jorge Aldaya was Penélope's brother?"

Nuria Monfort frowned. She looked disconcerted.

"Did you give Aldaya Julián's address in Paris?"

"No. He made me feel uneasy."

"What did he say?"

"He laughed at me, he said he'd find him some other way, and hung up."

Something seemed to be gnawing at her. I began to suspect where the conversation was taking us. "But you heard from him again, didn't you?"

She nodded nervously. "As I was telling you, shortly after Julián's disappearance that man turned up at Cabestany's firm. By then Mr. Cabestany could no longer work, and his eldest son had taken charge of the business. The visitor, Laín Coubert, offered to buy all the remaining stock of Julián's novels. I thought the whole thing was a joke in poor taste. Laín Coubert was a character in *The Shadow of the Wind*."

"The devil."

Nuria Monfort nodded again.

"Did you actually see Laín Coubert?"

She shook her head and lit her third cigarette. "No. But I heard part of the conversation with the son in Mr. Cabestany's office."

She left the sentence in the air, as if she were afraid of finishing it or wasn't sure how to. The cigarette trembled in her fingers.

"His voice," she said. "It was the same voice as the man who phoned saying he was Jorge Aldaya. Cabestany's son, an arrogant idiot, tried to ask for more money. Coubert—or whoever he was—said he had to think about the offer. That very night Cabestany's warehouse in Pueblo Nuevo went up in flames, and Julián's books with it."

"Except for the ones you rescued and hid in the Cemetery of Forgotten Books."

"That's right."

"Have you any idea why anyone would have wanted to burn all of Julián Carax's books?"

"Why are books burned? Through stupidity, ignorance, hatred . . . goodness only knows."

"Why do you think?" I insisted.

"Julián lived in his books. The body that ended up in the morgue was only a part of him. His soul is in his stories. I once asked him who inspired him to create his characters, and his answer was no one. That all his characters were himself."

"So if somebody wanted to destroy him, he'd have to destroy those stories and those characters, isn't that right?"

The dispirited smile returned, a smile of defeat and tiredness. "You remind me of Julián," she said. "Before he lost his faith."

"His faith in what?"

"In everything."

She came up to me in the half-light and took my hand. She stroked my palm in silence, as if she wanted to read the lines on my skin. My hand was shaking under her touch. I caught myself tracing the shape of her body under those old, borrowed clothes. I wanted to touch her and feel her pulse burning under her skin. Our eyes had met, and I felt sure that she knew what I was thinking. I sensed that she was lonelier than ever. I raised my eyes and met her serene, open gaze.

"Julián died alone, convinced that nobody would remember him or his books and that his life had meant nothing," she said. "He would have liked to know that somebody wanted to keep him alive, that someone remembered him. He used to say that we exist as long as somebody remembers us."

I was filled by an almost painful desire to kiss that woman, an eagerness such as I had never before experienced, not even when I conjured up the ghost of Clara Barceló. She read my thoughts.

"It's getting late for you, Daniel," she murmured.

One part of me wanted to stay, to lose myself in this strange intimacy, to hear her say again how my gestures and my silences reminded her of Julián Carax.

"Yes," I mumbled.

She nodded but said nothing, and then escorted me to the door. The corridor seemed endless. She opened the door for me, and I went out onto the landing.

"If you see my father, tell him I'm well. Lie to him."

I said good-bye to her in a low voice, thanking her for her time and holding out my hand politely. Nuria Monfort ignored my formal gesture. She placed her hands on my arms, leaned forward, and kissed me on the cheek. We gazed at each other, and this time I searched her lips, almost trembling. It seemed to me that they parted a little, and that her fingers were reaching for my face. At the last moment, Nuria Monfort moved away and looked down.

"I think it's best if you leave, Daniel," she whispered.

I thought she was about to cry, but before I could say anything, she closed the door. I was left on the landing, feeling her presence on the other side of the door, motionless, asking myself what had happened in there. At the other end of the landing, the neighbor's peephole was blinking. I waved at her and attacked the stairs. When I reached the street, I could still feel Nuria Monfort's face, her voice, and her smell, deep in my soul. I carried the trace of her lips, of her breath on my skin through streets full of faceless people escaping from offices and shops. When I turned into Calle Canuda, an icy wind hit me, cutting through the bustle. I welcomed the cold air on my face and walked up toward the university. After crossing the Ramblas, I made my way toward Calle Tallers and disappeared into its narrow canyon of shadows, feeling that I was still trapped in that dark, gloomy dining room where I now imagined Nuria Monfort sitting alone, silently tidying up her pencils, her folders, and her memories, her eyes poisoned with tears.

21

DUSK FELL ALMOST SURREPTITIOUSLY, WITH A COLD BREEZE AND a mantle of purple light that slid between the gaps in the streets. I quickened my pace, and twenty minutes later the front of the university emerged like an ocher ship anchored in the night. In his lodge the porter of the Literature Faculty perused the words of the nation's most influential bylines in the afternoon edition of the sports pages. There seemed to be hardly any students left on the premises. The echo of my footsteps followed me through the corridors and galleries that led to the cloister, where the glow of two yellowish lights barely disturbed the shadows. It suddenly occurred to me that perhaps Bea had tricked me, that she'd arranged to meet me there at that untimely hour to avenge my presumption. The leaves on the orange trees in the cloister shimmered with tears of silver, and the sound of the fountain wove its way through the arches. I looked carefully around the patio, contemplating disappointment or maybe a certain cowardly sense of relief. There she was, sitting on one of the benches, her silhouette outlined against the fountain, her eyes looking up toward the vaults of the cloister. I stopped at the entrance to gaze at her, and for a moment I was reminded of Nuria Monfort daydreaming on her bench in the square. I noticed she didn't have her folder or her books with her, and I suspected she hadn't had any classes that afternoon. Perhaps she'd come here just to meet me. I swallowed hard and walked into the cloister. The sound of my foot-steps on the paving gave me away and Bea looked up, with a smile of sur-prise, as if my presence there were just a coincidence.

"I thought you weren't coming," said Bea.

"That's just what I thought," I replied.

She remained seated, upright, her knees tight together and her hands on her lap. I asked myself how I could feel so detached from her and at the same time see every line on her lips.

"I've come because I want to prove to you that you were wrong about what you said the other day, Daniel. I'm going to marry Pablo, and I don't care what you show me tonight. I'm off to El Ferrol as soon as he's finished his military service."

I looked at her as if I'd just missed a train. I realized I'd spent two days walking on air, and now my world seemed to be collapsing.

"And there I was, thinking you'd come because you felt like seeing me." I managed a weak smile.

I noticed her blushing self-consciously.

"I was only joking," I lied. "What I was serious about was my promise to show you a face of the city that you don't yet know. At least that will give you cause to remember me, or Barcelona, wherever you go."

There was a touch of sadness in Bea's smile, as she avoided my eyes. "I nearly went into the cinema, you know. So as not to see you today," she said.

"Why?"

Bea looked at me but said nothing. She shrugged her shoulders and raised her eyes as if she were trying to catch words that were escaping from her.

"Because I was afraid that perhaps you were right," she said at last.

I sighed. We were shielded by the evening light and that despondent si-lence that brings strangers together, and I felt daring enough to say anything that came to my head, even though it might be for the last time.

"Do you love him, or don't you?"

A smile came and went. "It's none of your business."

"That's true," I said. "It's only your business."

She gave me a cold look. "And what does it matter to you?"

"It's none of your business," I said.

She didn't smile. Her lips trembled. "People who know me know I'm very fond of Pablo. My family and—"

"But I'm almost a stranger," I interrupted. "And I would like to hear it from you."

"Hear what?"

"That you really love him. That you're not marrying him to get away from home, to put distance between yourself and Barcelona and your family, to go somewhere where they can't hurt you. That you're leaving and not running away."

Her eyes shone with angry tears. "You have no right to say that to me, Daniel. You don't know me."

"Tell me I'm mistaken and I'll leave. Do you love him?"

We looked at each other for a long while, without saying a word.

"I don't know," she murmured at last. "I don't know."

"Someone once said that the moment you stop to think about whether you love someone, you've already stopped loving that person forever," I said.

Bea looked for the irony in my expression. "Who said that?"

"Someone called Julián Carax."

"A friend of yours?"

I caught myself nodding. "Sort of."

"You're going to have to introduce him to me."

"Tonight, if you like."

We left the university under a bruised sky and wandered aimlessly, going nowhere in particular, just getting used to walking side by side. We took shelter in the only subject we had in common, her brother, Tomás. Bea spoke about him as if he were a virtual stranger, someone she loved but barely knew. She avoided my eyes and smiled nervously. I felt that she regretted what she had said to me in the university cloister, that the words still hurt and were still gnawing at her.

"Listen, what I said to you before," she said suddenly, "you won't mention a word to Tomás, will you?"

"Of course not. I won't tell anyone."

She laughed nervously. "I don't know what came over me. Don't be offended, but sometimes one feels freer speaking to a stranger than to people one knows. Why is that?"

I shrugged. "Probably because a stranger sees us the way we are, not as he wishes to think we are."

"Is that also from your friend Carax?"

"No, I've just made it up to impress you."

"And how do you see me?"

"Like a mystery."

"That's the strangest compliment anyone has ever paid me."

"It's not a compliment. It's a threat."

"What do you mean?"

"Mysteries must be solved, one must find out what they hide."

"You might be disappointed when you see what's inside."

"I might be surprised. And you, too."

"Tomás never told me you had so much cheek."

"That's because what little I have, I've reserved entirely for you."

"Why?"

Because I'm afraid of you, I thought.

We sought refuge in a small café next to the Poliorama Theater. Withdrawing to a table by the window, we asked for some *serrano* ham sandwiches and a couple of white coffees, to warm up. Soon thereafter the manager, a scrawny fellow with the face of an imp, came up to the table with an attentive expression.

"Did yer folks ask for the 'am sandwiches?

We nodded.

"Sorry to 'ave to announce, on behalf of the management 'ere, that there's not a scrap of 'am left. I can offer black, white, or mixed *butifarra,* meatballs, or *chistorra.* Top of the line, extra fresh. I also 'ave pickled sardines, if yer folks can't consume meat products for reasons of religious conscience. It being Friday . . ."

"I'll be fine with a white coffee, really," said Bea.

I was starving. "What if you bring two servings of spicy potatoes and some bread, too?"

"Right away, sir. And please, pardon the shortness of supplies. Usually I tend to 'ave everything, even Bolshevik caviar. But s'afternoon, it being the European Cup semifinal, we've had a lot of customers. Great game."

The manager walked away ceremoniously. Bea watched him with amusement.

"Where's that accent from? Jaén?"

"Much closer: Santa Coloma de Gramanet," I specified. "You don't often take the subway, do you?"

"My father says the subway is full of riffraff and that if you're on your own, the Gypsies feel you up."

I was about to say something but decided to keep my mouth shut. Bea laughed. As soon as the coffees and the food arrived, I fell on it all with no pretense at refinement. Bea didn't eat anything. With her hands spread around the steaming cup, she watched me with half a smile, somewhere between curiosity and amazement.

"So what is it you're going to show me today?"

"A number of things. In fact, what I'm going to show you is part of a story. Didn't you tell me the other day that what you like to do is read?"

Bea nodded, arching her eyebrows.

"Well, this is a story about books."

"About books?"

"About accursed books, about the man who wrote them, about a character who broke out of the pages of a novel so that he could burn it, about a betrayal and a lost friendship. It's a story of love, of hatred, and of the dreams that live in the shadow of the wind."

"You talk like the jacket blurb of a Victorian novel, Daniel."

"That's probably because I work in a bookshop and I've seen too many. But this is a true story. As real as the fact that this bread they served us is at least three days old. And, like all true stories, it begins and ends in a cemetery, although not the sort of cemetery you imagine."

She smiled the way children smile when they've been promised a riddle or a conjuror's trick. "I'm all ears."

I gulped down the last of my coffee and looked at her for a few moments without saying anything. I thought about how much I wanted to lose myself in those evasive eyes. I thought about the loneliness that would take hold of me that night when I said good-bye to her, once I had run out of tricks or stories to make her stay with me any longer. I thought about how little I had to offer her and how much I wanted from her.

"I can hear your brains clanking, Daniel. What are you planning?"

I began my story with that distant dawn when I awoke and could not remember my mother's face, and I didn't stop until I paused to recall the world of shadows I had sensed that very day in the home of Nuria Monfort. Bea listened quietly, making no judgment, drawing no conclusions. I told her about my first visit to the Cemetery of Forgotten Books and about the night I spent reading *The Shadow of the Wind*. I told her about my meeting with the faceless man and about the letter signed by Penélope Aldaya that I always carried with me without knowing why. I spoke about how I had never kissed Clara Barceló, or anyone, and of how my hands had trembled when I felt the touch of Nuria Monfort's lips on my skin, only a few hours before. I told her how until that moment I had not understood that this was a story about lonely people, about absence and loss, and that that was why I had taken refuge in it until it became confused with my own life, like someone who has escaped into the pages of a novel because those whom he needs to love seem nothing more than ghosts inhabiting the mind of a stranger.

"Don't say anything," whispered Bea. "Just take me to that place."

It was pitch dark when we stopped by the front door of the Cemetery of Forgotten Books, in the gloom of Calle Arco del Teatro. I lifted the devil-head knocker and knocked three times. While we waited, sheltering under the arch of the entrance, the cold wind smelled of charcoal. I met Bea's eyes, so close to mine. She was smiling. Soon we heard light footsteps approaching the door, and then the tired voice of the keeper.

"Who's there?" asked Isaac.

"It's Daniel Sempere, Isaac."

I thought I could hear him swearing under his breath. Then followed the thousand squeaks and groans from the intricate system of locks. Finally the door yielded an inch or two, revealing the vulturine face of Isaac Monfort in candlelight. When he saw me, the keeper sighed and rolled his eyes.

"Stupid of me. I don't know why I ask," he said. "Who else could it be at this time of night?"

Isaac was clothed in what seemed like a strange crossbreed of dressing gown, bathrobe, and Russian army coat. The padded slippers perfectly matched his checked wool cap, rather like a professor's cap, complete with tassel.

"I hope I didn't get you out of bed," I said.

"Not at all. I'd only just started saying my prayers. . . ."

He looked at Bea as if he'd just seen a pack of dynamite sticks alight at his feet. "For your own good, I hope this isn't what it looks like," he threatened.

"Isaac, this is my friend Beatriz, and with your permission I'd like to show her this place. Don't worry, she's completely trustworthy."

"Sempere, I've known toddlers with more common sense than you."

"It will only be a moment."

Isaac let out a snort of defeat and examined Bea carefully, like a suspicious policeman.

"Do you realize you're in the company of an idiot?" he asked.

Bea smiled politely. "I'm beginning to come to terms with it."

"Sublime innocence! Do you know the rules?"

Bea nodded. Isaac mumbled under his breath and let us in, scanning the shadows of the street, as usual.

"I visited your daughter, Nuria," I mentioned casually. "She's well. Working hard, but well. She sends you her love."

"Yes, and poisoned darts. You're not much good at making things up, Sempere. But I appreciate the effort. Come on in."

Once inside, Isaac handed me the candle and proceeded to lock the door.

"When you've finished, you know where to find me."

Under the mantle of darkness, we could only just make out the spectral forms of the book maze. The candle projected its bubble of steamy light at our feet. Bea paused, astonished, at the entrance to the labyrinth. I smiled, recognizing in her face the same expression my father must have seen in mine years before. We entered the tunnels and galleries of the maze; they creaked under our footsteps. The marks I had made during my last incursion were still there.

"Come, I want to show you something," I said.

More than once I lost my own trail and we had to go back a stretch in search of the last sign. Bea watched me with a mixture of alarm and fascination. My mental compass told me we were caught in a knot of spirals that rose slowly toward the very heart of the labyrinth. At last I managed to retrace my steps within the tangle of corridors and tunnels until I entered a narrow passage that felt like a gangway stretching out into the gloom. I knelt down by the last shelf and looked for my old friend hidden behind the row of dust-covered volumes—the layer of dust shining like frost in the candlelight. I took the book and handed it to Bea.

"Let me introduce you to Julián Carax."

"The Shadow of the Wind," Bea read, stroking the faded letters on the cover.

"Can I take it with me?" she asked.

"You can take any book but this one."

"But that's not fair. After all the things you've told me, this is precisely the one I want."

"One day, perhaps. But not today."

I took it from her hands and put it back in its hiding place.

"I'll come back without you and I'll take it away without you knowing," she said mockingly.

"You wouldn't find it in a thousand years."

"That's what you think. I've seen your notches, and I, too, know the story of the Minotaur."

"Isaac wouldn't let you in."

"You're wrong. He prefers me to you."

"And how do you know?"

"I can read people's eyes."

Despite myself, I believed her and turned mine away.

"Choose any other one. Here, this one looks promising. *The Castilian Hog, That Unknown Beast: In Search of the Roots of Iberian Pork,* by Anselmo Torquemada. I'm sure it sold more copies than any book by Julián Carax. Every part of the pig can be put to good use."

"I'm more attracted to this other one."

"*Tess of the d'Urbervilles*. It's the original. You're bold enough to read Hardy in English?"

She gave me a sidelong glance.

"All yours, then!"

"Don't you see? It feels as if it's been waiting for me. As if it has been hiding here for me since before I was born."

I looked at her in astonishment. Bea's lips crinkled into a smile. "What have I said?"

Then, without thinking, barely brushing her lips, I kissed her.

IT WAS ALMOST MIDNIGHT WHEN WE REACHED THE FRONT DOOR OF Bea's house. We had walked most of the way without speaking, not daring to turn our thoughts into words. We walked apart, hiding from each other. Bea walked upright with her *Tess* under her arm, and I followed a step behind, still tasting her lips. The way Isaac had glanced at me when we left the Cemetery of Forgotten Books was still on my mind. It was a look I knew well and had seen a thousand times in my father, a look that asked me whether I had the slightest idea what I was doing. The last hours I'd been lost in another world, a universe of touches and looks I did not understand, that blotted out both reason and shame. Now, back in the reality that always lies in wait among the shadows of the Ensanche quarter, the enchantment was lifting, and all I had left in me was a painful desire and an indescribable restlessness. And yet just looking at Bea was enough for me to realize that my doubts were but a breeze compared to the storm that was raging inside her. We stopped by her door and looked at each other without attempting to pretend. A mellifluous night watchman was walking up to us unhurriedly, humming boleros to the rhythmic jingle of his bunches of keys.

"Perhaps you'd rather we didn't see each other again," I suggested without much conviction.

"I don't know, Daniel. I don't know anything. Is that what you want?"

"No. Of course not. And you?"

She shrugged her shoulders and smiled faintly. "What do you think?" she asked. "I lied to you earlier, you know. In the cloister."

"What about?"

"About not wanting to see you today."

The night porter hung about, smirking at us, obviously indifferent to my first whispered exchange at a front door. To him, experienced in such matters, it must have seemed a string of clichés and banalities.

"Don't worry about me, there's no hurry," he said. "I'll have a smoke on the corner, and you just let me know."

I waited for the watchman to walk away.

"When will I see you again?"

"I don't know, Daniel."

"Tomorrow?"

"Please, Daniel. I don't know."

I nodded. She stroked my face. "You'd better leave now."

"You know where to find me, at least?"

She nodded.

"I'll be waiting."

"Me, too."

As I moved away, I couldn't take my eyes off her. The night watchman, an expert in these situations, was already walking up to open the door for her.

"You rascal," he whispered as he went by, not without admiration. "What a looker."

I waited until Bea had gone into the building and then set off briskly, turning to glance back at every step. Slowly I became possessed by the absurd conviction that everything was possible, and it seemed to me that even those deserted streets and that hostile wind smelled of hope. When I reached Plaza de Cataluña, I noticed that a flock of pigeons had congregated in the center of the square. They covered it all with a blanket of white feathers that swayed silently. I thought of going around them, but at that moment I noticed that the pigeons parted to let me pass, without flying off. I felt my way forward, as the pigeons broke ranks in front of me and re-formed behind me. When I got to the middle of the square, I heard the peal of the cathedral bells ringing out midnight. I paused for a moment, stranded in an ocean of silvery birds, and thought how this had been the strangest and most marvelous day of my life.

22

THE LIGHT WAS STILL ON IN THE BOOKSHOP WHEN I CROSSED THE street toward the shop window. I thought that perhaps my father had stayed on until late, getting up to date with his correspondence or finding some other excuse to wait up for me and pump me for information about my meeting with Bea. I saw a silhouette making a pile of books and recognized the gaunt, nervous profile of Fermín, lost in concentration. I rapped on the pane with my knuckles. Fermín looked out, pleasantly surprised, and signaled to me to pop in through the back-room door.

"Still working, Fermín? It's terribly late."

"I'm really just killing time until I go over to poor Don Federico's and watch over him. I'm taking turns with Eloy from the optician's. I don't sleep much anyhow. Two or three hours at the most. Mind you, you can't talk either, Daniel. It's past midnight, from which I infer that your meeting with the young lady was a roaring success."

I shrugged my shoulders. "The truth is I don't know," I admitted.

"Did you get to feel her up?"

"No."

"A good sign. Never trust girls who let themselves be touched right away. But even less those who need a priest for approval. Good sirloin steak—if you'll excuse the comparison—needs to be cooked until it's medium rare. Of course, if the opportunity arises, don't be prudish, and go for the kill. But if what you're looking for is something serious, like this thing with me and Bernarda, remember the golden rule."

"Is your thing serious?"

"More than serious. Spiritual. And what about you and this pumpkin, Beatriz? You can see a mile off that she's worth a million bucks, but the crux of the matter is this: is she the sort who makes one fall in love or the sort who merely stirs up the lower parts?"

"I haven't the slightest idea," I pointed out. "Both things, I'd say."

"Look, Daniel, this is like indigestion. Do you notice something here, in the mouth of the stomach—as if you'd swallowed a brick? Or do you just feel a general feverishness?"

"The brick thing sounds more like it," I said, although I didn't altogether discard the fever.

"That means it's a serious matter. God help us! Come on, sit down and I'll make you a linden-blossom tea."

We settled down around the table in the back room, surrounded by books. The city was asleep, and the bookshop felt like a boat adrift in a sea of silence and shadows. Fermín handed me a steaming hot cup and smiled at me a little awkwardly. Something was bothering him.

"May I ask you a personal question, Daniel?"

"Of course."

"I beg you to answer in all frankness," he said, and he cleared his throat. "Do you think I could ever be a father?"

He must have seen my puzzled expression, and he quickly added, "I don't mean biologically—I may look a bit rickety, but by good luck Providence has endowed me with the potency and the fury of a fighting bull. I'm referring to the other sort of father. A good father, if you see what I mean."

"A good father?"

"Yes. Like yours. A man with a head, a heart, and a soul. A man capable of listening, of leading and respecting a child, and not of drowning his own defects in him. Someone whom a child will not only love because he's his father but will also admire for the person he is. Someone he would want to grow up to resemble."

"Why are you asking me this, Fermín? I thought you didn't believe in marriage and families. The yoke and all that, remember?"

Fermín nodded. "Look, all that's for amateurs. Marriage and family are only what we make of them. Without that they're just a nest of hypocrisy. Garbage and empty words. But if there is real love, of the sort one doesn't go around telling everyone about, the sort that is felt and lived . . ."

"You're a changed man, Fermín."

"I am. Bernarda has made me want to be a better man."

"How's that?"

"So that I can deserve her. You cannot understand such things right now, because you're young. But in good time you'll see that sometimes what matters isn't what one gives but what one gives up. Bernarda and I have been talking. She's quite a mother hen, as you know. She doesn't say so, but I think the one thing in life that would make her truly happy is becoming a mother. And I fancy that woman more than peaches in syrup. Suffice it to say that for her I'm prepared to enter a church after thirty-two years of clerical abstinence and recite the psalms of Saint Seraph or whatever needs to be done."

"Aren't you getting a bit ahead of yourself, Fermín? You've only just met her. . . ."

"Look, Daniel, at my age either you begin to see things for what they are or you're pretty much done for. Only three or four things are worth living for; the rest is manure. I've already fooled around a lot, and now I know that the only thing I really want is to make Bernarda happy and die one day in her arms. I want to be a respectable man again, see? Not for my sake—as far as I'm concerned, I couldn't give a fly's turd for the respect of this choir of simians we call humanity—but for hers. Because Bernarda believes in such things—in radio soaps, in priests, in respectability and in Our Lady of Lourdes. That's the way she is, and I want her exactly like that. I even like those hairs that grow on her chin. And that's why I want to be someone she can be proud of. I want her to think, my Fermín is one hell of a man, like Cary Grant, Hemingway, or Manolete."

I crossed my arms, weighing up the situation. "Have you spoken about all this with her? About having a child together?"

"Goodness no. Who do you take me for? Do you think I go around telling women I want to get them knocked up? And it's not that I don't feel like it, eh? Take that silly Merceditas: I'd put some triplets in her right now and feel on top of the world, but—"

"Have you told Bernarda you'd like to have a family?"

"Those things don't need to be said, Daniel. They show on your face."

I nodded. "Well, then, for what my opinion is worth, I'm sure you'll be an excellent father and husband. And since you don't believe in those things, you'll never take them for granted."

His face melted into happiness. "Do you mean it?"

"Of course."

"You've taken a huge weight off my mind. Because just to remember my own father and to think that I might end up being for someone what he was for me, makes me want to get sterilized."

"Don't worry, Fermín. Besides, there's probably no treatment capable of crushing your procreative powers."

"Good point," he reflected. "Go on, go and get some sleep, I mustn't keep you any longer."

"You're not keeping me, Fermín. I have a feeling I'm not going to sleep a wink."

"Take a pain for a pleasure. . . . By the way, remember you mentioned that PO box?"

"Have you discovered anything?"

"I told you to leave it to me. This lunchtime I went up to the post office and had a word with an old acquaintance of mine who works there. PO Box 2321 is under the name of one José María Requejo, a lawyer with offices on Calle León XIII. I took the liberty of checking out the guy's address and wasn't surprised to discover that it doesn't exist, although I imagine you already know that. Someone has been collecting the letters addressed to that box for years. I know because some of the mail received from a property business comes as registered post and requires a signature on a small receipt and identification."

"Who is it? An employee of Requejo the lawyer?" I asked.

"I couldn't get that far, but I doubt it. Either I'm very mistaken or this

Requejo guy exists on the same plane as Our Lady of Fátima. All I can tell you is the name of the person who collects the mail: Nuria Monfort."

I felt the blood draining from me.

"Nuria Monfort? Are you sure, Fermín?"

"I myself saw some of those receipts. That name and the number of her identity card were on all of them. I deduce, from that sick look on your face, that this revelation surprises you."

"Quite a lot."

"May I ask who this Nuria Monfort is? The clerk I spoke to told me he remembered her clearly because she went there two weeks ago to collect the mail and, in his impartial opinion, she looked hotter than the *Venus de Milo* and with a firmer bust. I trust his assessment, because before the war he was a professor of aesthetics—but he was also a distant cousin of the Socialist leader Largo Caballero, so naturally he now licks one-peseta stamps."

"I was with that woman today, in her home," I murmured.

Fermín looked at me in amazement. "With Nuria Monfort? I'm beginning to think I was wrong about you, Daniel. You've become quite a rake."

"It's not what you're thinking, Fermín."

"That's your loss, then. At your age I was like El Molino music hall—morning, afternoon, and night shows."

I gazed at that small, gaunt, and bony man, with his large nose and his yellow skin, and I realized he was becoming my best friend.

"May I tell you something, Fermín? Something that's been on my mind for some time?"

"But of course. Anything. Especially if it's shocking and concerns this yummy maiden."

For the second time that night I began to tell the story of Julián Carax and the enigma of his death. Fermín listened very attentively, writing things down in a notebook and interrupting me every now and then to ask me some detail whose relevance escaped me. As I listened to myself, it became increasingly clear to me that there were many lacunae in that story. More than once my mind went blank and my thoughts became lost as I tried to work out why Nuria Monfort would have lied to me. What was the significance of all this? Why had she, for years, collected the mail directed to a nonexistent lawyers' office that was supposedly in charge of the Fortuny-Carax apartment on Ronda de San Antonio? I didn't realize I was voicing my doubts out loud.

"We can't yet know why that woman was lying to you," said Fermín. "But we can speculate that if she did so in this respect, she may have done so, and probably did, in many others."

I sighed, completely lost. "What do you suggest, Fermín?"

Fermín Romero de Torres sighed and put on his most Socratic expression. "I'll tell you what we can do. This coming Sunday, if you agree, we drop by San Gabriel's School, quite casually, and we make some inquiries concerning the origins of the friendship between this Carax fellow and the other lad, the rich boy. . . ."

"Aldaya."

"I have a way with priests, you'll see, even if it's just because I look like a roguish monk. I butter them up a little, and I get them eating out of my hand."

"Are you sure?"

"Positive. I guarantee this lot is going to sing like the Montserrat Boys' Choir."

· *23* ·

I SPENT THE SATURDAY IN A TRANCE, ANCHORED BEHIND THE BOOK-
shop counter in the hopes of seeing Bea come through the door as if
by magic. Every time the telephone rang, I rushed to answer it, grabbing
the receiver from my father or Fermín. Halfway through the afternoon, af-
ter about twenty calls from clients and no news from Bea, I began to accept
that the world and my miserable existence were coming to an end. My fa-
ther had gone out to price a collection in San Gervasio, and Fermín took
advantage of the situation to deliver another of his magisterial lectures on
the many mysteries of romance.

"Calm down or you'll grow a stone in your liver," Fermín advised me.
"This business of courtship is like a tango: absurd and pure embellishment.
But you're the man, and you must take the lead."

It was all beginning to look pretty grim. "The lead? Me?"

"What do you expect? One has to pay some price for being able to piss
standing up."

"But Bea implied that she would get back to me."

"You really don't understand women, Daniel. I bet you my Christmas
bonus that the little chick is in her house right now, looking languidly out of
the window like the Lady of the Camellias, waiting for you to come and res-

cue her from that idiot father of hers and drag her into an unstoppable spiral of lust and sin."

"Are you sure?"

"It's a mathematical certainty."

"What if she's decided she doesn't want to see me again?

"Look, Daniel. Women, with remarkable exceptions like your neighbor Merceditas, are more intelligent than we are, or at least more honest with themselves about what they want or don't want. Another question is whether they tell you or the world. You're facing the enigma of nature, Daniel. Womankind is an indecipherable maze. If you give her time to think, you're lost. Remember: warm heart, cold mind. The seducer's code."

Fermín was about to detail the particulars and techniques of the art of seduction when the doorbell tinkled and in walked my friend Tomás Aguilar. My heart missed a beat. Providence was denying me Bea but was sending me her brother. A fateful herald, I thought. Tomás had a somber expression and a certain despondent air.

"What a funereal appearance, Don Tomás," Fermín remarked. "You'll accept a small coffee at least, I hope?"

"I won't say no," said Tomás, with his usual reserve.

Fermín served him a cup of the concoction he kept in a thermos. It gave out an odor suspiciously like sherry.

"Is there a problem?" I asked.

Tomás shrugged. "Nothing new. My father is having one of his days, and I thought it best to get out and breathe some fresh air for a while."

I gulped. "Why's that?"

"Goodness knows. Last night my sister, Bea, arrived very late. My father was waiting up for her, a bit worked up as usual. She refused to say where she'd been or who she'd been with, and my father flew into a rage. He was screaming and yelling until four o'clock in the morning, calling her all sorts of names, a tart being the least of them. He swore he was going to send her to a nunnery and said that if she ever came back pregnant, he was going to kick her out into the goddamn street."

Fermín threw me a look of alarm. The beads of sweat already running down my back grew colder.

"This morning," Tomás continued, "Bea locked herself up in her room, and she hasn't come out all day. My father has plonked himself in the dining room to read his newspaper and listen to operettas on the radio, full blast. During the intermission of *Luisa Fernanda,* I had to go out because I was going crazy."

"Well, your sister was probably out with her fiancé, don't you think?" Fermín needled. "It would be perfectly natural."

I gave Fermín a kick under the counter, which he avoided with feline dexterity.

"Her fiancé is doing his military service," Tomás said. "He doesn't come back on leave for another two weeks. Besides, when she goes out with him, she's home by eight at the latest."

"And you have no idea where she was or who she was with?"

"He's already told you he doesn't, Fermín," I intervened, anxious to change the subject.

"Nor your father?" insisted Fermín, who was thoroughly enjoying himself.

"No. But he's sworn he'll find out and he'll break his legs and his face as soon as he knows who it is."

I felt myself going deathly pale. Fermín offered me a cup of his concoction without asking. I drank it down in one gulp. It tasted like tepid diesel fuel. Tomás watched me but said nothing—a dark, impenetrable look.

"Did you hear that?" Fermín suddenly said. "Sounded like a drumroll for a somersault."

"No."

"Yours truly's rumblings. Look, I'm suddenly terribly hungry. . . . Do you mind if I leave you two alone and run up to the baker's to grab myself a bun? Not to mention the new shop assistant who's just arrived from Reus: she looks so tasty you could eat her. She's called María Virtudes, but despite her name the girl is pure vice. . . . That way I'll leave you two to talk about your things, eh?"

In ten seconds Fermín had done a disappearing act, off for his snack and his meeting with the young woman. Tomás and I were left alone, enveloped in a silence as weighty as the Swiss franc. After several minutes I could no longer bear it.

"Tomás," I began, my mouth dry. "Last night your sister was with me."

He stared at me without even blinking.

I swallowed hard. "Say something," I said.

"You're not right in the head."

A minute went by, with muffled sounds coming in from the street. Tomás held his coffee, which he had not touched.

"Are you serious?" he asked.

"I've seen her only once."

"That's not an answer."

"Would you mind?"

He shrugged his shoulders. "You'd better know what you're doing. Would you stop seeing her just because I asked you to?"

"Yes," I lied. "But don't ask me to."

Tomás looked down. "You don't know Bea," he murmured.

I didn't reply. We let another few minutes go by without saying a word, looking at the gray figures that scanned the shop window, praying that one of them would decide to come in and rescue us from our poisoned silence. After a while Tomás abandoned his cup on the counter and made his way to the door.

"You're leaving already?"

He nodded.

"Shall we meet up tomorrow for a while?" I said. "We could go to the cinema, with Fermín, like before."

He stopped by the door. "I'll tell you only once, Daniel. Don't hurt my sister."

On his way out, he passed Fermín, who was returning laden with a bag full of steaming-hot buns. Fermín saw him go off into the dusk, shaking his head. He left the buns on the counter and offered me an *ensaimada* just out of the oven. I declined. I wouldn't have been able to swallow even an aspirin.

"He'll get over it, Daniel. You'll see. These things are common between friends."

"I don't know," I mumbled.

· 24 ·

Fermín and I met on Sunday at seven-thirty in the morning at the Canaletas Café. Fermín treated me to a coffee and brioches whose texture, even with butter spread on them, bore some resemblance to pumice stone. We were served by a waiter who sported a fascist badge on his lapel and a pencil mustache. He didn't stop humming to himself, and when we asked him the reason for his excellent mood, he explained that he'd become a father the day before. We congratulated him, and he insisted on giving us each a cigar to smoke during the day in honor of his firstborn. We said we would. Fermín kept looking at him out of the corner of his eye, frowning, and I suspected he was plotting something.

Over breakfast Fermín kicked off the day's investigations with a general outline of the mystery.

"It all begins with the sincere friendship between two boys, Julián Carax and Jorge Aldaya, classmates since early childhood, like Don Tomás and yourself. For years all is well. Inseparable friends with a whole life before them, the works. And yet at some point a conflict arises that ruins this friendship. To paraphrase some drawing-room dramatists, the conflict bears a woman's name: Penélope. Very Homeric. Do you follow me?"

The only thing that came to my mind was the last sentence spoken by

Tomás the previous evening in the bookshop: "Don't hurt my sister." I felt nauseous.

"In 1919, Julián Carax sets off for Paris, Odysseus-fashion," Fermín continued. "The letter, signed by Penélope, which he never receives, establishes that by then the young woman has been incarcerated in her own house, a prisoner of her family for reasons that are unclear, and that the friendship between Aldaya and Carax has ended. Moreover, according to Penélope, her brother, Jorge, has sworn that if he ever sees his old friend Julián again, he'll kill him. Grim words to mark the end of a friendship. One doesn't have to be Pasteur to deduce that the conflict is a direct consequence of the relationship between Penélope and Carax."

A cold sweat covered my forehead. I could feel the coffee and the few mouthfuls of brioche I'd swallowed rising up my throat.

"All the same, we must assume that Carax never gets to know what happened to Penélope, because the letter doesn't reach him. He vanishes from our sight into the mists of Paris, where he will lead a ghostly existence between his job as a pianist in a variety club and his disastrous career as a remarkably unsuccessful novelist. These years in Paris are a puzzle. All that remains of them today is a forgotten literary work that has virtually disappeared. We know that at some point he decides to marry a mysterious rich lady who is twice his age. The nature of such a marriage, if we are to go by what the witnesses say, seems more of an act of charity or friendship on behalf of an ailing lady than a love match. Whichever way you look at it, this patron of the arts, fearing for the financial future of her protégé, decides to leave him her fortune and bid farewell to this world with a roll in the hay to further her noble cause. Parisians are like that."

"Perhaps it was a genuine love," I suggested, in a tiny voice.

"Hey, Daniel, are you all right? You're looking very pale, and you're perspiring terribly."

"I'm fine," I lied.

"As I was saying. Love is a lot like pork: there's loin steak and there's bologna. Each has its own place and function. Carax had declared that he didn't feel worthy of any love, and indeed, as I far as we know, no romances were recorded during his years in Paris. Of course, working in a bordello, perhaps his basic instinctive urges were satisfied by fraternizing with the employees of the firm, as if it were a perk of the job, so to speak. But this is pure speculation. Let us return to the moment when the marriage between Carax and his protectress is announced. That is when Jorge Aldaya reappears on the map of this murky business. We know he makes contact with Carax's publisher in Barcelona to find out the whereabouts of the novelist. Shortly after, on the morning of his wedding day, Julián Carax fights a duel with an unknown person in Père Lachaise cemetery, and disappears. The wedding never takes place. From then on, everything becomes confused."

Fermín allowed for a dramatic pause, giving me his conspiratorial look. "Supposedly Carax crosses the border and, with yet another show of his proverbial sense of timing, returns to Barcelona in 1936 at the very outbreak of the Civil War. His activities and whereabouts in Barcelona during these weeks are hazy. We suppose he stays in the city for about a month and that during this time he doesn't contact any of his acquaintances. Neither his father nor his friend Nuria Monfort. Then he is found dead in the street, struck down by a bullet. It is not long before a sinister character makes his appearance on the scene. He calls himself Laín Coubert—a name he borrows from the last novel by Julián Carax—who, to cap it all, is none other than the Prince of Darkness. The supposed Lucifer states that he is prepared to obliterate what little is left of Carax and destroy his books forever. To round off the melodrama, he appears as a faceless man, disfigured by fire. A rogue from a gothic operetta in whom, just to confuse matters more, Nuria Monfort believes she recognizes the voice of Jorge Aldaya."

"Let me remind you that Nuria Monfort lied to me," I said.

"True. But even if Nuria Monfort lied to you, she might have done it more by omission and perhaps to disassociate herself from the facts. There are few reasons for telling the truth, but for lying the number is infinite. Listen, are you sure you're all right? Your face is the color of goat cheese."

I shook my head and dashed to the toilet.

I threw up my breakfast, my dinner, and a good amount of the anger I was carrying with me. I washed my face with freezing water from the sink and looked at my reflection in the blurry mirror on which someone had scrawled SHITHEAD FASCISTS with a wax crayon. When I got back to the table, I realized that Fermín was at the bar, paying the bill and discussing football with the waiter who had served us.

"Better?" he asked.

I nodded.

"That was a drop in your blood pressure," said Fermín. "Here. Have a Sugus candy, they cure everything."

On the way out of the café, Fermín insisted that we should take a taxi as far as San Gabriel's School and leave the subway for another day, arguing that the morning was as bright as a political mural and that tunnels were for rats.

"A taxi up to Sarriá will cost a fortune," I protested.

"The ride's on the Cretins' Savings Bank," Fermín put in quickly. "The proud patriot back there gave me the wrong change, and we're in business. And you're not up to traveling underground."

Equipped with ill-gotten funds, we positioned ourselves on a corner at the foot of Rambla de Cataluña and waited for a cab. We had to let a few go by, because Fermín stated that, since he so rarely traveled by car, he wanted to get into a Studebaker at the very least. It took us a quarter of an hour to find a vehicle to his liking, which Fermín hailed by waving his arms about like a windmill. Fermín insisted on traveling in the front seat, which gave him the chance to get involved in a discussion with the driver about Joseph Stalin, who was the taxi driver's idol and distant spiritual guide.

"There have been three great figures in this century: La Pasionaria, bull-fighter extraordinaire Manolete, and Joseph Stalin," the driver proclaimed, getting ready to unload upon us a life of the saintly comrade.

I was riding comfortably in the backseat, paying little attention to the tedious speech, with the window open and enjoying the fresh air. Delighted to be driving around in a Studebaker, Fermín encouraged the cabdriver's chatter, occasionally punctuating his emotive biography of the Soviet leader with matters of doubtful historic interest.

"I've heard he's been suffering badly from prostate trouble ever since he swallowed the pip of a loquat, and now he can only pee if someone hums 'The Internationale' for him," he put in.

"Fascist propaganda," the taxi driver explained, more devout than ever. "The comrade pees like a bull. The Volga might envy such a flow."

This high-level political debate accompanied us as we made our way along Vía Augusta toward the hills. Day was breaking, and a fresh breeze gave the sky an intense blue. When we reached Calle Ganduxer, the driver turned right, and we began the slow ascent toward Paseo de la Bonanova.

San Gabriel's School, its redbrick façade dotted with dagger-shaped windows, stood in the middle of a grove, at the top of a narrow, winding street that led up from the boulevard. The whole structure was crowned by arches and towers, and peered over a group of plane trees like a Gothic cathedral. We got out of the taxi and entered a leafy garden strewn with fountains that were adorned with mold-covered angels. Here and there cobbled paths meandered among the trees. On our way to the main door, Fermín gave me the background on the institution.

"Even though it may look to you like Rasputin's mausoleum, San Gabriel's School was, in its day, one of the most prestigious and exclusive institutions in Barcelona. During the Republic it went downhill because the nouveaux riches of the time, the new industrialists and bankers to whose children it had for years refused access because their surnames smelled too new, decided to create their own schools, where they would be treated with due reverence and where they, in turn, could refuse access to the sons of others. Money is like any other virus: once it has rotted the soul of the person who houses it, it sets off in search of new blood. In this world a surname is less lasting than a sugared almond. In its heyday—say, between 1880 and 1930, more or less—San Gabriel's School took in the flower of old, established families with bulging wallets. The Aldayas and company came to this sinister establishment as boarders, to fraternize with their equals, go to mass, and learn their history in order to be able to repeat it ad nauseam."

"But Julián Carax wasn't precisely one of them," I observed.

"Sometimes these illustrious institutions offer a scholarship or two for the sons of the gardener or the shoeshine man, just to show their magnanimity and Christian charity," Fermín proffered. "The most efficient way of rendering the poor harmless is to teach them to want to imitate the rich. That is the poison with which capitalism blinds the—"

"Please don't get carried away with social doctrine, Fermín. If one of these priests hears you, they'll kick us out of here." I realized that a couple of padres were watching us with a mixture of curiosity and concern from the top of the steps that led up to the front door of the school. I wondered whether they'd heard any of our conversation.

One of them moved forward with a courteous smile, his hands crossed over his chest like a bishop. He must have been in his early fifties, and his build and sparse hair lent him the air of a bird of prey. He had a penetrating gaze and gave off an aroma of fresh eau de cologne and mothballs.

"Good morning. I'm Father Fernando Ramos," he announced. "How can I help you?"

Fermín held out his hand. The priest examined it briefly before shaking it, shielded by his icy smile.

"Fermín Romero de Torres, bibliographic adviser to Sempere and Son. It is an enormous pleasure to greet Your Most Devout Excellency. Here, at my side, my collaborator and friend, Daniel, a young man of promise and much-recognized Christian qualities."

Father Fernando observed us without blinking. I wanted the earth to swallow me.

"The pleasure is all mine, Mr. Romero de Torres," he replied amicably. "May I ask what brings such a formidable duo to our humble institution?"

I decided to intervene before Fermín made some other outrageous comment and we had to make a quick exit. "Father Fernando, we're trying to locate two alumni from San Gabriel's School: Jorge Aldaya and Julián Carax."

Father Fernando pursed his lips and raised an eyebrow. "Julián died over fifteen years ago, and Aldaya went off to Argentina," he said dryly.

"Did you know them?" asked Fermín.

The priest's sharp gaze rested on each of us before he answered. "We were classmates. May I ask what your interest is in this matter?"

I was wondering how to answer the question, but Fermín beat me to it. "You see, it so happens that we have in our possession a number of articles that belong or belonged—for on this particular the legal interpretation leads to confusion—to the two persons in question."

"And what is the nature of these articles, if you don't mind my asking?"

"I beg Your Grace to accept our silence, for God knows there are abundant reasons of conscience and secrecy that have nothing to do with the unquestioning faith Your Excellency merits, as does the order which you represent with such measure of gallantry and piety," Fermín spewed out at great speed.

Father Fernando appeared to be almost in shock. I decided to take up the conversation again before Fermín had time to get his breath back.

"The articles Mr. Romero de Torres is referring to are of a personal nature, mementos and objects of purely sentimental value. What we would like to ask you, Father, if this isn't too much trouble, is to tell us what you remember about Julián and Aldaya from your days as schoolboys."

Father Fernando was still looking at us suspiciously. It became obvious to me that the explanations we'd given him were not enough to justify our interest and earn us his collaboration. I threw a look of desperation at Fermín, begging him to find some cunning argument with which to win over the priest.

"Do you know that you look a bit like Julián when he was young?" Father Fernando suddenly said to me.

Fermín's eyes lit up. Here he goes, I thought. All our luck's on this card.

"Very shrewd of you, Your Reverence," proclaimed Fermín, feigning surprise. "Your uncanny insight has unmasked us without pity. You'll end up a cardinal at least, or even a pope."

"What are you talking about?"

"Isn't it obvious and patent, Your Lordship?"

"Quite frankly, no."

"Can we count on the secrecy of the confessional?"

"This is a garden, not a confessional."

"It will be enough if you grant us your ecclesiastic discretion."

"You have it."

Fermín heaved a deep sigh and looked at me with a melancholy expression. "Daniel, we can't go on lying to this saintly soldier of Christ."

"Of course not . . ." I corroborated, completely lost.

Fermín went up to the priest and murmured in a confidential tone, "Father, we have most solid grounds to suspect that our friend Daniel here is none other than the secret son of the deceased Julián Carax. Hence our interest in reconstructing his past and recovering the memory of an illustrious person, whom the Fates tore away from the side of a poor child."

Father Fernando fixed his astounded eyes on me. "Is this true?"

I nodded. Fermín patted my back, his face full of sorrow.

"Look at him, poor lad, searching for a lost father in the mist of memory. What could be sadder than this? Tell me, Your Most Saintly Grace."

"Have you any proof to uphold your assertions?"

Fermín grabbed my chin and offered up my face as payment. "What further proof would the clergyman require than this little face, silent, irrefutable witness of the paternal fact in question?"

The priest seemed to hesitate.

"Will you help me, Father?" I implored cunningly. "Please . . ."

Father Fernando sighed uncomfortably. I don't suppose there's any harm in it," he said at last. "What do you want to know?"

"Everything," said Fermín.

· 25 ·

WE WENT INTO FATHER FERNANDO'S OFFICE, WHERE THE priest summoned up his memories, adopting the tone of a sermon. He sculpted his sentences neatly, measuring them out with a cadence that seemed to promise an ultimate moral that never emerged. Years of teaching had left him with that firm and didactic tone of someone used to being heard, but not certain of being listened to.

"If I remember correctly, Julián Carax started at San Gabriel's in 1914. I got along with him right away, because we both belonged to the small group of pupils who did not come from wealthy families. They called us "The Starving Gang," and each one of us had his own special story. I'd managed to get a scholarship place thanks to my father, who worked in the kitchens of this school for twenty-five years. Julián had been accepted thanks to the intercession of Mr. Aldaya, who was a customer of the Fortuny hat shop, owned by Julián's father. Those were different times, of course, and during those days power was still concentrated within families and dynasties. That world has vanished——the last few remains were swept away with the fall of the Republic, for the better, I suppose. All that is left of it are the names on the letterheads of companies, banks, and faceless consortiums. Like all old cities, Barcelona is a sum of its ruins. The great glories so many people are proud of——palaces, factories, and monuments, the emblems with which we identify—are nothing more than relics of an extinguished civilization."

Having reached this point, Father Fernando allowed for a solemn pause in which he seemed to be waiting for the congregation to answer with some empty Latin phrase or a response from the missal.

"Say amen, reverend Father. What great truth lies in those wise words," offered Fermín to fill the awkward silence.

"You were telling us about my father's first year at the school," I put in gently.

Father Fernando nodded. "In those days he already called himself Carax, although his paternal surname was Fortuny. At first some of the boys teased him for that, and for being one of The Starving Gang, of course. They also laughed at me because I was the cook's son. You know what kids are like. Deep down, God has filled them with goodness, but they repeat what they hear at home."

"Little angels," punctuated Fermín.

"What do you remember about my father?"

"Well, it's such a long time ago. . . . Your father's best friend at that time was not Jorge Aldaya but a boy called Miquel Moliner. Miquel's family was almost as wealthy as the Aldayas, and I daresay he was the most extravagant pupil this school has ever seen. The headmaster thought he was possessed by the devil because he recited Marx in German during mass."

"A clear sign of possession," Fermín agreed.

"Miquel and Julián got on really well. Sometimes we three would get together during the lunch break and Julián would tell us stories. Other times he would tell us about his family and the Aldayas. . . ."

The priest seemed to hesitate.

"Even after leaving school, Miquel and I stayed in touch for a time. Julián had already gone to Paris by then. I know that Miquel missed him. He often spoke about him, remembering secrets Julián had once confided in him. Later, when I entered the seminary, Miquel told me I'd gone over to the enemy. It was meant as a joke, but the fact is that we drifted apart."

"Do you remember hearing that Miquel married someone called Nuria Monfort?"

"Miquel, married?"

"Do you find that odd?"

"I suppose I shouldn't, but . . . I don't know. The truth is that I haven't heard from Miquel for years. Since before the war."

"Did he ever mention the name of Nuria Monfort?"

"No, never. Nor did he say he was thinking of getting married or that he had a fiancée. . . . Listen, I'm not at all sure that I should be talking to you about this. These are personal things Julián and Miquel told me, with the understanding that they would remain between us."

"And are you going to refuse a son the only possibility of discovering his father's past?" asked Fermín.

Father Fernando was torn between doubt and, it seemed to me, the wish to remember, to recover those lost days. "I suppose so many years have gone by that it doesn't matter anymore. I can still remember the day when Julián told us how he'd met the Aldayas and how, without realizing it, his life was forever changed. . . ."

. . . *In October 1914 an artifact that many took to be a pantheon on wheels stopped one afternoon in front of the Fortuny hat shop on Ronda de San Antonio. From it emerged the proud, majestic, and arrogant figure of Don Ricardo Aldaya, by then already one of the richest men not only in Barcelona but also in the whole of Spain. His textile empire took in citadels of industry and colonies of commerce along all the rivers of Catalonia. His right hand held the reins of banks and landed estates of half the province. His left hand, ever active, pulled at the strings of the provincial council, the city hall, various ministries, the bishopric, and the customs service at the port.*

That afternoon the man with exuberant mustache, kingly sideburns, and uncovered head whom everybody feared, needed a hat. He entered the shop of Don Antoni Fortuny, and, after a quick glance at the premises, he looked askance at the hatter and his assistant, the young Julián, and said as follows: "I've been told that, despite appearances, the best hats of Barcelona come out of this shop. Autumn looks nasty, and I'm going to need six top hats, a dozen bowler hats, hunting caps, and something to wear for the Cortes in Madrid. Are you making a note of this, or do you expect me to repeat it all?" That was the beginning of a laborious and lucrative process during which father and son combined their efforts to get the order completed for Don Ricardo Aldaya.

Julián, who read the papers, was well aware of Aldaya's position and told himself he could not fail his father now, at the most crucial and decisive moment of his business. From the moment the magnate had set foot in his shop, the hatter levitated with joy. Aldaya had promised him that if he was satisfied, he would recommend his establishment to all his friends. That meant that the Fortuny hat shop, from being a dignified but modest enterprise, would attain the highest spheres, covering heads large and small of parliamentary members, mayors, cardinals, and ministers. That week seemed to fly by in a cloud of enchantment. Julián skipped school and spent up to eighteen or twenty hours a day working in the back-room workshop. His father, exhausted by enthusiasm, hugged him every now and then and even kissed him without thinking. He even went so far as to give his wife, Sophie, a dress and a pair of new shoes for the first time in fourteen years. The hatter was unrecognizable. One Sunday he forgot to go to church, and that same afternoon, brimming with pride, he put his arms around Julián and said, with tears in his eyes, "Grandfather would have been proud of us."

One of the most complex processes of the now disappeared science of hatmaking, both technically and politically, was that of taking measurements. Don Ricardo Aldaya had a cranium that, according to Julián, bordered on the melon-shaped and was quite rugged. The hatter was aware of the difficulties as soon as he saw the great man's head, and that same evening, when Julián said it reminded him of certain peaks in the mountains of Montserrat, Fortuny couldn't help agreeing with him. "Father, with all due respect, you know that when it comes to taking measurements, I'm better at it than you, because you get nervous. Let me do it." The hatter readily agreed, and the following day, when Aldaya arrived in his Mercedes-Benz, Julián welcomed him and took him to the workshop. When Aldaya realized that he was going to be measured by a boy of fourteen, he was furious. "But what is this? A child? Are you pulling my leg?" Julián, who was aware of his client's social position but who wasn't in the least bit intimidated by him, answered, "Sir, I don't know about your leg, but there's not much to pull up here. This crown looks like a bullring, and if we don't hurry up and make you a set of hats, your head will soon be mistaken for a Barcelona street plan." When he heard those words, Fortuny wanted the ground to swallow him up. Aldaya, undaunted, fixed his gaze on Julián. Then, to everyone's surprise, he burst out laughing as he hadn't done in years.

"This child of yours will go far, Fortunato," declared Aldaya, who had not quite learned the hatter's surname.

· · ·

That is how they discovered that Don Ricardo Aldaya was fed up to his very back teeth with being feared and flattered by everyone, with having people throw themselves on the ground like doormats as he went by. He despised ass lickers, cowards, and anyone who showed any sort of weakness, be it physical, mental, or moral. When he came across a humble boy, barely an apprentice, who had the cheek and the spirit to laugh at him, Aldaya decided he'd hit on the ideal hat shop and immediately doubled his order. That week he gladly turned up every day for his appointment, so that Julián could take measurements and try on different models. Antoni Fortuny was amazed to see how the champion of Catalan society would fall about laughing at the jokes and stories told by that son who was for him a stranger, that boy he never spoke to and who for years had shown no sign of having any sense of humor. At the end of the week, Aldaya took the hatter aside, to a corner of the shop, and spoke to him confidentially.

"Let's see, Fortunato, this son of yours has great talent, and you've got him stuck here, bored out of his mind, dusting the cobwebs in a two-bit shop."

"This is a good business, Don Ricardo, and the boy shows a certain flair, even though he lacks backbone."

"Nonsense. What school does he attend?"

"Well, he goes to the local school. . . ."

"Nothing but a production line for workers. When one is young, talent——genius, if you like——must be cultivated, or it becomes twisted and consumes the person who possesses it. It needs direction. Support. Do you understand me, Fortunato?"

"You're mistaken about my son. He's nowhere near a genius. He can hardly pass his geography. His teachers tell me he's a scatterbrain and has a very bad attitude, just like his mother. But at least here he'll always have an honest job and——"

"Fortunato, you bore me. Today, without fail, I'll go to San Gabriel's School to see the admissions board, and I'll let them know that they are to accept the entry of your son in the same class as my eldest child, Jorge. Anything less would be miserly of me."

The hatter's eyes were as big as saucers. San Gabriel's School was the nursery for the cream of high society.

"But, Don Ricardo, I would be unable to finance——"

"*No one is asking you to pay anything. I'll take charge of the boy's education. You, as his father, only have to agree.*"

"*But of course, certainly, but——*"

"*That's decided, then. So long as Julián accepts, of course.*"

"*He'll do what he's told, naturally.*"

At this point in the conversation, Julián stuck his head around the door of the back room with a hat mold in his hands.

"*Don Ricardo, whenever you're ready . . .*"

"*Tell me, Julián, what are you doing this afternoon?*" Aldaya asked.

Julián looked alternatively at his father and at the tycoon.

"*Well, helping my father here, in the shop.*"

"*Apart from that.*"

"*I was thinking of going to the library. . . .*"

"*You like books, eh?*"

"*Yes, sir.*"

"*Have you read Conrad? Heart of Darkness?*"

"*Three times.*"

The hatter frowned, utterly lost. "*And who is this Conrad, if you don't mind my asking?*"

Aldaya silenced him with a gesture that seemed made for a shareholders' meeting.

"*In my house I have a library with fourteen thousand books, Julián. When I was young, I read a lot, but now I no longer have the time. Come to think of it, I have three copies signed by Conrad himself. My son Jorge can't even be dragged into the library. In the house the only person who thinks and reads is my daughter Penélope, so all those books are being wasted. Would you like to see them?*"

Julián nodded, speechless. The hatter observed the scene with a sense of unease he couldn't quite define. All those names were unknown to him. Novels, as everyone knew, were for women and for people who had nothing better to do. Heart of Darkness sounded to him like a mortal sin at least.

"*Fortunato, your son is coming with me. I want to introduce him to my son Jorge. Don't worry, we'll bring him back to you later. Tell me, young man, have you ever been in a Mercedes-Benz?*"

Julián presumed that was the name of the cumbersome, imperial-looking machine the industrialist used for getting around. He shook his head.

"Well, then, it's about time. It's like going to heaven, but without dying."

Antoni Fortuny saw them leave in that exceedingly luxurious carriage, and when he searched his heart, all he found was sadness. That night, while he had dinner with Sophie (who was wearing her new dress and shoes and had almost no bruises or scars), he asked himself where he had gone wrong this time. Just when God was returning a son to him, Aldaya was taking him away.

"Take off that dress, woman, you look like a whore. And don't let me see this wine on the table again. The watered-down sort is quite good enough for us. Greed will corrupt us all in the end."

Julián had never crossed over to the other side of Avenida Diagonal. That line of groves, empty plots of land, and palaces awaiting the expansion of the city was a forbidden frontier. Hamlets, hills, and mysterious places of wealth and legend extended beyond it. As they passed through them, Aldaya talked to him about San Gabriel's School, about new friends Julián had never set eyes on, about a future he had not thought possible.

"What do you aspire to, Julián? In life, I mean."

"I don't know. Sometimes I think I'd like to be a writer. A novelist."

"Like Conrad, eh? You're very young, of course. And tell me, doesn't banking tempt you?"

"I don't know, sir. The truth is that it hadn't even entered my head. I've never seen more than three pesetas together. High finance is a mystery to me."

Aldaya laughed. "There's no mystery, Julián. The trick is not to put pesetas together in threes, but in three million. That way there's no enigma, I can assure you. No Holy Trinity."

That afternoon, as he drove up Avenida del Tibidabo, Julián thought he was entering the doors of paradise. Mansions that seemed like cathedrals flanked the way. Halfway along the avenue, the driver turned, and they went through the gates of one of them. Instantly an army of servants set about receiving the master. All Julián could see was a large, majestic house with three floors. It had never occurred to him that real people could live in places like this. He let himself be taken through the lobby, then he crossed a vaulted hall from where a marble staircase rose, framed by velvet curtains, and finally entered a large room whose walls were a tapestry of books, from floor to ceiling.

"What do you think?" asked Aldaya.

Julián was barely listening.

"Damián, tell Jorge to come down to the library immediately."

The faceless and silent servants glided away at the slightest order from the master with the efficiency and submissiveness of a body of well-trained insects.

"You're going to need a new wardrobe, Julián. There are a lot of morons out there who only go by appearances. . . . I'll tell Jacinta to take care of that; you don't have to worry about it. And it's almost best if you don't mention it to your father, in case it annoys him. Look, here comes Jorge. Jorge, I want you to meet a wonderful kid who is going to be your new classmate. Julián Fortu—"

"Julián Carax," he corrected.

"Julián Carax," repeated a satisfied Aldaya. "I like the sound of it. This is my son Jorge."

Julián held out his hand, and Jorge Aldaya shook it. His touch was lukewarm, unenthusiastic, and his face had a pale, chiseled look that came from having grown up in that doll-like world. His clothes and shoes seemed to Julián like something out of a novel. His eyes gave off an air of bravado and arrogance, of disdain and sugary politeness. Julián smiled at him openly, reading insecurity, fear, and emptiness under that shell of vanity and complacency.

"Is it true you haven't read any of these books?"

"Books are boring."

"Books are mirrors: you only see in them what you already have inside you," answered Julián.

Don Ricardo Aldaya laughed again. "Well, I'll leave you two alone so you can get to know each other. Julián, you'll see that although he seems spoiled and conceited, underneath that mask Jorge isn't as stupid as he looks. He has something of his father in him."

Aldaya's words seemed to fall like knives on the boy, though he didn't let his smile fade at all. Julián regretted his answer and felt sorry for him.

"You must be the hatter's son," said Jorge, without malice. "My father talks about you a lot these days."

"It's the novelty. I hope you don't hold that against me. Under this mask of a know-it-all meddler, I'm not such an idiot as I seem."

Jorge smiled at him. Julián thought he smiled the way people smile who have no friends, with gratitude.

"Come, I'll show you the rest of the house."

They left the library behind them and went off toward the main door and the gardens. When they crossed the hall with the staircase, Julián looked up and glimpsed a figure ascending the stairs with a hand on the banister. He felt as if he were caught up in a vision. The girl must have been about twelve or thirteen and was escorted by a mature woman, small and rosy-cheeked, who had the air of a governess. The girl wore a blue satin dress. Her hair was the color of almonds, and the skin on her shoulders and slim neck seemed translucent. She stopped at the top of the stairs and turned around briefly. For a second their eyes met, and she offered him the ghost of a smile. Then the governess put her arms around the girl's shoulders and led her to the entrance of a corridor into which they both disappeared. Julián looked down and he fixed his eyes on Jorge's again.

"That's Penélope, my sister. You'll meet her later. She's a bit nutty. She spends all day reading. Come on, I want to show you the chapel in the basement. The cooks say it's haunted."

Julián followed the boy meekly, but he cared little about anything else. Now he understood. He had dreamed about her countless times, on that same staircase, with that same blue dress and that same movement of her ash-gray eyes, without knowing who she was or why she smiled at him. When he went out into the garden, he let himself be led by Jorge as far as the coach houses and the tennis courts that stretched out beyond. Only then did he turn around to look back and saw her in her window on the second floor. He could barely make out her shape, but he knew she was smiling at him and that somehow she, too, had recognized him.

That fleeting glimpse of Penélope Aldaya at the top of the staircase remained with him during his first weeks at San Gabriel's School. His new world was not all to his liking: the pupils of San Gabriel's behaved like haughty, arrogant princes, while their teachers were like docile and learned servants. The first friend Julián made there, apart from Jorge Aldaya, was a boy called Fernando Ramos, the son of one of the cooks at the school, who would never have imagined he would end up wearing a cassock and teaching in the same classrooms in which he himself had grown up. Fernando, whom the rest nicknamed "Kitchen Sweep," and whom they treated like a servant, was alert and intelligent but had hardly any friends among the schoolboys. His only companion was an eccentric boy called Miquel Moliner, who in time would become the best friend Julián ever made at the school. Miquel Moliner, who had too much brain and too little patience, enjoyed teasing his teachers by questioning all their statements, using clever arguments in which he displayed both ingenuity and a poisonous bite. The rest feared his sharp tongue and considered him a member of some other species. In a way this was not entirely mistaken, for despite his bohemian traits and the unaristocratic tone he affected, Miquel was the son of a businessman who had become obscenely rich through the manufacture of arms.

"Carax, isn't it? I'm told your father makes hats," he said when Fernando Ramos introduced them.

"Julián for my friends. I'm told yours makes cannons."

"He just sells them, actually. The only thing he knows how to make is money. My friends, among whom I count only Nietzsche and Fernando here, call me Miquel."

Miquel Moliner was a sad boy. He suffered from an unhealthy obsession with death and all matters funereal, a field to whose consideration he dedicated much of his time and talent. His mother had died three years earlier as a result of a strange domestic accident, which some foolish doctor had dared describe as suicide. It was Miquel who had discovered the shining body under the water of the well, in the summer mansion the family had in Argentona. When they pulled her out with ropes, they found that the pockets of the dead woman's coat were filled with stones. There was also a letter written in German, the mother's native tongue, but Mr. Moliner, who had never bothered to learn the language, burned it that same afternoon without allowing anyone to read it. Miquel Moliner saw death everywhere—in fallen leaves, in birds that had dropped out of their nests, in old people, and in the rain, which swept everything away. He was exceptionally talented at drawing and would often become distracted for hours with charcoal sketches in which a lady, whom Julián took to be his mother, always appeared against a background of mist and deserted beaches.

"What do you want to be when you grow up, Miquel?"

"I'll never grow up," he would answer enigmatically.

His main interest, apart from sketching and contradicting every living soul, was the works of a mysterious Austrian doctor who, in years to come, would become famous: Sigmund Freud. Thanks to his deceased mother, Miquel Moliner read and wrote perfect German, and he owned a number of books by the Viennese doctor. His favorite field was the interpretation of dreams. He was in the habit of asking people what they had dreamed, and he would then make a diagnosis. He always said he was go-ing to die young and that he didn't mind. Julián believed that, by thinking so much about death, he had ended up finding more sense in it than in life.

"The day I die, all that was once mine will be yours, Julián," he would say. "Ex-cept my dreams."

Besides Fernando Ramos, Moliner, and Jorge Aldaya, Julián also befriended a shy and rather unsociable boy called Javier, the only son of the caretakers of San Gabriel's, who lived in a modest house stationed at the entrance to the school gardens. Javier, who, like Fernando, was considered by the rest of the boys to be no more than an irri-tating lackey, prowled about alone in the gardens and courtyards of the compound. From so much wandering around the school, he ended up knowing every nook and cranny of the building, from the tunnels in the basements to the passages up to the towers, and all kinds of hiding places that nobody remembered anymore. They were his secret world and his refuge. He always carried with him a penknife he had re-moved from one of his father's drawers, and he liked to carve wooden figures with it, which he kept in the school dovecote. His father, Ramón, the caretaker, was a veteran from the Cuban War, where he had lost a hand and (it was rumored maliciously) his right testicle, as a result of a pellet shot from Theodore Roosevelt himself in the raid of the Bay of Cochinos. Convinced that idleness was the mother of all evils, "Ramón Oneball" (as the schoolboys nicknamed him) set his son the task of gathering up in a sack all fallen leaves from the pine grove and the courtyard around the fountains. Ramón was a good man, rather coarse and fatally given to choosing bad company, most notably his wife. Ramón Oneball had married a strapping, dim-witted woman with delusions of grandeur and the looks of a scullion, who was wont to dress skimpily in front of her son and the other boys, a habit that gave rise to no end of mirth and ridicule. Her Christian name was María Craponcia, but she called herself Yvonne, be-cause she thought it more elegant. Yvonne used to question her son about the possi-bilities of social advancement that his friends would provide, for she believed that he was making connections with the elite of Barcelona society. She would ask him about the fortune of this or that one, imagining herself dressed in the best silks and being received for tea in the great salons of good society.

Javier tried to spend as little time as possible in the house and was grateful for the jobs his father gave him, however hard they might be. Any excuse was good in order to be alone, to escape into his secret world and carve his wooden figures. When the schoolboys saw him from afar, some would laugh or throw stones at him. One day Julián felt so sorry for him when he saw how a stone had gashed his forehead and knocked him onto a pile of rubble that he decided to go to his aid and offer him his friendship. At first Javier thought that Julián was coming to finish him off while the others fell about laughing.

"My name is Julián," he said, stretching out his hand. "My friends and I were about to go and play chess in the pine grove, and I wondered whether you'd like to join us."

"I don't know how to play chess."

"Nor did I, until two weeks ago. But Miquel is a good teacher. . . ."

The boy looked at him suspiciously, expecting the prank, the hidden attack, at any moment.

"I don't know whether your friends will want me to be with you. . . ."

"It was their idea. What do you say?"

From that day on, Javier would sometimes join them after finishing the jobs he had been assigned. He didn't usually say anything but would listen and watch the others. Aldaya was slightly fearful of him. Fernando, who had himself experienced the rejection of others because of his humble origins, would go out of his way to be kind to the strange boy. Miquel Moliner, who taught him the rudiments of chess and watched him with a careful eye, was the most skeptical of all.

"This guy is a nutter. He catches cats and pigeons and tortures them for hours with his knife. Then he buries them in the pine grove. Delightful."

"Who says so?"

"He told me himself the other day while I was explaining the knight's moves to him. He also told me that sometimes his mother gets into his bed at night and fondles him."

"He must have been pulling your leg."

"I doubt it. This kid isn't right in the head, Julián, and it's probably not his fault."

Julián struggled to ignore Miquel's warnings and predictions, but the fact is that he was finding it difficult to establish a friendship with the son of the caretaker. Yvonne in particular did not approve of Julián or of Fernando Ramos. Of all the young men, those were the only ones who didn't have a single peseta. Rumor had it that Julián's father was a simple shopkeeper and that his mother had got only as far as being a music teacher. "Those people have no money, class, or elegance, my love," his mother would lecture him. "The one you should befriend is Aldaya. He comes from a very good family." "Yes, Mother," the boy would answer. "Whatever you say." As time went by, Javier seemed to start trusting his new friends. Occasionally he said a few words, and he was carving a set of chess pieces for Miquel Moliner, in appreciation for his lessons. One day, when nobody expected it or thought it possible, they discovered that Javier knew how to smile and that he had the innocent laugh of a child.

"You see? He's just a normal boy," Julián argued.

Miquel Moliner remained unconvinced, and he observed the strange lad with a rigorous scrutiny that was almost scientific.

"Javier is obsessed with you, Julián," he told him one day. "Everything he does is just to earn your approval."

"What nonsense! He has a mother and a father for that; I'm only a friend."

"Irresponsible, that's what you are. His father is a poor wretch who has trouble enough finding his own bum when he needs to move his bowels, and Doña Yvonne is a harpy with the brain of a flea who spends her time pretending to meet people by chance in her underwear, convinced that she is Venus incarnate or something far worse I'd rather not mention. The kid, quite naturally, looks for a parent substitute, and you, the savior angel, fall from heaven and give him your hand. Saint Julián of the Fountain, patron saint of the dispossessed."

"This Dr. Freud is rotting your head, Miquel. We all need friends. Even you."

"This kid doesn't have friends and never will. He has the heart of a spider. And if you don't believe me, time will tell. I wonder what he dreams . . . ?"

Miquel Moliner could not know that Francisco Javier's dreams were more like his friend Julián's than he would ever have thought possible. Once, some months before Julián had started at the school, the caretaker's son was gathering dead leaves from the courtyard with the fountains when Don Ricardo Aldaya's luxurious automobile arrived. That afternoon the tycoon had company. He was escorted by an apparition, an angel of light dressed in silk who seemed to levitate. The angel, who was none other than his daughter, Penélope, stepped out of the Mercedes and walked over to one of the fountains, waving her parasol and stopping to splash the water of the pond with her hands. As usual, her governess, Jacinta, followed her dutifully, observant of the slightest gesture from the girl. It wouldn't have mattered if an army of servants had guarded her: Javier had eyes only for the girl. He was afraid that if he blinked, the vision would vanish. He remained there, paralyzed, breathlessly spying on the mi-

rage. Soon after, as if the girl had sensed his presence and his furtive gaze, Penélope raised her eyes and looked in his direction. The beauty of that face seemed painful, unsustainable. He thought he saw the hint of a smile on her lips. Terrified, Javier ran off to hide at the top of the water tower, next to the dovecote in the attic of the school building, his favorite hiding place. His hands were still shaking when he gathered his carving utensils and began to work on a new piece in the form of the face he had just sighted. When he returned to the caretaker's home that night, hours later than usual, his mother was waiting for him, half naked and furious. The boy looked down, fearing that, if his mother read his eyes, she would see in them the girl of the pond and would know what he had been thinking about.

"And where've you been, you little shit?"

"I'm sorry, Mother. I got lost."

"You've been lost since the day you were born."

Years later, every time he stuck his revolver into the mouth of a prisoner and pulled the trigger, Chief Inspector Francisco Javier Fumero would remember the day he saw his mother's head burst open like a ripe watermelon near an outdoor bar in Las Planas and didn't feel anything, just the tedium of dead things. The Civil Guard, alerted by the manager of the bar, who had heard the shot, found the boy sitting on a rock holding a smoking shotgun on his lap. He was staring impassively at the decapitated body of María Craponcia, alias Yvonne, covered in insects. When he saw the guards coming up to him, he just shrugged his shoulders, his face splattered with blood, as if he were being ravaged by smallpox. Following the sobs, the Civil Guards found Ramón Oneball squatting by a tree, some thirty yards away, in the undergrowth. He was shaking like a child and was unable to make himself understood. The lieutenant of the Civil Guard, after much deliberation, reported that the event had been a tragic accident, and so he recorded it in the statement, though not on his conscience. When they asked the boy if there was anything they could do for him, Francisco Javier asked whether he could keep that old gun, because when he grew up, he wanted to be a soldier. . . .

"Are you feeling all right, Mr. Romero de Torres?"

The sudden appearance of Fumero in Father Fernando Ramos's narrative had stunned me, but the effect on Fermín had been devastating. He looked yellow, and his hands shook.

"A sudden drop in my blood pressure," Fermín improvised in a tiny voice. "This Catalan climate can be hell for us southerners."

"May I offer you a glass of water?" asked the priest in a worried tone.

"If Your Grace wouldn't mind. And perhaps a chocolate, for the glucose, you know . . ."

The priest poured him a glass of water, which Fermín drank greedily.

"All I have are some eucalyptus sweets. Will they be any help?"

"God bless you."

Fermín swallowed a fistful of sweets and after a while seemed to recover his natural complexion.

"This boy, the son of the caretaker who heroically lost his scrotum defending the colonies, are you sure his name was Fumero, Francisco Javier Fumero?"

"Yes. Quite sure. Do you know him?"

"No," we intoned in unison.

Father Fernando frowned. "It wouldn't have surprised me. Regrettably, Francisco Javier has ended up being a notorious character."

"We're not sure we understand you. . . ."

"You understand me perfectly. Francisco Javier Fumero is chief inspector of the Barcelona Crime Squad and is widely known. His reputation has even reached those of us who never leave this establishment, and I'd say that when you heard his name, you shrank a couple of inches."

"Now that you mention it, Your Excellency, the name does ring a bell. . . ."

Father Fernando looked sidelong at us. "This kid isn't the son of Julián Carax. Am I right?"

"Spiritual son, Your Eminency. Morally, that has more weight."

"What kind of mess are you two in? Who sends you?"

At that point I was dead certain we were about to be kicked out of the priest's office, and I decided to silence Fermín and, for once, play the honesty card.

"You're right, Father. Julián Carax isn't my father. But nobody has sent us. Years ago I happened to come across a book by Carax, a book that was thought to have disappeared, and from that time on, I have tried to discover more about him and clarify the circumstances of his death. Mr. Romero de Torres has helped me—"

"What book?"

"*The Shadow of the Wind.* Have you read it?"

"I've read all of Julián's novels."

"Have you kept them?"

The priest shook his head.

"May I ask what you did with them?"

"Years ago someone came into my room and set fire to them."

"Do you suspect anyone?"

"Of course. I suspect Fumero. Isn't that why you're here?"

Fermín and I exchanged puzzled looks.

"Inspector Fumero? Why would he want to burn the books?"

"Who else would? During the last year we spent together in the school, Francisco Javier tried to kill Julián with his father's shotgun. If Miquel hadn't stopped him . . ."

"Why did he try to kill him? Julián had been his only friend."

"Francisco Javier was obsessed with Penélope Aldaya. Nobody knew this. I don't think even Penélope had noticed the existence of this boy. He kept the secret for years. Apparently he used to follow Julián secretly. I think one day he saw him kiss her. I don't know. What I do know is that he tried to kill him in broad daylight. Miquel Moliner, who had never trusted Fumero, threw himself on him and stopped him at the last moment. The hole made by the bullet is still visible by the entrance. Every time I go past it, I remember that day."

"What happened to Fumero?"

"He and his family were thrown out of the place. I think Francisco Javier was sent to a boarding school for a while. We heard no more about him until a couple of years later, when his mother died in a hunting accident. There was no such accident. Francisco Javier Fumero is a murderer."

"If I were to tell you . . ." mumbled Fermín.

"It wouldn't be a bad thing if one of you did tell me something, but something true for a change."

"We can tell you that Fumero was not the person who burned your books."

"Who was it, then?"

"In all likelihood it was a man whose face is disfigured by burns, who calls himself Laín Coubert."

"Isn't that the one . . . ?"

I nodded. "The name of one of Carax's characters. The devil."

Father Fernando leaned back in his armchair, almost as confused as we were.

"What does seem increasingly clear is that Penélope Aldaya is at the center of all this business, and she's the person we know least about," Fermín remarked.

"I don't think I'd be able to help you there. I hardly ever saw her, and then only from a distance, two or three times. What I know about her is what Julián told me, which wasn't much. The only other person who I heard mention Penélope's name a few times was Jacinta Coronado."

"Jacinta Coronado?"

"Penélope's governess. She had raised Jorge and Penélope. She loved them madly, especially Penélope. Sometimes she would come to the school to collect Jorge, because Don Ricardo Aldaya wanted his children to be watched over at all times by some member of his household. Jacinta was an angel. She had heard that both Julián and I came from modest families, so she would always bring us afternoon snacks because she thought we went hungry. I would tell her that my father was the cook and not to worry, for I was never without something to eat. But she insisted. Sometimes I'd wait and talk to her. She was the kindest person I've ever met. She had no children or any boyfriend that I knew of. She was alone in the world and had devoted her life to the Aldaya children. She simply adored Penélope. She still talks about her. . . ."

"Are you still in touch with Jacinta?"

"I sometimes visit her in the Santa Lucía hospice. She doesn't have anyone. For reasons that we cannot comprehend, the Good Lord doesn't always reward us during our lifetime. Jacinta is now a very old woman and is as alone as she has always been."

Fermín and I exchanged looks.

"What about Penélope? Hasn't she ever visited Jacinta?"

Father Fernando's eyes grew dark and impenetrable. "Nobody knows what happened to Penélope. That girl was Jacinta's life. When the Aldayas left for America and she lost her, she lost everything."

"Why didn't they take her with them? Did Penélope also go to Argentina, with the rest of the Aldayas?" I asked.

The priest shrugged his shoulders. "I don't know. Nobody ever saw Penélope again or heard anything about her after 1919."

"The year Carax left for Paris," Fermín observed.

"You must promise me that you're not going to bother this poor old lady and make her unearth painful memories."

"Who do you take us for, Father?" asked Fermín with annoyance.

Suspecting that he would get no more from us, Father Fernando made us swear to him that we would keep him informed about any new discoveries we made. To reassure him, Fermín insisted on swearing on a New Testament that lay on the priest's desk.

"Leave the Gospels alone. Your word is enough for me."

"You don't let anything pass you, do you, Father? You're sharp as a nail."

"Come, let me go with you to the door."

He led us through the garden until we reached the spiked gate and then stopped at a reasonable distance from the exit, gazing at the street that wound its way down toward the real world, as if he were afraid he would evaporate if he ventured out a few steps farther. I wondered when Father Fernando had last left the school grounds.

"I was very sad when I heard that Julián had died," he said softly. "Despite everything that happened afterward and the fact that we grew apart as time went by, we were good friends: Miquel, Aldaya, Julián, and myself. Even Fumero. I always thought we were going to be inseparable, but life must know things that we don't know. I've never had friends like those again, and I don't imagine I ever will. I hope you find what you're looking for, Daniel."

· *26* ·

I T WAS ALMOST MIDMORNING WHEN WE REACHED PASEO DE LA BONA-nova, wrapped in our own thoughts. I had little doubt that Fermín's were largely devoted to the sinister appearance of Inspector Fumero in the story. I glanced over at him and noticed that he seemed consumed by anxiety. A veil of dark-red clouds bled across the sky, punctured by splinters of light the color of fallen leaves.

"If we don't hurry, we're going to get caught in a downpour," I said.

"Not yet. Those clouds look like nighttime, like a bruise. They're the sort that wait."

"Don't tell me you're also a cloud expert, Fermín."

"Living in the streets has unexpected educational side effects. Listen, just thinking about this Fumero business has stirred my juices. Would you object to a stop at the bar in Plaza de Sarriá to polish off two well-endowed omelette sandwiches, plus trimmings?"

We set off toward the square, where a knot of old folks hovered around the local pigeon community, their lives reduced to a ritual of spreading crumbs and waiting. We found ourselves a table near the entrance, and Fermín proceeded to wolf down the two sandwiches, his and mine, a pint of beer, two chocolate bars, and a triple coffee heavily laced with rum and sugar. For dessert he had a Sugus candy. A man sitting at the next table glanced at Fermín over his newspaper, probably thinking the same thing I was.

"I don't see how you fit it all in, Fermín."

"In my family we've always had a speedy metabolism. My sister Jesusa, may God rest her soul, was capable of eating a six-egg omelette with blood sausage in the middle of the afternoon and then tucking in like a Cossack at night. Poor thing. She was just like me, you know? Same face and same classic figure, rather on the lean side. A doctor from Cáceres once told my mother that the Romero de Torres family was the missing link between man and the hammerhead, for ninety percent of our organism is cartilage, mainly concentrated in the nose and the outer ear. Jesusa was often mistaken for me in the village, because she never grew breasts and began to shave before me. She died of consumption when she was twenty-two, a virgin to the end and secretly in love with a sanctimonious priest who, when he met her on the street, always said, 'Hello, Fermín, you're becoming quite a dashing young man.' Life's ironies."

"Do you miss them?"

"The family?"

Fermín shrugged his shoulders, caught in a nostalgic smile.

"What do I know? Few things are more deceptive than memories. Look at the priest. . . . And you? Do you miss your mother?"

I looked down. "A lot."

"Do you know what I remember most about mine?" Fermín asked. "Her smell. She always smelled clean, like a loaf of sweet bread. It didn't matter if she'd spent the day working in the fields or was wearing the same old rags she'd worn all week. She always smelled of the best things in this world. Mind you, she was pretty uncouth. She would swear like a trooper, but she smelled like a fairy-tale princess. Or at least that's what I thought. What about you? What is it you remember most about your mother, Daniel?"

I hesitated for a moment, clawing at the words that my lips couldn't shape.

"Nothing. For years now I haven't been able to remember my mother. I can't remember what her face was like, or her voice or her smell. I lost them on the day I discovered Julián Carax, and they haven't come back."

Fermín watched me cautiously, considering his reply. "Don't you have a photograph of her?"

"I've never wanted to look at them," I said.

"Why not?"

I'd never told anyone this, not even my father or Tomás. "Because I'm afraid. I'm afraid of looking for a photograph of my mother and discovering that she's a stranger. You probably think that's nonsense."

Fermín shook his head. "And is that why you believe that if you manage to unravel the mystery of Julián Carax and rescue him from oblivion, the face of your mother will come back to you?"

I looked at him. There was no irony or judgment in his expression. For a moment Fermín Romero de Torres seemed to me the wisest and most lucid man in the universe.

"Perhaps," I said without thinking.

At noon on the dot, we got on a bus that would take us back downtown. We sat in the front, just behind the driver, a circumstance Fermín used as an excuse to hold a discussion with the man about the many advances, both technical and cosmetic, that he had noticed in public transportation since the last time he'd used it, circa 1940—especially with regard to signposting, as was borne out by the notice that read SPITTING AND FOUL LANGUAGE ARE STRICTLY FORBIDDEN. Fermín looked briefly at the sign and decided to acknowledge it by energetically clearing his throat of phlegm. This granted us a sharp look of disapproval from of a trio of saintly ladies who traveled like a commando unit in the back of the bus, each one armed with a missal.

"You savage!" murmured the bigot on the eastern flank, who bore a remarkable likeness to the official portrait of Il Duce, but with curls.

"There they go," said Fermín. "Three saints has my Spain. Saint Holier-than-thou, Saint Holyshit, and Saint Holycow. Between us all, we've turned this country into a joke."

"You can say that again," agreed the driver. "We were better off with the Republic. To say nothing of the traffic. It stinks."

A man sitting in the back of the bus laughed, enjoying the exchange of views. I recognized him as the same fellow who had sat next to us in the bar.

His expression seemed to suggest that he was on Fermín's side and that he wanted to see him get merciless with the diehards. We exchanged a quick glance. He gave me a friendly smile and returned to his newspaper. When we got to Calle Ganduxer, I noticed that Fermín had curled up in a ball under his raincoat and was having a nap with his mouth open, an expression of bliss and innocence on his face.

The bus was gliding through the wealthy domains of Paseo de San Gervasio when Fermín suddenly woke up. "I've been dreaming about Father Fernando," he told me. "Except that in my dream he was dressed as the center forward for Real Madrid and he had the league cup next to him, shining like the Holy Grail."

"I wonder why?" I asked.

"If Freud is right, this probably means that the priest has sneaked in a goal for us."

"He struck me as an honest man."

"Fair enough. Perhaps too honest for his own good. All priests with the makings of a saint end up being sent off to the missions, to see whether the mosquitoes or the piranhas will finish them off."

"Don't exaggerate."

"What blessed innocence, Daniel. You'd even believe in the tooth fairy. All right, just to give you an example: the tall tale about Miquel Moliner that Nuria Monfort landed on you. I think this wench told you more whoppers than the editorial page of *L'Osservatore Romano*. Now it turns out that she's married to a childhood friend of Aldaya and Carax—isn't that a coincidence? And on top of that, we have the story of Jacinta, the good nurse, which might be true but sounds too much like the last act in a play by Alexandre Dumas the younger. Not to mention the star appearance of Fumero in the role of thug."

"Then do you think Father Fernando lied to us?"

"No. I agree with you that he seems honest, but the uniform carries a lot of weight, and he may well have kept an *ora pro nobis* or two up his sleeve, if you get my drift. I think that if he lied, it was by way of holding back and decorum, not out of spite or malice. Besides, I don't imagine him capable of inventing such a story. If he could lie better, he wouldn't be teaching algebra and Latin; he'd be in the bishopric by now, growing fat in an office like a cardinal's and plunging soft sponge cakes in his coffee."

"What do you suggest we do, then?"

"Sooner or later we're going to have to dig up the mummified corpse of the angelic granny and shake it from the ankles to see what falls out. For the time being, I'm going to pull a few strings and see what I can find out about this Miquel Moliner. And it wouldn't be a bad idea to keep an eye on that Nuria Monfort. I think she's turning out to be what my deceased mother called a sly old fox."

"You're mistaken about her," I claimed.

"You're shown a pair of nice boobs and you think you've seen Saint Teresa—which at your age can be excused but not cured. Just leave her to me, Daniel. The fragrance of the eternal feminine no longer overpowers me the way it mesmerizes you. At my age the flow of blood to the brain has precedence over that which flows to the loins."

"Look who's talking."

Fermín pulled out his wallet and started to count his money.

"You have a fortune there," I said. "Is all that the change from this morning?"

"Partly. The rest is legitimate. I'm taking my Bernarda out today, and I can't refuse that woman anything. If necessary, I would rob the Central Bank of Spain to indulge her every whim. What about you? What are your plans for the rest of the day?"

"Nothing special."

"And what about the girl?"

"What girl?"

"Little Bo Peep. Who do you think? Aguilar's sister."

"I don't know. I don't have any plans."

"What you don't have, to put it bluntly, is enough balls to take the bull by the horns."

At that the conductor made his way up to us with a tired expression, his mouth juggling a toothpick, which he twisted and turned through his teeth with circuslike dexterity.

"Excuse me, but these ladies over there want to know if you could use more respectable language."

"They can mind their own bloody business," answered Fermín in a loud voice.

The conductor turned toward the three ladies and shrugged, to indicate that he had done what he could and was not inclined to get involved in a scuffle over a matter of semantic modesty.

"People who have no life always have to stick their nose in the life of others," said Fermín. "What were we talking about?"

"About my lack of guts."

"Right. A textbook case. Trust you me, young man. Go after your girl. Life flies by, especially the bit that's worth living. You heard what the priest said. Like a flash."

"She's not *my* girl."

"Well, then, make her yours before someone else takes her, especially the little tin soldier."

"You talk as if Bea were a trophy."

"No, as if she were a blessing," Fermín corrected. "Look, Daniel. Destiny is usually just around the corner. Like a thief, a hooker, or a lottery vendor: its three most common personifications. But what destiny does not do is home visits. You have to go for it."

I spent the rest of the journey considering this pearl of wisdom while Fermín had another snooze, an occupation for which he had a Napoleonic talent. We got off the bus on the corner of Gran Vía and Paseo de Gracia under a leaden sky that stole the light of day. Buttoning his raincoat up to his neck, Fermín announced that he was departing in a hurry toward his *pensión*, to smarten up for his meeting with Bernarda.

"You must understand that with rather modest looks such as mine, basic beautification entails at least ninety minutes. You won't get far without some looks; that's the sad truth about these dishonest times. *Vanitas peccata mundi.*"

I saw him walk away down Gran Vía, barely a sketch of a little man sheltering himself in a drab raincoat that flapped in the wind like a ragged flag.

I started off for home, where I planned to recruit a good book and hide away from the world. When I turned the corner of Puerta del Ángel and Calle Santa Ana, my heart missed a beat. As usual, Fermín had been right. Destiny was waiting for me in front of the bookshop, clad in a tight gray wool suit, new shoes, and nylon stockings, studying her reflection in the shop window.

"My father thinks I've gone to twelve o'clock mass," said Bea without looking up from her own image.

"You could as well be there. There's been a continuous performance since nine o'clock in the morning less than twenty yards from here, in the Church of Santa Ana."

We spoke like two strangers who have casually stopped by a shop window, looking for each other's eyes in the pane.

"Let's not make a joke of it. I've had to pick up a church leaflet to see what the sermon was about. He's going to ask me for a detailed synopsis."

"Your father thinks of everything."

"He's sworn he'll break your legs."

"Before that he'll have to find out who I am. And while they're still in one piece, I can run faster than him."

Bea was looking at me tensely, glancing over her shoulder at the people who drifted by behind us in puffs of gray and wind.

"I don't know what you're laughing at," she said. "He means it."

"I'm not laughing. I'm scared shitless. It's just that I'm so happy to see you."

A suggestion of a smile, nervous, fleeting. "Me, too," Bea admitted.

"You say it as if it were an illness."

"It's worse than that. I thought that if I saw you again in daylight, I might come to reason."

I wondered whether that was a compliment or a condemnation.

"We can't be seen together, Daniel. Not like this, in full view of everyone."

"If you like, we can go into the bookshop. There's a coffeepot in the back room and—"

"No. I don't want anyone to see me go into or come out of this place. If anyone sees me talking to you now, I can always say I've bumped into my brother's best friend by chance. If we are seen together more than once, we'll arouse suspicion."

I sighed. "And who's going to see us? Who cares what we do?"

"People always have eyes for what is none of their business, and my father knows half of Barcelona."

"So why have you come here to wait for me?"

"I haven't come to wait for you. I've come to church, remember? You yourself said so. Twenty yards from here . . ."

"You scare me, Bea. You lie even better than I do."

"You don't know me, Daniel."

"So your brother tells me."

Our eyes met in the reflection.

"The other night you showed me something I'd never seen before," murmured Bea. "Now it's my turn."

I frowned, intrigued. Bea opened her bag, pulled out a folded card, and handed it to me.

"You're not the only person in Barcelona who knows secrets, Daniel. I have a surprise for you. I'll wait for you at this address today at four. Nobody must know that we have arranged to meet there."

"How will I know that I've found the right place?"

"You'll know."

I looked at her briefly, praying that she wasn't just making fun of me.

"If you don't come, I'll understand," Bea said. "I'll understand that you don't want to see me anymore."

Without giving me a second to answer, she turned around and walked hurriedly off toward the Ramblas. I was left holding the card, my words still hanging on my lips, gazing at her until she melted into the heavy shadows that preceded the storm. I opened the card. Inside, in blue handwriting, was an address I knew well.

Avenida del Tibidabo, 32

· 27 ·

THE STORM DIDN'T WAIT UNTIL NIGHTFALL TO SHOW ITS TEETH. The first flashes of lightning caught me by surprise shortly after taking a bus on Line 22. As we went around Plaza Molina and started up Calle Balmes, the city was already beginning to fade behind curtains of liquid velvet, reminding me that I hadn't even thought of taking an umbrella with me.

"That's what I call courage," said the conductor when I asked for the stop.

It was already ten minutes past four when the bus left me in the middle of nowhere—somewhere at the end of Calle Balmes—at the mercy of the storm. Opposite, Avenida del Tibidabo disappeared in a watery mirage. I counted up to three and started to run. Minutes later, soaked to the bone and shivering, I stopped under a doorway to get my breath back. I scrutinized the rest of the route. The storm's icy blast blurred the ghostly outline of mansions and large, rambling houses veiled in the mist. Among them rose the dark and solitary tower of the Aldaya mansion, anchored among the swaying trees. I pushed my soaking hair away from my eyes and began to run toward it, crossing the deserted avenue.

The small door encased within the gates swung in the wind. Beyond it, a path wound its way up to the house. I slipped in through the door and made my way across the property. Through the undergrowth I could make out the pedestals of statues that had been knocked down. As I neared the mansion I noticed that one of the statues, the figure of an avenging angel, had been dumped into the fountain that was the centerpiece of the garden. Its blackened marble shone ghostlike beneath the sheet of water that flowed over the edge of the bowl. The hand of that fiery angel emerged from the water; an accusing finger, as sharp as a bayonet, pointed toward the front door of the house. The carved oak door looked ajar. I pushed it and ventured a few steps into a cavernous entrance hall, its walls flickering under the gentle light of a candle.

"I thought you weren't coming," said Bea.

The corridor was entombed in shadows, and her silhouette stood out against the pallid light of a gallery that opened up beyond. She was sitting on a chair against the wall, a candle at her feet.

"Close the door," she told me without getting up. "The key is in the lock."

I obeyed. The lock creaked with a deathly echo. I heard Bea's steps approaching me from behind and felt her touch on my soaking clothes.

"You're trembling. Is it fear or cold?"

"I haven't decided yet. Why are we here?"

She smiled in the dark and took my hand. "Don't you know? I thought you would have guessed. . . ."

"This was the house of the Aldayas, that's all I know. How did you manage to get in, and how did you know . . . ?"

"Come, we'll light a fire to warm you up."

She led me through the corridor to the gallery, which presided over the inner courtyard of the house. The marble columns and naked walls of the sitting room crept up to the coffered ceiling, which was falling to pieces. One could make out the spaces where paintings and mirrors had once covered the walls, and there were markings on the marble floor where furniture had stood. At one end of the room was a fireplace laid with a few logs. A pile of old newspapers stood by the poker. The air from the fireplace smelled of recent flames and charcoal. Bea knelt down by the hearth and started to place a few sheets of newspaper among the logs. She pulled out a match and lit them, quickly conjuring up a crown of flames, and her hands stirred the logs with confidence. I imagined she was thinking that I was dying of curiosity and impatience, so I decided to adopt a nonchalant air, making it very clear that if she wanted to play mystery games with me, she had every chance of losing. But she wore a triumphant smile. Perhaps my trembling hands did not help my acting.

"Do you often come around here?" I asked.

"This is the first time. Intrigued?"

"Vaguely."

She spread out a clean blanket that she took out of a canvas bag. It smelled of lavender.

"Come on, sit here, by the fire. You might catch pneumonia, and it would be my fault."

The heat from the blaze revived me. Bea gazed silently at the flames, bewitched.

"Are you going to tell me the secret?" I finally asked.

Bea sighed and sat on one of the chairs. I remained glued to the fire, watching the steam rise from my clothes like a fleeing soul.

"What you call the Aldaya mansion has in fact got its own name. The house is called 'The Angel of Mist,' but hardly anyone knows this. My father's firm has been trying to sell this property for fifteen years without any luck. The other day, while you were telling me the story of Julián Carax and Penélope Aldaya, I didn't think of it. Later, at home that night, I put two and two together and remembered I'd occasionally heard my father talk about the Aldaya family, and about this house in particular. Yesterday I went over to my father's office, and his secretary, Casasús, told me the story of the house. Did you know that in fact this wasn't their official residence but one of their summer houses?"

I shook my head.

"The Aldayas' main house was a mansion that was knocked down in 1925 to erect a block of apartments, on the site where Calle Bruch and Calle Mallorca cross today. The building had been designed by Puig i Cadafalch and commissioned by Penélope and Jorge's grandfather Simón Aldaya, in 1896, when that area was no more than fields and irrigation channels. The eldest son of the patriarch Simón, Don Ricardo Aldaya, bought this summer residence at the turn of the century from a rather bizarre character—at a ridiculous price, because the house had a bad name. Casasús told me it was cursed and that even the sellers didn't dare show it and would dodge the issue with any old pretext. . . ."

THAT AFTERNOON, AS I WARMED MYSELF BY THE FIRE, BEA TOLD ME the story of how The Angel of Mist had come into the possession of the Aldaya family. It had all the makings of a lurid melodrama that could well have come from the pen of Julián Carax. The house was built in 1899 by the architectural partnership of Naulí, Martorell i Bergadà, for a prosperous and extravagant Catalan financier called Salvador Jausà, who would live in it for only a year. The tycoon, an orphan since the age of six and of humble origins, had amassed most of his fortune in Cuba and Puerto Rico. People said that he was one of the many shady figures behind the plot that led to the fall of Cuba and the war with the United States, in which the last of the colonies were lost. He brought back rather more than a fortune from the New World: with him were an American wife—a fragile damsel from Philadelphia high society who didn't speak a word of Spanish—and a mulatto maid who had been in his service since his first years in Cuba and who traveled with a caged macaque in harlequin dress and seven trunks of luggage. At first they moved into a few rooms in the Hotel Colón, while they waited to acquire a residence that would suit the tastes and desires of Jausà.

Nobody doubted in the least that the maid—an ebony beauty endowed with eyes and a figure that, according to the society pages, could make heart rates soar—was in fact his lover, the guide to innumerable illicit pleasures.

It was assumed, moreover, that she was a witch and a sorceress. Her name was Marisela, or that's what Jausà called her. Her presence and her air of mystery soon became the favorite talking point at gatherings that wellborn ladies held to sample sponge fingers and kill time and the autumn blues. Unconfirmed rumors circulated at these tea parties that the woman, like a vision from hell, fornicated on top of the male, that is to say, rode him like a mare in heat, which violated at least five of six recognized mortal sins. In consequence, more than one person wrote to the bishopric asking for a special blessing and protection for the untainted, immaculate souls of all respectable families in Barcelona. And to crown it all, Jausà had the audacity to go out for a ride in his carriage on Sundays, in the middle of the morning, with his wife and with Marisela, parading this Babylonian spectacle of depravity in front of the eyes of any virtuous young man who might happen to be strolling along Paseo de Gracia on his way to the eleven o'clock mass. Even the newspapers noted the haughty look of the strapping woman, who gazed at the Barcelona public "as a queen of the jungle might gaze at a collection of pygmies."

Around that time the fever of Catalan modernism was raging in Barcelona, but Jausà made it quite clear to the architects he had engaged to build his new home that he wanted something different. In his book "different" was the highest praise. Jausà had spent years strolling past the row of neo-Gothic extravagances that the great tycoons of the American industrial age had erected on Fifth Avenue's Mansion Row in New York City. Nostalgic for his American days of glory, the financier refused to listen to any argument in favor of building in accordance with the fashion of the moment, just as he had refused to buy a box in the Liceo, which was de rigueur, labeling the opera house a Babel for the deaf, a beehive of undesirables. He wanted his home to be far from the city, in the still relatively isolated area of Avenida del Tibidabo. He wanted to gaze at Barcelona from a distance, he said. The only company he sought was a garden filled with statues of angels, which, according to his instructions (conveyed by Marisela), must be placed on each of the points of a six-point star—no more, no less. Resolved to carry out his plans, and with his coffers bursting with money with which to satisfy his every whim, Salvador Jausà sent his architects to New York for three months to study those exhilarating structures built to house Commodore Vanderbilt, the Astors, Andrew Carnegie, and the rest of the fifty golden families. He instructed them to assimilate the style and techniques of the Stanford, White & McKim firm and strongly warned them not to bother to knock on his door with a project that would please what he called "pork butchers and button manufacturers."

A year later the three architects turned up at his sumptuous rooms at the Hotel Colón to submit their proposal. Jausà, in the company of the Cuban Marisela, listened to them in silence and, at the end of the presentation, asked them what it would cost to carry out the work in six months. Frederic Martorell, the leading member of the architectural partnership, cleared his throat and, out of decorum, wrote down a figure on a piece of paper and handed it to the tycoon. The latter, without even blinking, wrote out a check for the total sum and dismissed the delegation with a vague gesture. Seven months later, in July 1900, Jausà, his wife, and the maid Marisela moved into the house. By August the two women would be dead and the police would find a dazed Salvador Jausà naked and handcuffed to the armchair in his study. The report made by the sergeant in charge of the case remarked that all the walls in the house were bloodstained, that the statues of the angels surrounding the garden had been mutilated—their faces painted like tribal masks—and that traces of black candles had been found on the pedestals. The inquiry lasted eight months. By then Jausà had fallen silent.

The police investigations concluded that by all indications Jausà and his wife had been poisoned by some herbal extract that had been administered to them by Marisela, in whose rooms various bottles of the lethal substance had been found. For some reason Jausà had survived the poison, although the aftermath had been terrible, for he gradually lost his power of speech and his hearing, part of his body was paralyzed, and he suffered pains so horrendous they condemned him to live the rest of his days in constant agony. Mrs. Jausà had been discovered in her bedroom, lying on her bed with nothing on but her jewels, one of which was a diamond bracelet. The police believed that once Marisela had committed the crime, she had slashed her own wrists with a knife and had wandered about the house spreading her blood on the walls of the corridors and rooms until she collapsed in her attic room. The motive, according to the police, had been jealousy. It seems that the tycoon's wife was pregnant at the time of her death. Marisela, it was said, had sketched a skeleton on the woman's naked belly with hot red wax. The case, like Salvador Jausà's lips, was sealed forever a few months later. Barcelona's high society observed that nothing like this had ever happened in the history of the city, and that the likes of rich colonials and other rabble arriving from across the pond was ruining the moral fiber of the country. Behind closed doors many were delighted that the eccentricities of Salvador Jausà had come to an end. As usual, those people were mistaken: they had just begun.

The police and Jausà's lawyers were responsible for closing the file on the case, but the nabob Jausà wanted to continue. It was at this point that he met Don Ricardo Aldaya—by then a rich industrialist with a colorful reputation for his womanizing and his leonine temper—who offered to buy the property off him with the intention of knocking it down and reselling for a healthy profit: the value of land in that area was soaring. Jausà did not agree to sell, but he invited Ricardo Aldaya to visit the house and observe what he called a scientific and spiritual experiment. No one had entered the property since the investigation had ended. What Aldaya witnessed in the house left him speechless. Jausà had completely lost his mind. The dark shadow of Marisela's blood still covered the walls. Jausà had summoned an inventor, a pioneer in the technological novelty of the moment, the cinematograph. His name was Fructuós Gelabert, and he'd agreed to Jausà's demands in exchange for funds with which to build a film studio in the Vallés region, for he felt sure that, during the twentieth century, moving pictures would supplant organized religion. Apparently Jausà was convinced that the spirit of Marisela had remained in the house. He asserted that he could feel her presence, her voice, her smell, and even her touch in the dark. When they heard these stories, Jausà's servants immediately fled in search of less stressful employment, in neighboring Sarriá, where there were plenty more mansions and families incapable of filling up a bucket of water or darning their own socks.

Jausà, left on his own, sank further into his obsession with his invisible specters. He decided that the answer to his woes lay in making the invisible

visible. He had already had a chance to see some of the results of the invention of cinematography in New York, and he shared the opinion of the deceased Marisela that the camera swallowed up souls. Following this line of reasoning, he commissioned Fructuós Gelabert to shoot yards and yards of film in the corridors of The Angel of Mist, in search of signs and visions from the other world. Despite the cinematographer's noble efforts, the scientific pursuit of Jausà's phantoms proved futile.

Everything changed when Gelabert announced that he'd received a new type of sensitive film material straight from the Thomas Edison factory in Menlo Park, New Jersey. The new stock made it possible to shoot in extremely low light conditions—below candlelight—something unheard of at the time. Then, in circumstances that were never made clear, one of the assistants in Gelabert's laboratory had accidentally poured some sparkling Xarelo wine from the Penedés region into the developing tray. As a result of the chemical reaction, strange shapes began to appear on the exposed film. This was the film Jausà wanted to show Don Ricardo Aldaya the night he invited him to his ghostly abode at number 32, Avenida del Tibidabo.

When Aldaya heard this, he supposed that Gelabert was afraid of losing Jausà's funding and had resorted to such an elaborate ruse to keep his patron's interest alive. Whatever the truth, Jausà had no doubt about the reliability of the results. Moreover, where others saw shapes and shadows, he saw revenants. He swore he could see the silhouette of Marisela materializing under a shroud, a shadow that then mutated into a wolf and walked upright. Alas, all Ricardo Aldaya could see during the screening were large stains. He also maintained that both the film itself and the technician who operated the projector stank of wine and other entirely earthly spirits. Nonetheless, being a sharp businessman, the industrialist sensed that he could turn the situation to his advantage. A mad millionaire who was alone and obsessed with capturing ectoplasms on film constituted an ideal victim. So Aldaya agreed with him and encouraged him to continue with his enterprise. For weeks Gelabert and his men shot miles of film that they then developed in different tanks, using chemical solutions of developing liquids diluted with exotic liqueurs, red wine blessed in the Ninot parish church, and all kinds of *cava* from the Tarragona vineyards. Between screenings, Jausà transferred powers, signed authorizations, and conferred the control of his financial reserves to Ricardo Aldaya.

Jausà vanished one November night of that year during a storm. Nobody knew what had become of him. Apparently he was exposing one of Gelabert's special rolls of film himself when he met with an accident. Don Ricardo Aldaya asked Gelabert to recover the roll. After viewing it in private, Aldaya opted to set fire to it personally. Then, with the help of a very generous check, he suggested to the technician that he should forget all about the incident. By then Aldaya was already the owner of most of the properties of the vanished Jausà. There were those who said that the deceased Marisela had returned to take Jausà with her to hell. Others pointed out that a beggar, who greatly resembled the deceased millionaire, was seen for a few months afterward on the grounds of Ciudadela Park, until a black carriage with drawn curtains ran over him in the middle of the day, without bothering to stop. The stories spread: the dark legend of the rambling mansion, like the invasion of Cuban music in the city's dance halls, could not be contained.

A few months later, Don Ricardo Aldaya moved his family to the house in Avenida del Tibidabo, where, two weeks after their arrival, the couple's youngest child, Penélope, was born. To celebrate the occasion, Aldaya renamed the house "Villa Penélope." The new name, however, never stuck. The house had its own character and proved immune to the influence of its new owners. The recent arrivals complained about noises and banging on the walls at night, sudden putrid smells and freezing drafts that seemed to roam through the house like wandering sentinels. The mansion was a compendium of mysteries. It had a double basement, with a sort of crypt, as yet unused, on the lower level. On the higher floor, a chapel was dominated by a large polychrome figure of Christ crucified, which the servants thought looked disturbingly like Rasputin—a very popular character in the press of the time. The books in the library were constantly appearing rearranged or turned back to front. There was a room on the third floor, a bedroom that was never used because of the unaccountable damp stains that showed up on the walls and seemed to form blurry faces, where fresh flowers would wilt in just a few minutes and one could always hear the drone of flies, although it was impossible to see them.

The cooks swore that certain items, such as sugar, disappeared from the larder as if by magic and that the milk took on a red hue at every new moon. Occasionally they found dead birds or small rodents at the door of some of the rooms. Other times things went missing, especially jewels and buttons from clothes kept in cupboards and drawers. Sometimes the missing objects would mysteriously reappear, months later, in remote corners of the house or buried in the garden. But usually they were never seen again. Don Ricardo was of the opinion that these incidents were but pranks and nonsense. In his view a week's fasting would have curbed his family's fears. What he didn't regard so philosophically were the thefts of his dear wife's jewelry. More than five maids were sacked when different items from the lady's jewelry box disappeared, though they all cried their hearts out, swearing they were innocent. Those in the know tended to think there was no mystery involved: the explanation lay in Don Ricardo's regrettable habit of slipping into the bedrooms of the younger maids at midnight for playful extramarital purposes. His reputation in this field was almost as notorious as his fortune, and there were those who said that at the rate his exploits were taking place, the illegitimate children he left behind would organize their own union.

The fact was that not only jewels disappeared. In time the family lost its joie de vivre entirely. The Aldaya family was never happy in the house that had been acquired through Don Ricardo's dark arts of negotiation. Mrs. Aldaya pleaded constantly with her husband to sell the property and move them to a home in the town or even return to the residence that Puig i Cadafalch had built for Grandfather Simón, the patriarch of the clan. Ricardo Aldaya flatly refused. Since he spent most of his time traveling or in the family's factories, he saw no problem with the house. On one occasion little Jorge disappeared for eight hours inside the mansion. His mother and the servants looked for him desperately, but without success. When he reappeared, pale and dazed, he said he'd been in the library the whole time, in the company of a mysterious black woman who had been showing him old photographs and had told him that all the females in the family would die in that house to atone for the sins of the males. The mysterious lady even revealed to little Jorge the date on which his mother would die: April 12, 1921. Needless to say, the so-called black lady was never found, but years later, on April 12, 1921, at first light, Mrs. Aldaya would be discovered lifeless on her bed. All her jewels had disappeared. When the pond in the courtyard was drained, one of the servant boys found them in the mud at the bottom, next to a doll that had belonged to her daughter, Penélope.

A week later Don Ricardo Aldaya decided to get rid of the house. By then his financial empire was already in its death throes, and there were those who insinuated that it was all due to that accursed house, which brought misfortune to whoever occupied it. Others, the more cautious ones, simply asserted that Aldaya had never understood the changing trends of the market and that all he had accomplished during his lifetime was to ruin the robust business created by the patriarch Simón. Ricardo Aldaya announced that he was leaving Barcelona and moving with his family to Argentina, where his textile industries were allegedly doing splendidly. Many believed he was fleeing from failure and shame.

In 1922 The Angel of Mist was put up for sale at a ridiculously low price. At first there was a strong interest in buying it, as much for its notoriety as for the growing prestige of the neighborhood, but none of the potential buyers made an offer after visiting the house. In 1923 the mansion was closed. The deed was transferred to a real-estate company high up on the long list of Aldaya's creditors, so that it could arrange for its sale or demolition. The house was on the market for years, but the firm was unable to find a buyer. The said company, Botell i Llofré S.L., went bankrupt in 1939 when its two partners were sent to prison on unknown charges. After the unexplained fatal accident that befell both men in the San Viçens jail in 1940, the company was taken over by a financial group, among whose shareholders were three fascist generals and a Swiss banker. This company's executive director turned out to be a certain Mr. Aguilar, father of Tomás and Bea. Despite all their efforts, none of Mr. Aguilar's salesmen were able to place the house, not even by offering it far beneath its already low asking price. Nobody had been back on the property for over ten years.

"Until today," said Bea quietly, withdrawing into herself for a moment. "I wanted to show you this place, you see? I wanted to give you a surprise. I told myself I had to bring you here, because this was part of your story, of the story of Carax and Penélope. I borrowed the key from my father's office. Nobody knows we're here. It's our secret. I wanted to share it with you. And I was asking myself whether you'd come."

"You knew I would."

She smiled as she nodded. "I believe that nothing happens by chance. Deep down, things have their secret plan, even though we don't understand it. Like you finding that novel by Julián Carax in the Cemetery of Forgotten Books or the fact that you and I are here now, in this house that belonged to the Aldayas. It's all part of something we cannot comprehend, something that owns us."

While she spoke, my hand had slipped awkwardly down to Bea's ankle and was sliding toward her knee. She watched it as if she were watching an insect climbing up her leg. I asked myself what Fermín would have done at that moment. Where was his wisdom when I most needed it?

"Tomás says you've never had a girlfriend," said Bea, as if that explained me.

I removed my hand and looked down, defeated. I thought Bea was smiling, but I preferred not to make sure.

"Considering he's so quiet, your brother is turning out to be quite a big-mouth. What else does the newsreel say about me?"

"He says that for years you were in love with an older woman and that the experience left you brokenhearted."

"All I had broken was a lip and my pride."

"Tomás says you haven't been out with any other girl because you compare them all with that woman."

Good old Tomás and his hidden blows. "Her name is Clara," I proffered.

"I know. Clara Barceló."

"Do you know her?"

"Everyone knows a Clara Barceló. The name is the least of it."

We fell silent for a while, watching the fire crackle.

"After I left you, I wrote a letter to Pablo," said Bea.

I swallowed hard. "To your lieutenant boyfriend? What for?"

Bea took an envelope out of her blouse and showed it to me. It was closed and sealed.

"In the letter I tell him I want us to get married very soon, in a month's time, if possible, and that I want to leave Barcelona forever."

Almost trembling, I faced her impenetrable eyes.

"Why are you telling me this?"

"Because I want you to tell me whether I should send it or not. That's why I've asked you to come here today, Daniel."

I examined the envelope that she twirled in her hand like a playing card.

"Look at me," she said.

I raised my eyes and met her gaze. I didn't know what to answer. Bea lowered her eyes and walked away toward the end of the gallery. A door led to the marble balustrade that opened onto the inner courtyard of the house. I watched her silhouette fade into the rain. I went after her and stopped her, snatching the envelope from her hands. The rain beat down on her face, sweeping away the tears and the anger. I led her back into the mansion and to the heat of the blaze. She avoided my eyes. I took the envelope and threw it into the flames. We watched the letter breaking up among the hot coals and the pages evaporating in spirals of smoke, one by one. Bea knelt down next to me, with tears in her eyes. I embraced her and felt her breath on my throat.

"Don't let me fall, Daniel," she murmured.

The wisest man I ever knew, Fermín Romero de Torres, had told me that there is no experience in life comparable to the first time a man undresses a woman. For all his wisdom, though he had not lied to me, he hadn't told me all the truth either. He hadn't told me anything about that strange trembling of the hands that turned every button, every zip, into a superhuman challenge. Nor had he told me about that bewitchment of pale, tremulous skin, that first brush of the lips, or about the mirage that seemed to shimmer in every pore of the skin. He didn't tell me any of that because he knew that the miracle happened only once and, when it did, it spoke in a language of secrets that, were they disclosed, would vanish again forever. A thousand times I've wanted to recover that first afternoon with Bea in the rambling house of Avenida del Tibidabo, when the sound of the rain washed the whole world away with it. A thousand times I've wished to return and lose myself in a memory from which I can rescue only one image stolen from the heat of the flames: Bea, naked and glistening with rain, lying by the fire, with open eyes that have followed me since that day. I leaned over her and passed the tips of my fingers over her belly. Bea lowered her eyelids and smiled, confident and strong.

"Do what you like to me," she whispered.

She was seventeen, her entire life shining on her lips.

· *29* ·

Darkness enveloped us in blue shadow as we left the mansion. The storm was receding, now barely an echo of cold rain. I wanted to return the key to Bea, but her eyes told me she wanted me to be the one to keep it. We strolled down toward Paseo de San Gervasio, hoping to find a taxi or a bus. We walked in silence, holding hands and hardly looking at each other.

"I won't be able to see you again until Tuesday," Bea said in a tremulous voice, as if she suddenly doubted my desire to see her again.

"I'll be waiting for you here," I said.

I took for granted that all my meetings with Bea would take place between the walls of that rambling old house, that the rest of the city did not belong to us. It even seemed to me that the firmness of her touch decreased as we moved away, that her strength and warmth diminished with every step we took. When we reached the avenue, we realized that the streets were almost deserted.

"We won't find anything here," said Bea. "We'd better go down along Balmes."

We started off briskly down Calle Balmes, walking under the trees to shelter from the drizzle. It seemed to me that Bea was quickening her pace at every step, almost dragging me along. For a moment I thought that if I let go of her hand, Bea would start running. My imagination, still intoxicated by her touch and her taste, burned with a desire to corner her on a bench, to seek her lips and recite a predictable string of nonsense that would have made anyone within hearing burst out laughing, anyone but me. But Bea was withdrawing into herself, fading a world away from me.

"What's the matter?" I murmured.

She gave me a broken smile, full of fear and loneliness. I then saw myself through her eyes: just an innocent boy who thought he had conquered the world in an hour but didn't yet realize that he could lose it again in an instant. I kept on walking, without expecting an answer. Waking up at last. Soon we heard the rumbling of traffic, and the air seemed to light up like a flame of gas with the heat from the streetlamps and traffic lights. They made me think of invisible walls.

"We'd better separate here," said Bea, letting go of my hand.

The lights from a taxi rank could be seen on the corner, a procession of glowworms.

"As you wish."

Bea leaned over and brushed my cheek with her lips. Her hair still smelled of candle wax.

"Bea," I began, almost inaudibly. "I love you. . . ."

She shook her head but said nothing, sealing my lips with her hand as if my words were wounding her.

"Tuesday at six, all right?" she asked.

I nodded again. I saw her leave and disappear into a taxi, almost a stranger. One of the drivers, who had followed the exchange as if he were an umpire, observed me with curiosity. "What do you say? Shall we head for home, chief?"

I got into the taxi without thinking. The taxi driver's eyes examined me through the mirror. I lost sight of the car that was taking Bea away, two dots of light sinking into a well of darkness.

I DIDN'T MANAGE TO GET TO SLEEP UNTIL DAWN CAST A HUNDRED TONES of dismal gray on my bedroom window. Fermín woke me up, throwing tiny pebbles at my window from the church square. I put on the first thing I found and ran down to open the door for him. Fermín was full of the insufferable enthusiasm of the early bird. We pushed up the grilles and hung up the OPEN sign.

"Look at those rings under your eyes, Daniel. They're as big as a building site. May we assume the owl got the pussycat to go out to sea with him?"

When I returned to the back room, I put on my blue apron and handed him his, or rather threw it at him angrily. Fermín caught it in midflight, with a sly smile.

"The owl drowned, period. Happy?" I snapped.

"Intriguing metaphor. Have you been dusting off your Verlaine, young man?"

"I stick to prose on Monday mornings. What do you want me to tell you?"

"I leave that up to you. The number of *estocadas* or the laps of honor."

"I'm not in the mood, Fermín."

"O youth, flower of fools! Oh, well, don't get irritated with me. I have fresh news concerning our investigation on your friend Julián Carax."

"I'm all ears."

He gave me one of his cloak-and-dagger looks, one eyebrow raised.

"Well, it turns out that yesterday, after leaving Bernarda back home with her virtue intact but a nice couple of well-placed bruises on her backside, I was assailed by a fit of insomnia—due to those evening erotic arousals—which gave me the pretext to walk down to one of the information centers of the Barcelona underworld—i.e., the tavern of Eliodoro Salfumán, aka 'Coldprick,' situated in a seedy but rather colorful establishment in Calle Sant Jeroni, pride of the Raval quarter."

"The abridged version, Fermín, for goodness' sake."

"Coming. The fact is that once I was there, ingratiating myself with some of the usual crowd, old chums from troubled times of yore, I began to make inquiries about this Miquel Moliner, the husband of your Mata Hari Nuria Monfort and a supposed inmate at the local penitential hotels."

"Supposed?"

"With a capital S. There are no slips at all 'twixt cup and lip in this case, if you see what I mean. I know from experience that when it comes to the census of the prison population, my informants in Coldprick's tabernacle are much more accurate than the pencil pushers in the law courts, and I can guarantee, Daniel, my friend, that nobody has heard mention of the name Miquel Moliner as an inmate, visitor, or any other living soul in the prisons of Barcelona, for at least ten years."

"Perhaps he's serving in some other prison."

"Yeah. Alcatraz, Sing Sing, or the Bastille. Daniel, that woman lied to you."

"I suppose she did."

"Don't suppose; accept it."

"So what now? Miquel Moliner is a dead end."

"Or this Nuria is very crafty."

"What are you suggesting?"

"At the moment we must explore other avenues. It wouldn't be a bad idea to call on the good nanny in the story the priest foisted on us yesterday morning."

"Don't tell me you also suspect that the governess has vanished."

"No, but I do think it's time we stopped fussing about and knocking on doors as if we were begging for alms. In this line of business, one must go in through the back door. Are you with me?"

"You know that to me you walk on holy ground, Fermín."

"Well, then, start dusting your altar-boy costume. This afternoon, as soon as we've closed the shop, we're going to make a charitable visit to the old lady in the Hospice of Santa Lucía. And now tell me, how did it go yesterday with the young filly? Don't be secretive. If you hold back, may you sprout virulent pimples."

I sighed in defeat and made my confession, down to the last detail. At the end of my narrative, after listing what I was sure were just the existential anxieties of a moronic schoolboy, Fermín surprised me with a sudden heartfelt hug.

"You're in love," he mumbled, full of emotion, patting me on the back. "Poor kid."

That afternoon we left the bookshop precisely at closing time, a move that earned us a steely look from my father, who was beginning to suspect that we were involved in some shady business, with all this coming and going. Fermín mumbled something incoherent about a few errands that needed doing, and we quickly disappeared. I told myself that sooner or later I'd have to reveal part of all this mess to my father; what part, exactly, was a different question.

On our way, with his usual flair for tales, Fermín briefed me on where we were heading. The Santa Lucía hospice was an institution of dubious reputation housed within the ruins of an ancient palace on Calle Moncada. The legend surrounding the place made it sound like a cross between purgatory and a morgue, with sanitary conditions worse than in either. The story was, to say the very least, peculiar. Since the eleventh century, the palace had housed, among other things, various residences for well-to-do families, a prison, a salon for courtesans, a library of forbidden manuscripts, a barracks, a sculptor's workshop, a sanatorium for plague sufferers, and a convent. In the middle of the nineteenth century, when it was practically crumbling down in bits, the palace had been turned into a museum of circus freaks and atrocities by a bombastic impresario who called himself Laszlo de Vicherny, Duke of Parma and private alchemist to the House of Bourbon. His real name turned out to be Baltasar Deulofeu i Carallot, the bastard of a salted-pork entrepreneur and a fallen debutante, who was mostly known for his escapades as a professional gigolo and con artist.

The man took pride in owning Spain's largest collection of humanoid fetuses in different stages of deformity, preserved in jars of embalming fluid, and somewhat less pride in his even larger collection of warrants issued by some of Europe's and America's finest law-enforcement agencies. Among other attractions, "The Tenebrarium" (as Deulofeu had renamed the palace) offered séances, necromancy, fights (with cocks, rats, dogs, big strapping women, imbeciles, or some combination of the above), as well as betting, a brothel that specialized in cripples and freaks, a casino, a legal and financial consultancy, a workshop for love potions, a stage for regional folklore and puppet shows, and parades of exotic dancers. At Christmas a Nativity play was staged, sparing no expenses and featuring the troupe from the museum and the whole collection of prostitutes. Its fame reached the far ends of the province.

The Tenebrarium was a roaring success for fifteen years, until it was discovered that Deulofeu had seduced the wife, the daughter, *and* the mother-in-law of the military governor of the province within a single week. The blackest infamy descended on the place and its owner. Before Deulofeu was able to flee the city and don another of his multiple identities, a band of masked thugs seized him in the backstreets of the Santa María quarter and proceeded to hang him and set fire to him in the Ciudadela Park, leaving his body to be devoured by wild dogs that roamed in the area. After two decades of neglect, during which time nobody bothered to remove the collection of horrors of the ill-fated Laszlo, the Tenebrarium was transformed into a charitable institution under the care of an order of nuns.

"The Ladies of the Final Ordeal, or something equally morbid," said Fermín. "The trouble is, they're very obsessive about the secrecy of the place (bad conscience, I'd say), which means we'll have to think of some ruse for getting in."

In more recent times, the occupants of the Hospice of Santa Lucía were being recruited from the ranks of dying, abandoned, demented, destitute old people who made up the crowded underworld of Barcelona. Luckily for them, they mostly lasted only a short time after they had been taken in; neither the conditions of the establishment nor the company encouraged longevity. According to Fermín, the deceased were removed shortly before dawn and made their last journey to the communal grave in a covered wagon donated by a firm in Hospitalet that specialized in meat packing and delicatessen products of doubtful reputation——a firm that occasionally would be involved in grim scandals.

"You're making all this up," I protested, overwhelmed by the horrific details of Fermín's story.

"My inventiveness does not go that far, Daniel. Wait and see. I visited the building on one unfortunate occasion about ten years ago, and I can tell you that it looked as if they'd hired your friend Julián Carax as an interior decorator. A shame we didn't bring some laurel leaves to stifle the aromas. But we'll have enough trouble as it is just being allowed in."

With my expectations thus shaped, we turned into Calle Moncada, by that time of day already transformed into a dark passage flanked by old mansions that had been turned into storehouses and workshops. The litany of bells coming from the basilica of Santa María del Mar mingled with the echo of our footsteps. Soon a penetrating, bitter odor permeated the cold winter breeze.

"What's that smell?"

"We've arrived," announced Fermín.

· *30* ·

A FRONT DOOR OF ROTTED WOOD LET US INTO A COURTYARD guarded by gas lamps that flickered above gargoyles and angels, their features disintegrating on the old stone. A staircase led to the first floor, where a rectangle of light marked the main entrance to the hospice. The gaslight radiating from this opening gave an ocher tone to the miasma that emanated from within. An angular, predatory figure observed us coolly from the shadows of the door's archway, her eyes the same color as her habit. She held a steaming wooden bucket that gave off an indescribable stench.

"Hail-Mary-Full-of-Grace-Conceived-Without-Sin!" Fermín called out enthusiastically.

"Where's the coffin?" answered the voice from up high, serious and taciturn.

"Coffin?" Fermín and I replied in unison.

"Aren't you from the undertaker's?" asked the nun in a weary voice.

I wondered whether that was a comment on our appearance or a genuine question. Fermín's face lit up at such a providential opportunity.

"The coffin is in the van. First we'd like to examine the customer. Pure technicality."

I felt overpowered by nausea.

"I thought Mr. Collbató was going to come in person," said the nun.

"Mr. Collbató begs to be excused, but a rather complicated embalming has cropped up at the last moment. A circus strongman."

"Do you work with Mr. Collbató in the funeral parlor?"

"We're his right and left hands, respectively. Wilfred the Hairy at your service, and here, at my side, my apprentice and student, Sansón Carrasco."

"Pleased to meet you," I rounded off.

The nun gave us a brief looking-over and nodded, indifferent to the pair of scarecrows reflected in her eyes.

"Welcome to Santa Lucía. I'm Sister Hortensia, the one who called you. Follow me."

We followed Sister Hortensia without a word through a cavernous corridor whose smell reminded me of the subway tunnels. It was flanked by doorless frames through which one could make out candlelit halls filled with rows of beds, piled up against the wall and covered with mosquito nets that moved in the air like shrouds. I could hear groans and see glimpses of human shapes through the netting.

"This way," Sister Hortensia beckoned, a few yards ahead of us.

We entered a wide vault, where I found no difficulty in situating the stage for the Tenebrarium described by Fermín. The darkness obscured what at first seemed to me a collection of wax figures, sitting or abandoned in corners, with dead, glassy eyes that shone like tin coins in the candlelight. I thought that perhaps they were dolls or remains of the old museum. Then I realized that they were moving, though very slowly, even stealthily. It was impossible to tell their age or gender. The rags covering them were the color of ash.

"Mr. Collbató said not to touch or clean anything," said Sister Hortensia, looking slightly apologetic. "We just placed the poor thing in one of the boxes that was lying around here, because he was beginning to drip, but that's done."

"You did the right thing. You can't be too careful," agreed Fermín.

I threw him a despairing look. He shook his head calmly, indicating that I should leave him in charge of the situation. Sister Hortensia led us to what appeared to be a cell with no ventilation or light, at the end of a narrow passage. She took one of the gas lamps that hung from the wall and handed it to us.

"Will you be long? I'm rather busy."

"Don't worry about us. You get on with your things, and we'll take him away."

"All right. If you need anything I'll be down in the basement, in the gallery for the bedridden. If it's not too much bother, take him out through the back door. Don't let the others see him. It's bad for the patients' morale."

"We quite understand," I said in a faltering voice.

Sister Hortensia gazed at me for a moment with vague curiosity. When I saw her more closely, I noticed that she was quite an age, almost an elderly woman. Few years separated her from the hospice's guests.

"Listen, isn't the apprentice a bit young for this sort of work?" she asked.

"The truths of life know no age, Sister," remarked Fermín.

The nun nodded and smiled at me sweetly. There was no suspicion in that look, only sadness.

"Even so," she murmured.

She wandered off into the shadows, carrying her bucket and dragging her shadow like a bridal veil. Fermín pushed me into the cell. It was a dismal room built into the walls of a cave that sweated with damp. Chains ending in hooks hung from the ceiling, and the cracked floor was broken up by a sewage grating. In the center of the room, on a grayish marble table, was a wooden crate for industrial packaging. Fermín raised the lamp, and we caught a glimpse of the deceased between the straw padding. Parchment features, incomprehensible, jagged and frozen. The swollen skin was purple. The eyes were open: white, like broken eggshells.

The sight made my stomach turn, and I looked away.

"Come on, let's get down to work," ordered Fermín.

"Are you mad?"

"I mean we have to find this Jacinta woman before we're found out."

"How?"

"How do you think? By asking."

We peered into the corridor to make sure Sister Hortensia had vanished. Then we scurried back to the hall we had previously crossed. The wretched figures were still observing us, with looks that ranged from curiosity to fear and, in some cases, to greed.

"Watch it, some of these would sink their teeth in you if they could, to become young again," said Fermín. "Age makes them all look as meek as lambs, but there are as many sons of bitches in here as out there, or more. Because these are the ones who have lasted and buried the rest. Don't feel sorry for them. Go on, begin with the ones in the corner—they look toothless."

If those words were meant to give me courage for the mission, they failed miserably. I looked at the group of human remains that languished in the corner and smiled at them. It occurred to me that their very presence was testimony to the moral emptiness of the universe and the mechanical brutality with which it destroys the parts it no longer needs. Fermín seemed able to read these profound thoughts and nodded gravely.

"Mother Nature is the meanest of bitches, that's the sad truth," he said. "Be courageous, and go for it."

My first round of inquiries as to the whereabouts of Jacinta Coronado produced only empty looks, groans, burps, and ravings. Fifteen minutes later I called it a day and joined Fermín to see whether he'd had better luck. His discouragement was all too obvious.

"How are we going to find Jacinta Coronado in this shithole?"

"I don't know. This is a cauldron of idiots. I've tried the Sugus candy trick, but they seem to think they're suppositories."

"What if we ask Sister Hortensia? We tell her the truth and have done with it."

"Telling the truth should be kept as a last resort, Daniel, even more so to a nun. Let's use up all our powder first. Look at that little group over there. They seem quite jolly. I'm sure they're very articulate. Go and question them."

"And what are you planning to do?"

"I'll keep watch in the rear guard, in case the penguin returns. You get on with your business."

With little or no hope of success, I went up to a group of patients occupying another corner of the room.

"Good evening," I said, realizing instantly how absurd my greeting was, because in there it was always nighttime. "I'm looking for Señora Jacinta Coronado. Co-ro-na-do. Do any of you know her, or could you tell me where to find her?"

I was confronted by four faces corrupted by greed. There's something here, I thought. Maybe all's not lost.

"Jacinta Coronado?" I insisted.

The four patients exchanged looks and nodded to one another. One of them, a potbellied man without a single hair to be seen on his body, seemed to be their leader. His appearance and manner made me think of a happy Nero, plucking his harp while Rome was rotting at his feet. With a majestic gesture, the Nero figure smiled at me playfully. I returned the smile, hopefully.

The guy gestured at me to come closer, as if he wanted to whisper something in my ear. I hesitated, then leaned forward.

I lent my ear to the patient's lips—so close that I could feel his fetid, warm breath on my skin. "Can you tell me where I can find Señora Jacinta Coronado?" I asked for the last time. I was afraid he'd bite me. Instead he emitted a violently loud fart. His companions burst out laughing and clapped with joy. I took a few steps back, but it was too late: the flatulent vapors had already hit me. It was then I noticed, close to me, an old man, all hunched up, with a prophet's beard, thin hair, and fiery eyes, who leaned on a walking stick and gazed at the others with disdain.

"You're wasting your time, young man. Juanito only knows how to let off farts, and those who are with him can only laugh and sniff them. As you see, the social structure here isn't very different from that of the outside world."

The ancient philosopher spoke in a solemn voice and with perfect diction. He looked me up and down, taking the measure of me.

"You're looking for Jacinta, I think I heard?"

I nodded, astounded by the appearance of intelligent life in that den of horrors.

"And what for?"

"I'm her grandson."

"And I'm the Marquis of Crèmebrûlée. You're a terrible liar, that's what you are. Tell me what you want to see her for or I'll play the madman. It's easy here. And if you intend to ask these poor wretches one by one, you'll soon see what I mean."

Juanito and his gang of inhalers were still howling with laughter. The soloist then gave off an encore, more muted and prolonged than the previous one. It sounded like a hiss, emulating the puncture of a tire, and proved that Juanito's control over his sphincter verged on virtuosity. I yielded to the facts.

"You're right. I'm not a relative of Señora Coronado, but I need to speak to her. It's a matter of the utmost importance."

The old man came up to me. He had a wicked, catlike smile, the smile of a mischievous child, and his eyes were branded with cunning.

"Can you help me?" I begged.

"That depends on how much you can help me."

"If it's in my power, I'll be delighted to help you. Would you like me to deliver a message to your family?"

The old man laughed bitterly. "It's my family who's stuck me in this hole. They're a load of leeches, likely to steal my underpants while they're still warm. Hell can take them—or the city hall. I've kept them and put up with them for long enough. What I want is a woman."

"Excuse me?"

The old man looked at me impatiently.

"Being young is no excuse for slow wit, kid. I'm telling you I want a woman. A female, a maid, or a young filly of a top breed. Young—under fifty-five, that is—and healthy, with no sores or fractures."

"I'm not sure if I understand. . . ."

"You understand me perfectly. I want to have it off with a woman who has teeth and won't pee on me, before I depart for the other world. I don't mind whether she's good-looking or not; I'm half blind, and at my age any girl who has anything to hold onto is a Venus. Am I making myself clear?"

"Crystal. But I don't see how I'm going to find a woman for you. . . ."

"When I was your age, there was something in the service sector called ladies of easy virtue. I know the world changes, but never in essence. Find one for me, plump and fun-loving, and we'll do business. And if you're asking yourself about my ability to enjoy a lady, I want you to know I'm quite content to pinch her backside and feel up her bumpers. That's the advantage of experience."

"Technicalities are your affair, sir, but right now I can't bring a woman to you here."

"I might be a dirty old man, but I'm not stupid. I know that. Your promise is good enough for me."

"And how do you know I won't say yes just to get you to tell me where Jacinta Coronado is?"

The old man gave me a sly smile. "You give me your word, and leave any problems of conscience to me."

I looked around me. Juanito was starting on the second half of his recital. Hope was ebbing away. Fulfilling this horny granddad's request seemed to be the only thing that made any sense in that purgatory. "I give you my word. I'll do what I can."

The old man smiled from ear to ear. I counted three teeth.

"Blond, even if it's peroxide. Pneumatically endowed and skilled at talking dirty, if possible. Of all senses, the one I preserve best is my hearing."

"I'll see what I can do. Now, tell me where I can find Jacinta Coronado."

Y OU'VE PROMISED *WHAT* TO THAT OLD METHUSELAH?"

"You heard."

"You meant it as a joke, I hope."

"I don't lie to an old man who is at death's door, no matter how fresh he turns out to be."

"And that does you credit, Daniel, but how do you think you're going to slip a whore into this holy house?"

"Paying three times as much, I suppose. I leave all specific details to you."

Fermín shrugged resignedly. "Oh, well, a deal's a deal. We'll think of something. But remember, next time a negotiation of this nature turns up, let me do the talking."

"Agreed."

Just as the crafty old devil had instructed, we found Jacinta Coronado in a loft that could be reached only from a staircase on the third floor. According to the old man, the attic was the refuge for the few patients whom fate had not yet had the decency to deprive of understanding. Apparently this hidden wing had, in its day, housed the rooms of Baltasar Deulofeu, aka Laszlo de Vicherny, from where he governed the Tenebrarium's activities and cultivated the arts of love newly arrived from the East, amid scented vapors and oils. And there was no lack of scent now, though of a very different nature. A woman who could only be Jacinta Coronado languished in a wicker chair, wrapped in a blanket.

"Señora Coronado? I asked, raising my voice, in case the poor thing was deaf, half-witted, or both.

The elderly woman examined us carefully, with some reserve. Her eyes looked blurred, and only a few wisps of whitish hair covered her head. I noticed that she gave me a puzzled look, as if she'd seen me before but couldn't remember where. I was afraid Fermín was going to rush into introducing me as the son of Carax or some similar lie, but all he did was kneel down next to the old lady and take her shaky, wrinkled hand.

"Jacinta, I'm Fermín, and this handsome young lad is my friend Daniel. Father Fernando Ramos sends us. He wasn't able to come today because he had twelve masses to say—you know what the calendar of saints' days is like—but he sends you his best regards. How are you feeling?"

The old woman smiled sweetly at Fermín. My friend stroked her face and her forehead. She appreciated the touch of another skin like a purring cat. I felt a lump in my throat.

"What a stupid question, wasn't it?" Fermín went on. "What you'd like is to be out there, dancing a fox-trot. You have the looks of a dancer; everyone must tell you that."

I had never seen him treat anyone with such delicacy, not even Bernarda. His words were pure flattery, but the tone and expression on his face were sincere.

"What pretty things you say," she murmured in a voice that was broken from not having had anyone to speak to or anything to say.

"Not half as pretty as you, Jacinta. Do you think we could ask you some questions? Like on a radio contest, you know?"

The old woman just blinked for an answer.

"I'd say that's a yes. Do you remember Penélope, Jacinta? Penélope Aldaya? It's her we'd like to ask you about."

Jacinta's eyes suddenly lit up and she nodded.

"My girl," she murmured, and it looked like she was going to burst into tears.

"The very one. You do remember, don't you? We're friends of Julián.

Julián Carax, the one who told scary stories. You remember that, too, don't you?"

The old woman's eyes shone, as if those words and the touch on her skin were bringing life back to her by the minute.

"Father Fernando, from San Gabriel's, told us you adored Penélope. He loves you very much, too, and thinks of you every day, you know. If he doesn't come more often, it's just because the new bishop, who is a social climber, loads him with such a quota of masses that his voice gives out."

"Are you sure you eat enough?" the old lady suddenly asked, with a worried expression.

"I eat like a horse, Jacinta. The trouble is, I have a very manly metabolism and I burn it all up. But believe me, under these clothes it's all pure muscle. Feel, feel. Like Charles Atlas, only hairier."

Jacinta nodded and looked reassured. She couldn't take her eyes off Fermín. She had forgotten about me completely.

"What can you tell us about Penélope and Julián?"

"Between them all, they took her from me," she said. "My girl."

I took a step forward and was about to say something, but Fermín threw me a look that told me to remain silent.

"Who took Penélope from you, Jacinta? Do you remember?"

"The master," she said, raising her eyes fearfully, as if she thought someone might hear us.

Fermín seemed to be gauging the emphasis of the old woman's gesture and followed her eyes to the ceiling, weighing up possibilities.

"Are you referring to God Almighty, emperor of the heavens, or did you mean the master, the father of Miss Penélope, Don Ricardo?"

"How's Fernando?" asked the old woman.

"The priest? Splendid. When we least expect it, he'll be made pope and will set you up in the Sistine Chapel. He sends you all the best."

"He's the only one who comes to see me, you know. He comes because he knows I don't have anyone else."

Fermín gave me a sidelong look, as if he were thinking what I was thinking. Jacinta Coronado was much saner than her appearance suggested. Her body was fading away, but her mind and her soul were still blazing with anguish in that place of wretchedness. I wondered how many more people like her, or like the lusty little old man who had shown us how to find her, were trapped in there.

"He comes because he's very fond of you, Jacinta. Because he remembers how well you looked after him and how you fed him when he was a child. He's told us all about that. Do you remember, Jacinta? Do you remember those days, when you went to collect Jorge from school, do you remember Fernando and Julián?"

"Julián . . ."

She dragged out that whispered word, but her smile betrayed her.

"Do you remember Julián Carax, Jacinta?"

"I remember the day Penélope told me she was going to marry him. . . ."

Fermín and I looked at each other in astonishment.

"Marry? When was that, Jacinta?"

"The day she saw him for the first time. She was thirteen and didn't know who he was or what he was called."

"Then how did she know she was going to marry him?"

"Because she'd seen him. In dreams."

As a child, María Jacinta Coronado was convinced that the world ended on the outskirts of Toledo and that beyond the town limits there was nothing but darkness and oceans of fire. Jacinta had got that idea from a dream she had during a fever that had almost killed her when she was four years old. The dreams began with that mysterious fever, which some blamed on the sting of a huge red scorpion that appeared in the house one day and was never seen again, and others on the evil designs of a mad nun who crept into houses at night to poison children and who, years later, was to be garroted reciting the Lord's Prayer backward with her eyes popping out of their sockets, while a red cloud spread over the town and discharged a storm of dead cockroaches. In her dreams Jacinta perceived the past and the future and, at times, saw revealed to her the secrets and mysteries of the old streets of Toledo. One of the characters she would see repeatedly in her dreams was someone called Zacarías, an angel who was always dressed in black and who was accompanied by a dark cat with yellow eyes whose breath smelled of sulfur. Zacarías knew everything: he had predicted the day and the hour of her uncle Benancio's death—the hawker of ointments and holy water. He had revealed the place where her mother, a sanctimonious churchgoer, hid a bundle of letters from an ardent medical student with few financial resources but a solid knowledge of anatomy, and in whose bedroom in the alleyway of Santa María she had discovered the doors of paradise in advance. Zacarías had announced to Jacinta that there was something evil fixed in her stomach, a dead spirit that wished her ill, and that she would know the love of only one man: an empty, selfish love that would break her soul in two. He had augured that in her lifetime she would behold the death of everything she most loved, and that before she reached heaven, she would visit hell. On the day of her first period, Zacarías and his sulfuric cat disappeared from her dreams, but years later Jacinta would remember the visits of the black angel with tears in her eyes, because all his prophecies had come true.

So when the doctors diagnosed that she would never be able to have children, Jacinta wasn't surprised. Nor was she surprised, although she almost died of grief, when her husband of three years announced that he was going to leave her because she was like a wasteland that produced no fruit, because she wasn't a woman. In the absence of Zacarías (whom she took for an emissary of the heavens, for, whether or not he was dressed in black, he was still a luminous angel and the best-looking man she had ever seen or dreamed of), Jacinta spoke to God on her own, hiding in corners, without seeing Him or expecting Him to bother with a reply, because there was a lot of pain in the world and her troubles were, in the end, only small matters. All her monologues with God dealt with the same theme: she wanted only one thing in life, to be a mother, to be a woman.

One day, while she was praying in the cathedral, a man, whom she recognized as Zacarías, came up to her. He was dressed as he always was and held his malicious cat on his lap. He did not look a single day older and still sported magnificent nails, like the nails of a duchess, long and pointed. The angel admitted that he was there because God didn't plan to answer her prayers. But he told her not to worry because, one way or another, he would send her a child. He leaned over her, murmured the word "Tibidabo," and kissed her very tenderly on the lips. At the touch of those fine, honeyed lips, Jacinta had a vision: she would have a daughter without further knowledge of a man (which, judging from the three years of bedroom experience with her husband, who insisted on doing his thing while covering her head with a pillow and mumbling "Don't look, you slut," was a relief). This girl would come to her in a very faraway city, trapped between a moon of mountains and a sea of light, a city filled with buildings that could exist only in dreams. Later Jacinta was unable to tell whether Zacarías's visit had been another of her dreams or whether the angel had really come to her in Toledo Cathedral, with his cat and his scarlet manicured nails. What she didn't doubt for a moment was the truth of those predictions. That very afternoon she consulted with the parish deacon, who was a well-read man and had seen the world (it was said that he had gone as far as Andorra and that he spoke a little Basque). The deacon, who claimed not to know the angel Zacarías among the winged legions of the heavens, listened attentively to Jacinta's vision. After much consideration of the matter, and going by the description of some sort of cathedral that, in the words of the clairvoyant, sounded like a large hair comb made of melting chocolate, the wise man said, "Jacinta, what you've seen is Barcelona, the great enchantress, and the Expiatory Temple of the Sagrada Familia. . . ." Two weeks later, armed with a bundle of clothes, a missal, and her first smile in five years, Jacinta was on her way to Barcelona, convinced that everything the angel had described to her would come true.

Months of great hardships passed before Jacinta would find a permanent job in one of the stores of Aldaya and Sons, near the pavilions of the old 1888 Universal Exhibition in Ciudadela Park. The Barcelona of her dreams had changed into a sinister, hostile city, full of closed palaces, full of factories that poured forth a foggy breath, poisoning the skin with coal and sulfur. Jacinta knew from the start that this city was a woman, cruel and vain; she learned to fear her and never look her in the eye. She lived alone in a pensión in the Ribera quarter, where her pay barely afforded her a miserable room with no windows, whose only source of light came from the candles she stole from the cathedral. She kept these alight all night to scare away the rats that had already gnawed at the ears and fingers of a six-month-old baby, the child of Ramoneta—a prostitute who rented the room next door and the only friend Jacinta had managed to make in Barcelona in eleven months. That winter it rained almost every day, and the rain was blackened by soot. Soon Jacinta began to fear that Zacarías had deceived her, that she had come to that terrible city to die of cold, of misery and oblivion.

Jacinta was prepared to survive. She went to the store every day before dawn and did not come out until well after nightfall. There Don Ricardo Aldaya happened to notice her looking after the daughter of one of the foremen, who had fallen ill with consumption. When he saw the dedication and the tenderness that the young girl exuded, he decided to take her home with him to look after his wife, who was pregnant *with what would be his firstborn. Jacinta's prayers had been answered. That night Jacinta saw Zacarías again in her dreams. The angel was no longer dressed in black. He was naked, and his skin was covered in scales. He didn't have his cat with him anymore, but a white snake coiled around his torso. His hair had grown down to his waist, and his smile, the honeyed smile she had kissed in Toledo Cathedral, was now lined with triangular, serrated teeth, like those she'd seen in some of the deepsea fish that thrashed their tails in the fish market. Years later the young woman would reveal this vision to an eighteen-year-old Julián Carax, recalling how the day she left the pensión in the Ribera quarter and moved to the Aldaya mansion, she was told that her friend Ramoneta had been stabbed to death in the doorway the night before and that Ramoneta's baby had died of cold in her arms. When they heard the news, the guests at the pensión came to blows, shouting and scratching over the meager belongings of the dead woman. The only thing they left was what had been Ramoneta's greatest treasure: a book. Jacinta recognized it, because often, at night, Ramoneta had asked her to read her one or two pages. She herself had never learned to read.*

Four months later Jorge Aldaya was born, and although Jacinta was to offer him all the affection that the mother never knew how to give him, or never wished to— for she was an ethereal lady, Jacinta thought, who always seemed trapped in her own reflection in the mirror—the governess realized that this was not the child Zacarías had promised her. During those years Jacinta gave up her youth and became a different woman. The other Jacinta had been left behind in the pensión of the Ribera quarter, as dead as Ramoneta. Now she lived in the shadow of the Aldayas' luxuries, far from that dark city that she had come to hate so much and into which she did not venture, not even on her monthly day off. She learned to live through others, through a family that sat on top of a fortune the size of which she could scarcely conceive. She lived in the expectation of that child, who would be female, like the city, and to whom she would give all the love with which God had poisoned her soul. Sometimes Jacinta asked herself whether that dreamy peace that filled her days, that absence of consciousness, was what some people called happiness, and she wanted to believe that God, in His infinite silence, had, in His way, answered her prayers.

Penélope Aldaya was born in the spring of 1902. By then Don Ricardo Aldaya had already bought the house on Avenida del Tibidabo, that rambling mansion that Jacinta's fellow servants were convinced lay under the influence of some powerful spell, but which Jacinta did not fear, because she knew that what others took to be magic was nothing more than a presence that only she could capture in dreams: the shadow of Zacarías, who hardly resembled the man she remembered and who now only manifested himself as a wolf walking on his two hind legs.

Penélope was a fragile child, pale and slender. Jacinta saw her grow like a flower in winter. For years she watched over her every night, personally prepared every one of her meals, sewed her clothes, was by her side when she went through her many illnesses, when she said her first words, when she became a woman. Mrs. Aldaya was one more figure in the scenery, a prop that came on- and offstage according to the dictates of decorum. Before going to bed, she would come and say good night to her daughter and tell her she loved her more than anything in the world, that she was the most important thing in the universe to her. Jacinta never told Penélope that she loved her. The nurse knew that those who really love, love in silence, with deeds and not with words. Secretly Jacinta despised Mrs. Aldaya, that vain, empty creature who grew old in the corridors of the mansion, weighed down by the jewels with which her husband—who for years had set anchor in foreign ports—kept her quiet. She hated her because, of all women, God had chosen her to give birth to Penélope while her own womb, the womb of the true mother, remained barren. In time, as if the words of her husband had been prophetic, Jacinta even lost her womanly shape. She grew thin and austere in appearance, she wore the look of tired skin and tired bone. Her breasts withered until they were but scraps of skin, her hips were like the hips of a boy, and her flesh, hard and angular, didn't even catch the eye of Don Ricardo Aldaya, who only needed to sense a hint of liveliness to set him off in a frenzy—as all the maids in the house and in the houses of his close friends knew only too well. Better this way, thought Jacinta. She had no time for nonsense.

All her time was for Penélope. She read to her, she accompanied her everywhere, she bathed her, dressed her, undressed her, combed her hair, took her out for walks, put her to bed and woke her up. But above all she spoke to her. Everyone took her for a batty nurse, a spinster with nothing in her life other than her job in the house, but nobody knew the truth: Jacinta was not only Penélope's mother, she was her best friend. From the moment the girl began to speak and articulate her thoughts, which was much sooner than Jacinta remembered in any other child, they shared their secrets and their lives.

The passing of time only strengthened this union. When Penélope reached adolescence, they were already inseparable friends. Jacinta saw Penélope blossom into a woman whose beauty and radiance were evident to more eyes than just hers. When that mysterious boy called Julián came to the house, Jacinta noticed that from the very first moment a current flowed between him and Penélope. They were joined by a bond, similar to the one that joined her to Penélope, but also different. More intense. Dangerous. At first she thought she would come to hate the boy, but soon she realized that she did not hate Julián Carax and would never be able to. As Penélope fell under Julián's spell, she, too, allowed herself to be dragged into it and in time desired only what Penélope desired. Nobody had noticed, nobody had paid attention, but, as usual, the essential part of the matter had been settled before the story had begun, and by then it was too late.

Many months of wistful looks and longings would pass before Julián Carax and Penélope were able to be alone. Their lives were ruled by chance. They met in corridors, they looked at each other from opposite ends of the table, they brushed silently against each other, they felt each other's absence. They exchanged their first words in the library of the house on Avenida del Tibidabo one stormy afternoon when "Villa Penélope" was suddenly filled with the dim light of candles—only a few seconds stolen from the darkness in which Julián thought he saw in the girl's eyes the certainty that they both felt the same, that the same secret was devouring them. Nobody seemed to notice. Nobody but Jacinta, who saw with growing anxiety the game of furtive glances that Penélope and Julián were playing in the shadow of the Aldayas. She feared for them.

By then Julián had begun to have sleepless nights, writing stories for Penélope from midnight to dawn. Then, after going up to the house on Avenida del Tibidabo with any old excuse, he would look for the moment when he could slip into Jacinta's room and give her his pages so that she, in turn, could give them to the girl. Sometimes Jacinta would hand him a note that Penélope had written for him, and he would spend days rereading it. That game went on for months. While time brought them no good fortune, Julián did whatever was necessary to be close to Penélope. Jacinta helped him, to see Penélope happy, to keep that light glowing. Julián, for his part, felt that the casual innocence of the beginning was now fading and it was necessary to start giving way. That is how he began to lie to Don Ricardo about his plans for the future, to fake an enthusiasm for a career in banking and finance, to feign an affection and an attachment for Jorge Aldaya that he did not feel, in order to justify his almost constant presence in the house on Avenida del Tibidabo; to say only what he knew others wanted to hear him say, to read their looks and their hopes, to put aside honesty and sincerity, to feel that he was selling his soul away in pieces, and to fear that if he ever did come to deserve Penélope, there would be nothing left of the Julián who saw her the first time. Sometimes Julián would wake up at dawn, burning with anger, longing to tell the world his real feelings, to face Don Ricardo Aldaya and tell him he had no interest whatsoever in his fortune, his opportunities for the future, or his company; that he only wanted his daughter, Penélope, and was thinking of taking her as far away as possible from that empty, shrouded world in which her father had imprisoned her. The light of day dispelled his courage.

There were times when Julián opened his heart to Jacinta, who was beginning to love the boy more than she would have wished. She would often leave Penélope for a moment and, with the pretext of going to collect Jorge from school, would see Julián and deliver Penélope's messages to him. That is how she met Fernando, who, many years later, would be her only remaining friend while she awaited death in the hell of Santa Lucía—the hell that had been prophesied by the angel Zacarías. Sometimes the nurse would mischievously take Penélope with her to the school and facilitate a brief encounter between the two youngsters, watching a love grow between them such as she had never known, which had been denied to her. It was also about this time that Jacinta noticed the somber and disturbing presence of that quiet boy whom everyone called Francisco Javier, the son of the caretaker at San Gabriel's. She would catch him spying on them, reading their gestures from afar and devouring Penélope with his eyes.

Jacinta kept a photograph of Julián and Penélope taken by Recasens, the official portrait photographer of the Aldayas, by the door of the hat shop in Ronda de San Antonio. It was an innocent image, taken at midday in the presence of Don Ricardo and of Sophie Carax. Jacinta always carried it with her. One day, while she was waiting for Jorge outside the school, the governess absentmindedly left her bag by one of the fountains, and, when she went back for it, found young Fumero prowling around the area, looking at her nervously. That night she looked for the photograph but couldn't find it and was certain that the boy had stolen it. On another occasion, a few weeks later, Francisco Javier Fumero went up to Jacinta and asked her whether she could give Penélope something from him. When Jacinta asked what this thing was, the boy pulled out a piece of cloth in which he had wrapped what looked like a figure carved in pinewood. Jacinta recognized Penélope in the figure and felt a shiver. Before she was able to say anything, the boy left. On her way back to the house on *Avenida del Tibidabo*, Jacinta threw the figure out of the car window, as if it were a piece of stinking carrion. More than once Jacinta was to wake up at dawn, covered in sweat, plagued by nightmares in which that boy with a troubled look threw himself on Pené-lope with the cold and indifferent brutality of some strange insect.

Some afternoons, when Jacinta went to fetch Jorge and he was late, the governess would talk to Julián. He, too, was beginning to love that severe-looking woman. Soon, when a problem cast a shadow over his life, she and Miquel Moliner were always the first, and sometimes the last, to know. Once Julián told Jacinta he had seen his mother and Don Ricardo Aldaya talking in the fountain courtyard while they waited for the pupils to come out. Don Ricardo seemed to be enjoying Sophie's company, and Julián felt a little uneasy, because he was aware of the magnate's reputation as a Don Juan and of his voracious appetite for the delights of the female sex—with no distinction of class or condition—to which only his saintly wife seemed immune. "I was telling your mother how much you like your new school," Don Ricardo told him. When he said good-bye to them, Don Ricardo gave them a wink and walked off laughing bois-terously. His mother was quiet during the journey home, clearly offended by the com-ments Don Ricardo Aldaya had made to her.

Sophie was suspicious of Julián's growing bond with the Aldayas and the way he had abandoned his old neighborhood friends and his family. She was not alone. Whereas his mother showed her displeasure in sadness and silence, the hatter dis-played bitterness and spite. His initial enthusiasm about the widening of his clien-tele to include the flower of Barcelona society had evaporated. He hardly ever saw his son now and soon had to employ Quimet, a local boy and one of Julián's former friends, as a helper and apprentice in the shop. Antoni Fortuny was a man who felt he could talk openly only about hats. He locked his deeper feelings in the prison of his heart for months on end, until they became hopelessly embittered. He grew ever more bad-tempered and irritable. He found fault with everything—from the efforts of poor Quimet to learn the trade to Sophie's attempts to make light of Julián's seem-ing abandonment of them.

"Your son thinks he's someone because those rich guys treat him like a performing monkey," he'd say in a depressed tone, full of resentment.

One day, almost three years to the day since Don Ricardo Aldaya's first visit to the Fortuny and Sons hat shop, the hatter left Quimet in charge of the shop and told him *he'd be back at noon. He boldly presented himself at the offices of Aldaya's consortium on Paseo de Gracia and asked to see Don Ricardo.*

"And whom have I the honor to announce?" asked a clerk in a haughty manner.

"His personal hatter."

Don Ricardo received him, somewhat surprised but well disposed, imagining that perhaps Fortuny was bringing him a bill—small shopkeepers never quite understood the protocol when it comes to money.

"So tell me, what can I do for you, Fortunato, old fellow?"

Without further delay, Antoni Fortuny proceeded to explain to Don Ricardo that he was very much mistaken concerning his son, Julián.

"My son, Don Ricardo, is not the person you think he is. Quite the contrary, he is an ignorant, lazy boy, with no more talent than the pretentiousness his mother has put into his head. He'll never get anywhere, believe me. He lacks ambition and character. You don't know him. He can be very clever at sweet-talking strangers, making them believe he knows a lot about everything, when in fact he knows nothing about anything. He's a mediocre person. But I know him better than anyone, and I thought I should warn you."

Don Ricardo Aldaya listened to the speech in silence, without blinking.

"Is that all, Fortunato?"

Seeing that it was, the industrialist pressed a button on his desk. A few moments later, the secretary who had received Fortuny on arrival appeared at the office door.

"Our friend Fortunato is leaving, Balcells," Don Ricardo announced. "Please accompany him to the door."

The icy tone of the industrialist did not please the hatter.

"If you don't mind, Don Ricardo: it's Fortuny, not Fortunato."

"Whatever. You're a very sad man, Fortuny. I'd appreciate it if you didn't come by here again."

When Fortuny found himself back on the street, he felt more alone than ever, more convinced that everyone was against him. Only a few days later, the smart clients brought in by his relationship with Aldaya began to send messages canceling their orders and settling their bills. In just a few weeks, he had to dismiss Quimet, because there wasn't enough work for both in the shop. The boy wasn't much use anyhow, he told himself. He was mediocre and lazy, like all of them.

It was around this time that people in the neighborhood began to mention that

Mr. Fortuny was looking much older, lonelier, more bitter. He barely spoke to anyone anymore and spent hours on end shut up in the shop, with nothing to do, watching people go by on the other side of the counter, feelings of disdain mingling with hope. Later people said that fashions changed, that young people no longer wore hats, and that those who did would rather go to other shops, where they sold hats ready made in different sizes, with more modern designs, and at a cheaper price. The Fortuny and Sons hat shop slowly sank into a sad, silent slumber.

You're all waiting for me to die, Fortuny said to himself. Well, I might just give you that pleasure. In fact, he had started to die long before.

Julián threw himself even more into the world of the Aldayas, into the only future he could conceive of, one with Penélope in it. Almost two years went by, in which the two of them walked on a tightrope of secrecy together. In his own way, Zacarías had warned him long ago. Shadows spread around Julián, and soon they would close in on him.

The first sign came one day in April 1918. Jorge Aldaya was going to be eighteen, and Don Ricardo, playing the role of great patriarch, had decided to organize (or, rather, to give orders for someone to organize) a monumental birthday party that his son did not want and from which he, Don Ricardo, would be absent: with the excuse of important business commitments, he would be meeting with a delicious lady, newly arrived from St. Petersburg, in the blue suite of the Hotel Colón. The house on Avenida del Tibidabo was turned into a circus pavilion for the occasion: hundreds of lanterns, pennants, and stalls were set up in the gardens to delight the guests.

Almost all Jorge Aldaya's school companions from San Gabriel's had been invited. At Julián's suggestion, Jorge had included Francisco Javier Fumero. Miquel Moliner warned them that the son of the school caretaker would feel out of place in such pompous, pretentious surroundings. Francisco Javier received his invitation but, anticipating exactly the same thing, decided to turn it down. When Doña Yvonne, his mother, learned that her son was going to decline an invitation to the Aldayas' luxurious mansion, she was on the point of skinning him alive. What could that invitation be but a sign that she herself would soon enter high society? The next step could only be an invitation to afternoon tea with Mrs. Aldaya and other ladies of unquestionable distinction. Doña Yvonne took the savings she had been scraping together out of her husband's pay and went to buy a pretty sailor suit for her son.

Francisco Javier was already seventeen at the time, and that blue suit with short trousers, tailored to appeal to the none-too-refined sensibility of Doña Yvonne, looked grotesque and humiliating on the boy. Pressed by his mother, Francisco Javier accepted the invitation and spent a week carving a letter opener, which he intended to give Jorge as a present. On the day of the party, Doña Yvonne insisted on accompanying her son to the door of the Aldayas' house. She wanted to scent royalty and bask in the glory of seeing her son cross the doors that would soon open for her. When the moment came to put on his awful sailor suit, Francisco Javier discovered it was too small for him. Yvonne decided to adjust it somehow. They arrived late. In the meantime, taking advantage of the hubbub and of Don Ricardo's absence—who no doubt was at that very moment celebrating in his own way—Julián had slipped away from the party. He and Penélope had arranged to meet in the library, where they didn't risk running into any partygoers. They were too busy devouring each other's lips to notice the couple approaching the front door of the house. Francisco Javier, dressed in a first-communion sailor suit and purple with shame, was almost being dragged by Doña Yvonne, who for the occasion had decided to resurrect a broad-brimmed hat and a matching dress adorned with pleats and garlands; they made her look like a candy stand or, in the words of Miquel Moliner, who sighted her from afar, a bison dressed up as Madame Récamier. The two servants guarding the door didn't seem very impressed by the visitors. Doña Yvonne announced that her son, Don Francisco Javier Fumero de Sotoceballos, was making his entrance. The two servants answered, in a sarcastic tone, that the name did not ring a bell. Irritated, but keeping the composure of a woman of importance, Yvonne told her son to show them the invitation. Unfortunately, when the suit was being fixed, the card had been left on Doña Yvonne's sewing table.

Francisco Javier tried to explain the circumstances, but he stammered, and the laughter of the two servants did not help clear up the misunderstanding. Mother and son were invited to get the hell out of there. Doña Yvonne was inflamed with anger and announced that the servants didn't know who they were dealing with. The servants replied that the floor cleaner's position was already taken.

From her bedroom window, Jacinta watched Francisco Javier turn to leave, then suddenly stop. Beyond the scene his mother was creating, shouting herself hoarse at the arrogant servants, the boy saw them: Julián kissing Penélope by the large window of the library. They were kissing with the intensity of those who belong to each other, unaware of the world around them.

The following day, during the midday break, Francisco Javier appeared unexpect-edly. News of the previous day's scene had already spread among the pupils: he was met with laughter and questioned about what he'd done with his little sailor suit. The laughter ended abruptly when the boys noticed he was carrying his father's gun in his hand. Silence reigned, and many of them moved away. Only the circle formed by Al-daya, Moliner, Fernando, and Julián turned around and stared at the boy, without understanding. Francisco Javier gave no warning: he raised his rifle and aimed. Later, witnesses said there was no irritation or anger in his expression. Francisco Javier dis-played the same automatic coolness with which he performed his cleaning jobs in the garden. The first bullet scraped past Julián's head. The second would have gone through his throat had Miquel Moliner not thrown himself on the caretaker's son, punched him, and wrenched the gun from him. Julián Carax watched the scene in as-tonishment, paralyzed. Everyone thought the shots were aimed at Jorge Aldaya in re-venge for the humiliation Javier had suffered the day before. Only later, when the Civil Guards were taking the boy away and the caretakers were being almost literally kicked out of their home, did Miquel Moliner go up to Julián and tell him, without any pride, that he had saved his life.

It was the last year for Julián and his companions at San Gabriel's School. Most of them were already talking about their plans, or about the plans their respective families had set up for them for the following year. Jorge Aldaya already knew that his father was sending him to study in England, and Miquel Moliner took it for granted that he would go to Barcelona University. Fernando Ramos had mentioned more than once that perhaps he would enter the seminary of the Society of Jesus, a prospect his teachers considered the wisest in his particular situation. As for Francisco Javier Fumero, all one knew about the boy was that, thanks to Don Ricardo Aldaya, who interceded on his behalf, he had been taken to a reformatory school high in a re-mote valley of the Pyrenees, where a long winter awaited him. Seeing that all his friends had found some direction in life, Julián wondered what would become of him-self. His literary dreams and ambitions seemed further away and more unfeasible than ever. All he longed for was to be near Penélope.

While he asked himself about his future, others were planning it for him. Don Ri-cardo Aldaya was already preparing a post for him in his firm to initiate him into the business. The hatter, for his part, had decided that if his son did not want to continue in the family business, he could forget about sponging off him. He had secretly started procedures to send Julián to the army, where a few years of military life would cure him of his delusions of grandeur. Julián was unaware of such plans, and by the time he found out what others had arranged for him, it would be too late. Only Penélope occupied his thoughts, and now the feigned distance and the clandestine meetings no longer satisfied him. He insisted on seeing her more often, increasingly risking discovery. Jacinta did what she could to cover them: she lied repeatedly and concocted a thousand and one ruses to give them a few moments on their own. She understood that this was not enough for Penélope and Julián. The governess had for some time now recognized in their looks the defiance and arrogance of desire: a blind desire to be discovered, a hope that their secret would become an open scandal so that they would no longer have to hide in corners and attics, to love each other in the dark. Sometimes, when Jacinta tucked Penélope up at night, the girl would burst into floods of tears and confess how she longed to flee with Julián, to catch the first train and escape to a place where nobody would know them. Jacinta, who remembered the sort of world that existed beyond the iron gates of the Aldaya mansion, shuddered and tried to dissuade her. Penélope was docile by nature, and the fear she saw in Jacinta's face was enough to soothe her. Julián was another matter.

During that last spring at San Gabriel's, Julián was unnerved to discover that Don Ricardo Aldaya and his mother sometimes met secretly. At first he feared that the industrialist might have decided to add the conquest of Sophie to his collection, but soon he realized that the meetings, which always took place in cafés in the center of town and were carried out with the utmost propriety, were limited to conversation. Sophie kept silent about these meetings. When at last Julián decided to go up to Don Ricardo and ask him what was going on between him and his mother, the magnate laughed.

"Nothing gets by you, does it, Julián? The fact is, I was going to talk to you about this matter. Your mother and I are discussing your future. She came to see me a few weeks ago. She was worried because your father wants to send you to the army next year. Your mother, quite naturally, wants the best for you, and she came to me to see whether, between the two of us, we could do anything. Don't worry; you have Don Ricardo Aldaya's word that you won't become cannon fodder. Your mother and I have great plans for you. Trust us."

Julián wanted to trust him, yet Don Ricardo inspired anything but trust. When he consulted with Miquel Moliner, the boy agreed with Julián.

"*If what you want to do is elope with Penélope, and may God help you, what you need is money.*"

Money is what Julián didn't have.

"That can be arranged," Miquel told him. "That's what rich friends are for."

That is how Miquel and Julián began to plan the lovers' escape. The destination, at Miquel's suggestion, would be Paris. Moliner was of the opinion that, if Julián was set on being a starving bohemian artist, at least a Paris setting couldn't be improved upon. Penélope spoke a little French, and for Julián, who had learned it from his mother, it was his second language.

"Besides, Paris is large enough to get lost in but small enough to offer opportunities," Miquel reasoned.

Miquel managed to put together a small fortune, joining his savings from many years to what he was able to get out of his father using the most outlandish excuses. Only he knew where the money was going.

"And I plan to go dumb the minute you two board that train."

That same afternoon, after finalizing details with Moliner, Julián went to the house on Avenida del Tibidabo to tell Penélope about the plan.

"You mustn't tell anyone what I'm about to tell you. No one. Not even Jacinta," Julián began.

The girl listened to him in astonishment, enthralled. Moliner's plan was impeccable. Miquel would buy the tickets under a false name and hire a third party to collect them at the ticket office in the station. If by any chance the police discovered him, all he'd be able to offer would be the description of someone who did not look like Julián. Julián and Penélope would meet on the train. There would be no waiting on the platform, where they might be seen. The escape would take place on a Sunday, at midday. Julián would make his own way to the Estación de Francia. Miquel would be waiting for him there, with the tickets and the money.

The most delicate part of the plan concerned Penélope. She had to deceive Jacinta and ask her to invent an excuse for taking her out of the eleven o'clock mass and returning home. On the way Penélope would ask Jacinta to let her go and meet Julián, promising to be back before the family had returned to the mansion. This would be Penélope's opportunity to get to the station. They both knew that if they told her the truth, Jacinta would not allow them to leave. She loved them too much.

"It's the perfect plan, Miquel," Julián said.

Miquel nodded sadly. "Except in one detail. The pain you are going to cause a lot of people by going away forever."

Julián nodded, thinking of his mother and Jacinta. It did not occur to him that Miquel Moliner was talking about himself.

The most difficult thing was convincing Penélope of the need to keep Jacinta in the dark. Only Miquel would know the truth. The train would depart at one in the afternoon. By the time Penélope's absence was noticed, they would have crossed the border. Once in Paris, they would settle in a hostel as man and wife, using a false name. They would then send Miquel Moliner a letter addressed to their families, confessing their love, telling them they were well, that they loved them, announcing their church wedding, and asking for forgiveness and understanding. Miquel Moliner would put the letter in a second envelope to do away with the Paris postmark and would see to it that it was posted from some nearby town.

"When?" asked Penélope.

"In six days' time," said Julián. "This coming Sunday."

Miquel reckoned it would be best if Julián didn't see Penélope during the days left prior to the elopement, so as not to arouse suspicions. They should both agree not to see each other again until they met on that train on their way to Paris. Six days without seeing her, without touching her, seemed interminable to Julián. They sealed the pact, the secret marriage, with their lips.

It was then that Julián took Penélope to Jacinta's bedroom on the third floor of the house. Only the servants' quarters were on that floor, and Julián was sure nobody would discover them. They undressed feverishly, with an angry passion, scratching each other's skin and melting into silences. They learned each other's bodies by heart and buried all thoughts of those six days of separation. Julián penetrated her with fury, pressing her against the floorboards. Penélope received him with open eyes, her legs hugging his torso, her lips half open with yearning. There was not a glimmer of fragility or childishness in her eyes or in her warm body. Later, with his face still resting on her stomach and his hands on her white, tremulous breasts, Julián knew he had to say good-bye. He had barely had time to sit up when the door of the room was slowly opened and a woman's shape appeared in the doorway. For a second, Julián thought it was Jacinta, but he soon realized it was Mrs. Aldaya. She was watching them, spellbound, with a mixture of fascination and disgust. All she managed to mumble was "Where's Jacinta?" Then she just turned and walked away without say-

ing a word, while Penélope crouched on the ground in mute agony and Julián felt the world collapsing around him.

"Go now, Julián. Go before my father comes."

"But . . ."

"Go."

Julián nodded. "Whatever happens, I'll wait for you on Sunday on that train."

Penélope managed a faint smile. "I'll be there. Now go. Please . . ."

She was still naked when he left her and slid down the servants' staircase toward the coach houses and out into the coldest night he could remember.

The days that followed were agony. Julián had spent all night awake, expecting that at any moment Don Ricardo's hired assassins would come for him. The following day, in school, he didn't notice any change of attitude in Jorge Aldaya. Devoured by anguish, Julián told Miquel Moliner what had happened. Miquel shook his head.

"You're crazy, Julián, but that's nothing new. What's strange is that there hasn't been an upheaval in the Aldayas' house. Which, come to think of it, isn't so surprising. If, as you say, Mrs. Aldaya discovered you, it might be that she herself still doesn't know what to do. I've had three conversations with her in my life and came to two conclusions from them: one, Mrs. Aldaya has the mental age of a twelve-year-old; two, she suffers from a chronic narcissism that makes it impossible for her to see or understand anything that is not what she wants to see or believe, especially if it concerns herself."

"Spare me the diagnosis, Miquel."

"What I mean is that she's probably still wondering what to say, how to say it, when, and to whom. First she must think of the consequences for herself, the potential scandal, her husband's fury. . . . The rest, I daresay, she couldn't care less about."

"So you think she won't say anything?"

"She might take a day or two. But I don't think she's capable of keeping such a secret from her husband. What about the escape plan? Is it still on?"

"More than ever."

"I'm glad to hear that. Because I really believe that now there's no turning back."

The week stretched out interminably. Julián went to school every day with uncertainty hard on his heels. He passed the time merely pretending to be there, barely able to exchange glances with Miquel Moliner, who was beginning to be just as worried as him, or more so. Jorge Aldaya said nothing. He was as polite as ever. Jacinta had not turned up again to collect Jorge from school. Don Ricardo's chauffeur came every afternoon. Julián felt like dying, wishing that whatever was going to happen did happen, so that the time of waiting would come to an end. On Thursday afternoon, after classes, Julián began to think that luck was on his side. Mrs. Aldaya had not said anything, perhaps out of shame, stupidity, or for any of the reasons Miquel suspected. It mattered little. All that mattered was that she kept the secret until Sunday. That night, for the first time in a number of days, he was able to sleep.

On Friday morning, when he went to class, Father Romanones was waiting for him by the gate.

"Julián, I have to speak to you."

"What is it, Father?"

"I always knew this day would come, and I must confess I'm happy to be the one who will break the news to you."

"What news, Father?"

Julián Carax was no longer a pupil at San Gabriel's. His presence in the precinct, the classrooms, and even the gardens was strictly forbidden. His school items, textbooks, and all other belongings were now school property.

"The technical term is 'immediate and total expulsion,'" Father Romanones summed up.

"May I ask the reason?"

"I can think of a dozen, but I'm sure you'll know how to choose the most appropriate one. Good day, Carax. And good luck in your life. You're going to need it."

Some thirty yards away, in the fountain courtyard, a group of pupils was watching him. Some were laughing, waving good-bye. Others looked at him with pity and bewilderment. Only one smiled sadly: his friend Miquel Moliner, who simply nodded and silently mouthed some words that Julián thought he could read in the air: "See you on Sunday."

When he got back to the apartment on Ronda de San Antonio, Julián noticed Don Ricardo's Mercedes-Benz parked outside the hat shop. He stopped on the corner and waited. After a while Don Ricardo came out of his father's shop and got into the car. Julián hid in a doorway until the car had set off toward Plaza Universidad. Only then did he rush up the stairs to his home. His mother, Sophie, was waiting there, in floods of tears.

"What have you done, Julián?" she murmured without anger.

"Forgive me, Mother. . . ."

Sophie held her son close to her. She had lost weight and had aged, as if between them all they had stolen her life and her youth. *I more than anyone,* thought Julián.

"Listen to me carefully, Julián. Your father and Don Ricardo Aldaya have got everything set up to send you to the army in a few days' time. Aldaya has influences. . . . You have to go, Julián. You have to go where neither of them can find you. . . ."

Julián thought he saw a shadow in his mother's eyes that seemed to take hold of her.

"Is there anything else, Mother? Something you haven't told me?"

Sophie gazed at him with trembling lips. *"You must go. We must both go away from here forever."*

Julián held her tight and whispered in her ear, *"Don't worry about me, Mother. Don't you worry."*

Julián spent the Saturday shut up in his room, among his books and his drawing pads. The hatter had gone down to the shop just after dawn and didn't return until the early hours. *He doesn't have the courage to tell me to my face,* thought Julián. That night, his eyes blurred with tears, Julián said farewell to the years he had spent in that dark, cold room, lost amid dreams that he now knew would never come true. Sunday, at daybreak, armed with only a bag containing a few clothes and books, he kissed Sophie's forehead, as she lay curled under blankets in the dining room, and left. The streets seemed enveloped in a blue haze. Flashes of copper sparkled on the flat roofs of the old town. He walked slowly, saying good-bye to every door, to every street corner, wondering whether the illusions of time would turn out to be true and in days to come he would be able to remember only the good things, forget the solitude that had so often hounded him in those streets.

The Estación de Francia was deserted; the platforms, reflecting the burning light of dawn, curved off into the mist like glistening sabers. Julián sat on a bench under the vaulted ceiling and took out his book. He let the hours go by lost in the magic of words, shedding his skin and his name, feeling like another person. He allowed himself to be carried away by the dreams of shadowy characters, the only refuge left for him. By then he knew that Penélope wouldn't come. He knew he would board that train with no other company than his memories. When, just before noon, Miquel Mo-

278 · The Shadow of the Wind

liner arrived in the station and gave him his ticket and all the money he had been able to gather, the two friends embraced without a word. Julián had never seen Miquel Moliner cry. Clocks were everywhere, counting the minutes that flew by.

"There's still time," Miquel murmured with his eyes fixed on the station entrance.

At five past one, the stationmaster gave the last call for passengers traveling to Paris. The train had already started to slide along the platform when Julián turned around to say good-bye to his friend. Miquel Moliner stood there watching him, his hands sunk in his pockets.

"Write," he said.

"I'll write to you as soon as I get there," answered Julián.

"No. Not to me. Write books. Not letters. Write them for me, for Penélope."

Julián nodded, realizing only then how much he was going to miss his friend.

"And keep your dreams," said Miquel. "You never know when you might need them."

"Always," murmured Julián, but the roar of the train had already stolen his words.

"The night her mother caught them in my bedroom, Penélope told me what had happened. The following day Mrs. Aldaya called me and asked me what I knew about Julián. I said I didn't know anything, except that he was a nice boy, a friend of Jorge's. . . . She ordered me to keep Penélope in her room until she was given permission to come out. Don Ricardo was away in Madrid and didn't come back until early on Friday. As soon as he arrived, Mrs. Aldaya told him what she'd witnessed. I was there. Don Ricardo jumped up from his armchair and slapped his wife so hard she fell on the floor. Then, shouting like a madman, he told her to repeat what she had just said. Mrs. Aldaya was terrified. We had never seen Mr. Aldaya like that. Never. He looked as if he were possessed by all the devils in hell. Seething with anger, he went up to Penélope's bedroom and pulled her out of her bed, dragging her by the hair. I tried to stop him, but he kicked me aside. That same evening he called the family doctor and had him examine Penélope. When the doctor had finished, he spoke to Mr. Aldaya. They locked Penélope up in her room, and Mrs. Aldaya told me to collect my things.

"They didn't let me see Penélope. I never said good-bye to her. Don Ricardo threatened to report me to the police if I told anyone what had happened. That very night they threw me out, with nowhere to go, after eighteen years of uninterrupted service in the house. Two days later, in a *pensión* on Calle Muntaner, I had a visit from Miquel Moliner, who told me that Julián had gone to Paris. He wanted me to tell him what had happened, why Penélope hadn't come as arranged to the station. For weeks I returned to the house, begging for a chance to see her, but I wasn't even allowed to cross the gates. I would position myself on the opposite corner every day for days on end, hoping to see them come out. I never saw her. She didn't come out of the house. Later on, Mr. Aldaya called the police and, with the help of his high-powered friends, managed to get me committed to the lunatic asylum in Horta, claiming that nobody knew me, that I was some demented woman who harassed his family and children. I spent two years there, caged like an animal. The first thing I did when I got out was go to the house on Avenida del Tibidabo to see Penélope.

"Did you manage to see her?" Fermín asked.

"The house was locked and up for sale. Nobody lived there. I was told the Aldayas had gone to Argentina. I wrote to the address I was given. The letters were returned to me unopened. . . ."

"What happened to Penélope? Do you know?"

Jacinta shook her head, in a state of near collapse. "I never saw her again."

The old woman moaned and began to weep uncontrollably. Fermín held her in his arms and rocked her. Jacinta Coronado had shrunk to the size of a little girl, and next to her Fermín looked like a giant. I had questions burning in my head, but my friend signaled to me that the interview was over. I saw him gazing about him at that dirty, cold hovel where Jacinta Coronado was spending her last days.

"Come on, Daniel. We're leaving. You go first."

I did what I was told. As I walked away, I turned for a moment and saw Fermín kneel down by the old lady and kiss her on the forehead. She gave him a toothless smile.

"Tell me, Jacinta," I heard Fermín saying. "You like Sugus candies, don't you?"

. . . .

ON OUR CIRCUITOUS PATH BACK TO THE EXIT, WE PASSED THE REAL undertaker and his two cadaverous assistants carrying a cheap pine coffin, rope, and what looked suspiciously like a recycled shroud. The committee gave off a sinister smell of formaldehyde and cheap eau de cologne. The men's bloodless skin framed gaunt, canine smiles. Fermín pointed to the cell where the body of the deceased awaited and proceeded to bless the trio, who nodded respectfully and made the sign of the cross.

"Go in peace," mumbled Fermín, dragging me toward the exit, where a nun holding an oil lamp saw us off with a harsh, condemnatory look.

Once we were out of the building, the grim canyon of stone and shadow that was Calle Moncada seemed to me a valley of hope and glory. Fermín breathed deeply, with relief, and I knew I wasn't the only one to be rejoicing at having left that place behind. Jacinta's story weighed on our consciences more than we would have wished to admit.

"Listen, Daniel. What would you say to some ham croquettes and a couple of glasses of sparkling wine here in the Xampañet, just to take away the bad taste left in our mouths?"

"I wouldn't say no, quite frankly."

"Didn't you arrange to meet up with the girl today?"

"Tomorrow."

"Ah, you devil . . . you're playing hard to get, eh? We're learning fast. . . ."

We hadn't taken ten steps toward the noisy tavern, just a few doors down the street, when three silhouettes materialized out of the shadows and intercepted us. Two positioned themselves behind us, so close I could feel their breath on the nape of my neck. The third, smaller but much more menacing, blocked our way. It was him. He wore the usual raincoat, and his oily smile oozed irrepressible glee.

"Why, who have we here? If it's not my old friend, the man of the thousand faces!" cried Inspector Fumero.

It seemed to me I could hear all Fermín's bones shudder with terror at the apparition. My loquacious friend could manage only a stifled groan. The two thugs, who I guessed were two agents from the Crime Squad, grabbed us by the scruff of our necks and held our right wrists, ready to twist our arms at the slightest hint of a movement.

"I see from your look of surprise that you thought I'd lost track of you long ago, eh? Surely you didn't think a piece of shit like you was going to be able to crawl out of the gutter and pass for a decent citizen. You might be stupid, but not *that* stupid. Besides, I'm told you're poking your nose—and it's quite a nose—in a whole pile of things that are none of your business. That's a bad sign. . . . What is it with you and those little nuns? Are you having it off with one of them? How much do they charge these days?"

"I respect other people's asses, Inspector, especially if they are cloistered. Perhaps if you became inclined to do the same, you would save yourself a hefty bill in penicillin and improve the number and ease of your bowel movements."

Fumero let out a little laugh streaked with anger.

"That's right. Balls of steel. It's what I say. If all crooks were like you, my work would be a party. Tell me, what are you calling yourself these days, you little son of a bitch? Gary Cooper? Come on, tell me what you're up to, sticking that big nose of yours in the Hospice of Santa Lucía, and I might let you go with just a warning. Come, spell it out. What brings you two here?"

"A private matter. We came to visit a relative."

"Sure, your fucking mother. Look here, you happen to have caught me on a good day, otherwise I'd be taking you to headquarters and giving you another session with the welding torch. Come on, be a good boy and tell your pal Inspector Fumero the truth about what the fuck you and your friend are doing here. Damn it, just cooperate a bit, and you'll save me going over this smart little kid you've chosen as a sponsor."

"You touch a single hair of his and I swear that—"

"You scare me to bits, really. I just shat in my pants."

Fermín swallowed, as if to hold in all the courage that was seeping out of him. "Those wouldn't be the same sailor-boy pants that your esteemed mother, the Illustrious Kitchen Maid, made you wear? That would be a shame; I'm told the outfit really suited you."

Inspector Fumero's face paled, and all expression left his eyes. "What did you say, motherfucker?"

"I was saying it looks like you've inherited the taste and the charm of Doña Yvonne Sotoceballos, a high-society lady. . . ."

Fermín was not a heavy man, and the first punch was enough to knock him off his feet and into a puddle of water. He lay curled up in a ball as Fumero meted out a flurry of kicks to his stomach, kidneys, and face. I lost count after the fifth. Fermín lost his breath and then, a moment later, the ability to protect himself from the blows. The two policemen who were holding me down with iron hands were laughing dutifully.

"Don't you get involved," one of them whispered to me. "I don't feel like breaking your arm."

I tried in vain to wriggle out of his grip, and, as I struggled, I caught a glimpse of him. I recognized his face immediately. He was the man in the raincoat with the newspaper who was in the bar of Plaza de Sarriá a few days earlier, the same man who had followed us in the bus and laughed at Fermín's jokes.

"Look, the one thing that really pisses me off is people who stir up the shit from the past!" Fumero cried out. "Things from the past have to be left alone, do you understand? And that goes for you and your dumb friend. Look and learn, kid. You're next."

The whole time I watched Inspector Fumero destroy Fermín with his kicks under the slanted light of the streetlamp, I was unable to utter a word. I remember the dull, terrible impact of the blows raining down mercilessly on my friend. They hurt me still. All I did was take refuge in the policemen's convenient grasp, trembling and shedding silent tears of cowardice.

When Fumero tired of striking a dead weight, he opened up his raincoat, unzipped his fly, and began to urinate on Fermín. My friend didn't move; he looked like a bundle of old clothes in a puddle. While Fumero discharged his generous, steamy cascade over Fermín, I still couldn't speak. When he'd finished, the inspector zipped up his trousers and came over to me, sweaty-faced and panting. One of the police officers handed him a handkerchief, and he mopped his face and neck. He came closer, until his face was only a couple of inches from mine, and he fixed me with his stare.

"You weren't worth that beating, kid. That's the problem with your friend: he always backs the wrong side. Next time I'm going to fuck him up like I never have before, and I'm sure it's going to be your fault."

I thought he was going to hit me then, that my turn had come. For some reason I was glad. I wanted to believe that his blows would cure me of the shame I felt for not having raised a finger to help Fermín, when the only thing he was trying to do, as usual, was protect me.

But no blow came. All Fumero did was pat me on the cheek.

"It's okay, boy. I don't dirty my hands with cowards."

The two policemen chuckled, more relaxed now that they knew the show was over. Their desire to leave the scene was obvious. They went off laughing in the dark.

By the time I went to his aid, Fermín was trying in vain to get up and find the teeth he'd lost in the dirty water of the puddle. His mouth, nose, ears, and eyelids were all bleeding. When he saw that I was unharmed, he attempted to smile and I thought he was going to die on the spot. I knelt beside him and held him in my arms. The first thought that crossed my mind was that he weighed less than Bea.

"Fermín, for God's sake, we must get you to a hospital right away."

He shook his head energetically. "Take me to her."

"To who, Fermín?"

"To Bernarda. If I'm going to go, I'd rather it was in her arms."

· 32 ·

THAT NIGHT I RETURNED TO PLAZA REAL, TO THE APARTMENT that I'd sworn years ago I would never set foot in again. A couple of regulars who had witnessed the beating from the door of the Xampañet Tavern offered to help me take Fermín to a taxi rank in Calle Princesa while a waiter called the number I had given him, to give warning of our arrival. The taxi ride seemed endless. Fermín had lost consciousness before we set off. I held him in my arms, clutching him against my chest and trying to warm him up. I could feel his tepid blood soaking my clothes. I whispered in his ear that we were nearly there, that he was going to be all right. My voice trembled. The driver shot me furtive looks through the mirror.

"Listen, I don't want trouble, do you hear? If he dies, you get out."

"Just floor it and shut up."

By the time we reached Calle Fernando, Gustavo Barceló and Bernarda were waiting by the main door of the building, along with Dr. Soldevila. When she saw us covered in blood and dirt, Bernarda started to scream in panic. The doctor quickly took Fermín's pulse and assured us that the patient was alive. Between the four of us, we managed to carry Fermín up the stairs and into Bernarda's room, where a nurse, who had come along with the doctor, was getting everything ready. Once the patient was laid on the bed, the nurse began to undress him. Dr. Soldevila insisted that we all leave the room and let him get on with his work. He closed the door on us with a brief "He'll live."

In the corridor Bernarda sobbed inconsolably. She moaned that now that she'd found a good man, for the first time in her life, God came along and wrenched him away from her without mercy. Don Gustavo Barceló took her in his arms and led her to the kitchen, where he proceeded to ply her with brandy until the poor thing could hardly stand up. Once the maid's words became unintelligible, the bookseller poured a glass for himself and downed it in one gulp.

"I'm sorry. I didn't know where to go . . ." I began.

"That's all right. You've done the right thing. Soldevila is the best orthopedic surgeon in Barcelona." He spoke without addressing anyone in particular.

"Thank you," I murmured.

Barceló sighed and poured me a good shot of brandy in a tumbler. I declined his offer, and it was passed on to Bernarda, past whose lips it disappeared as if by magic.

"Will you please go and have a shower and put on some clean clothes," Barceló said. "If you go back home looking like that, your father will die of cardiac arrest."

"It's all right. . . . I'm okay," I said.

"In that case stop trembling. Go on, you can use my bathroom, it's got a water heater. You know the way. In the meantime I'm going to call your father and tell him . . . well, I don't know what I'll tell him. I'll think of something."

I nodded.

"This is still your home, Daniel," said Barceló as I wandered off down the corridor. "We've missed you."

I found Gustavo Barceló's bathroom, but not the light switch. I took off my filthy, bloodstained clothes and hauled myself into Gustavo Barceló's imperial bathtub. A pearly mist filtered in through the window that gave onto the inner courtyard of the building, with enough light to reveal the outline of the room and the pattern of the enameled tiles on the floor and walls. The water came out boiling hot and with much greater pressure than our modest bathroom on Calle Santa Ana could offer; it seemed worthy of a luxury hotel such as I'd never set foot in. I stood under the shower's steamy rays for a few minutes without moving.

The echo of the blows raining on Fermín still hammered in my ears. I couldn't get Fumero's words out of my mind, or the face of that policeman who had held me down. After a while I noticed that the water was beginning to get cold, and I assumed the reserve in my host's boiler was coming to an end. When I had finished the last drop of lukewarm water, I turned off the tap. The steam rose up my body like silk threads. Through the shower curtains, I noticed a still figure standing by the door, her marble gaze shining like the eyes of a cat.

"You can come out. There's nothing to worry about, Daniel. Despite all my evil doings, I still can't see you."

"Hello, Clara."

She held out a clean towel toward me. I stretched out my hand and took it, wrapping myself in it with the modesty of a schoolgirl. Even in the steamy darkness, I could see that Clara was smiling, guessing at my movements.

"I didn't hear you come in."

"I didn't call. Why are you taking a shower in the dark?"

"How do you know the light isn't on?"

"The buzzing of the bulb," she said. "You never came back to say good-bye."

Yes, I did come back, I thought, but you were very busy. The words died on my lips; their animosity seemed distant, ridiculous.

"I know. I'm sorry."

I got out of the shower and stood on the mat. The steamy air glowed with specks of silver, and the pale light from the window was a white veil on Clara's face. She hadn't changed a bit. Four years of absence had not helped me.

"Your voice has changed," she said. "Have you changed, too, Daniel?"

"I'm just as stupid as before, if that's what you're wondering."

And more of a coward, I thought. She still had that same broken smile that hurt, even in the dark. She stretched out her hand, and, just as on that afternoon in the Ateneo library some eight years before, I understood immediately. I guided her hand to my damp face and felt her fingers rediscovering me, her lips shaping words in silence.

"I never wanted to hurt you, Daniel. Forgive me."

I took her hand and kissed it in the dark. "No: you must forgive me."

Any possibility of a melodrama was shattered when Bernarda stuck her head around the door. Despite being quite drunk, she realized that I was naked, dripping, and holding Clara's hand against my lips with the light out.

"For the love of Christ, Master Daniel, have you no shame? Jesus, Mary, and Joseph. Some people never learn. . . ."

In her embarrassment Bernarda beat a retreat, and I hoped that once the effects of the brandy wore off, the memory of what she had seen would fade from her mind like the traces of a dream. Clara moved away a few steps and handed me the clothes she held under her left arm.

"My uncle gave me this suit for you to put on. It's from his younger days. He says you've grown a lot and it will fit you. I'll leave you, so you can get dressed. I shouldn't have come in without knocking."

I took the change of clothes she was offering me and started to put on the underwear, which was clean-smelling and warm, then the pale pink cotton shirt, the socks, the waistcoat, the trousers, and jacket. The mirror showed me a door-to-door salesman whose smile had abandoned him. When I returned to the kitchen, Dr. Soldevila had come out of the bedroom to give us all a bulletin on Femín's condition.

"For the moment the worst is over," he announced. "No need to worry. These things always look more serious than they are. Your friend has a broken left arm and two broken ribs, he's lost three teeth, and he presents a large number of bruises, cuts, and contusions. But luckily there's no internal bleeding and no symptoms of any brain lesion. The folded newspapers the patient wore under his clothes to keep him warm and accentuate his figure, as he puts it, served as armor and cushioned the blows. A few moments ago, when he recovered consciousness, the patient asked me to tell you that he's feeling like a twenty-year-old, that he wants blood sausage sandwiches with fresh garlic, a chocolate bar, and some lemon Sugus candies. I see no problem with that, though I think it would be better to start off with fruit juices, yogurt, and perhaps a bit of boiled rice. Moreover, as proof of his vigor and presence of mind, he has asked me to transmit to you that, when Nurse Amparito was putting a few stitches in his leg, he had an iceberg of an erection."

"It's just that he's very manly," Bernarda murmured apologetically.

"When will we be able to see him?" I asked.

"Not just yet. Perhaps by daybreak. It will do him good to rest a bit. Tomorrow, at the latest, I'd like him to be taken along to the Hospital del Mar so he can have a brain scan, just for our peace of mind. But I think we can rest assured that Mr. Romero de Torres will be as good as new within a few days. Judging from the marks and scars on his body, this man has got out of tighter spots. He's a true survivor. If you need a copy of the report to take along to the police—"

"It won't be necessary," I interrupted.

"Young man, let me warn you that this could have been very serious. You must report it to the police immediately."

Barceló was watching me attentively. I looked back at him, and he nodded.

"There'll be plenty of time for that, Doctor, don't worry," said Barceló. "What's important now is to make sure the patient is well. I myself will report this incident tomorrow morning, first thing. Even the authorities have a right to a little peace and quiet at night."

It was obvious that the doctor took a dim view of my suggestion to keep the incident from the police, but when he realized that Barceló was taking responsibility for the matter, he shrugged his shoulders and returned to the bedroom to continue with his treatments. As soon as the doctor had disappeared, Barceló told me to follow him to his study. Bernarda sighed on her stool, numb with brandy and shock.

"Bernarda, keep yourself busy. Make some coffee. Nice and strong."

"Yes, sir. Right away."

I followed Barceló to his study, a cave blanketed in clouds of tobacco smoke, which curled around columns of books and papers. Echoes of Clara's piano reached us in discordant spurts. It was obvious that Maestro Neri's lessons hadn't done much good, at least in the field of music. The bookseller pointed me to a chair and proceeded to fill his pipe.

"I've phoned your father and told him that Fermín had a minor accident and that you'd brought him here."

"Did he believe you?"

"I don't think so."

"Right."

The bookseller lit his pipe and sat back in the armchair behind his desk. At the other end of the apartment, Clara was tormenting Debussy. Barceló rolled his eyes.

"What happened to the music teacher?" I asked.

"He got fired. Seems like there were not enough keys on the piano to keep his fingers busy."

"Right."

"Are you sure you haven't had a beating too? You're being pretty monosyllabic. When you were a kid, you were much more talkative."

The study door opened, and Bernarda came in carrying a tray with two steaming cups of coffee and a sugar bowl. She was swaying from side to side as she walked, and I was afraid of getting caught under a shower of boiling-hot coffee.

"May I come in? Will you take yours with a dash of brandy, sir?"

"I think the bottle of Lepanto has earned itself a break for tonight, Bernarda. And you, too. Come on, off you go to sleep. Daniel and I will stay up in case anything is needed. Since Fermín is in your bedroom, you can use mine."

"Oh, no, sir, I wouldn't hear of it."

"It's an order. And no arguing. I want you to be asleep in the next five minutes."

"But, sir . . ."

"Bernarda, you're risking your Christmas bonus."

"Whatever you say, Mr. Barceló. But I'll sleep on top of the cover. That goes without saying."

Barceló waited ceremoniously for Bernarda to retire. He helped himself to seven lumps of sugar and began to stir the coffee with the spoon, his cat-like smile discernible behind dark clouds of Dutch tobacco.

"As you see, I must run my house with a firm hand."

"Yes, you're certainly a tough one, Don Gustavo."

"And you're a smooth talker. Tell me, Daniel, now that nobody can hear us. Why isn't it a good idea to report what has happened to the police?"

"Because they already know."

"You mean . . . ?"

I nodded.

"What kind of trouble are you two in, if you don't mind my asking?"

I sighed.

"Anything I can help with?"

I looked up. Barceló smiled at me without malice, for once putting aside his ironic stance.

"Does all this have, by some chance, anything to do with that book by Carax you didn't want to sell me when you should have?"

The question caught me totally by surprise.

"I could help you," he offered. "I have a surplus of what you both lack: money and common sense."

"Believe me, Don Gustavo, I've already got too many people involved in this business."

"One more won't make much difference, then. Come on, confide in me. Imagine that I'm your father confessor."

"I haven't been to confession for years."

"It shows on your face."

· 33 ·

GUSTAVO BARCELÓ HAD A WAY OF LISTENING THAT SEEMED BOTH contemplative and Solomonic, like a doctor or a pope. He observed me with his hands joined under his chin and his elbows on his desk, as if in prayer. His eyes were wide open, and he nodded here and there, as if he could detect symptoms in the flow of my narrative and was composing his own diagnosis. Every time I paused, the bookseller raised his eyebrows inquisitively and beckoned with his right hand for me to continue unraveling my jumbled story, which seemed to amuse him enormously. Every now and then, he would raise a hand and take notes, or he would stare into space as if he wanted to consider the implications of what I was telling him. More often than not, he would lick his lips and smile ironically, a gesture I attributed either to my ingenuousness or to the foolishness of my conjectures.

"Listen, if you think this is nonsense, I'll shut up."

"On the contrary. Fools talk, cowards are silent, wise men listen."

"Who said that? Seneca?"

"No. Braulio Recolons, who runs a pork butcher's on Calle Avignon and has a great talent for both making sausages and composing witty aphorisms. Please continue. You were telling me about this lively girl. . . ."

"Bea. And that is my business and has nothing to do with everything else."

Barceló tried to keep his laughter to himself. I was about to continue the narration of my adventures when Dr. Soldevila poked his head around the door of the study looking tired and out of breath.

"Please excuse me. I'm leaving now. The patient is well, and, for lack of a better expression, he's full of beans. This gentleman will outlive us all. He's even saying that the sedatives have gone to his head and given him a high. He refuses to rest and insists that he must have a word with Daniel about matters he has not wished to explain to me, claiming that he doesn't believe in the Hippocratic, or hypocritical, oath, as he calls it."

"We'll go and see him right away. And please forgive poor Fermín. He's obviously still in shock."

"Perhaps, but I wouldn't rule out shamelessness. There was no way of stopping him pinching the nurse's bottom and reciting rhymed couplets in praise of her firm and shapely thighs."

We escorted the doctor and his nurse to the door and thanked them effusively for their good offices. When we went into the bedroom, we discovered that, after all, Bernarda had challenged Barceló's orders and was lying next to Fermín on the bed. The fright, the brandy, and the exhaustion had finally sent her to sleep. Covered in bandages, dressings, and slings, Fermín held her tenderly, stroking her hair. His face carried a bruise that hurt to look at, and from it emerged his large, unharmed nose, two ears like sails, and the eyes of a dispirited mouse. His toothless smile, through lips covered in cuts, was triumphant, and he greeted us with his right hand raised in the sign of victory.

"How are you feeling, Fermín?" I asked.

"Twenty years younger," he said in a low voice, so as not to wake Bernarda.

"Stop pretending, damn it. You look like shit, Fermín. You scared me to death. Are you sure you're all right? Isn't your head spinning? Aren't you hearing voices?"

"Now you mention it, sometimes I thought I could hear a discordant and arrhythmic murmur, as if a macaque was trying to play the piano."

Barceló frowned. Clara went on tinkling at the piano in the distance.

"Don't worry, Daniel. I've survived worse sticks and stones. That guy Fumero can't even kick a bad habit."

"So the person who's sculpted you a new face is none other than Inspector Fumero," said Barceló. "I see you two move about in the highest circles."

"I hadn't got to that part of the story," I said.

Fermín looked at me in alarm.

"It's all right, Fermín. Daniel is filling me in about this little play that you two are taking part in. I must admit, it's all very interesting. What about you, Fermín, how are you on confessions? I warn you I spent two years in a seminary."

"I would have said at least three, Don Gustavo."

"Some things get lost along the way. Shame, for a start. This is the first time you come to my house, and you end up in bed with the maid."

"Look at her, poor little thing, my angel. You must understand that my intentions are honest, Don Gustavo."

"Your intentions are your business and Bernarda's. She's quite old enough. And now, let's be frank. What kind of charade are you involved in?"

"What have you told him, Daniel?"

"We got to act two: enter the femme fatale," Barceló explained.

"Nuria Monfort?" Fermín asked.

Barceló smacked his lips with delight. "But is there more than one? This sounds like *The Abduction from the Seraglio.*"

"Please lower your voice. My fiancée is present."

"Don't worry, your fiancée has half a bottle of brandy in her veins. The trumpets of doom wouldn't wake her. Go on, ask Daniel to tell me the rest. Three heads think better than two, especially if the third one is mine."

Fermín attempted to shrug his shoulders under dressings and slings. "I'm not against it, Daniel. It's your call."

Having resigned myself to have Don Gustavo on board, I continued with my narrative until I reached the point when Fumero and his men came upon us on Calle Moncada a few hours earlier. When the story ended, Barceló got up and began pacing up and down the room, pondering. Fermín and I observed him cautiously. Bernarda snored like a baby calf.

"Little angel," whispered Fermín, entranced.

"A few things have caught my attention," the bookseller said at last.

"Evidently Inspector Fumero is in this up to his neck, although how and why is something that escapes me. On the one hand, there's this woman—"

"Nuria Monfort."

"Then there's the business of Julián Carax's return to Barcelona and his murder in the streets of the city—after a month in which nobody knows anything about him. It's obvious that the woman is lying through her teeth. Even about the time of day."

"That's what I've been saying from the start," said Fermín, casting a glance at me. "Trouble is, some of us suffer from an excess of juvenile ardor and a lack of strategic grasp of the situation."

"Look who's talking: Saint John of the Cross."

"That's enough. Let's calm down and stick to the facts. There's one thing in Daniel's narrative that seemed very strange to me, even stranger than the rest of it. It has nothing to do with the gothic spin of this whole saga, but with an essential and apparently banal detail," Barceló said.

"Dazzle us, Don Gustavo."

"Well, here it is: this business about Carax's father refusing to identify Carax's body, claiming that he didn't have a son. That seems very odd to me. Almost unnatural. No father in the world would do that. Never mind the bad blood there might have been between them. Death does that: it makes everyone feel sentimental. When we stand in front of a coffin, we all see only what is good or what we want to see."

"What a great quote, Don Gustavo," Fermín said. "Do you mind if I add it to my repertoire?"

"There can always be exceptions," I objected. "From what we know, Mr. Fortuny was rather peculiar."

"All we know about him is thirdhand gossip," said Barceló. "When everyone is determined to present someone as a monster, there are two possibilities: either he's a saint or they themselves are not telling the whole story."

"The trouble is, you've taken a shining to the hatter just because he's dense," said Fermín.

"With all due respect to the profession, when the description of a rogue is based solely on the caretaker's statement, my first instinct is not to trust it."

"But that means we can't be sure of anything. Everything we know is, as you say, third-, or even fourth-hand. Caretakers or otherwise."

"Never trust he who trusts everyone," Barceló added.

"What an evening you're having, Don Gustavo," Fermín applauded. "Pearls of wisdom offered in abundance. Would that I had your crystalline insight—"

"The only crystalline thing in all this is that you need my help—logistical and probably monetary as well—if you're hoping to bring this Christmas play to a conclusion before Inspector Fumero reserves a suite for you in San Sebas Prison. Fermín, I assume you're with me?"

"I follow Daniel's orders. If he orders it, I'd even play the part of Baby Jesus."

"Daniel, what do you say?"

"You two are doing all the talking. What do you propose, Don Gustavo?"

"This is my plan: as soon as Fermín has recovered, you, Daniel, pay a casual visit to Nuria Monfort and put your cards on the table. You let her see that you know she's lied to you and that she's hiding something, a lot or a little—that remains to be seen."

"What for?"

"To see how she reacts. She won't say anything to you, of course. Or she'll lie to you again. The important thing is to thrust the *banderilla* into her—forgive the bullfighting image—to see where the bull will lead us or, should I say, the young heifer. And that's where you come in, Fermín. While Daniel is sticking his neck out, you position yourself discreetly where you can keep watch on the suspect and wait for her to take the bait. Once she's done that, you follow her."

"You're assuming she's going to go somewhere," I protested.

"O ye of little faith! She will. Sooner or later. And something tells me that in this case it will be sooner rather than later. It's the basis of feminine psychology."

"And in the meantime, what are you planning to do, Dr. Freud?" I asked.

"That's my business, and in good time you'll know. And you'll thank me for it."

I looked for reassurance in Fermín's eyes, but the poor man had slowly been falling asleep hugging Bernarda while Barceló was drawing up his triumphant plan. Fermín's head was tilted to one side, and dribble was leaking onto his chest from the edge of a beatific smile. Bernarda was snoring loudly.

"I do hope this one proves good," Barceló murmured.

"Fermín is a great guy," I said.

"He must be, because I don't think he can have won her over with his looks. Come on, let's go."

We turned out the light and left the room quietly, closing the door and leaving the two lovers in the hands of sleep. I thought I could see the first glimmer of daybreak through the gallery windows at the end of the corridor.

"Suppose I say no," I said in a low voice. "Suppose I tell you to forget this."

Barceló smiled. "Too late, Daniel. You should have sold me that book years ago, when you had the chance."

Day was dawning when I reached home, dragging myself in that absurd loaned suit through damp streets that shone with a scarlet hue. I found my father asleep in his dining-room armchair, with a blanket over his legs and his favorite book open in his hands—a copy of Voltaire's *Candide,* which he reread a couple of times a year, the only times I heard him laugh heartily. I observed him: his hair was gray, thinning, and the skin on his face had begun to sag around his cheekbones. I looked at that man whom I had once imagined almost invincible; he now seemed fragile, defeated without knowing it. Perhaps we were both defeated. I leaned over to cover him with the blanket he had been promising to give away to charity for years, and I kissed his forehead, as if by doing so I could protect him from the invisible threads that kept him away from me, from that tiny apartment, and from my memories, as if I believed that with that kiss I could deceive time and convince it to pass us by, to return some other day, some other life.

· 34 ·

I SPENT NEARLY ALL MORNING DAYDREAMING IN THE BACK ROOM, conjuring up images of Bea. I visualized her naked skin under my hands, and it seemed to me that I could almost savor her sweet breath. I caught myself remembering with maplike precision every contour of her body, the glistening of my saliva on her lips and on that line of fair hair, so fair it was almost transparent, that ran down her belly and that my friend Fermín, in his improvised lectures on carnal logistics, liked to call "the little road to Jerez."

I looked at my watch for the umpteenth time and realized to my horror that there were still a few hours to go before I could see, and touch, Bea. I tried to sort out the month's invoices, but the rustle of the sheets of paper reminded me of the sound of underwear slipping down the pale hips and thighs of Doña Beatriz Aguilar, sister of my childhood friend.

"Daniel, you've got your head in the clouds. Is anything worrying you? Is it Fermín?" my father asked.

I nodded, ashamed of myself. My best friend had lost a few ribs to save my skin a few hours earlier, and all I could think of was the fastener of a bra.

"Speaking of the devil . . ."

I raised my eyes, and there he was. Fermín Romero de Torres, the one and only, wearing his best suit and with that ragged posture of a cheap cigar.

He was coming in through the shop door with a victorious smile and a fresh carnation in his lapel.

"But what are you doing here? Weren't you supposed to be resting?"

"Rest takes care of itself. I'm a man of action. And if I'm not here, you two won't even sell a catechism."

Ignoring the doctor's advice, Fermín had come along determined to take up his post again. His face was yellow and covered in bruises; he limped badly and moved like a broken puppet.

"You're going straight to bed, Fermín, for God's sake," said my horrified father.

"Wouldn't hear of it. Statistics prove it: more people die in bed than in the trenches."

All our protests went unheeded. After a while my father gave in, because something in poor Fermín's eyes suggested that even though his bones hurt him terribly, the prospect of being alone in his *pensión* room was even more painful.

"All right, but if I see you lifting anything besides a pencil, I'll give you an earful."

"Yes, sir! You have my word of honor that I won't even lift a finger."

Fermín proceeded to put on his blue overalls and arm himself with a rag and a bottle of alcohol. He set himself up behind the counter, planning to clean the covers and spines of the fifteen secondhand books that had arrived that morning. They were all copies of a much-sought-after title, *The Three-Cornered Hat: A History of the Civil Guard in Alexandrine Verse,* by the exceedingly young graduate Fulgencio Capón, acclaimed as a prodigy by critics all over the country. While he devoted himself to his task, Fermín kept throwing me surreptitious looks, winking like a scheming devil.

"Your ears are as red as peppers, Daniel."

"It must be from hearing you talk so much nonsense."

"Or from the fever that's gripped you. When are you seeing the young maid?"

"None of your business."

"You look really bad. Are you avoiding spicy food? Hot spices are fatal; they dilate your blood vessels."

"Piss off."

It was going to be a long, miserable day.

THE AFTERNOON WAS CLOSING IN WHEN THE SUBWAY TRAIN LEFT ME AT the foot of Avenida del Tibidabo. I could distinguish the shape of the blue tram, moving away through folds of violet mist. I decided not to wait for its return but to make my way on foot in the twilight. Soon I discerned the outline of The Angel of Mist. I pulled out the key Bea had given me and opened the small door within the gate. I stepped into the property, leaving the door almost closed, so that it looked shut but was ready to be opened by Bea. I had arrived early deliberately. I knew that Bea would take at least half an hour or forty-five minutes more. I wanted to feel the presence of the house on my own and explore it before Bea arrived and made it hers. I stopped for a moment to look at the fountain and the hand of the angel rising from the waters that were tinted scarlet. The accusing index finger seemed sharp as a dagger. I went up to the edge of the bowl. The sculpted face, with no eyes and no soul, quivered beneath the water.

I walked up the wide staircase that led to the entrance. The main door was slightly ajar. I felt a pang of anxiety, because I thought I'd closed it when I left the place the other night. I examined the lock, which didn't seem to have been tampered with, and came to the conclusion that I must have forgotten to close the door. I pushed it gently inward, and felt the breath from inside the house brushing my face, a whiff of burned wood, damp, and dead flowers. I pulled out a box of matches I'd picked up before leaving the bookshop and knelt down to light the first of the candles Bea had left. A copper-colored bubble lit up in my hands and revealed the dancing shapes of the walls that wept with tears of dampness, the fallen ceilings and dilapidated doors.

I proceeded to the second candle and lit it. Slowly, almost ritualistically, I followed the trail of the candles and lit them one by one, conjuring up a halo of amber light that seemed to float in the air like a cobweb trapped between mantles of impenetrable darkness. My journey ended by the sitting-room fireplace, by the blankets that were still lying on the floor, stained with ash. I sat there, facing the rest of the room. I had expected silence, but the house exhaled a thousand sounds. The creaking of wood, the brush of the wind over the roof tiles, a thousand and one tapping sounds inside the walls, under the floor, moving from place to place.

After about thirty minutes, I noticed that the cold and the dark were beginning to make me feel drowsy. I stood up and began to walk up and down the room to get warm. There was only the charred husk of a log in the hearth. By the time Bea arrived, the temperature inside the old mansion would have gone down enough to chill from my mind the feverish ideas I had been harboring for days and fill me with pure and chaste thoughts. Having found an aim more practical than the contemplation of the ruins of time, I picked up one of the candles and set off to explore the house in search of something to burn.

My notions of Victorian literature suggested that the most logical place to begin searching was the cellar, which must have once housed the cookers and a great coal bunker. With this idea in mind, I spent almost five minutes trying to find a door or staircase leading to the lower floor. I chose a large door made of carved wood, at the end of a passage. It looked like a piece of exquisite cabinetmaking, with reliefs in the shape of angels and a large cross in the center. The handle was in the middle of the door, under the cross. I tried unsuccessfully to turn it. The mechanism was probably jammed or simply ruined by rust. The only way that door would yield would be by forcing it open with a crowbar or knocking it down with an ax, alternatives I quickly ruled out. I studied the large piece of wood by candlelight and thought that somehow it looked more like a sarcophagus than a door. I wondered what was hidden behind it.

A closer examination of the carved angels discouraged me from looking any further, and I left the place. I was about to give up my search for a way down to the cellar when, by chance, I came across a tiny door at the other end of the passage, which at first I took for the door of a broom closet. I tested the doorknob, and it gave way instantly. On the other side, a steep staircase plunged into a pool of blackness. A powerful smell of wet earth hit me. It seemed a strangely familiar smell, and as I stood there with my eyes on the black well in front of me, I was seized by a memory I had kept since my childhood, buried behind curtains of fear.

A rainy afternoon on the eastern slope of Montjuïc, looking at the sea through a forest of incomprehensible mausoleums, a forest of crosses and gravestones carved with skulls and faces of children with no lips or eyes, a place that stank of death; and the silhouettes of about twenty adults that I could remember only as black suits that were dripping with rain, and my father's hand holding mine too tightly, as if by doing so he could stop his weeping, while a priest's empty words fell into that marble tomb into which three faceless gravediggers pushed a gray coffin. The downpour slithered like melted wax over the coffin, and I thought I heard my mother's voice calling me from within, begging me to free her from that prison of stone and darkness, but all I could do was tremble and ask my father in a voiceless whisper not to hold my hand so tight, tell him he was hurting me, and that smell of fresh earth, earth of ash and rain, was devouring everything, a smell of death and emptiness.

I opened my eyes and went down the steps almost blindly, because the light from the candle dispelled only an inch or two of darkness. When I reached the bottom, I held the candle up high and looked about me. I found no kitchen, no closet full of dry wood. A narrow passage extended before me, ending in a semicircular chamber. In the chamber stood a figure, its face lined with tears of blood from two hollow eyes, its arms unfolded like wings and a serpent of thorns sprouting from its temples. I felt an icy cold stabbing me in the nape of the neck. At some point I regained my composure and realized I was staring at an effigy of Christ carved in wood on the wall of a chapel. I stepped forward a few yards and beheld a ghostly sight. A dozen naked female torsos were piled up in one corner of the old chapel. Their heads and arms were missing, and they were supported by tripods. Each one was shaped differently, replicating the figures of women of varying ages and constitutions. On their bellies were words written in charcoal: "Isabel, Eugenia, Penélope." For once my Victorian reading came to the rescue, and I realized that what I was beholding was none other than the remains of an old custom no longer in use, the echo of an era when the homes of the wealthy had mannequins made to measure for different members of the family, used for tailoring their dresses and trousseaux. Despite Christ's threatening, grim look, I could not resist the temptation of stretching out my hand and touching the torso with Penélope Aldaya's name written on it.

At that moment I thought I heard footsteps on the floor above. I imagined that Bea had arrived and was wandering through the old mansion, looking for me. Relieved, I left the chapel and made my way back to the staircase. I was about to go up when I noticed that at the other end of the corridor there was a boiler and a central heating system that seemed to be in good order. It seemed incongruent with the rest of the cellar. I remembered Bea's mentioning that the estate agency, which for years had tried to sell the Aldaya mansion, had carried out some renovation work, hoping to attract potential buyers. I went up to examine the contraption more closely and saw that it consisted of a radiator system fed by a small boiler. At my feet I found a few pails full of charcoal, bits of plywood, and a few tins that I presumed must contain kerosene. I opened the boiler latch and had a look inside. Everything seemed to be in order. The idea of being able to get that old machine to work after so many years struck me as a bit far-fetched, but that didn't stop me filling the boiler with bits of charcoal and wood and spraying them with a good shower of kerosene. While I was doing this, I thought I heard the creaking of old wood, and for a moment I turned my head to look behind me. Suddenly I had a vision of bloodstained thorns being pulled out of the wood, and as I faced the darkness, I was afraid of seeing the figure of Christ emerge only a few steps away, coming toward me with a wolfish smile.

When I put the candle to it, the boiler lit up with a sudden blaze that provoked a metallic roar. I closed the latch and moved back a few steps, becoming increasingly unsure about the soundness of my plan. The boiler appeared to be drawing with some difficulty, so I decided to return to the ground floor and check whether my efforts were yielding any practical results. I went up the stairs and returned to the large room, hoping to find Bea there, but there was no trace of her. I calculated that an hour must have passed since my arrival, and my fear that the object of my desires might never turn up grew more acute. To kill that anxiety, I decided to continue with my plumbing and set off in search of radiators that might confirm whether the resurrection of the boiler had been a success. All the ones I found proved resistant to my hopes; they were icy cold. But then, in a small room of no more than four or five square yards, a bathroom that I supposed must be situated immediately above the boiler, I could feel a little warmth. I knelt down and realized joyfully that the floor tiles were lukewarm. That is how Bea found me, crouching on the floor, feeling the tiles of the bathroom like an idiot, with an asinine smile plastered on my face.

WHEN I LOOK BACK AND TRY TO RECONSTRUCT THE EVENTS OF THAT night in the Aldaya mansion, the only excuse that occurs to me that might justify my behavior is to allege that when you're eighteen, in the absence of subtlety and greater experience, an old bathroom can seem like paradise. It only took me a couple of minutes to persuade Bea that we should take the blankets from the sitting room and lock ourselves in that minute bathroom, with only two candles and some bathroom fittings that looked like museum pieces. My main argument—climatological—soon convinced Bea, the warmth that emanated from those floor tiles making her put aside her initial fear that my crazy invention might burn the house down. Later, in the reddish half-light of the candles, as I undressed her with trembling fingers, she smiled, her eyes searching mine and proving that then and forever afterward anything that might occur to me had already occurred to her.

I remember her sitting with her back against the closed door of that room, her arms hanging down beside her, the palms of her hands opened toward me. I remember how she held her face up, defiant, while I stroked her throat with the tips of my fingers. I remember how she took my hands and placed them on her breasts, and how her eyes and lips quivered when, enraptured, I took her nipples between my fingers and squeezed them, how she slid down to the floor while I searched out her belly with my lips and her white thighs received me.

"Had you ever done this before, Daniel?"

"In dreams."

"Seriously."

"No. Had you?"

"No. Not even with Clara Barceló?"

I laughed. Probably at myself. "What do you know about Clara Barceló?"

"Nothing."

"I know less than nothing," I said.

"I don't believe you."

I leaned over her and looked into her eyes. "I have never done this with anybody."

Bea smiled. My hand found its way between her thighs, and I threw myself on her, searching her lips, convinced by now that cannibalism was the supreme incarnation of wisdom.

"Daniel?" said Bea in a tiny voice.

"What?" I asked.

The answer never came to her lips. Suddenly a shaft of cold air whistled under the door, and in that endless moment before the wind blew out all the candles, our eyes met and we felt that the passion of that moment had been shattered. An instant was enough for us to know that there was somebody on the other side of the door. I saw fear sketched on Bea's face, and a second later we were covered in darkness. The bang on the door came later. Brutal, like a steel fist hammering on the door, almost pulling it off its hinges.

I felt Bea's body jump in the dark, and I put my arms around her. We moved to the other end of the room just before the second blow hit the door, throwing it with tremendous force against the wall. Bea screamed and shrank back against me. For a moment all I could see was the blue mist that crept up from the corridor and the snakes of smoke from the candles as they were blown out, rising in a spiral. The doorframe cast fanglike shadows, and I thought I saw an angular figure in the threshold of darkness.

I peered into the corridor, fearing, or perhaps hoping, that I would find only a stranger, a tramp who had ventured into the ruined mansion looking for shelter on an unpleasant night. But there was no one there, only ribbons of blue air that seemed to blow in through the windows. Huddled in a corner of the room, trembling, Bea whispered my name.

"There's nobody here," I said. "Perhaps it was a gust of wind."

"The wind doesn't beat on doors, Daniel. Let's go."

I went back to the room and gathered up our clothes.

"Here, get dressed. We'll go and have a look."

"We'd better leave."

"Yes, right away. I just want to check one thing."

We dressed hurriedly in the dark. In a matter of seconds, we could see our breath forming puffs in the air. I picked up one of the candles from the floor and lit it again. A draft of cold air glided through the house, as if someone had opened doors and windows.

"You see? It's the wind."

Bea shook her head but kept silent. We made our way back toward the sitting room, shielding the flame with our hands. Bea followed close behind me, holding her breath.

"What are we looking for, Daniel?"

"It'll only take a minute."

"No, let's leave right away."

"All right."

We turned to walk toward the exit, and it was then that I noticed. The large sculpted door at the end of a corridor, which I had tried unsuccessfully to open, was ajar.

"What's the matter?" asked Bea.

"Wait for me here."

"Daniel, please . . ."

I walked down the corridor, holding the candle that flickered in gusts of cold air. Bea sighed and followed me reluctantly. I stopped in front of the door. Marble steps were just visible, descending into the darkness. I started to go down them. Petrified, Bea stood at the entrance holding the candle.

"Please, Daniel, let's go now. . . ."

I descended, step by step, to the bottom of the staircase. The ghostly aura from the candle that was raised behind me seemed to scratch at the shape of a rectangular room, made of bare stone walls that were covered in crucifixes. The icy cold in that chamber took my breath away. Before me stood a marble slab, and on top of it I saw what looked like two similar white objects in different sizes, lined up one next to the other. They reflected the tremor of the candle with more intensity than the rest of the room, and I guessed they were made of lacquered wood. I took one more step forward, and only then did I understand. The two objects were white coffins. One of them was scarcely two feet long. I felt a shiver. It was a child's sarcophagus. I was in a crypt.

Without realizing what I was doing, I got closer to the marble stone until I was near enough to stretch out my hand and touch it. I then noticed that on each coffin a cross and a name had been carved. A blanket of ash obscured them. I put my hand on one of the coffins, the larger one. Slowly, almost in a trance, without stopping to think what I was doing, I brushed off the ashes that covered the lid. I could barely read the words in the dim red candlelight.

†

PENÉLOPE ALDAYA

1902—1919

I froze. Something or somebody was moving about in the dark. I could feel the cold air sliding down my skin, and only then did I retreat a few steps.

"Get out of here," murmured a voice in the shadows.

I recognized him immediately. Laín Coubert. The voice of the devil.

I charged up the stairs, and as soon as I reached the ground floor, I grabbed Bea by the arm and dragged her as fast as I could toward the exit. We had lost the candle and were running blindly. Bea was frightened and unable to comprehend my sudden alarm. She hadn't seen anything. She hadn't heard anything. I didn't pause to give her an explanation. I expected that at any moment something would jump out from the shadows and block our way, but the main door was waiting for us at the end of the corridor, forming a rectangle of light around the cracks in the doorframe.

"It's locked," Bea whispered.

I felt my pockets for the key. I turned my head for a fraction of a second and was sure that two shining points were slowly advancing toward us from the other end of the passageway. Eyes. My fingers found the key. I inserted it desperately into the lock, opened the door, and pushed Bea out roughly. Bea must have sensed the fear in me, because she rushed toward the gate in the garden and didn't stop until we were both on the pavement of Avenida del Tibidabo, breathless and covered in cold sweat.

"What happened down there, Daniel? Was there someone there?"

"No."

"You look pale."

"I've always been pale. Come on. Let's go."

"What about the key?"

I had left it inside, stuck in the lock. I felt no desire to go back and look for it.

"I think I dropped it on the way out. We'll look for it some other day."

We walked briskly away down the avenue, crossed over to the other side, and did not slow down until we were a good hundred yards from the mansion and its outline could hardly be distinguished in the dark. It was then I noticed that my hand was still stained with ashes. I was thankful for the mantle of the night, for it concealed the tears of terror running down my cheeks.

WE DESCENDED CALLE BALMES TO PLAZA NÚÑEZ DE ARCE, WHERE WE found a solitary taxi. As we drove down Balmes to Consejo de Ciento, we hardly spoke a word. Bea held my hand, and a couple of times I caught her gazing at me with glassy, impenetrable eyes. I leaned over to kiss her, but she didn't part her lips.

"When will I see you again?"

"I'll call you tomorrow, or the next," she said.

"Do you promise?"

She nodded.

"You can call me at home or at the bookshop. It's the same number. You have it, don't you?"

She nodded again. I asked the driver to stop for a moment on the corner of Muntaner and Diputación. I offered to see Bea to her front door, but she refused and walked away without letting me kiss her again, or even brush her hand. She started to run as I looked on from the taxi. The lights were on in the Aguilars' apartment, and I could clearly see my friend Tomás watching me from his bedroom window, where we had spent so many afternoons together chatting or playing chess. I waved at him, forcing a smile that he probably could not see. He didn't return the greeting. He remained static, glued to the windowpane, gazing at me coldly. A few seconds later, he moved away and the window went dark. He was waiting for us, I thought.

· *35* ·

W HEN I GOT HOME, I FOUND THE REMAINS OF A DINNER FOR
two on the table. My father had already gone to bed, and I won-
dered whether, by chance, he had plucked up the courage to invite Mer-
ceditas around for dinner. I tiptoed off toward my room and went in
without turning on the light. The moment I sat on the edge of the mattress,
I realized there was someone else in the room, lying on the bed in the dark
like a dead body with his hands crossed over his chest. I felt an icy spasm in
my stomach, but soon I recognized the snoring, and the profile of that in-
comparable nose. I turned on the light on the bedside table and found Fer-
mín Romero de Torres lying on the bedspread, lost in a blissful dream and
moaning gently with pleasure. I sighed, and the sleeper opened his eyes.
When he saw me, he looked surprised. He was obviously expecting some
other company. He rubbed his eyes and looked about him, taking in his sur-
roundings more closely.

"I hope I didn't scare you. Bernarda says that when I'm asleep, I look like
a Spanish Boris Karloff."

"What are you doing on my bed, Fermín?"

He half closed his eyes with longing.

"Dreaming of Carole Lombard. We were in Tangier, in some Turkish baths, and I was covering her in oil, the sort they sell for babies' bottoms. Have you ever covered a woman with oil, from head to toe, completely and meticulously?"

"Fermín, it's half past midnight, and I'm dead on my feet."

"Please forgive me, Daniel. It's just that your father insisted that I come up and have dinner with him, and afterward I felt terribly drowsy. Beef has a narcotic effect on me, you see. Your father suggested that I lie down here for a while, insisting that you wouldn't mind. . . ."

"And I don't mind, Fermín. It's just that you've caught me by surprise. Keep the bed and go back to Carole Lombard; she must be waiting for you. And get under the sheets. It's a foul night, and if you stay on top you'll catch something. I'll go to the dining room."

Fermín nodded meekly. The bruises on his face were beginning to swell up, and his head, covered with two days of stubble and that sparse hair, looked like some ripe fruit fallen from a tree. I took a blanket from the chest of drawers and handed another one to Fermín. Then I turned off the light and went back to the dining room, where my father's favorite armchair awaited me. I wrapped myself in the blanket and curled up, as best I could, convinced that I wouldn't sleep a wink. The image of the two white coffins in the dark was branded on my mind. I closed my eyes and did my best to delete the sight. In its place I conjured up the image of Bea in the bathroom, lying naked on the blankets, in candlelight. As I abandoned myself to these thoughts, it seemed to me that I could hear the distant murmur of the sea, and I wondered whether, without my knowing it, I had already succumbed to sleep. Perhaps I was sailing toward Tangier. Soon I realized that the sound was only Fermín's snoring. A moment later the world was turned off. In all my life, I've never slept so well or so deeply as that night.

MORNING CAME, AND IT WAS POURING. STREETS WERE FLOODED, AND the rain beat angrily against the windows. The telephone rang at seven-thirty. I jumped out of the armchair to answer, with my heart in my mouth.

Fermín, in a bathrobe and slippers, and my father, holding the coffeepot, exchanged that look I was already growing used to.

"Bea?" I whispered into the receiver, with my back to them.

I thought I heard a sigh on the line.

"Bea, is that you?"

There was no answer, and a few seconds later the line went dead. I stayed there for a minute, staring at the telephone, hoping it would ring again.

"They'll call back, Daniel. Come and have some breakfast now," said my father.

She'll call again later, I told myself. Someone must have caught her phoning. It couldn't be easy to break Mr. Aguilar's curfew. There was no reason to be alarmed. With this and other excuses, I dragged myself to the table to pretend I was going to have breakfast with Fermín and my father. It might have been the rain, but the food had lost all its flavor.

It rained all morning. Shortly after we opened the bookshop, there was a general power cut in the whole neighborhood that lasted until noon.

"That's all we needed," sighed my father.

At three the first leaks began. Fermín offered to go up to Merceditas's apartment to borrow some buckets, dishes, or any other hollow receptacle. My father strictly forbade him to go. The deluge persisted. To alleviate my nervousness, I told Fermín what had happened the day before, though I kept to myself what I'd seen in the crypt. Fermín listened with fascination, but despite his insistence, I refused to describe to him the consistency, texture, and shape of Bea's breasts. The day wore slowly on.

After dinner, on the pretext of going out to stretch my legs, I left my father reading and walked up to Bea's house. When I got there, I stopped on the corner to look up at the large windows of the apartment. I asked myself what I was doing. Spying, meddling, or making a fool of myself were some of the answers that went through my mind. Even so, as lacking in dignity as in appropriate clothes for such icy weather, I took shelter from the wind in a doorway on the other side of the street for about half an hour, watching the windows and seeing the silhouettes of Mr. Aguilar and his wife as they passed by. But not a trace of Bea.

It was almost midnight when I got back home, shivering with cold and carrying the world on my shoulders. She'll call tomorrow, I told myself a thousand times while I tried to fall asleep. Bea didn't call the next day. Or the next. She didn't call that whole week, the longest and the last of my life.

IN SEVEN DAYS' TIME, I WOULD BE DEAD.

ONLY SOMEONE WHO HAS BARELY A WEEK LEFT TO LIVE COULD waste his time the way I wasted mine during those days. All I did was watch over the telephone and gnaw at my soul, so much a prisoner of my own blindness that I wasn't even capable of guessing what destiny was already taking for granted. On Monday at noon, I went over to the Literature Faculty in Plaza Universidad, hoping to see Bea. I knew she wouldn't be amused if I turned up there and we were seen together, but facing her anger was preferable to continuing with my uncertainty.

I asked in the office for Professor Velázquez's lecture room and decided to wait for the students to come out. I waited for about twenty minutes, until the doors opened and I saw the arrogant, well-groomed countenance of Professor Velázquez, as usual surrounded by his small group of female admirers. Five minutes later there was still no sign of Bea. I decided to walk up to the door of the lecture room and take a look. A trio of girls were huddled together like a Sunday-school group, chatting and exchanging either lecture notes or secrets. The one who seemed like the leader of the congregation noticed my presence and interrupted her monologue to fire me an inquisitive look.

"I'm sorry. I'm looking for Beatriz Aguilar. Do you know whether she comes to this class?"

The girls traded venomous glances.

"Are you her fiancé?" one of them asked. "The officer?"

I smiled blankly, and they took this to mean agreement. Only the third girl smiled back at me, shyly, averting her eyes. The other two were more forward, almost defiant.

"I imagined you different," said the one who seemed to be the head commando.

"Where's the uniform?" asked the second in command, observing me with suspicion.

"I'm on leave. Do you know whether she's already left?"

"Beatriz didn't come to class today," the chief informed me.

"Oh, didn't she?"

"No," confirmed the suspicious lieutenant. "If you're her fiancé, you should know."

"I'm her fiancé, not a Civil Guard."

"Come on, let's go, this guy's a twit," the chief said.

They both walked past me, eyeing me sideways with disdain. The third one lagged behind. She stopped for a moment before leaving and, making quite sure the others didn't see her, whispered in my ear, "Beatriz didn't come on Friday either."

"Do you know why?"

"You're not her fiancé, are you?"

"No. Only a friend."

"I think she's ill."

"Ill?"

"That's what one of the girls who phoned her said. Now I must go."

Before I was able to thank her for her help, the girl went off to join the other two, who were waiting for her with withering looks at the far end of the cloister.

"DANIEL, SOMETHING MUST HAVE HAPPENED. A GREAT-AUNT HAS DIED, or a parrot has got the mumps, or she's caught a cold from so much going around without enough clothes to cover her bum—goodness knows what.

Contrary to what you firmly believe, the earth does not revolve around the desires of your crotch. Other factors influence the evolution of mankind."

"You think I'm not aware of that? You don't seem to know me, Fermín."

"My dear, if God had wished to give me wider hips, I might even have given birth to you: that's how well I know you. Pay attention to me. Throw off those thoughts and get some fresh air. Waiting is the rust of the soul."

"So I seem absurd to you."

"No. You seem fretful. I know that at your age these things look like the end of the world, but everything has a limit. Tonight you and I are going on a binge in a club on Calle Platería, which is apparently all the rage. I hear there are some new Scandinavian girls straight from Ciudad Real that are real knockouts. It's on me."

"And what will Bernarda say?"

"The girls are for you. I'll be waiting in the hall, reading a magazine and looking at the nice bundles of stuff from afar, because I'm a convert to monogamy, if not *in mentis,* at least de facto."

"I'm very grateful, Fermín, but—"

"A young boy of eighteen who refuses such an offer is not in his right mind. Something must be done immediately. Here."

He searched in his pockets and handed me some coins. I wondered whether that was the enormous sum with which he was going to finance the visit to the sumptuous seraglio of Iberian nymphs.

"With this we won't even get a 'Good evening,' Fermín."

"You're one of those people who fall off a tree and never quite reach the ground. Do you really think that I'm going to take you to a whorehouse and bring you back, covered with gonorrhea, to your dear father, who is the saintliest man I have ever met? I told you about the chicks to see whether you'd react, appealing to the only part of your person that seems to be in working order. This is for you to go to the telephone on the corner and call your beloved with a bit of privacy."

"Bea told me quite clearly not to phone her."

"She also told you she'd call you on Friday. It's already Monday. It's up to you. It is one thing to believe in women, and another to believe what they say."

Convinced by his arguments, I slipped out of the bookshop, walked over to the public telephone on the street corner, and dialed the Aguilars' number. At the fifth ring, someone lifted the telephone on the other end and listened in silence, without answering. Five eternal seconds went by.

"Bea?" I murmured. "Is that you?"

The voice that answered struck my stomach like a hammer.

"You son of a bitch, I swear I'm going to beat your brains out."

It was the steely tone of pure, contained anger. Icy and serene. That is what scared me most. I could picture Mr. Aguilar holding the telephone in the entrance hall of his apartment, the same one I had often used to call my father and tell him I would be late because I'd spent the afternoon with Tomás. I stayed where I was, listening to the breathing of Bea's father, dumb, wondering whether he'd recognized my voice.

"I see you don't even have the balls to talk, you swine. Any little shit is capable of doing what you've done, but a man would at least have the guts to show his face. I would die of shame if I thought that a seventeen-year-old girl was ballsier than me—because she hasn't revealed your name and she's not going to. I know her. And since you don't have the courage to show your face for Beatriz's sake, she's going to have to pay for what you've done."

When I hung up, my hands were shaking. I wasn't conscious of what I'd done until I left the booth and dragged my feet back toward the bookshop. I hadn't stopped to consider that my call would only make things worse for Bea. My only concern had been to remain anonymous and hide my face, disowning those whom I professed to love and whom I only used. I had done this already when Inspector Fumero had beaten up Fermín. I had done it again when I'd abandoned Bea to her fate. I would do it again as soon as circumstances provided me with another opportunity. I stayed out on the street for ten minutes, trying to calm down before returning to the bookshop. Perhaps I should call again and tell Mr. Aguilar that yes, it was me. That I was crazy about his daughter, end of story. If he then felt like coming by in his general's uniform and beating me up, he had every right to do so.

I was on my way back when I noticed that somebody was watching me from a doorway on the other side of the street. At first I thought it was Don Federico, the watchmaker, but a quick glance was enough to make me realize this was a taller, more solid-looking individual. I stopped to return his gaze, and, to my surprise, he nodded, as if he wished to greet me and prove that he didn't mind at all that I'd noticed his presence. The light from one of the streetlamps fell on his face. His features seemed familiar. He took a step forward, buttoning his raincoat to his neck; he smiled at me and walked away toward the Ramblas, mingling with other passersby. Then I recognized him: the police officer who had held me down while Inspector Fumero attacked Fermín.

When I entered the bookshop, Fermín looked at me inquisitively.

"What's that face for?"

"Fermín, I think we have a problem."

That same evening we put into action the plan we had conceived with Don Gustavo Barceló.

"The first thing is to make sure that you are right and we're under police surveillance. We'll walk over to Els Quatre Gats, casually, to see whether that guy is still out there, lying in wait. But not a word of all this to your father, or he'll end up with a kidney stone."

"And what do I tell him? He's suspicious enough as it is."

"Tell him you're going out to buy sunflower seeds or something."

"And why do we need to go to Els Quatre Gats, precisely?"

"Because there they serve the best ham sandwiches in a three-mile radius, and we have to talk somewhere. Don't be a wet blanket—do as I say, Daniel."

Welcoming any activity that would distract me from my thoughts, I obeyed meekly, and a couple of minutes later was on my way out into the street, having assured my father that I'd be back in time for dinner. Fermín was waiting for me on the corner. As soon as I joined him, he raised his eyebrows to indicate that I should start walking.

"We've got the rattlesnake about twenty yards behind us. Don't turn your head."

"Is it the same one?"

"I don't think so, unless he's shrunk with this wet weather. This one looks like a novice. He's carrying a sports page that's six days old. Fumero must be recruiting apprentices from the charity hospice."

When we got to Els Quatre Gats, our plainclothes policeman sat at a table a few yards from ours and pretended to reread last week's football-league report. Every twenty seconds he would throw us a furtive glance.

"Poor thing, look how he's sweating," said Fermín, shaking his head. "You seem rather distant, Daniel. Did you speak to the girl or didn't you?"

"Her father answered the phone."

"And you had a friendly and civil conversation?"

"It was more like a monologue."

"I see. Must I therefore infer that you don't address him as *papá* yet?"

"He told me verbatim that he was going to beat my brains out."

"Surely that was a rhetorical flourish."

At that moment the waiter's frame hovered over us. Fermín asked for enough food to feed a regiment, rubbing his hands with anticipation.

"And you don't want anything, Daniel?"

I shook my head. When the waiter returned with two trays full of tapas, sandwiches, and various glasses of beer, Fermín handed him a handsome sum and told him to keep the change.

"Listen, boss," he added. "Do you see that guy sitting at the table by the window—the one dressed like Jiminy Cricket with his head buried in his newspaper, as if it were a cone?"

The waiter nodded with an air of complicity.

"Could you please go and tell him that there's an urgent message from Inspector Fumero? He must go immediately to the Boquería Market to buy twenty duros' worth of boiled chickpeas and take them without delay to Police Headquarters (in a taxi if necessary)—or he must prepare to present his balls to him on a plate. Would you like me to repeat it?"

"That won't be necessary, sir. Twenty duros' worth of chickpeas or his balls on a plate."

Fermín handed him another coin. "God bless you."

The waiter nodded respectfully and set off toward our pursuer's table to deliver the message. When the watchman heard the instructions, his face dropped. He remained at the table for another fifteen seconds, torn, and then galloped off into the street. Fermín didn't bat an eyelid. In other circumstances I would have enjoyed the episode, but that night I was unable to get Bea out of my mind.

"Daniel, come down from the clouds, we have work to discuss. Tomorrow, without delay, you must go and visit Nuria Monfort, as we said."

"And when I'm there, what do I say to her?"

"You'll find some topic of conversation. The plan is to follow Mr. Barceló's very sensible suggestion. You make her aware that you know she lied to you knowingly about Carax, that her so-called husband Miquel Moliner is not in prison as she pretends, that you've discovered that she is the evil hand responsible for collecting the mail from the old Fortuny-Carax family apartment, using a PO box in the name of a nonexistent solicitors' firm. . . . You tell her whatever is necessary to light a fire under her feet. All in a melodramatic tone and with a biblical expression. Then, just for the effect, you leave her to stew for a while in her own juices of unease."

"And in the meantime . . ."

"In the meantime I'll be waiting to follow her, an objective I plan to put into practice using the latest techniques in camouflage."

"It's not going to work, Fermín."

"O ye of little faith! Come on, what has this girl's father said to you to get you into this frame of mind? Is it the threat you're worried about? Don't pay any attention to him. Let's see, what did this lunatic say to you?"

I answered without thinking. "The truth."

"The truth according to Saint Daniel the Martyr?"

"You can laugh as much as you like. It serves me right."

"I'm not laughing, Daniel. It's just that I feel bad seeing you punish yourself. Anyone would say you're about to put on a hair shirt. You haven't done anything wrong. Life has enough torturers as it is, without you going around moonlighting as a Grand Inquisitor against yourself."

"Do you speak from experience?"

Fermín shrugged.

"You've never told me how you came across Fumero," I said.

"Would you like to hear a story with a moral?"

"Only if you want to tell it."

Fermín poured himself a glass of beer and swigged it down in one gulp. "Amen," he said to himself. "What I can tell you about Fumero is common knowledge. The first time I heard him mentioned, the future inspector was a gunman working for the anarchist syndicate, the FAI. He had earned himself quite a reputation, because he had no fear and no scruples. All he needed was someone's name, and he'd finish him off on the street with a shot in the face, in the middle of the day. Such talents are greatly valued in times of unrest. The other things he didn't have were loyalty or beliefs. He didn't give a damn what cause he was serving, so long as the cause would help him climb the ladder. There are plenty of riffraff like him in the world, but few of them have Fumero's talent. From the anarchists he went on to serve the communists, and from there to the fascists was only a step. He spied and sold information from one faction to the other, and he took money from all of them. I'd had my eye on him for a long time. I was working for the government of the Generalitat at the time. Sometimes I was mistaken for the ugly brother of President Companys, which would fill me with pride."

"What did you do?"

"A bit of everything. In today's radio soaps, it would be called espionage, but in wartime we're all spies. Part of my job was to keep an eye on types like Fumero. Those are the most dangerous. They're like vipers, with no creed and no conscience. In a war they appear everywhere. In times of peace, they put on their masks. But they're still there. Thousands of them. The fact is that sooner or later I discovered what his game was. Rather later than sooner, I'd say. Barcelona fell in a matter of days, and the boot was on the other foot now. I became a persecuted criminal, and my superiors were forced to hide like rats. Naturally, Fumero was already in charge of the "cleanup" operation. The purge was carried out openly, with shootings on the streets or in Montjuïc Castle. I was arrested in the port while attempting to obtain passage to France on a Greek cargo ship for some of my superiors. I was taken to Montjuïc and held for two days in a pitch-dark cell, with no water or ventilation. The next light I saw was the flame of a welding torch. Fumero and a guy who spoke only German had me hung upside down by my feet. The German first got rid of my clothes by burning them with the torch. It seemed to me that he was well practiced. When I was left stark naked and with all the hairs on my body singed, Fumero told me that if I didn't tell him where my superiors were hiding, the fun would begin in earnest. I'm not a brave man, Daniel. I never have been, but what little courage I possess I used to tell him to go screw himself. At a sign from Fumero, the German injected something into my thigh and waited a few minutes. Then, while Fumero smoked and watched me, smiling, he began to roast me thoroughly with the welding torch. You've seen the marks. . . ."

I nodded. Fermín spoke in a calm tone, with no emotion.

"These marks are the least important. The worst ones remain inside. I held out for an hour under the torch, or perhaps it was just one minute. I don't know. But I ended up giving them the first names, surnames, and even the shirt sizes of all my superiors and even of those who were not. They abandoned me in an alleyway in Pueblo Seco, naked and with my skin burned. A good woman took me into her home and looked after me for two months. The communists had shot her husband and her two sons dead on her doorstep. She didn't know why. When I was able to get up and go out to the street, I learned that all my superiors had been arrested and executed just hours after I had informed on them."

"Fermín, if you don't want to tell me all this . . ."

"No, no. I'd rather you heard it and knew who you're dealing with. When I returned to my home, I was told it had been expropriated by the government, with all my possessions. Without knowing it, I had become a beggar. I tried to get work. I was rejected. The only thing I could get was a bottle of cheap wine for a few céntimos. It's a slow poison that burns your guts up like acid, but I hoped that sooner or later it would work. I told my-self I would return to Cuba one day, to my mulatto girl. I was arrested when I tried to board a freighter going to Havana. I've forgotten how long I spent in prison. After the first year, one begins to lose everything, even one's mind. When I came out, I began to live on the streets, where you found me an eternity later. There were many others like me, colleagues from prison or parole. The lucky ones had somebody they could count on outside, somebody or something they could go back to. The rest of us would join the army of the dispossessed. Once you're given a card for that club, you never cease to be a member. Most of us came out only at night, when the world isn't looking. I met many like me. Rarely did I see them again. Life on the streets is short. People look at you in disgust, even the ones who give you alms, but this is nothing compared to the revulsion you feel for yourself. It's like being trapped in a walking corpse, a corpse that's hungry, stinks, and refuses to die. Every now and then, Fumero and his men would arrest me and accuse me of some absurd theft or of pestering girls on their way out of a convent school. Another month in La Modelo Prison, more beatings, and out into the streets again. I never understood the point of those farces. Apparently the police thought it convenient to have a census of suspects at their disposal, which they could resort to whenever necessary. In one of my meetings with Fumero, who by now was quite the respectable figure, I asked him why he hadn't killed me, as he'd killed the others. He laughed and told me there were worse things than death. He never killed an informer, he said. He let him rot alive."

"Fermín, you're not an informer. Anyone in your place would have done the same. You're my best friend."

"I don't deserve your friendship, Daniel. You and your father have saved my life, and my life belongs to you both. Whatever I can do for you, I'll do. The day you got me out of the streets, Fermín Romero de Torres was born again."

"That's not your real name, is it?"

Fermín shook his head. "I saw that one on a poster at the Arenas bullring. The other is buried. The man who used to live within these bones died, Daniel. Sometimes he comes back, in nightmares. But you've shown me how to be another man, and you've given me a reason for living once more: my Bernarda."

"Fermín . . ."

"Don't say anything, Daniel. Just forgive me, if you can."

I embraced him without a word and let him cry. People were giving us funny looks, and I returned their looks with eyes of fire. After a while they decided to ignore us. Later, while I walked with Fermín to his *pensión,* my friend recovered his voice.

"What I've told you today . . . I beg you not to tell Bernarda. . . ."

"I won't tell Bernarda or anyone else. Not one word, Fermín."

We said farewell with a handshake.

· *37* ·

I COULDN'T SLEEP AT ALL THAT NIGHT. I LAY ON MY BED WITH THE light on, staring at my smart Montblanc pen, which hadn't written anything for years—it was fast becoming the best pair of gloves ever given to someone with no hands. More than once I felt tempted to go over to the Aguilars' apartment and, for want of a better outcome, give myself up. But after much meditation, I decided that to burst into Bea's home in the early hours of the morning was not going to improve whatever situation she was in. By daybreak exhaustion and uncertainty helped me to conclude that the best thing to do was let the water flow; in time the river would carry the bad blood away.

The morning dripped by with little activity in the bookshop, and I took advantage of the circumstance to doze, standing up, with what my father described as the grace and balance of a flamingo. At lunchtime, as arranged with Fermín the night before, I pretended I was going out for a walk, and he claimed he had an appointment at the outpatients' department to have a few stitches removed. As far as I could tell, my father swallowed both lies whole. The idea of systematically lying to my father was beginning to unnerve me, and I said as much to Fermín halfway through the morning, while my father was out on an errand.

"Daniel, the father-son relationship is based on thousands of little white lies. Presents from the Three Kings, the tooth fairy, meritocracy, and many others. This is just one more. Don't feel guilty."

WHEN THE TIME CAME, I LIED AGAIN AND MADE MY WAY TO THE HOME of Nuria Monfort, whose touch and smell remained indelible in my memory. The cobblestones of Plaza de San Felipe Neri had been taken over by a flock of pigeons, but otherwise the square was deserted. I crossed the paving under the watchful eye of dozens of pigeons and looked around in vain for Fermín, disguised as heaven knows what—he had refused to reveal his planned ruse. I went into the building and saw that the name of Miquel Moliner was still on the letterbox; I wondered whether that would be the first flaw I was going to point out in Nuria Monfort's story. As I went up the stairs in the dark, I almost hoped she wouldn't be at home. Nobody can feel more compassion for a fibber than another fibber. When I reached the fourth-floor landing, I stopped to gather up courage and devise some excuse with which to justify my visit. The neighbor's radio was still thundering at the other end of the landing, this time broadcasting a game show on which contestants tested their knowledge of religious lore. It went by the name *With a Little Help from the Lord,* and reputedly held the whole of Spain spellbound every Tuesday at noon.

And now, for five points, and with a little help from the Lord, can you tell us, Bartolomé, how does the Evil One disguise his appearance in front of the wise men of the Tabernacle, in the parable of the archangel and the gourd, in the Book of Joshua? a) as a young goat, b) as a jug vendor, or c) as an acrobat with a monkey?

Riding on the wave of applause from the audience in the studios of Radio Nacional, I planted myself in front of Nuria Monfort's door and pressed the bell for a few seconds. I listened to the echo spread through the apartment and heaved a sigh of relief. I was about to leave when I heard footsteps coming up to the door. The peephole lit up like a tear of light. I smiled. As the key turned in the lock, I breathed deeply.

· *38* ·

D ANIEL."
The blue smoke of her cigarette coiled around her face. Her lips
shone with dark lipstick; they were moist and left marks that looked like
bloodstains on the filter she held between her index and ring fingers. There
are people you remember and people you dream of. For me, Nuria Mon-
fort was like a mirage: you don't question its veracity, you simply follow it
until it vanishes or until it destroys you. I followed her to the narrow, shad-
owy room where she had her desk, her books, and that collection of lined-
up pencils, like an accident of symmetry.

"I thought I wouldn't see you again."

"I'm sorry to disappoint you."

She sat on the chair by her desk, crossing her legs and leaning backward.
I tore my eyes away from her throat and concentrated on a damp spot on the
wall. I went up to the window and had a quick glance around the square. No
sign of Fermín. I could hear Nuria Monfort breathing behind my back,
could feel her eyes brushing my neck. I spoke without taking my eyes off
the window.

"A few days ago, a good friend of mine discovered that the property
administrator responsible for the old Fortuny-Carax apartment had been
sending his correspondence to a PO box in the name of a firm of solicitors,

which, apparently, doesn't exist. This same friend discovered that the person who for years has been collecting the mail to this PO box has been using your name, Señora Monfort—"

"Shut up."

I turned around and saw her retreating into the shadows.

"You judge me without knowing me," she said.

"Then help me to get to know you."

"Have you told anyone about this? Who else knows what you've said to me?"

"More people than you'd think. The police have been following me for a long time."

"Fumero?"

I nodded. It seemed to me that her hands were trembling.

"You don't know what you've done, Daniel."

"You tell me," I answered with a harshness I didn't feel.

"You think that because you chance upon a book you have a right to enter the lives of people you don't know and meddle in things you cannot understand and don't belong to you."

"They belong to me now, whether I like it or not."

"You don't know what you're saying."

"I was in the house of the Aldayas. I know that Jorge Aldaya hides there. I know he was the person who murdered Carax." I didn't know I believed these words until I heard myself saying them.

She looked at me for a long time, choosing her words carefully. "Does Fumero know this?"

"I don't know."

"You'd better know. Did Fumero follow you to that house?"

The anger in her eyes burned me. I had made my entrance playing the role of accuser and judge, but with every minute that passed, I felt more like the culprit.

"I don't think so. Did you know? Did you know that it was Aldaya who killed Julián and that he's hiding in that house? Why didn't you tell me?"

She smiled bitterly. "You don't understand anything, do you?"

"I understand that you lied in order to defend the man who murdered the person you call your friend, that you've been covering up this crime for years, protecting a man whose only aim is to erase any traces of the existence of Julián Carax, who burns his books. I understand that you lied to me about your husband, who is not in prison and clearly isn't here either. That's what I understand."

Nuria Monfort shook her head slowly. "Go away, Daniel. Leave this house and don't return. You've done enough."

I walked away toward the door, leaving her in the dining room. I stopped halfway and looked back. Nuria Monfort was sitting on the floor, her back against the wall, all concern for appearances gone.

I CROSSED THE SQUARE WITH DOWNCAST EYES. I CARRIED WITH ME THE pain I had received from the lips of that woman, a pain I felt I deserved, though I didn't understand why. "You don't know what you've done, Daniel." All I wanted was to get away from that place. As I walked past the church, I didn't at first notice the presence of a gaunt, large-nosed priest standing at the entrance holding a missal and a rosary. He blessed me unhurriedly as I passed.

· *39* ·

I WALKED INTO THE BOOKSHOP ALMOST FORTY-FIVE MINUTES LATE. When my father saw me, he frowned disapprovingly and looked at the clock.

"What time do you think it is? You know I have to go out to visit a client in San Cugat and you leave me here alone."

"What about Fermín? Isn't he back yet?"

My father shook his head with that haste that seemed to take over when he was in a bad mood. "By the way, there's a letter for you. I've left it next to the till."

"Dad, I'm sorry but—"

He waved my excuses aside, threw on raincoat and hat, and went out of the door without saying good-bye. Knowing him, I guessed his anger would evaporate before he reached the train station. What I found odd was Fermín's absence. Since I'd seen him dressed up as a vaudeville priest in Plaza de San Felipe Neri, waiting for Nuria Monfort to come rushing out and lead him to the heart of the mystery, my faith in that strategy had crumbled away. I imagined that if Nuria Monfort did go down to the street, Fermín must have ended up following her to the pharmacist's or the baker's. A grand plan! I went over to the till to have a look at the letter my father had mentioned. The envelope was white and rectangular, like a tombstone, and in the place of a crucifix it bore a return address that managed to crush what little spirit I had left for that day.

Military Government of Barcelona
Recruitment Office

"Hallelujah," I mumbled.

I knew the contents of the letter without having to open it, but even so I did, just to wallow in my misery. The letter was concise: two paragraphs of that prose, poised somewhere between a strident proclamation and the aria from an operetta, that characterizes all military correspondence. It was announced to me that in two months' time I, Daniel Sempere, would have the honor and pride of fulfilling the most sacred and edifying duty that could befall an Iberian male: to serve the Motherland and wear the uniform of the national crusade for the defense of the spiritual bulwark of the West. I hoped that at least Fermín would be able to see the funny side of it and make us laugh a bit with his rhymed version of *The Fall of the Judeo-Masonic Conspiracy.* Two months. Eight weeks. Sixty days. I could always divide up the time into seconds and get a mile-long number. I had 5,184,000 seconds left of freedom. Perhaps Don Federico, who according to my father could build a Volkswagen, could make me a clock with disc brakes. Perhaps someone could explain to me how I was going to manage not to lose Bea forever. When I heard the tinkle of the doorbell, I thought it would be Fermín, returning after having finally persuaded himself that our efforts as detectives were no more than a bad joke.

"Well, if it's not the crown prince himself watching over his castle—and so he should be, even if his face is as long as a cat's tail. Cheer up, Little Boy Blue," said Gustavo Barceló. He sported a camel-hair coat and his customary ivory walking stick, which he didn't need and which he brandished like a cardinal's miter. "Isn't your father in, Daniel?"

"I'm sorry, Don Gustavo. He went out to visit a customer, and I don't suppose he'll be back until—"

"Perfect. Because it's not your father I've come to see, and it's better if he doesn't hear what I have to tell you."

He winked at me, pulling off his gloves and looking around the shop.

"Where's our colleague Fermín? Is he around?"

"Missing in action."

"While applying his talents to the Carax case, I imagine."

"Body and soul. The last time I saw him, he was wearing a cassock and was offering the benediction *urbi et orbi*."

"I see. . . . It's my fault for egging you on. I wish I hadn't opened my mouth."

"You seem rather worried. Has anything happened?"

"Not exactly. Or yes, in a way."

"What did you want to tell me, Don Gustavo?"

The bookseller smiled at me meekly. His usual haughty expression was nowhere to be seen. Instead he looked serious and concerned.

"This morning I met Don Manuel Gutiérrez Fonseca. He's fifty-nine, a bachelor, and has been a city employee at the municipal morgue of Barcelona since 1924. Thirty years' service in the threshold of darkness. His words, not mine. Don Manuel is a gentleman of the old school—courteous, pleasant, and obliging. For the last fifteen years, he's been living on Calle Ceniza, in a rented room he shares with a dozen parakeets that have learned how to hum the funeral march. He has a season ticket at the Liceo. He likes Verdi and Donizetti. He told me that in his job the important thing is to follow the rules. The rules make provisions for everything, especially on occasions when one doesn't know what to do. Fifteen years ago Don Manuel opened a canvas bag brought in by the police, and in it he found his best childhood friend. The rest of the body came in a separate bag. Don Manuel, holding back his feelings, followed the rules."

"Would you like a coffee, Don Gustavo? You're looking a bit pale."

"Please."

I went in search of the thermos and poured him a cup with eight lumps of sugar. He gulped it down.

"Better?"

"Getting there. Well, then, the fact is that Don Manuel was on duty the day they brought the body of Julián Carax to the autopsy department, in

September of 1936. Of course, Don Manuel couldn't remember the name, but a look through the archives and a hundred-peseta donation toward his retirement fund refreshed his memory remarkably. Do you follow me?"

I nodded, almost in a trance.

"Don Manuel remembers all the details of that day because, as he told me, it was one of the few times when he skipped the rules. The police claimed that the body had been found in an alleyway of the Raval quarter, shortly before dawn. The body reached the morgue by midmorning. On it were only a book and a passport, which identified him as Julián Fortuny Carax, born in Barcelona in 1900. The passport had been stamped at the border post of La Junquera, showing that Carax had come into the country a month earlier. The cause of death was, apparently, a bullet wound. Don Manuel isn't a doctor, but over the years he had learned what to look for. In his opinion the gunshot, just above the heart, had been delivered at point-blank range. Thanks to the passport, they were able to locate Mr. Fortuny, Carax's father, who came to the morgue that very evening to identify the body."

"Up to here it all tallies with what Nuria Monfort said."

Barceló nodded. "That's right. What Nuria Monfort didn't tell you is that he—my friend Don Manuel—sensing that the police did not seem very interested in the case, and having realized that the book found in the pocket of the corpse bore the name of the deceased, decided to act on his own initiative and called the publishing house that very afternoon, while they awaited the arrival of Mr. Fortuny, to inform them about what had happened."

"Nuria Monfort told me that the employee at the morgue phoned the publishers three days later, when the body had already been buried in a common grave."

"According to Don Manuel, he called on the same day as the body was delivered to the morgue. He tells me he spoke to a young woman who said she was grateful to him for having called. Don Manuel remembers that he was slightly shocked by the attitude of the young lady. In his own words: 'It sounded as if she already knew.'"

"What about Mr. Fortuny? Is it true that he refused to identify his son?"

"That's what intrigued me most of all. Don Manuel tells me that at the end of the afternoon, a little man arrived, trembling, escorted by two policemen. It was Mr. Fortuny. According to Don Manuel, that is the one thing that one never gets used to, the moment when those closest to the loved one come to identify the body. He says it's a situation he wouldn't wish on anyone. Worst of all, he says, is when the deceased is a young person and it's the parents, or a young spouse, who have to identify him. Don Manuel remembers Mr. Fortuny well. He says that when he arrived at the morgue, he could scarcely stand, that he cried like a child, and that the two policemen had to hold him up by his arms. He kept on moaning: 'What have they done to my son? What have they done to my son?'"

"Did he get to see the body?"

"Don Manuel told me that he was on the point of asking the police officers whether they might skip the procedure. It's the only time it occurred to him to question the rules. The corpse was in a bad state. The victim had probably been dead for over twenty-four hours when the body reached the morgue, and not since dawn that day, as the police claimed. Manuel was afraid that when that little old man saw it, he would break down. Mr. Fortuny kept on repeating that it couldn't be, that his Julián couldn't be dead. . . . Then Don Manuel removed the shroud that covered the body, and the two policemen asked Mr. Fortuny formally whether that was his son, Julián."

"And?"

"Mr. Fortuny was dumbfounded. He stared at the body for almost a minute. Then he turned on his heels and left."

"He left?"

"In a hurry."

"What about the police? Didn't they stop him? Wasn't he there to identify the body?"

Barceló smiled roguishly. "In theory. But Don Manuel remembers there was someone else in the room, a third policeman, who had come in quietly while the other two were preparing Mr. Fortuny. He was watching the scene without saying a word, leaning against the wall, with a cigarette in his mouth. Don Manuel remembers him because when he told him that the regulations strictly forbade smoking in the morgue, one of the officers signaled to him to be quiet. According to Don Manuel, as soon as Mr. Fortuny had left, the third policeman went up to the body, glanced at it, and spit on its face. Then he kept the passport and gave orders for the body to be sent to Montjuïc, to be buried in a common grave at daybreak."

"It doesn't make sense."

"That's what Don Manuel thought. Especially as none of it tallied with the rules. 'But we don't know who this man is,' he said. The two other policemen didn't say anything. Don Manuel rebuked them angrily: 'Or do you know only too well? Because it is quite clear to us all that he's been dead for at least a day.' Don Manuel was obviously referring to the regulations and was no fool. According to him, when the third policeman heard his protests, he went up to him, looked straight into his eyes, and asked him whether he'd care to join the deceased on his last voyage. Don Manuel was terrified. That man had the eyes of a lunatic, and Don Manuel didn't doubt for one moment that he meant what he said. He mumbled that he was only trying to comply with the regulations, that nobody knew who that man was, and that, consequently, he couldn't be buried yet. 'This man is whoever I say he is,' answered the policeman. Then he picked up the register form and signed it, closing the case. Don Manuel says he'll never forget that signature, because during the war years, and for a long time afterward, he would come across it on dozens of death certificates for bodies that arrived from goodness knows where—bodies that nobody managed to identify. . . ."

"Inspector Francisco Javier Fumero . . ."

"The pride and glory of Central Police Headquarters. Do you realize what this means, Daniel?"

"That we've been lashing out blindly from the very beginning."

Barceló took his hat and stick and walked over to the door, tut-tutting under his breath. "No, it means the lashings are about to start."

· 40 ·

I SPENT THE AFTERNOON KEEPING WATCH OVER THE GRIM LETTER announcing my draft, hoping for signs of life from Fermín. Half an hour after our closing time, Fermín's whereabouts remained unknown. I picked up the telephone and called the *pensión* on Calle Joaquín Costa. Doña Encarna answered, her voice thick with alcohol. She said she hadn't seen Fermín since that morning.

"If he's not back within the next half hour, he'll have to have his supper cold. This isn't the Ritz, you know. I hope nothing's happened to him?"

"Don't worry, Doña Encarna. He had some errand to do and must have got delayed. In any case, if you do see him before going to bed, I'll be really grateful if you could ask him to call me. It's Daniel Sempere, the neighbor of your friend Merceditas."

"Sure, but I must warn you that I turn in for the night at half past eight."

After that I phoned Barceló's home, hoping that Fermín might have turned up there to empty Bernarda's larder or carry her off into the ironing room. It hadn't occurred to me that Clara might answer the phone.

"Daniel, what a surprise."

You stole my line, I thought. Talking to her in a roundabout manner worthy of Don Anacleto, the high-school teacher, I let drop the reason for my call, but in a very casual manner, almost in passing.

"No, Fermín hasn't come by all day. And Bernarda has been with me all afternoon, so I would know. We've been talking about you, you know."

"What a boring conversation."

"Bernarda says you look very handsome, quite grown up."

"I take lots of vitamins."

A long silence.

"Daniel, do you think we could become friends again someday? How many years will it take you to forgive me?"

"We are friends already, Clara, and I don't have to forgive you for anything. You know that."

"My uncle says you're still investigating Julián Carax. Why don't you come by some afternoon for tea and tell me the latest. I've also got things to tell you."

"One of these days, I promise."

"I'm getting married, Daniel."

I stared at the receiver. I felt as if my feet were sinking into the ground or I had shrunk a few inches.

"Daniel, are you there?"

"Yes."

"You're surprised."

I swallowed—my saliva had the consistency of concrete. "No. What surprises me is that you're not yet married. You can't have lacked for suitors. Who's the lucky fellow?"

"You don't know him. His name is Jacobo. He's a friend of Uncle Gustavo. A director of the Bank of Spain. We met at an opera recital organized by my uncle. Jacobo is enthusiastic about opera. He's a bit older than me, but we're very good friends, and that's what matters, don't you think?"

My mouth was full of words of malice, but I bit my tongue. It tasted like poison. "Of course . . . So listen, congratulations."

"You'll never forgive me, will you, Daniel? For you I'll always be the perfidious Clara Barceló."

"To me you'll always be Clara Barceló, period. And you know that as well as I do."

There was another silence, of the kind in which gray hairs seem to creep up on you.

"What about you, Daniel? Fermín tells me you have a beautiful girl-friend."

"I have to go, Clara, a client has just come in. I'll call you one of these days, and we'll arrange to meet for tea. Congratulations once again."

I put down the phone and sighed.

My father returned from his visit to the client, looking dejected and not in the mood for conversation. He got dinner ready while I set the table, without even asking after Fermín or how the day had gone in the bookshop. We stared at our plates during the meal, hiding behind the chatter of the news on the radio. My father hardly ate. He just stirred the watery, tasteless soup with his spoon, as if he were looking for gold in the bottom.

"You haven't touched your food," I said.

My father shrugged his shoulders. The radio continued to bombard us with nonsense. My father got up and turned it off.

"What did the letter from the army say?" he finally asked.

"I have to join up in two months' time."

His face seemed to age ten years.

"Barceló says he'll try to pull some strings so that I get transferred to the Military Government in Barcelona, after the training. I'll even be able to come home to sleep," I added.

My father replied with an anemic nod. I found it painful to hold his gaze, so I got up to clear the table. My father remained seated, his eyes lost and his hands clasped under his chin. I was about to wash up the dishes when I heard footsteps pounding on the stairs. Firm, hurried footsteps that struck the floor and spoke a terrible message. I looked up and exchanged glances with my father. The footsteps stopped on our landing. My father stood up, looking anxious. A second later we heard banging on the door and a furious booming voice that sounded vaguely familiar.

"Police! Open up!"

A thousand daggers stabbed at my mind. Another volley of banging made the door shake. My father went to the door and lifted the cover of the peephole.

"What do you want at this time of night?"

"Open the door or we'll kick it down, Sempere. Don't make me have to repeat this."

I recognized the voice as Fumero's, and an icy breath seemed to enter me. My father threw me a questioning look. I nodded. Suppressing a sigh, he opened the door. Fumero and his two henchmen were silhouetted against the yellowish light of the landing, ashen-faced puppets in gray raincoats.

"Where is he?" shouted Fumero, swiping my father aside and pushing his way into the dining room.

My father tried to stop him, but one of the policemen who was covering the inspector's back grabbed him by the arm and pushed him against the wall, holding him with the coldness and efficiency of a man accustomed to the task. It was the same man who had followed me and Fermín, the same one who had held me while Fumero beat up my friend outside the Hospice of Santa Lucía, the same one who had kept watch on me a couple of nights before. He gave me an empty, deadpan look. I went up to Fumero, displaying all the calm I was able to muster. The inspector's eyes were bloodshot. A recent scratch ran down his left cheek, edged with dry blood.

"Where?"

"Where what?"

Fumero looked down suddenly and shook his head, mumbling to himself. When he raised his face, he had a wolfish grimace on his lips and a revolver in his hand. Without taking his eyes off mine, he banged the butt of his revolver against the vase of withered flowers on the table. The vase smashed into small fragments, spilling the water and the shriveled stalks over the tablecloth. Despite myself, I shivered. My father was shouting in the entrance hall, held firmly in the grip of the two policemen. I could barely decipher his words. All I could absorb was the icy pressure of the gun's barrel sunk into my cheek, and the smell of gunpowder.

"Don't fuck with me, you little shit, or your father will have to pick your brains off the floor. Do you hear?"

I nodded. I was shaking. Fumero pressed the barrel hard against my cheek. I could feel it cutting my skin, but I didn't even dare blink.

"This is the last time I'll ask you. Where is he?"

I saw myself reflected in the black pupils of the inspector's eyes. They slowly contracted as he tightened the hammer with his thumb.

"Not here. I haven't seen him since lunchtime. It's the truth."

Fumero stood still for almost half a minute, digging the gun into my face and smacking his lips.

"Lerma," he ordered. "Have a look."

One of the policemen hurried off to inspect the apartment. My father struggled in vain with the third officer.

"If you've lied to me and we find him in this house, I swear I'll break both your father's legs," whispered Fumero.

"My father doesn't know anything. Leave him alone."

"You're the one who doesn't even know what he's playing at. But as soon as I grab hold of your friend, the game's over. No judges, no hospitals, no fucking nothing. This time I'll see to it personally that he's put out of circulation. And I'm going to enjoy doing it, believe me. I'm going to take my time. You can tell him if you see him. Because I'm going to find him even if I have to turn over every stone in the city. And you're next on the list."

The officer called Lerma reappeared in the dining room and gave a slight shake of the head. Fumero loosened the hammer and removed the revolver.

"Pity," said Fumero.

"What has he done? Why are you looking for him?"

Fumero turned his back on me and went up to the two policemen, who, at a signal from him, let go of my father.

"You're going to remember this," spit my father.

Fumero's eyes rested on his. Instinctively, my father took a step back. I feared that Inspector Fumero's visit had only just begun, but suddenly the man shook his head, laughing under his breath, and left the apartment. Lerma followed him. The third policeman, my perpetual sentinel, paused for a moment in the doorway. He looked silently at me, as if he wanted to say something.

"Palacios!" yelled Fumero, his voice fading into the echo of the stairwell.

Palacios lowered his eyes and disappeared around the door. I went out to the landing. I could see blades of light emerging from the half-open doors of the neighbors, their frightened faces peeping out into the dark. The three shadowy shapes of the policemen vanished down the stairs, and the angry sound of their footsteps receded like a poisoned tide, leaving behind it a residue of fear.

It was about midnight when we heard more bangs on the door, this time weaker, almost fearful. My father, who was dabbing iodine on the bruise left on my cheek by Fumero's gun, suddenly froze. Our eyes met. There were three more knocks.

For a moment I thought it was Fermín, who had perhaps witnessed the whole incident hidden in some dark corner of the staircase.

"Who's there?" asked my father.

"Don Anacleto, Mr. Sempere."

My father gave out a sigh. We opened the door to find the teacher, looking paler than ever.

"Don Anacleto, what's the matter? Are you all right?" my father asked, letting him in.

The teacher was holding a folded newspaper. He handed it to us with a horrified look. The paper was still warm, the ink still damp.

"It's tomorrow's edition," murmured Don Anacleto. "Page six."

What first caught my eye were the two photographs under the heading. The first was a picture of Fermín, with a fuller figure and more hair, perhaps fifteen or twenty years younger. The second showed the face of a woman with her eyes closed and skin like marble. It took me a few seconds to recognize her, because I'd got used to seeing her in the half-light.

TRAMP MURDERS WOMAN
IN BROAD DAYLIGHT

BARCELONA/PRESS AGENCY

Police are looking for the tramp who stabbed a woman to death this afternoon. Her name was Nuria Monfort Masdedeu, and she lived in Barcelona.

The crime took place in midafternoon in the neighborhood of San Gervasio, where the victim was assaulted by the tramp with no apparent motive. According to the Central Police Headquarters, it would appear that the tramp had been following her for reasons that have not yet been made clear.

It seems that the murderer, fifty-five-year-old Antonio José Gutiérrez Alcayete, from Villa Inmunda in the province of Cáceres, is a well-known criminal with a long record of mental illness, who escaped from La Modelo Prison six years ago and has managed to elude the authorities by assuming different identities. At the moment of the crime, he was dressed in a cassock. He is armed, and the police describe him as highly dangerous. It is not yet known whether the victim and her murderer knew each other, although sources from Police Headquarters indicate that everything points toward that hypothesis; nor is it known what may have been the motive behind the crime. The victim was stabbed six times in her stomach, chest, and throat. The attack, which took place close to a school, was witnessed by a number of pupils, who alerted the teachers. These in turn called the police and an ambulance. According to the police report, death was caused by multiple wounds. The victim was pronounced dead on arrival at the Hospital Clínico of Barcelona, at 6:15 PM.

· 41 ·

WE HAD NO NEWS FROM FERMÍN ALL DAY. MY FATHER INSISTED on opening the bookshop as usual to offer a show of normality and innocence. The police had posted an officer by the door to our stairs, and another watched over Plaza de Santa Ana, sheltering beneath the church door like the effigy of a saint. We could see them shivering under the intense rain that had arrived with the dawn, the steam from their breath becoming less visible as the day wore on, their hands buried in the pockets of their raincoats. A few neighbors walked straight past, with a quick glance through the shop window, but not a single buyer ventured in.

"The rumor must have spread," I said.

My father only nodded. He'd spent all morning without speaking to me, expressing himself only with gestures. The page with the news of Nuria Monfort's murder lay on the counter. Every twenty minutes he would wander over and reread it with an inscrutable expression. All day long he had been bottling up his anger, letting it accumulate inside him.

"However many times you read the article, it's not going to be true," I said.

My father raised his head and looked at me severely. "Did you know this person? Nuria Monfort?"

"I'd spoken to her a couple of times."

Nuria Monfort's face took over my thoughts. My lack of honesty was nauseating. I was still haunted by her smell and the touch of her lips, the image of that desk so impeccably tidy and her sad, wise eyes. "A couple of times."

"Why did you have to speak to her? What did she have to do with you?"

"She was an old friend of Julián Carax. I went to see her to ask her what she remembered about Carax. That's all. She was the daughter of Isaac, the keeper. It was he who gave me her address."

"Did Fermín know her?"

"No."

"How can you be sure?"

"How can you doubt him and believe these fabrications? All Fermín knew about that woman was what I told him."

"And is that why he was following her?"

"Yes."

"Because you'd asked him to."

I didn't answer. My father heaved a sigh.

"You don't understand, Dad."

"You can be sure of that. I don't understand you, or Fermín, or—"

"Dad, from what we know of Fermín, what it says there is impossible."

"And what do we know about Fermín, eh? To begin with, it turns out that we didn't even know his real name."

"You're mistaken about him."

"No, Daniel. You're the one who's mistaken, in many things. Who asks you to go digging up other people's lives?"

"I'm free to speak to whoever I want."

"I suppose you also feel free from the consequences."

"Are you insinuating that I'm responsible for this woman's death?"

"This woman, as you call her, had a first name and a last name, and you knew her."

"There's no need to remind me," I answered with tears in my eyes.

My father looked at me sadly, shaking his head. "Oh, God, I don't even want to think how poor Isaac must be feeling."

"It's not my fault that she's dead," I said in a tiny voice, thinking that perhaps if I repeated those words often enough, I would end up believing them.

My father retired to the back room, still shaking his head.

"You must know what you're responsible for and what you're not, Daniel. Sometimes I no longer know who you are."

I grabbed my raincoat and escaped into the street and the rain, where nobody would know me.

I GAVE MYSELF UP TO THE FREEZING RAIN, GOING NOWHERE IN particular. I walked with my eyes downcast, dragging with me the image of Nuria Monfort, lifeless, stretched out on a cold marble slab, her body riddled with stab wounds. I passed a crossing with Calle Fontanella and didn't stop to look at the traffic lights. It was only when a strong gust of wind hit my face that I turned to see a wall of metal and light hurtling toward me at full speed. At the last moment, a passerby behind me pulled me back and moved me out of the bus's path. I gazed at the metal behemoth that shimmered only an inch or two from my face, what could have been certain death zooming by, a tenth of a second away. By the time I realized what had happened, the person who had saved my life was walking away over the pedestrian crossing, just a silhouette in a gray raincoat. I remained rooted to the spot, breathless. Through the curtain of rain, I noticed that my savior had stopped on the other side of the street and was watching me under the downpour. It was the third policeman, Palacios. A thick wall of traffic slid by between us, and when I looked again, Officer Palacios was no longer there.

I set off toward Bea's house, incapable of waiting any longer. I needed to recall what little good there was in me, what she had given me. I rushed up the stairs and stopped outside the door of the Aguilars' apartment, almost out of breath. I held the door knocker and gave three loud knocks. While I waited, I gathered my courage and became aware of my appearance: soaked to the skin. I pushed the hair back from my forehead and told myself that the dice had been cast. If Mr. Aguilar was to turn up ready to break my legs and smash my face, the sooner the better. I knocked again and after a while heard footsteps approaching. The peephole opened a fraction. A dark, suspicious eye stared at me.

"Who's there?"

I recognized the voice of Cecilia, one of the maids who worked for the Aguilar family.

"It's Daniel Sempere, Cecilia."

The peephole closed, and within a few seconds the bolts and latches began to perform their sounds. The large door opened slowly, and I was received by Cecilia in her cap and uniform, holding a candle in a candleholder. From her alarmed expression, I gathered that I looked like a ghost.

"Good afternoon, Cecilia. Is Bea in?"

She looked at me without understanding. In her experience of the household routine, my presence, which lately had been an unusual occurrence, was associated only with Tomás, my old school friend.

"Miss Beatriz isn't here. . . ."

"Has she gone out?"

Cecilia, who at the best of times was a frightened soul, nodded.

"Do you know when she's coming back?"

The maid shrugged. "She went with Mr. and Mrs. Aguilar to the doctor, about two hours ago."

"To the doctor? Is she ill?"

"I don't know, sir."

"And what doctor did they go to?"

"That I don't know, sir."

I decided not to go on tormenting the poor maid. The absence of Bea's parents opened up other avenues. "What about Tomás? Is he in?"

"Yes, Master Daniel. Come in, I'll call him."

I went into the hall and waited. In the past I would have gone straight to my friend's room, but I hadn't been to that house for so long that I felt like a stranger. Cecilia disappeared down the corridor wrapped in an aura of light, abandoning me to the dark. I thought I could hear Tomás's voice in the distance and then some steps approaching. I made up a pretext with which to explain my unannounced visit to my friend. But the figure that appeared at the door of the entrance hall was again Cecilia's. She looked at me contritely, and my forced smile vanished.

"Master Tomás says he's very busy and cannot see you right now."

"Did you tell him who I was? Daniel Sempere."

"Yes, Master Daniel. He told me to tell you to go away."

A stab of cold steel in my stomach cut my breath.

"I'm sorry, sir," said Cecilia.

I nodded, not knowing what to say. The maid opened the door of the residence that, until not very long ago, I had considered my second home.

"Does the young master want an umbrella?"

"No thank you, Cecilia."

"I'm, sorry, Master Daniel," the maid repeated.

I smiled weakly. "Don't worry, Cecilia."

The door closed, leaving me in the shadows. I stayed there a few moments and then dragged myself down the stairs. The rain was still pouring relentlessly. I walked off down the street. When I reached the corner, I stopped and turned around for a moment. I looked up at the apartment of the Aguilars. I could see the silhouette of my old friend Tomás outlined against his bedroom window. He was staring at me, motionless. I waved my hand at him. He didn't return the greeting. A few seconds later, he moved away to the back of the room. I waited almost five minutes, hoping he would reappear, but he didn't.

· 42 ·

ON MY WAY BACK TO THE BOOKSHOP, I CROSSED THE STREET BY the Capitol Cinema, where two painters standing on a scaffold watched with dismay as their freshly painted placard became streaked under the rain. In the distance I made out the stoical figure of the sentinel on duty stationed opposite the bookshop. When I got to Don Federico Flaviá's shop, I noticed that the watchmaker was standing in the doorway observing the downpour. The scars from his stay at Police Headquarters still showed on his face. He wore an impeccable gray wool suit and held a cigarette that he hadn't bothered to light. I raised a hand to him, and he smiled back.

"What have you got against umbrellas, Daniel?"

"What could be more beautiful than the rain, Don Federico?"

"Pneumonia. Come on in, I have your repair ready."

I looked at him without understanding. Don Federico's eyes were fixed on mine, and his smile hadn't diminished. I nodded and followed him into his marvelous bazaar. As soon as we were inside, he handed me a small brown paper bag.

"You'd better leave right away. The scarecrow watching over the book-shop hasn't taken his eyes off us."

I looked inside the bag. It contained a small, leather-bound book. A missal. The missal Fermín held in his hands the last time I'd seen him. Don

Federico, pushing me back toward the street, vowed me to silence with a solemn nod. Once I was outside again, he recovered his happy expression and raised his voice.

"And remember, don't force the key when you wind it up, or it'll come loose again, all right?"

"Don't worry, Don Federico, and thanks."

I walked away with a knot in my stomach that tightened with every step I took toward to the plainclothes policeman guarding the bookshop. When I passed in front of him, I greeted him with the same hand in which I held the bag given to me by Don Federico. The policeman looked at it with vague interest. I slipped into the bookshop. My father was still standing behind the counter, as if he hadn't moved since I'd left. He gave me a troubled look.

"Listen Daniel, about what I said . . ."

"Don't worry. You were right."

"You're trembling."

I nodded casually and saw him go off in search of the thermos. I seized the moment to go into the small toilet by the back room and examine the missal. Fermín's note slipped out, fluttering about like a butterfly. I caught it in the air. The message was written on an almost transparent piece of cigarette paper in minute writing, and I had to hold it up against the light to be able to decipher it.

Dear Daniel,

Don't believe one word of what the newspapers say about the murder of Nuria Monfort. As usual, it's nothing but a tall tale. I'm safe and sound, hiding in a secure place. Don't try to find me or send me messages. Destroy this note as soon as you've read it. No need to swallow it, just burn it or tear it up into small pieces. I'll use my wits to get in touch with you—and the good offices of friendly intermediaries. I beg you to transmit the essence of this message, in code and with all discretion, to my beloved. Don't you do anything. Your friend, the third man,

FRdT

I was beginning to reread the note when someone's knuckles rapped on the toilet door.

"May I come in?" asked an unknown voice.

My heart missed a beat. Not knowing what else to do, I scrunched up the cigarette paper and put it in my mouth. I pulled the chain, and while the water thundered through pipes and cisterns, I swallowed the little paper ball. It tasted of wax and Sugus candy. When I opened the door, I encountered the reptilian smile of the police officer who had been stationed in front of the bookshop.

"Excuse me. I don't know whether it's listening to the rain all day, but suddenly it seems there's something of an emergency building down there, and when nature calls . . ."

"But of course," I said, making way for him. "It's all yours."

"Much obliged."

The policeman, who, in the light of the bare bulb, made me think of a small weasel, looked me up and down. His ratlike eyes paused on the missal I held in my hands.

"If I don't have something to read, I just can't go," I explained.

"It's the same with me. And people say Spaniards don't read. May I borrow it?"

"On top of the cistern, you'll find the latest Critics' Prize," I said, cutting him short. "It's infallible."

I walked away without losing my composure and joined my father, who was pouring me a cup of white coffee.

"What's he doing here?" I asked.

"He swore on his mother's grave he was on the verge of crapping his pants. What was I supposed to do?"

"Leave him in the street and let him warm up with it."

My father frowned.

"If you don't mind, I'm going up to the apartment."

"Of course I don't mind. And put on some dry clothes. You're going to catch your death."

The apartment was cold and silent. I went into my bedroom and peeped out the window. The second sentinel was still there, by the door of the

Church of Santa Ana. I took off my soaking clothes and put on some thick pajamas and a dressing gown that had belonged to my grandfather. I lay down on the bed without bothering to turn on the light and abandoned myself to the darkness and the sound of the rain on the windowpanes. I closed my eyes and tried to conjure up the image of Bea, her touch and smell. The night before I hadn't slept at all, and soon I was overcome by exhaustion. In my dreams the hooded figure of Death rode over Barcelona, a ghostly apparition that hovered like haze above the towers and roofs, trailing black ropes that held hundreds of small white coffins. The coffins left behind them their own trail of black flowers on whose petals, written in blood, was the name Nuria Monfort.

I awoke at the break of a gray dawn. The windows were steamed up. I dressed for the cold weather and put on some calf-length boots, then went out into the corridor and groped my way through the apartment. I slipped out through the door and walked down to the street. The newsstands in the Ramblas were already lighting up in the distance. I steered a course toward the one that was anchored at the mouth of Calle Tallers and bought the first edition of the day's paper, which still smelled of warm ink. I rushed through the pages until I found the obituary section. Nuria Monfort's name lay printed under a cross, and I couldn't bring myself to look at it. I walked away with the newspaper folded under my arm, in search of darkness. The funeral was that afternoon, in Montjuïc Cemetery. After walking around the block, I returned home. My father was still asleep, and I went back into my room. I sat at my desk and took the Meinsterstück pen out of its case, then took a blank sheet of paper and hoped the nib would guide me. In my hands the pen had nothing to say. In vain I tried to conjure up the words I wanted to offer Nuria Monfort, but I was incapable of writing or feeling anything except the terror of her absence, of knowing she was lost, wrenched away. I knew that one day she would return to me, in months or years to come, that I would always relive her memory in the touch of a stranger, in the recollection of images that no longer belonged to me.

· *43* ·

Shortly before three o'clock, I got on a bus on Paseo de Colón that would take me to the cemetery on Montjuïc. Through the window I could see the forest of masts and fluttering pennants at the docks. The bus, which was almost empty, circled Montjuïc Mountain and started up the road that led to the eastern gates of the boundless Barcelona cemetery. I was the last passenger.

"What time does the last bus leave?" I asked the driver before getting off.

"At half past four."

The driver left me by the cemetery gates. An avenue of cypress trees rose in the mist. Even from there, at the foot of the mountain, one could already begin to see the vast city of the dead that scaled the slope to the very top: avenues of tombs, walks lined with gravestones, and alleyways of mausoleums, towers crowned by fiery angels and whole forests of sepulchers that seemed to grow against one another. The city of the dead was a pit of palaces guarded by an army of rotting stone statues sinking into the mud. I took a deep breath and entered the labyrinth. My mother lay buried a hundred yards away from the path along which I walked. With every step I took, I could feel the cold, the emptiness, and the fury of that place, the horror of its silence, of the faces trapped in the old photographs that had been abandoned to the company of candles and dead flowers. After a while

I caught a glimpse of distant gas lamps lit around a grave, the shapes of half a dozen people lined up against an ashen sky. I quickened my step and stopped where I could hear the words of the priest.

The coffin, an unpolished pinewood box, rested on the mud. Two gravediggers guarded it, leaning on spades. I scanned those present. Old Isaac, the keeper of the Cemetery of Forgotten Books, had not come to his daughter's funeral. I recognized the neighbor who lived opposite. She shook her head, sobbing, while a man stroked her back with a resigned air. Her husband, I imagined. Next to them was a woman of about forty, dressed in gray and carrying a bunch of flowers. She cried quietly, looking away from the grave with tight lips. I had never seen her. Separated from the group, clad in a dark raincoat and holding his hat behind his back, was the policeman who had saved my life the day before. Palacios. He raised his eyes and observed me for a few seconds without blinking. The blind, senseless words of the priest were all that separated us from the terrible silence. I stared at the mud-splattered coffin. I imagined her lying inside it, and I didn't realize I was crying until that woman in gray came up to me and offered me one of the flowers from her bunch. I remained there until the group dispersed. At a sign from the priest, the gravediggers got ready to do their work by the lamplight. I kept the flower in my coat pocket and walked away, unable to express my final farewell.

It was beginning to get dark by the time I reached the cemetery gates, and I assumed I'd missed the last bus. I was about to start a long walk, under the shadow of the necropolis, following the road that skirted the port on the way back to Barcelona. A black car was parked about twenty yards ahead of me, its lights on. Inside, a figure smoked a cigarette. As I drew near, Palacios opened the passenger door.

"Get in. I'll take you home. You won't find any buses or taxis around here at this time of day."

I hesitated for a moment. "I'd rather walk."

"Don't be silly. Get in."

He spoke in the steely tone of someone used to giving orders and being obeyed instantly. "Please," he added.

I got into the car, and the policeman started the engine.

"Enrique Palacios," he said, holding his hand out to me.

I didn't shake it. "If you leave me in Colón, that's fine."

The car sped off. We joined the traffic on the road and traveled a good stretch without uttering a single word.

"I want you to know I'm very sorry about Señora Monfort."

Coming from him, those words seemed an obscenity, an insult.

"I'm grateful to you for saving my life the other day, but I must tell you I don't care a shit what you feel, Mr. Enrique Palacios."

"I'm not what you think, Daniel. I'd like to help you."

"If you expect me to tell you where Fermín is, you can leave me right here."

"I don't give a damn where your friend is. I'm not on duty now."

I didn't reply.

"You don't trust me, and I don't blame you. But at least listen to me. This has already gone too far. There was no reason why this woman should have died. I beg you to let this matter be and to put this man, Carax, out of your mind forever."

"You speak as if I'm in control of what's happening. I'm only a spectator. The whole show has been staged by your boss and all you lot."

"I'm tired of funerals, Daniel. I don't want to have to go to yours."

"All the better, because you're not invited."

"I'm serious."

"Me, too. Please stop and leave me here."

"We'll be in Colón in two minutes."

"I don't care. This car smells of death, like you. Let me out."

Palacios slowed down and stopped on the hard shoulder. I got out of the car and banged the door shut, eluding Palacios's eyes. I waited for him to leave, but the police officer didn't drive off. I turned around and saw him lowering the car window. I thought I read honesty, even pain, in his face, but I refused to believe it.

"Nuria Monfort died in my arms, Daniel," he said. "I think her last words were a message for you."

"What did she say?" I asked, my voice gripped by an icy cold. "Did she mention my name?"

"She was delirious, but I think she was referring to you. At one point she said there were worse prisons than words. Then, before dying, she asked me to tell you to let her go."

I looked at him without understanding. "To let who go?"

"Someone called Penélope. I imagined she must be your girlfriend."

Palacios looked down and set off into the twilight. I remained there, staring disconcertedly at the lights of the car as they disappeared into the blue-and-red dusk. Then I walked on toward Paseo de Colón, repeating to myself those last words of Nuria Monfort but finding no meaning to them. When I reached the square called Portal de la Paz, I stopped next to the pleasure boats' dock to gaze at the port. I sat on the steps that disappeared under the murky water, in the same place where, on a night that was now in the distant past, I had met Laín Coubert, the man without a face.

"There are worse prisons than words," I murmured.

Only then did I understand that the message from Nuria Monfort was not meant for me. It wasn't I who had to let Penélope go. Her last words hadn't been for a stranger, but for a man she had loved in silence for twenty years: Julián Carax.

· *44* ·

NIGHT WAS FALLING WHEN I REACHED PLAZA DE SAN FELIPE Neri. The bench on which I had first caught sight of Nuria Monfort stood at the foot of a streetlamp, empty and tattooed by penknives with names of lovers, with insults and promises. I looked up to the windows of Nuria Monfort's home on the third floor and noticed a dim, flickering copper light. A candle.

I entered the gloomy foyer and groped my way up the stairs. My hands shook when I reached the third-floor landing. A sliver of reddish light ran under the frame of the half-open door. I placed my hand on the doorknob and remained there motionless, listening. I thought I heard a whisper, a choked voice coming from within. For a moment I thought that if I opened that door, I'd find her waiting for me on the other side, smoking by the balcony, her legs tucked under her, leaning against the wall, anchored in the same place where I'd left her. Gently, fearing I might disturb her, I opened the door and went into the apartment. In the dining room, the balcony curtains swayed. A figure was sitting by the window, unmoving, holding a burning candle in its hands. I couldn't make out the face against the light, but a bright pearl slid down its skin, shining like fresh resin, then falling on the figure's lap. Isaac Monfort turned, his face streaked with tears.

"I didn't see you this afternoon at the funeral," I said.

He shook his head, drying his tears with the back of his lapel.

"Nuria wasn't there," he murmured after a while. "The dead never go to their own funeral."

He looked around him, as if his daughter was in that room, sitting next to us in the dark, listening to us.

"Do you know that I've never been in this house?" he asked. "Whenever we met, it was always Nuria who came to me. 'It's easier for you, Father,' she would say. 'Why go up all those stairs?' I'd always say to her, 'All right, if you don't invite me, I won't go,' and she'd answer, 'I don't need to invite you to my home, Father. One only invites strangers. You can come whenever you like.' In over fifteen years, I didn't go to see her once. I always told her she'd chosen a bad neighborhood. Not enough light. An old building. She would just nod in agreement. Like when I used to tell her she'd chosen a bad life. Not much future. A jobless husband. It's funny how we judge others and don't realize the extent of our disdain until they are no longer there, until they are taken from us. They're taken from us because they've never been ours. . . ."

The old man's voice, deprived of its veil of irony, faltered and seemed almost as weary as his look.

"Nuria loved you very much, Isaac. Don't doubt it for an instant. And I know she also felt loved by you," I said.

Old Isaac shook his head again. He smiled, but his silent tears did not stop falling. "Perhaps she loved me, in her own way, as I loved her, in mine. But we didn't know one another. Perhaps because I never allowed her to know me, or I never took any steps toward getting to know her. We spent our lives like two strangers who see each other every single day and greet one another out of politeness. And I think she probably died without forgiving me."

"Isaac, I can assure you—"

"Daniel, you're young and you try hard, but even though I've had a bit to drink and I don't know what I'm saying, you still haven't learned to lie well enough to fool an old man whose heart has been broken by misfortune."

I looked down.

"The policeman says that the man who killed her is a friend of yours," Isaac ventured.

"The police are lying."

Isaac assented. "I know."

"I can assure you—"

"There's no need, Daniel. I know you're telling the truth," said Isaac, pulling out an envelope from his coat pocket.

"The afternoon before she died, Nuria came to see me, as she used to do years ago. I remember we used to go and eat in a café on Calle Guardia, where I would take her when she was a child. We always talked about books, about old books. She would sometimes tell me things about her work, trifles, the sort of things one tells a stranger on a bus. . . . Once she told me she was sorry she'd been a disappointment to me. I asked her where she'd got that ridiculous idea. 'From your eyes, Father, from your eyes,' she said. Not once did it occur to me that perhaps I'd been an even greater disappointment to her. Sometimes we think people are like lottery tickets, that they're there to make our most absurd dreams come true."

"Isaac, with all due respect, you've been drinking like a fish, and you don't know what you're saying."

"Wine turns the wise man into a fool and the fool into a wise man. I know enough to understand that my own daughter never trusted me. She trusted more in you, Daniel, and she'd seen you only a couple of times."

"I can assure you you're wrong."

"The last afternoon we saw each other, she brought me this envelope. She was restless, worried about something that she didn't want to talk about. She asked me to keep this envelope and, should anything happen, to give it to you."

"Should anything happen?"

"Those were her words. She looked so distressed that I suggested we go together to the police, that, whatever the problem, we'd find a solution. Then she said that the police was the last place she could go to for help. I begged her to let me know what it was about, but she said she had to leave and made me promise that I'd give you this envelope if she didn't come back for it within a couple of days. She asked me not to open it."

Isaac handed me the envelope. It was open. "I lied to her, as usual," he said.

I examined the envelope. It contained a wad of handwritten sheets of paper. "Have you read them?" I asked.

The old man nodded slowly.

"What do they say?"

The old man looked up. His lips were trembling. He seemed to have aged a hundred years since the last time I'd seen him.

"It's the story you were looking for, Daniel. The story of a woman I never knew, even though she bore my name and my blood. Now it belongs to you."

I put the envelope into my coat pocket.

"I'm going to ask you to leave me alone here, with her, if you don't mind. A while ago, as I was reading those pages, it seemed to me that I was seeing her again. However hard I try, I can only remember her the way she was as a little girl. She was very quiet then, you know. She looked at everything pensively, and never laughed. What she liked best were stories, and I don't think any child has ever learned to read so early. She used to say she wanted to be an author and write encyclopedias and treatises on history and philosophy. Her mother said it was all my fault. She said that Nuria adored me and because she thought her father loved only books, she wanted to write books to make her father love her."

"Isaac, I don't think it's a good idea to be on your own tonight. Why don't you come home with me? Spend the night with us, and that way you can keep my father company."

Isaac shook his head again. "I have things to do, Daniel. You go home and read those pages. They belong to you."

The old man looked away, and I took a few steps toward the door. I was in the doorway when Isaac's voice called me, barely a whisper.

"Daniel?"

"Yes?"

"Take great care."

When I got out into the street, it seemed as if darkness were creeping along the paving in pursuit of me. I quickened my pace and didn't slow down until I reached the apartment on Calle Santa Ana. I found my father in his armchair with an open book on his lap. It was a photograph album. On seeing me, he got up with an expression of great relief.

"I was beginning to get worried," he said. "How was the funeral?"

I shrugged, and my father nodded gravely.

"I got a bit of dinner ready for you. If you like, I could warm it up and—"

"Thanks, but I'm not hungry. I had a bite to eat out there."

He fixed his gaze on me and nodded again. He turned to remove the plates he'd placed on the table. It was then, without quite knowing why, that I went up to him and hugged him. My father, surprised, hugged me back.

"Daniel, are you all right?"

I held my father tightly in my arms.

"I love you," I murmured.

The cathedral bells were ringing when I began to read Nuria Monfort's manuscript. Her small, neat writing reminded me of her impeccable desk. Perhaps she had been trying to find in these words the peace and safety that life had not granted her.

Nuria Monfort:

Remembrance

of the Lost

1933–1955

· 1 ·

There are no second chances in life, except to feel remorse. Julián Carax and I met in the autumn of 1933. At that time I was working for the publisher Toni Cabestany, who had discovered him in 1927 in the course of one of his "book-scouting" trips to Paris. Julián earned his living playing piano at a hostess bar in the afternoons, and he wrote at night. The owner of the establishment, one Irene Marceau, knew most of the Paris publishers, and, thanks to her entreaties, favors, or threats of disclosure, Julián Carax had managed to get a number of novels published, though with disastrous commercial results. For a giveaway price, Cabestany acquired the exclusive rights to publish Carax's works in Spain and Latin America, with the translation of the French originals into Spanish by the author himself. Cabestany hoped to sell around three thousand copies per novel, but the first two titles he published in Spain turned out to be a total flop: barely a hundred copies of each sold. Despite these dismal results, every two years we received a new manuscript from Julián, which Cabestany accepted without any objections, saying that he'd signed an agreement with the author, that profit wasn't everything, and that good literature had to be supported no matter what.

One day I was intrigued enough to ask him why he continued to publish Julián Carax's novels as a loss-making venture. In answer to my question,

Cabestany ceremoniously walked over to his bookshelf, took one of Julián's books, and invited me to read it. I did. Two weeks later I'd read them all. This time my question was, how we could possibly sell so few copies of those novels.

"I don't know, dear," replied Cabestany. "But we'll keep on trying."

Such a noble and admirable gesture didn't quite fit the picture I had formed of Mr. Cabestany. Perhaps I had underestimated him. I found the figure of Julián Carax increasingly intriguing as everything related to him seemed to be shrouded in mystery. At least twice a month, someone would call asking for his address. I soon realized that it was always the same person, using a different name each time. But I would tell him only what could be read on the back cover of his novels, that Julián lived in Paris. After a time he stopped calling. Just in case, I deleted Carax's address from the company files. I was the only one who wrote to him, and I knew the address by heart.

Months later I chanced upon the bills sent by the printers to Mr. Cabestany. Glancing through them, I noticed that the expense of the editions of Julián Carax's books was defrayed, in its entirety, by someone outside our firm whose name I had never heard before: Miquel Moliner. Moreover, the costs of printing and shipping these books were substantially lower than the sum of money invoiced to Mr. Moliner. The numbers didn't lie: the publishing firm was making money by printing books that went straight to a warehouse. I didn't have the courage to question Cabestany's financial irregularities. I was afraid of losing my job. What I did do was take down the address to which we sent Miquel Moliner's invoices, a mansion on Calle Puertaferrissa. I kept that address for months before I plucked up the courage to visit him. Finally my conscience got the better of me, and I turned up at his house to tell him that Mr. Cabestany was swindling him. He smiled and told me he already knew.

"We all do what we're best at."

I asked him whether he was the person who had phoned so often asking for Carax's address. He said he wasn't, and told me with a worried look that I should never give that address to anyone. Ever.

Miquel Moliner was a bit of a mystery. He lived on his own in a cavernous, crumbling mansion that was part of the inheritance from his father, an industrialist who had grown rich through arms manufacture and, it was said, war mongering. Far from living among luxuries, Miquel led an almost monastic existence, dedicated to squandering his father's money, which he considered bloodstained, on the restoration of museums, cathedrals, schools, libraries, and hospitals, and on ensuring that the works of his childhood friend, Julián Carax, were published in his native city.

"I have more money than I need, but not enough friends like Julián" was his only explanation.

He hardly kept in touch with his siblings or the rest of the family, whom he referred to as strangers. He hadn't married and he seldom left the grounds of his mansion, of which he occupied only the top floor. There he had set up his office, where he worked feverishly, writing articles and columns for various newspapers and magazines in Madrid and Barcelona, translating technical texts from German and French, copyediting encyclopedias and school textbooks. Miquel Moliner suffered from that affliction of those who feel guilty when not working; although he respected and even envied the leisure others enjoyed, he fled from it. Far from gloating about his manic work ethic, he would joke about his obsessive activity and dismiss it as a minor form of cowardice.

"While you're working, you don't have to look life in the eye."

Almost without realizing it, we became good friends. We had a lot in common, probably too much. Miquel liked to talk to me about books, about his beloved Dr. Freud, about music, but above all about his old friend Julián. We saw each other almost every week. Miquel would tell me stories about the days when Julián was at San Gabriel's School. He kept a collection of old photographs of, and stories written by, a teenage Julián. Miquel adored Julián, and, through his words and his memories, I came to know him, or at least to create an image in his absence. A year after we had met, Miquel confessed that he'd fallen in love with me. I did not wish to hurt him, but neither did I want to deceive him. It was impossible to deceive Miquel. I told him I was extremely fond of him, that he'd become my best friend, but I wasn't in love with him. Miquel told me he already knew.

364 · *The Shadow of the Wind*

"You're in love with Julián, but you don't yet know."

In August 1933, Julián wrote to inform me that he'd almost finished the manuscript of another novel, called *The Cathedral Thief.* Cabestany had some contracts with Gallimard that were due for renewal in September. He'd been paralyzed for several weeks with a vicious attack of gout and, as a reward for my dedication, decided that I should travel to France in his place to negotiate the new contracts. At the same time, I could visit Julián Carax and collect his new opus. I wrote to Julián telling him of my visit, which was planned for mid-September, and asking him whether he could recommend a reliable, inexpensive hotel. Julián replied saying that I could stay at his place, a modest apartment in the Saint-Germain quarter, and keep the hotel money for other expenses. The day before I left, I went to see Miquel to ask him whether he had any message for Julián. For a long while he seemed to hesitate, and then he said he didn't.

The first time I saw Julián in person was at the Gare d'Austerlitz. Autumn had sneaked up early in Paris, and the station vault was thick with fog. I waited on the platform while the other passengers made their way toward the exit. Soon I was left alone and then saw a man wearing a black coat, standing at the entrance to the platform and watching me through the smoke of his cigarette. During the journey I had often wondered how I would recognize Julián. The photographs I'd seen of him in Miquel Moliner's collection were at least thirteen or fourteen years old. I looked up and down the platform. There was nobody there except that figure and me. I noticed that the man was looking at me with some curiosity: perhaps he, too, was waiting for someone. It couldn't be him. According to my calculations, Julián would be thirty-three, and that man seemed older. His hair was gray, and he looked sad or tired. Too pale and too thin, or maybe it was just the fog and the wearying journey or that the only pictures in my mind were of an adolescent Julián. Tentatively, I went up to the stranger and looked straight into his eyes.

"Julián?"

The stranger smiled and nodded. Julián Carax possessed the most charming smile in the world. It was all that was left of him.

Julián lived in an attic in Saint-Germain. The apartment had only two rooms: a living room with a minute kitchen and a tiny balcony from which you could see the towers of Notre-Dame looming out of a jungle of rooftops and mist, and a bedroom with no windows and a single bed. The bathroom was at the end of a corridor on the floor below, and he shared it with the neighbors. The whole of the apartment was smaller than Mr. Cabestany's office. Julián had cleaned it up and got everything ready to welcome me with simple modesty. I pretended to be delighted with the apartment, which still smelled of disinfectant and furniture wax, applied by Julián with more determination than skill. The sheets on the bed looked brand-new. They appeared to have a pattern of dragons and castles. Children's sheets. Julián excused himself: he'd bought them at a very reduced price, but they were top quality. The ones with no pattern were twice the price, he explained, and they were boring.

In the sitting room, an old wooden desk faced the view of the cathedral towers. On it stood the Underwood typewriter that Julián had bought with Cabestany's advance and two piles of writing paper, one blank and the other written on both sides. Julián shared the attic apartment with a huge white cat he called Kurtz. The animal watched me suspiciously as he lay at his master's feet, licking his paws. I counted two chairs, a coatrack, and little else. The rest was all books. Books lined the walls from floor to ceiling, in double rows. Seeing me inspect the place, Julián sighed.

"There's a hotel two blocks away. Clean, affordable, and respectable. I took the liberty of making a reservation."

I thought about it but was afraid of offending him.

"I'll be fine here, so long as it's not a bother for you, or for Kurtz."

Kurtz and Julián exchanged glances. Julián shook his head, and the cat imitated him. I hadn't noticed how alike they looked. Julián insisted on letting me have his bedroom. He hardly slept, he explained, and would set himself up in the sitting room on a folding bed, lent to him by his neighbor, Monsieur Darcieu—an old conjuror who read young ladies' palms in exchange for a kiss. That first night I slept right through, exhausted after the journey. I woke up at dawn and discovered that Julián had gone out. Kurtz was asleep on top of his master's typewriter. He snored like a mastiff. I went up to the desk and saw the manuscript of the new novel that I had come to collect.

The Cathedral Thief

On the first page, as in all Julián's other novels, was the handwritten dedication:

For P

I was tempted to start reading. I was about to pick up the second page when I noticed that Kurtz was looking at me out of the corner of his eye. I shook my head the way I'd seen Julián do. The cat, in turn, shook his head, and I put the pages back in their place. After a while Julián appeared, bringing with him freshly baked bread, a thermos of coffee, and some cheese. We had breakfast by the balcony. Julián spoke incessantly but avoided my eyes. In the light of dawn, he seemed to me like an aged child. He had shaved and put on what I imagined must be his only decent outfit, a cream-colored cotton suit that looked worn but elegant. I listened to him as he talked about the mysteries of Notre-Dame and about a ghostly barge that was said to cleave the waters of the Seine at night, gathering up the souls of desperate lovers who had ended their lives by jumping into the frozen waters. I listened to a thousand and one magic tales he invented as he went along just to keep me from asking him any questions. I watched him silently, nodding, searching in him for the man who had written the books I knew almost by heart from so much rereading, the boy whom Miquel Moliner had described to me so often.

"How many days are you going to be in Paris?" he asked.

My business with Gallimard would take me about two or three days, I said. My first meeting was that afternoon. I told him I'd thought of taking a couple of days off to get to know the city before returning to Barcelona.

"Paris requires more than two days," said Julián. "It won't listen to reason."

"I don't have any more time, Julián. Mr. Cabestany is a generous employer, but everything has a limit."

"Cabestany is a pirate, but even he knows that one can't see Paris in two days, or in two months, or even in two years."

"I can't spend two years in Paris, Julián."

For a long while, he looked at me without speaking, and then he smiled. "Why not? Is someone waiting for you?"

The dealings with Gallimard and my courtesy calls to various other publishers with whom Cabestany had agreements took up three whole days, just as I had foreseen. Julián had assigned me a guide and protector, a young boy called Hervé who was barely thirteen and knew the city intimately. Hervé would accompany me from door to door, making sure I knew which cafés to stop at for a bite, which streets to avoid, which sights to take in. He would wait for me for hours at the door of the publishers' offices without losing his smile or accepting any tips. Hervé spoke an amusing broken Spanish, which he mixed with overtones of Italian and Portuguese.

"Signore Carax, he already pay, with tuoda generosidade for meus serviços. . . ."

From what I gathered, Hervé was the orphan of one of the ladies at Irene Marceau's establishment, in whose attic he lived. Julián had taught him to read, write, and play the piano. On Sundays he would take him to the theater or a concert. Hervé idolized Julián and seemed prepared to do anything for him, even guide me to the end of the world if necessary. On our third day together, he asked me whether I was the girlfriend of Signore Carax. I said I wasn't, that I was only a friend on a visit. He seemed disappointed.

Julián spent most nights awake, sitting at his desk with Kurtz on his lap, going through pages or simply staring at the cathedral towers silhouetted in the distance. One night, when I couldn't sleep either because of the noise of the rain pattering on the roof, I went into the sitting room. We looked at each other without saying a word, and Julián offered me a cigarette. For a long time we stared silently at the rain. Later, when the rain stopped, I asked him who P was.

"Penélope," he answered.

I asked him to talk to me about her, about those fourteen years of exile in Paris. In a whisper, in the half-light, Julián told me Penélope was the only woman he had ever loved.

ONE NIGHT, IN THE WINTER OF 1921, IRENE MARCEAU FOUND JULIÁN wandering in the Paris streets, unable to remember his name and coughing up blood. All he had on him were a few coins and some folded sheets of paper with writing on them. Irene read them and thought she'd come across some famous author who had drunk too much, and that perhaps a generous publisher would reward her when he recovered consciousness. That, at least, was her version, but Julián knew she'd saved him out of compassion. He spent six months recovering in an attic room of Irene's brothel. The doctors warned Irene that if that man poisoned himself again, they would not be held responsible for him. He had ruined his stomach and his liver and was going to have to spend the rest of his days eating only milk, cottage cheese, and fresh bread. When Julián was able to speak again, Irene asked him who he was.

"Nobody," answered Julián.

"Well, nobody lives at my expense. What can you do?"

Julián said he could play the piano.

"Prove it."

Julián sat at the drawing-room piano and, facing a rapt audience of fifteen-year-old prostitutes in underwear, played a Chopin nocturne. They all clapped except for Irene, who told him that what she had just heard was music for the dead and they were in the business of the living. Julián played her a ragtime tune and a couple of pieces by Offenbach.

"That's better. Let's keep it upbeat."

His new job earned him a living, a roof, and two hot meals a day.

He survived in Paris thanks to Irene Marceau's charity, and she was the only person who encouraged him to keep on writing. Her favorite books were romantic novels and biographies of saints and martyrs, which intrigued her enormously. In her opinion Julián's problem was that his heart was poisoned; that was why he could only write those stories of horror and darkness. Despite her objections, it was thanks to Irene that Julián had found a publisher for his first novels. She was the one who had provided him with that attic in which he hid from the world, the one who dressed him and took him out to get a bit of sun and fresh air, who bought him books and made him go to mass with her on Sundays, followed by a stroll through the Tuileries. Irene Marceau kept him alive without asking for anything in return except his friendship and the promise that he would continue writing. In time she would allow him, occasionally, to take one of her girls up to the attic, even if they were only going to sleep hugging each other. Irene joked that the girls were almost as lonely as he was, and all they wanted was a bit of affection.

"My neighbor, Monsieur Darcieu, thinks I'm the luckiest man in the universe," he told me.

I asked him why he had never returned to Barcelona in search of Penélope. He fell into a long, deep silence, and when I looked at his face in the dark, I saw it was lined with tears. Without quite knowing what I was doing, I knelt down next to him and hugged him. We remained like that, embracing, until dawn caught us by surprise. I no longer know who kissed whom first, nor whether it matters. I know I found his lips and let him caress me without realizing that I, too, was crying and didn't know why. That dawn, and all the ones that followed in the two weeks I spent with Julián, we made love to each other on the floor, never saying a word. Later, sitting in a café or strolling through the streets, I would look into his eyes and know, without any need to question him, that he still loved Penélope. I remember that during those days I learned to hate that seventeen-year-old girl (for Penélope was always seventeen to me) whom I had never met and who now haunted my dreams. I invented excuses for cabling Cabestany to prolong my stay. I no longer cared whether I lost my job or the gray existence I had left behind in Barcelona. I have often asked myself whether I arrived in Paris with such an empty life that I fell into Julián's arms like Irene Marceau's girls, who, despite themselves, craved affection. All I know is that those two weeks I spent with Julián were the only time in my life when I felt, for once, that I was myself, when I understood with the hopeless clarity of what cannot be explained that I would never be able to love another man the way I loved Julián, even if I spent the rest of my days trying.

One day Julián fell asleep in my arms, exhausted. The previous afternoon, as we passed by a pawnshop, he had stopped to show me a fountain pen that had been on display there for years. According to the pawnbroker, it had once belonged to Victor Hugo. Julián had never owned even a fraction of the means to buy that pen, but he would stop and look at it every day. I dressed quietly and went down to the pawnshop. The pen cost a fortune, which I didn't have, but the pawnbroker said that he'd accept a check in pesetas on any Spanish bank with a branch in Paris. Before she died, my mother had promised me she would save up to buy me a wedding dress. Victor Hugo's pen took care of that, veil and all, and although I knew it was madness, I have never spent any sum of money with more satisfaction. When I left the shop with the fabulous case, I noticed that a woman was following me. She was a very elegant lady, with silvery hair and the bluest eyes I have ever seen. She came up to me and introduced herself. She was Irene Marceau, Julián's patron. Hervé, my guide, had spoken to her about me. She only wanted to meet me and ask me whether I was the woman Julián had been waiting for all those years. I didn't have to reply. Irene nodded in sympathy and kissed my cheek. I watched her walking away down the street, and at that moment I understood that Julián would never be mine. I went back to the attic with the pen case hidden in my bag. Julián was awake and waiting for me. He undressed me without saying anything, and we made love for the last time. When he asked me why I was crying, I told him they were tears of joy. Later, when Julián went down for some food, I packed my bags and placed the case with the pen on his typewriter. I put the manuscript of the novel in my suitcase and left before Julián returned. On the landing I came upon Monsieur Darcieu, the old conjuror who read the palms of young ladies in exchange for a kiss. He took my left hand and gazed at me sadly.

"*Vous avez poison au coeur, mademoiselle.*"

When I tried to pay him his fee, he shook his head gently, and instead it was he who kissed my hand.

I GOT TO THE GARE D'AUSTERLITZ JUST IN TIME TO CATCH THE TWELVE o'clock train to Barcelona. The ticket inspector who sold me the ticket asked me whether I was feeling all right. I nodded and shut myself up in the compartment. The train was already leaving when I looked out the window and caught a glimpse of Julián on the platform, in the same place I'd seen him for the first time. I closed my eyes and didn't open them again until we had lost sight of the station and that bewitching city to which I could never return. I arrived in Barcelona the following morning, as day was breaking. It was my twenty-fourth birthday, and I knew that the best part of my life was already behind me.

· 2 ·

AFTER I RETURNED TO BARCELONA, I LET SOME TIME PASS BEFORE visiting Miquel Moliner again. I needed to get Julián out of my head, and I realized that if Miquel were to ask me about him, I wouldn't know what to say. When we did meet again, I didn't need to tell him anything. Miquel just looked me in the eyes and knew. He seemed to me thinner than before my trip to Paris; his face had an almost unhealthy pallor, which I attributed to the enormous workload with which he punished himself. He admitted that he was going through financial difficulties. He had spent almost all the money from his inheritance on his philanthropic causes, and now his brothers' lawyers were trying to evict him from his home, claiming that a clause in old Mr. Moliner's will specified that he could live there only providing he kept it in good condition and could prove he had the financial means for the upkeep of the property. Otherwise the Puertaferrissa mansion would pass into the custody of his brothers.

"Even before dying, my father sensed that I was going to spend his money on all the things he most detested in life, down to the last céntimo."

His income as a newspaper columnist and translator was far from enough to maintain that sort of residence.

"Making money isn't hard in itself," he complained. "What's hard is to earn it doing something worth devoting one's life to."

372 · The Shadow of the Wind

I suspected that he was beginning to drink secretly. Sometimes his hands shook. Every Sunday I went over to see him and made him come out into the street and get away from his desk and his encyclopedias. I knew it hurt him to see me. He acted as if he didn't remember that he'd offered to marry me and I'd refused him, but at times I'd catch him gazing at me with a look of mingled yearning and defeat. My sole excuse for submitting him to such cruelty was purely selfish: only Miquel knew the truth about Julián and Penélope Aldaya.

During those months I spent away from Julián, Penélope Aldaya became a specter that stole my sleep and my thoughts. I could still remember the expression of disappointment on the face of Irene Marceau when she realized I was not the woman Julián was waiting for. Penélope Aldaya, treacherously absent, was too powerful an enemy for me. She was invisible, so I imagined her as perfect. Next to her I was unworthy, vulgar, all too real. I had never thought it possible to hate someone so much and so despite myself—to hate someone I didn't even know, whom I had never seen in my life. I suppose I thought that if I met her face-to-face, if I could prove to myself that she was flesh and blood, her spell would break and Julián would be free again. And I with him. I wanted to believe that it was only a matter of time and patience. Sooner or later Miquel would tell me the truth. And the truth would liberate me.

One day, as we strolled through the cathedral cloister, Miquel once again hinted at his interest in me. I looked at him and saw a lonely man, devoid of hope. I knew what I was doing when I took him home and let myself be seduced by him. I knew I was deceiving him and that he knew, too, but had nothing else in the world. That is how we became lovers, out of desperation. I saw in his eyes what I would have wanted to see in Julián's. I felt that by giving myself to him I was taking revenge on Julián and Penélope and on everything that was denied to me. Miquel, who was ill with desire and loneliness, knew that our love was a farce, but even so he couldn't let me go. Every day he drank more heavily and often could hardly make love to me. He would then joke bitterly that, after all, we'd turned into the perfect married couple in record time. We were hurting each other through spite and cowardice. One night, almost a year after I had returned from Paris, I asked him to tell me the truth about Penélope. Miquel had been drinking, and he became violent, as I'd never seen him before. In his rage he insulted me and accused me of never having loved him, of being a vulgar whore. He tore my clothes off me, shredding them in the process, and when he tried to force himself on me, I lay down, offering my body without resistance, crying to myself. Miquel broke down and begged me to forgive him. How I wished I were able to love him and not Julián, able to choose to remain by his side. But I couldn't. We embraced in the dark, and I asked forgiveness for all the pain I had caused him. He then told me that if it mattered so much to me, he would tell me the truth about Penélope Aldaya. Another one of my mistakes.

That Sunday in 1919, when Miquel Moliner went to the station to give his friend Julián his ticket to Paris and see him off, Miquel already knew that Penélope would not be coming to the rendezvous. Two days earlier, when Don Ricardo Aldaya had returned from Madrid, his wife had confessed that she'd surprised Julián and their daughter, Penélope, in the governess's room. Jorge Aldaya had revealed this to Miquel the next day, making him swear he would never tell anyone. Jorge explained how, when he was given the news, Don Ricardo exploded with anger and rushed up to Penélope's room, shouting like a madman. When she heard her father's yells, Penélope locked her door and wept with terror. Don Ricardo kicked in the door and found his daughter on her knees, trembling and begging for mercy. Don Ricardo then slapped her in the face so hard that she fell down. Not even Jorge was able to repeat the words Don Ricardo hurled at her in his fury. All the members of the family and the servants waited downstairs, terrified, not knowing what to do. Jorge hid in his room, in the dark, but even there he could hear Don Ricardo's shouts. Jacinta was dismissed that same day. Don Ricardo didn't even deign to see her. He ordered the servants to throw her out of the house and threatened them with a similar fate if any of them had any contact with her again.

When Don Ricardo went down to the library, it was already midnight. He'd left Penélope locked up in what had been Jacinta's bedroom and strictly forbade anyone, whether members of his staff or family, to go up to see her. From his room Jorge heard his parents talking on the ground floor. The doctor arrived in the early hours. Mrs. Aldaya led him to Jacinta's room and waited by the door while the doctor examined Penélope. When he came out, the doctor only nodded and collected his fee. Jorge heard Don Ricardo telling him that if he made any comments to anyone about what he'd seen there, he would personally ensure that his reputation was ruined and he was unable to practice medicine ever again. Jorge knew what that meant.

Jorge admitted that he was very worried about Penélope and Julián. He had never seen his father so beside himself with rage. Even taking into account the offense committed by the lovers, he could not understand the intensity of his father's anger. There had to be something else, he said. Don Ricardo had already ordered San Gabriel's School to expel Julián and had got in touch with the boy's father, the hatter, about sending him off to the army immediately. When Miquel heard all this, he decided he couldn't tell Julián the truth. If he disclosed to Julián that Don Ricardo was keeping Penélope locked up and that she might be carrying their child, Julián would never take that train to Paris. He knew that if his friend remained in Barcelona, that would be the end of him. So he decided to deceive him and let him go to Paris without knowing what had happened; he would let him think that Penélope was going to join him later. When he said good-bye to Julián that day in the Estación de Francia, even Miquel wanted to believe that not all was lost.

Some days later, when it was discovered that Julián had disappeared, all hell broke loose. Don Ricardo Aldaya was seething. He set half the police department in pursuit of the fugitive, but without success. He then accused the hatter of having sabotaged the plan they had agreed on and threatened him with total ruin. The hatter, who couldn't understand what was going on, in turn accused his wife, Sophie, of having plotted the escape of that despicable son and threatened to throw her out of their home. It didn't occur to anyone that it was Miquel Moliner who had planned the whole thing—to anyone except Jorge Aldaya, who went to see him a fortnight later. He no longer exuded the fear and anxiety that had gripped him earlier. This was a different Jorge Aldaya, an adult robbed of all innocence. Whatever it was that hid behind Don Ricardo's anger, Jorge had discovered it. The reason for his visit was clear: he knew it was Miquel who had helped Julián to escape. He told him their friendship was over, that he didn't ever want to see him again, and he threatened to kill him if he told anyone what he, Jorge, had revealed to him two weeks before.

A few weeks later, Miquel received a letter, with a false sender's name, posted by Julián in Paris. In it he gave him his address, told him he was well and missed him, and inquired after his mother and Penélope. He included a letter addressed to Penélope, for Miquel to post from Barcelona, the first of many that Penélope would never read. Miquel prudently allowed a few months to go by. He wrote to Julián once a week, mentioning only what he felt was suitable, which was almost nothing. Julián, in turn, told him about Paris, about how difficult everything was turning out to be, how lonely and desperate he felt. Miquel sent him money, books, and his friendship. In every letter Julián would include another one for Penélope. Miquel mailed them from different post offices, even though he knew it was useless. In his letters Julián never stopped asking after Penélope. Miquel couldn't tell him anything. He knew from Jacinta that Penélope had not left the house on Avenida del Tibidabo since her father had locked her in the room on the third floor.

One night Jorge Aldaya waylaid Miquel in the dark, two blocks from his home. "Have you come to kill me already?" asked Miquel. Jorge said that he had come to do him and his friend Julián a favor. He handed him a letter and advised him to make sure it reached Julián, wherever he was hiding. "For everyone's sake," he declared portentously. The envelope contained a sheet of paper handwritten by Penélope Aldaya.

Dear Julián,

I'm writing to notify you of my forthcoming marriage and to entreat you not to write to me anymore, to forget me and rebuild your life. I don't bear you any grudge, but I wouldn't be honest if I didn't confess to you that I have never loved you and never will be able to love you. I wish you the best, wherever you may be.

Penélope

Miquel read and reread the letter a thousand times. The handwriting was unmistakable, but he didn't believe for a moment that Penélope had

376 · The Shadow of the Wind

written that letter willingly: ". . . wherever you may be." Penélope knew
perfectly well where Julián was: in Paris, waiting for her. If she pretended
not to know his whereabouts, Miquel reflected, it was to protect him. For
that same reason, Miquel couldn't understand what could have induced her
to write those words. What further threats could Don Ricardo Aldaya bring
down on her, on top of keeping her locked up for months in that room like
a prisoner? More than anyone, Penélope knew that her letter was a poi-
soned dagger for Julián's heart: a young boy of nineteen, lost in a distant
and hostile city, abandoned by all, surviving only through his false hopes of
seeing her again. What did she want to protect him from by pushing him
away in that way? After much consideration, Miquel decided not to send the
letter. Not without first knowing the reason for it. Without a good reason,
it wouldn't be his hand that would plunge that dagger into his friend's soul.

Some days later he found out that Don Ricardo Aldaya, tired of seeing
Jacinta waiting like a sentry at the doors of his house, begging for news of
Penélope, had used his contacts to get her admitted into the Horta lunatic
asylum. When Miquel Moliner tried to see her, he was denied access. Ja-
cinta Coronado was to spend the first three months in solitary confinement.
After three months of silence and darkness, he was told by one of the doc-
tors—a young, cheerful individual—the patient's submission was guaran-
teed. Following a hunch, Miquel decided to pay a visit to the *pensión* where
Jacinta had been staying after her dismissal. When he identified himself, the
landlady remembered that Jacinta had left a note for him and still owed her
three weeks' rent. He paid the debt, whose existence he doubted, and took
the note. In it the governess explained that she had been informed that
Laura, one of the Aldayas' servants, had been dismissed when it was dis-
covered that she had secretly posted a letter from Penélope to Julián. Miquel
deduced that the only address to which Penélope, from her captivity, would
have sent the letter was the apartment of Julián's parents on Ronda de San
Antonio, hoping that they, in turn, would make sure it reached him in Paris.

So he decided to visit Sophie Carax to recover the letter and forward it
to Julián. When he arrived at the home of the Fortunys, Miquel was in for
an unpleasant surprise: Sophie Carax no longer lived there. She had aban-
doned her husband a few days earlier—that, at least, was the rumor that

was doing the rounds of the neighbors. Miquel then tried to speak to the hatter, who spent his days shut away in his shop, consumed by anger and humiliation. Miquel told him that he'd come to collect a letter that must have arrived for his son, Julián, a few days earlier.

"I have no son" was the only answer he received.

Miquel Moliner went away without knowing that the letter in question had ended up in the hands of the caretaker and that many years later, you, Daniel, would find it and read the words Penélope had meant for Julián, this time straight from her heart: words that he never received.

When Miquel left the Fortuny hat shop, one of the residents in the block of apartments, who identified herself as Viçenteta, went up to him and asked him whether he was looking for Sophie. Miquel said he was and told her he was a friend of Julián's.

Viçenteta informed him that Sophie was staying in a boardinghouse hidden in a small street behind the post office building, waiting for the departure of the boat that would take her to America. Miquel went to that address, where he found a narrow, miserable staircase almost devoid of light and air. At the top of the dusty spiral of sloping steps, he found Sophie Carax, in a damp, dark, fourth-floor room. Julián's mother was facing the window, sitting on the edge of a makeshift bed on which two closed suitcases were lying like coffins containing her twenty-two years in Barcelona.

When she read the letter signed by Penélope that Jorge Aldaya had given Miquel, Sophie shed tears of anger.

"She knows," she murmured. "Poor kid, she knows. . . ."

"Knows what?" asked Miquel.

"It's my fault," said Sophie. "It's my fault."

Miquel held her hands, without understanding. Sophie didn't dare meet his eyes.

"Julián and Penélope are brother and sister," she whispered.

· 3 ·

YEARS BEFORE BECOMING ANTONI FORTUNY'S SLAVE, SOPHIE CARAX had been a woman who made a living from her talents. She was only nineteen when she arrived in Barcelona in search of a promised job that never materialized. Before dying, her father had obtained the necessary references for her to go into the service of the Benarenses, a prosperous family of merchants from Alsace who had established themselves in Barcelona.

"When I die," he urged her, "go to them, and they'll take you in like a daughter."

The warm welcome she received was part of the problem. Monsieur Benarens indeed received her with open arms—all too open, in the opinion of his wife. Madame Benarens gave Sophie one hundred pesetas and turned her out of the house, not without showing some pity toward her and her bad luck.

"You have your whole life ahead of you, but I have only this miserable, lewd husband."

A music school on Calle Diputación agreed to give Sophie work as a private music and piano tutor. In those days it was considered desirable for girls of well-to-do families to be taught proper social graces and a smattering of music for the drawing room, where the polonaise was less dangerous than conversation or questionable literature. That is how Sophie Carax began her visits to palatial mansions, where starched, silent maids would lead her to the music rooms. There the hostile offspring of the industrial aristocracy would be waiting for her, to laugh at her accent, her shyness, or her lowly position—the fact that she could read music didn't alter that. Gradually Sophie learned to concentrate on that tiny number of pupils who rose above the status of perfumed vermin and to forget the rest of them.

At about that time, Sophie met a young hatter (for so he liked to be referred to, with professional pride) called Antoni Fortuny, who seemed determined to court her, whatever the price. Antoni Fortuny, for whom Sophie felt a warm friendship and nothing else, did not take long to propose to her, an offer Sophie refused—and kept refusing, a dozen times a month. Every time they parted, Sophie hoped she wouldn't see him again, because she didn't want to hurt him. The hatter, brushing aside her refusals, stayed on the offensive, inviting her to dance, take a stroll, or have a hot chocolate with sponge fingers on Calle Canuda. Being alone in Barcelona, Sophie found it difficult to resist his enthusiasm, his company, and his devotion. She only had to look at Antoni Fortuny to know that she would never be able to love him. Not the way she dreamed she would love somebody one day. But she found it hard to cast aside the image of herself that she saw reflected in the hatter's besotted eyes. Only in them did she see the Sophie she would have wished to be.

And so, through need or through weakness, Sophie continued to entertain the hatter's advances, in the belief that one day he would meet a girl who would return his affection and his life would take a more rewarding course. In the meantime, being desired and appreciated was enough to alleviate her loneliness and the longing she felt for everything she had left behind. She saw Antoni on Sundays, after mass. The rest of the week was taken up by her music lessons. Her favorite pupil was a highly talented girl called Ana Valls, the daughter of a prosperous manufacturer of textile machinery who had built his fortune from nothing, by dint of great efforts and sacrifices, mostly other people's. Ana expressed her desire to become a great composer and would make Sophie listen to small pieces she composed, imitating motifs by Grieg and Schumann—not without skill. Although Mr. Valls was convinced that women were incapable of creating anything but knitted garments or crocheted bedspreads, he approved of his daughter's becoming a competent interpreter on the keyboard, for he had plans of marrying her off to some heir with a good surname, and he knew that refined people liked to discover unusual qualities in marriageable girls, besides submissiveness and the fecundity of youth.

It was in the Valls residence that Sophie met one of Mr. Valls's greatest benefactors and financial godfathers: Don Ricardo Aldaya, inheritor of the Aldaya empire, by then already the great white hope of the Catalan oligarchy of the end of the century. A few months earlier, Don Ricardo Aldaya had married a rich heiress, a dazzling beauty with an unpronounceable name, attributes that wagging tongues held to be true, despite the fact that her newlywed husband seemed to see no beauty in her at all and never bothered to mention her name. It had been a match between families and banks, not any sentimental nonsense, said Mr. Valls, for whom it was very clear that one thing was the bed and the other the head.

Sophie had only to exchange one look with Don Ricardo Aldaya to know she was doomed. Aldaya had wolfish eyes, hungry and sharp, the eyes of a man who knew where and when to strike. He kissed her hand slowly, caressing her knuckles with his lips. Just as the hatter exuded kindness and warmth, Don Ricardo radiated cruelty and power. His canine smile made it clear that he could read her thoughts and desires and found them laughable. Sophie felt for him that species of contempt that is awakened in us by the things we most desire without knowing it. She immediately told herself she would not see him again, would stop teaching her favorite pupil if that was what it took to avoid any future encounters with Ricardo Aldaya. Nothing had ever terrified her so much as sensing that animality under her own skin, the prey's instinctive recognition of her predator, dressed in elegant linen. It took her only a few seconds to make up a flimsy excuse for leaving the room, to the puzzlement of Mr. Valls, the amusement of Aldaya, and the dejection of little Ana, who understood people even better than she did music and knew she had irretrievably lost her teacher.

A week later Sophie saw Don Ricardo Aldaya waiting for her at the entrance of the music school on Calle Diputación, smoking and leafing through a newspaper. They exchanged glances, and, without saying a word,

he led her to a building two blocks away. It was a new building, still unin-
habited. They went up to the first floor. Don Ricardo opened the door and
ushered her in. Sophie entered the apartment, a maze of corridors and gal-
leries, bare of any furniture, paintings, lamps, or any other object that might
have identified it as a dwelling. Don Ricardo Aldaya shut the door, and they
looked at each other.

"I haven't stopped thinking about you all week. Tell me you haven't done
the same and I'll let you go, and you won't ever see me again," said Ricardo.

Sophie shook her head.

Their secret meetings lasted ninety-six days. They met in the after-
noons, always in that empty apartment on the corner of Diputación and
Rambla de Cataluña. Tuesdays and Thursdays at three. Their meetings
never lasted more than an hour. Sometimes Sophie stayed on alone once Al-
daya had left, crying or shaking in a corner of the bedroom. Then, when
Sunday came, Sophie looked desperately into the hatter's eyes for traces of
the woman who was disappearing, yearning for both devotion and decep-
tion. The hatter didn't see the marks on her skin, the cuts and burns that
peppered her body. The hatter didn't see the despair in her smile, in her
meekness. The hatter didn't see anything. Perhaps for that reason, she ac-
cepted his promise of marriage. By then she already suspected that she was
carrying Aldaya's child, but was afraid of telling him, almost as much as she
was afraid of losing him. Once again it was Aldaya who saw in Sophie what
she was incapable of admitting. He gave her five hundred pesetas and an ad-
dress on Calle Platería and ordered her to get rid of the baby. Sophie re-
fused. Don Ricardo Aldaya slapped her until her ears bled, then threatened
to have her killed if she dared mention their meetings or admit that the
child was his. When Sophie told the hatter that some thugs had assaulted
her in Plaza del Pino, he believed her. When she told him she wanted to be
his wife, he believed her. On the day of her wedding, someone erroneously
sent a funeral wreath to the church. Everyone laughed nervously when they
saw the florist's mistake. All except Sophie, who knew perfectly well that
Don Ricardo Aldaya had not forgotten her on her wedding day.

· 4 ·

Sophie Carax never imagined that years later she would see Ricardo again (a mature man by now, heading up the family empire, and a father of two), nor that he would return to meet the boy he had wished to erase with five hundred pesetas.

"Perhaps it's because I'm growing old," he explained, "but I want to get to know this kid and give him the opportunities in life that a son of my flesh and blood deserves. It had not crossed my mind to think of him in all these years, and now, strangely enough, I'm unable to think of anything else."

Ricardo Aldaya had decided that he couldn't see himself in his firstborn, Jorge. The boy was weak, reserved, and lacked his father's steadfast spirit. He lacked everything, except the right surname. One day Don Ricardo had woken up in the maid's bed feeling that his body was getting old, that God had removed His blessing. Seized with panic, he ran to look at himself naked in the mirror and felt that the mirror was lying. That man was not Ricardo Aldaya.

He now wanted to find the man who had been stolen from him. For years he had known about the hatter's son. Nor had he forgotten Sophie, in his own way. Don Ricardo Aldaya never forgot anything. The moment had arrived to meet the boy. It was the first time in fifteen years that he had come across someone who wasn't afraid of him, who dared to defy him and even laugh at him. He recognized gallantry in the child, the silent ambition that fools can't see but is there all the same. God had given him back his youth. Sophie, only an echo of the woman he remembered, didn't even have the strength to come between them. The hatter was just a buffoon, a spiteful and resentful yokel whose complicity Aldaya counted on buying. He decided to tear Julián away from that stifling world of mediocrity and poverty and open the doors of his financial paradise to him. He would be educated in San Gabriel's School, would enjoy all the privileges of his class, and would be initiated into the pursuits his father had chosen for him. Don Ricardo wanted a successor worthy of himself. Jorge would always live in the shadow of his entitlements, hiding from his mediocrity in creature comforts. Penélope, the beautiful Penélope, was a woman, and therefore a treasure, not a treasurer. Julián, who had the soul of a poet, and therefore the soul of a murderer, fulfilled all the requirements. It was only a question of time. Don Ricardo estimated that within ten years he would have stamped his image on the boy. Never, in all the time Julián spent with the Aldayas as one of the family (as the chosen one, even), did it occur to Don Ricardo that the only thing Julián wanted from him was Penélope. It didn't occur to him for an instant that Julián secretly despised him, that his affection was a sham, only a pretext to be close to Penélope. To possess her wholly and utterly. They did resemble each other in that.

When his wife told him she'd discovered Julián and Penélope naked in unequivocal circumstances, his entire world went up in flames. Horror at this treason, the rage of knowing that he had been unspeakably affronted, outwitted at his own game, humiliated and stabbed in the back by the one person he had learned to adore as the image of himself—all these feelings assailed him with such fury that nobody was able to understand the magnitude of his pain. When the doctor who came to examine Penélope confirmed that the girl had been deflowered and that she was possibly pregnant, Don Ricardo's soul dissolved into the thick, viscous liquid of blind hatred. He saw his own hand in Julián's hand, the hand that had plunged the dagger deep into his heart. He didn't know it yet, but the day he ordered Penélope to be locked up in the third-floor bedroom was the day he began to die. Everything he did from then on was only the final agony of his self-destruction.

In collaboration with the hatter, whom he had so deeply despised, he arranged Julián's removal from Barcelona and his entry into the army, where Aldaya had given orders that he should meet with an "accidental" death. He forbade that anyone—doctors, servants, even members of the family, except himself and his wife—should see Penélope during the months when the girl remained imprisoned in that room that smelled of illness and death. By then Aldaya's partners had secretly withdrawn their support and were maneuvering behind his back to seize his power, using the fortune that he himself had made available to them. By then the Aldaya empire was silently crumbling, at secret board meetings in Madrid, in hushed corridors, in Geneva banks. Julián, as Aldaya should have suspected, had escaped. Deep down he secretly felt proud of the boy, even though he wished him dead. Julián had done what he would have done in his place. Someone else would pay for Julián's actions.

Penélope Aldaya gave birth to a stillborn baby boy on September 26, 1919. If a doctor had been able to examine her, he would have said that the baby had already been in danger for some days and must be delivered by cesarean. If a doctor had been present, perhaps he would have been able to stop the hemorrhage that took Penélope's life, while she shrieked and scratched at the locked door, on the other side of which her father wept in silence and her mother cowered staring at her husband. If a doctor had been present, he would have accused Don Ricardo Aldaya of murder, for there was no other word that could describe the scene within that dark, blood-stained cell. But there was nobody there, and when at last they opened the door and found Penélope lying dead in a pool of her own blood, hugging a shining, purple-colored baby, nobody was capable of uttering a single word. The two bodies were buried in the basement crypt, with no ceremony or witnesses. The sheets and the afterbirth were thrown into the boilers, and the place was sealed with a brick wall.

When Jorge Aldaya, drunk with guilt and shame, told Miquel Moliner what had happened, Miquel decided to send Julián the letter, signed by Penélope, in which she declared that she didn't love him, begged him to forget her, and announced a fictitious wedding. He preferred to have Julián believe that lie and rebuild his life in the shadow of a betrayal than have to present him with the truth. When, two years later, Mrs. Aldaya died, there were those who blamed her death on the curse that lay on the mansion, but her son, Jorge, knew that what had killed her was the fire that raged inside her, Penélope's screams and her desperate banging on that door that hammered incessantly in her head. By then the family had already fallen from grace, and the Aldaya fortune was collapsing like a sand castle, swept away by a combination of greed and revenge. Secretaries and accountants devised the flight to Argentina, the beginning of a new, more modest, business. The important thing was to get away. Away from the specters that scurried through the corridors of the Aldaya mansion, as they had always done.

They departed one dawn of 1926, traveling under false names on board the ship that would take them across the Atlantic to the port of La Plata. Jorge and his father shared a cabin. Old Aldaya, foul-smelling and dying, could barely stand up. The doctors whom he had not permitted to see Penélope feared him too much to tell him the truth, but he knew that death had boarded the ship with them, and that his body, which God had begun to steal from him on the morning he decided to look for his son Julián, was wasting away. Throughout that long crossing, sitting on the deck, shivering under the blankets and facing the ocean's infinite emptiness, he knew that he would never see land. Sometimes, sitting on the stern, he would watch the school of sharks that had been following them since they left Tenerife. He heard one of the officers say that such a sinister escort was normal in transatlantic cruises. The beasts fed on the animal remains that the ship left in its wake. But Don Ricardo thought otherwise. He was convinced that those devils were following him. You're waiting for me, he thought, seeing in them God's true face. It was then he approached his son Jorge, whom he had so often despised and whom he now saw as his last resort, and made him swear he would carry out his dying wish. "You will find Julián Carax and you'll kill him. Swear that you will."

One dawn, two days before reaching Buenos Aires, Jorge woke up and saw that his father's berth was empty. He went out to look for him; the deck was deserted, bathed in mist and spray. He found his father's dressing gown, still warm, abandoned on the stern of the ship. The ship's wake disappeared into a cloud of scarlet, a stain on the calm waters, as if the ocean itself were bleeding. It was then he noticed that the sharks had stopped following them. He saw them, in the distance, their dorsal fins flapping as they danced in a circle. During the remainder of the crossing, no passenger sighted the school of dogfish again.

When Jorge Aldaya disembarked in Buenos Aires and the customs officer asked him whether he was traveling alone, he nodded in assent. He had been traveling alone for a long time.

· 5 ·

Ten years after disembarking in Buenos Aires, Jorge Aldaya, or the spent force he had become, returned to Barcelona. The misfortunes that had started to eat away at the Aldaya family in the Old World had only grown in Argentina. Jorge was left on his own to face the world, a fight for which he had neither his father's strength nor his composure. Jorge had reached Buenos Aires with a numb heart, shot through with remorse. America, he would later say, by way of apology or epitaph, is a mirage, a land of savage predators, and he'd been educated into the privileges and frivolous refinements of Old Europe—a dead continent held together by inertia. In only a few years, he lost everything, starting with his reputation and ending with the gold watch his father had given him for his first communion. Thanks to the watch, he was able to buy himself a return ticket. The man who came back to Spain was almost a beggar, a bundle of bitterness and failure, poisoned by the memory of what he felt had been snatched from him and the hatred for the person on whom he blamed his ruin: Julián Carax.

The promise he had made to his father was still branded on his mind. As soon as he arrived, he tried to pick up Julián's trail, only to discover that, like him, Carax also seemed to have vanished from Barcelona. It was then, through chance or fate, that he encountered a familiar character from his youth. After a prominent career in reformatories and state prisons, Francisco Javier Fumero had joined the army, attaining the rank of lieutenant. There were many who envisaged him as a future general, but

a murky scandal caused his expulsion from the army. Even then his reputation out-
lasted his rank. He was talked about a great deal, but above all he was feared. Fran-
cisco Javier Fumero, that shy, disturbed boy who once gathered dead leaves from the
courtyard at San Gabriel's, was now a murderer. It was rumored that he killed off no-
torious characters for money, that he dispatched political figures on request. Fumero
was said to be death itself.

Aldaya and he recognized each other instantly through the haze of the Novedades
Café. Aldaya was ill, stricken by a strange fever that he blamed on the insects of South
American jungles. "There, even the mosquitoes are sons of bitches," he complained.
Fumero listened to him with a mixture of fascination and revulsion. He revered mos-
quitoes and all insects in general. He admired their discipline, their fortitude and or-
ganization. There was no laziness in them, no irreverence or racial degeneration. His
favorite species were spiders, blessed with that rare science for weaving a trap in which
they awaited their prey with infinite patience, knowing that sooner or later the prey
would succumb, through stupidity or slackness. In his opinion society had a lot to
learn from insects. Aldaya was a clear case of moral and physical ruin. He had aged
noticeably and looked shabby, with no muscle tone. Fumero couldn't bear people with
no muscle tone. They nauseated him.

"Javier, I feel dreadful," Aldaya pleaded. "Could you help me out for a few days?"

Fumero agreed to take Jorge Aldaya to his home. He lived in a gloomy apartment
in the Raval quarter, on Calle Cadena, in the company of numerous insects stored in
pharmacy jars, and half a dozen books. Fumero detested books as much as he loved
insects, but those were no ordinary volumes: they were the novels of Julián Carax pub-
lished by Cabestany. Two prostitutes lived in the apartment opposite—a mother and
daughter duo who allowed themselves to be pinched and burned with cigars when
business was slow, especially at the end of the month. Fumero paid them to take care
of Aldaya while he was away at work. He had no desire to see him die. Not yet.

Francisco Javier Fumero had joined the Crime Squad. There was always work there
for qualified personnel capable of confronting the most awkward situations, the sorts
of situations that needed to be solved discreetly so that respectable citizens could
continue living in blissful ignorance. Words to that effect had been said to him by
Lieutenant Durán, a man given to solemn pronouncements, under whose command
Fumero had joined the police force.

"Being a policeman isn't a job, it's a mission," Durán would proclaim. "Spain needs more balls and less chatter."

Unfortunately, Lieutenant Durán was soon to die in a lamentable accident during a police raid in the district of La Barceloneta: in the confusion of an encounter with a group of anarchists, he fell through a skylight, and plunged five floors to his death. Everyone agreed that Spain had lost a great man, a national hero with a vision of the future, a thinker who did not fear action. Fumero took over his post with pride, knowing that he had done the right thing by pushing him, for Durán was getting too old for the job. Fumero found old men revolting—as he did crippled men, Gypsies, and queers—whether or not they had muscle tone. Sometimes God made mistakes. It was the duty of every upright citizen to correct these small failings and keep the world looking presentable.

In March 1932, a few weeks after their meeting in the Novedades Café, Jorge Aldaya began to feel better and opened his heart to Fumero. He begged forgiveness for the way he had treated him in their school days. With tears in his eyes, he told him his whole story, without omitting anything. Fumero listened silently, nodding, taking it in, all the while wondering whether he should kill Aldaya then and there, or wait. He wondered whether Aldaya would be so weak that the blade would meet only a tepid resistance from that stinking flesh, softened by indolence. He decided to postpone the vivisection. He was intrigued by the story, especially insofar as it concerned Julián Carax.

He knew, from the information he obtained at the publishing house, that Carax lived in Paris, but Paris was a very large city, and nobody in Cabestany's company seemed to know the exact address. Nobody except for a woman called Monfort, who kept it to herself. Fumero had followed her two or three times on her way out of the office, without her realizing. He had even traveled in a tram at half a yard's distance from her. Women never noticed him, and if they did, they turned their faces the other way, pretending not to have seen him. One night, after following her right up to her front door in Plaza de San Felipe Neri, Fumero went back to his home and masturbated furiously; as he did so, he imagined himself plunging his knife into that woman's body, an inch or so at a time, slowly, methodically, his eyes fixed on hers. Maybe then she would deign to give him Carax's address and treat him with the respect due to a police officer.

390 · *The Shadow of the Wind*

Julián Carax was the only person whom Fumero had failed to kill once he'd made up his mind. Perhaps because he had been Fumero's first, and it takes time to master your game. When Fumero heard that name again, he smiled in a way his neighbors, the prostitutes, found so frightening: without blinking, and slowly licking his upper lip. He could still remember Carax kissing Penélope Aldaya in the large mansion on Avenida del Tibidabo. His Penélope. His had been a pure love, a true love, like the ones you saw in movies. Fumero was very keen on movies and went to the cinema at least twice a week. It was in a cinema that he had understood that Penélope had been the love of his life. The rest, especially his mother, had been nothing but tarts. As he listened to the last snippets of Aldaya's story, he decided that, after all, he was not going to kill him. In fact, he was pleased that fate had reunited them. He had a vision, like the ones in the films he so enjoyed: Aldaya was going to hand him the others on a platter. Sooner or later they would all end up ensnared in his web.

· 6 ·

IN THE WINTER OF 1934, THE MOLINER BROTHERS FINALLY MANAGED
to evict Miquel from the house on Calle Puertaferrissa, which still re-
mains empty and in a derelict state. All they wanted was to see him on the
street, shorn of what little he had left, his books and the freedom and inde-
pendence that offended them and filled them with such deep hatred. He
didn't tell me anything or come to me for help. I only discovered he'd be-
come a virtual beggar when I went to look for him in what had been his
home and found his brothers' hired legal thugs drawing up an inventory of
the property and selling off the few objects that had belonged to him.
Miquel had already been spending a few nights in a *pensión* on Calle Canuda,
a dismal, damp hovel that looked and smelled like a brothel. When I saw the
room in which he was confined, a sort of coffin with no windows and a pris-
oner's bunk, I grabbed hold of him and took him home. He couldn't stop
coughing, and he looked emaciated. He said it was a lingering cold, a spin-
ster's complaint that would go away when it got bored. Two weeks later he
was worse.

As he always dressed in black, it took me some time to realize that those
stains on his sleeves were bloodstains. I called a doctor, and after he exam-
ined Miquel, he asked me why I'd waited so long to call him. Miquel had tu-
berculosis. Bankrupt and ill, he now lived only for memories and regrets.

He was the kindest and frailest man I had ever known, my only friend. We got married one cold February morning in a county court. Our honeymoon consisted of taking the bus up to Güell Park and gazing down on Barcelona—a little world of fog—from its sinuous terraces. We didn't tell anyone we'd got married, not Cabestany, or my father, or Miquel's family, who believed him to be dead. Eventually I wrote a letter to Julián, telling him about it, but I never mailed it. Ours was a secret marriage. A few months after the wedding, someone knocked on our door saying his name was Jorge Aldaya. He looked like a shattered man, and his face was covered in sweat despite the biting cold. When he saw Miquel again after more than ten years, Aldaya smiled bitterly and said, "We're all cursed, Miquel. You, Julián, Fumero, and me." The alleged reason for the visit was an attempt to make up with his old friend Miquel, who he hoped would now let him know how to get in touch with Julián Carax, because he had a very important message for him from his deceased father, Don Ricardo Aldaya. Miquel said he didn't know where Carax was.

"We lost touch years ago," he lied. "The last thing I heard was that he was living in Italy."

Aldaya was expecting such an answer. "You disappoint me, Miquel. I had hoped that time and misfortune would have made you wiser."

"Some disappointments honor those who inspire them."

Shriveled up, on the verge of collapsing into a heap of bile, Aldaya laughed.

"Fumero sends you his most heartfelt congratulations on your marriage," he said on his way to the door.

Those words froze my heart. Miquel didn't wish to speak, but that night, while I held him close and we both pretended to fall asleep, I knew that Aldaya had been right. We were cursed.

A few months went by without any news from either Julián or Aldaya. Miquel was still writing regular pieces for the press in Barcelona and Madrid. He worked without pause, sitting at the typewriter and pouring out what he considered drivel to feed commuters on the tram. I kept my job at the publishing house, perhaps because that was where I felt closest to Julián. He had sent me a brief note saying he was working on a new novel, called

The Shadow of the Wind, which he hoped to finish within a few months. The letter made no mention at all of what had happened in Paris. The tone was colder and more distant than before. But my attempts at hating him were unsuccessful. I began to believe that Julián was not a man, he was an illness.

Miquel had no illusions about my feelings. He offered me his affection and devotion without asking for anything in exchange except my company and perhaps my discretion. No reproach or complaint ever passed his lips. In time I came to feel an immense tenderness for him, beyond the friendship that had brought us together and the compassion that had later doomed us. Miquel opened a savings account in my name, into which he deposited almost all the income he earned from his journalism. He never said no to an article, a review, or a gossip column. He wrote under three different pseudonyms, fourteen or sixteen hours a day. When I asked him why he worked so hard, he just smiled or else he said that if he didn't do anything, he'd be bored. There were never any deceits between us, not even wordless ones. Miquel knew he would die soon.

"You must promise that if anything happens to me, you'll take that money and get married again, that you'll have children, and that you'll forget us all, starting with me."

"And who would I marry, Miquel? Don't talk nonsense."

Sometimes I'd catch him looking at me with a gentle smile, as if the very sight of my presence were his greatest treasure. Every afternoon he would come to meet me on my way out of the office, his only moment of leisure in the whole day. He feigned strength, but I saw how he stooped when he walked, and how he coughed. He would take me for a snack or to look at the shop windows on Calle Fernando, and then we'd go back home, where he would continue working until well after midnight. I silently blessed every minute we spent together, and every night he would fall asleep embracing me, while I hid the tears caused by the anger I felt at having been incapable of loving that man the way he loved me, incapable of giving him what I had so pointlessly abandoned at Julián's feet. Many a night I swore to myself that I would forget Julián, that I would devote the rest of my life to making that poor man happy and returning to him some small part of what he had given me. I was Julián's lover for two weeks, but I would be Miquel's wife the rest of my life. If some day these pages should reach your hands and you should judge me, as I have judged myself when writing them, looking at my reflection in this mirror of curses and remorse, remember me like this, Daniel.

The manuscript of Julián's last novel arrived toward the end of 1935. I don't know whether out of spite or out of fear, I handed it to the printer without even reading it. Miquel's last savings had financed the edition in advance, months earlier, so Cabestany, who at the time was already having health problems, paid little attention. That week the doctor who was attending Miquel came to see me at the office, looking very concerned. He told me that if Miquel didn't slow down and give himself some rest, there was little left he could do to help him fight the tuberculosis.

"He should be in the mountains, not in Barcelona breathing in clouds of bleach and charcoal. He's not a cat with nine lives, and I'm not a nanny. Make him listen to reason. He won't pay any attention to me."

That lunchtime I decided to go home and speak to him. Before I opened the door of the apartment, I heard voices leaking out from inside. Miquel was arguing with someone. At first I assumed it was someone from the newspaper, but then I thought I caught Julián's name in the conversation. I heard footsteps approaching the door, and I ran up to hide on the attic landing. From there I was able to catch a glimpse of the visitor.

It was a man dressed in black, with somewhat indifferent features and thin lips, like an open scar. His eyes were black and expressionless, fish eyes. Before he disappeared down the stairs, he looked up into the darkness. I leaned against the wall, holding my breath. The visitor remained there for a few moments, as if he could smell me, licking his lips with a doglike grin. I waited for his steps to fade away completely before I left my hiding place and went into the apartment. A smell of camphor drifted in the air. Miquel was sitting by the window, his arms hanging limply on either side of the chair. His lips trembled. I asked him who that man was and what he wanted.

"It was Fumero. He came with news of Julián."

"What does he know about Julián?"

Miquel looked at me, more dispirited than ever. "Julián is getting married."

The news left me speechless. I fell into a chair, and Miquel took my hands. He seemed tired and spoke with difficulty. Before I was able to open my mouth, he began to give me a summary of the events Fumero had related to him, and what could be inferred from them. Fumero had made use of his contacts in the Paris police to discover Julián Carax's whereabouts and keep a watch on him. This could have taken place months or even years earlier, Miquel said. What worried him wasn't that Fumero had found Carax—that was just a question of time—but that he should have decided to tell Miquel about it now, together with some bizarre news of an improbable marriage. The wedding, it seemed, was going to take place in the early summer of 1936. All that was known about the bride was her name, which in this case was more than sufficient: Irene Marceau, the owner of the club where Julián had worked as a pianist for years.

"I don't understand," I murmured. "Julián is marrying his patron?"

"Exactly. This isn't a wedding. It's a contract."

Irene Marceau was twenty-five or thirty years older than Julián. Miquel suspected she had decided on the marriage so that she could transfer her assets to Julián and secure his future.

"But she already helps him. She always has."

"Perhaps she knows she's not going to be around forever," Miquel suggested.

The echo of those words cut us to the quick. I knelt down next to him and held him tight. I bit my lips because I didn't want him to see me cry.

"Julián doesn't love this woman, Nuria," he said, thinking that was the cause of my sorrow.

"Julián doesn't love anyone but himself and his damned books," I muttered.

I looked up to find Miquel wearing the wise smile of an old child.

"And what does Fumero hope to gain from bringing all this out into the open now?"

It didn't take long for us to find out. Two days later a ghostlike, hollow-eyed Jorge Aldaya turned up at our home, inflamed with anger. Fumero had told him that Julián was going to marry a rich woman in a ceremony of romantic splendor. Aldaya had spent days obsessed with the thought that the man responsible for his misfortunes was now clothed in glitter, sitting astride a fortune, while his had been lost. Fumero had not told him that

Irene Marceau, despite being a woman of some means, was the owner of a brothel and not a princess in a fairy tale. He had not told him that the bride was thirty years older than Carax and that, rather than a real marriage, this was an act of charity toward a man who had reached the end of the road. He had not told him when or where the wedding was going to take place. All he had done was sow the seeds of a fantasy that was devouring what little energy remained in Jorge's wizened, polluted body.

"Fumero has lied to you, Jorge," said Miquel.

"And you, king of liars, you dare accuse your brother!" cried a delirious Aldaya.

There was no need for Aldaya to disclose his thoughts. In a man so withered, they could be read like words beneath the scrawny skin that covered his haunted face. Miquel saw Fumero's game clearly. He had shown him how to play chess twenty years earlier in San Gabriel's School. Fumero had the strategy of a praying mantis and the patience of the immortals. Miquel sent Julián a warning note.

When Fumero decided the moment was right, he took Aldaya aside and told him Julián was getting married in three days' time. Since he was a police officer, he explained, he couldn't get involved in this sort of matter. But Aldaya, as a civilian, could go to Paris and make sure that the wedding in question would never take place. How? a feverish Aldaya would ask, smoldering with hatred. Challenging him to a duel on the very day of his wedding. Fumero even supplied him with the weapon with which Jorge was convinced he would perforate the stony heart that had ruined the Aldaya dynasty. The report from the Paris police would later state that the weapon found at his feet was faulty and could never have done more than what it did: blow up in Jorge's hands. Fumero already knew this when he handed it to him in a case on the platform of the Estación de Francia. He knew perfectly well that even if fever, stupidity, and blind anger didn't prevent Aldaya from killing Julián Carax in a duel with pistols at dawn after a sleepless night, the weapon he carried would. It wasn't Carax who had to die in Père Lachaise cemetery, but Aldaya.

Fumero also knew that Julián would never agree to confront his old friend, dying as Aldaya was, reduced to a whimper. That is why Fumero carefully coached Aldaya on every step he must take. He would have to admit to Julián that the letter Penélope had written to him years ago, announcing her wedding and asking him to forget her, was a lie. He would have to disclose that it was he, Jorge Aldaya, who had forced his sister to write that string of lies while she cried in despair, protesting her undying love for Julián. He would have to tell Julián that she had been waiting for him, with a broken soul and a bleeding heart, since then, dying of loneliness. That would be enough. Enough for Carax to pull the trigger and shoot him in the face. Enough for him to forget any wedding plan and think of nothing else but returning to Barcelona in search of Penélope. And, once in Barcelona, his cobweb, Fumero would be waiting for him.

JULIÁN CARAX CROSSED THE FRENCH BORDER A FEW DAYS BEFORE
the start of the Civil War. The first and only edition of *The Shadow of the
Wind* had left the press two weeks earlier, bound for the anonymity of its
predecessors. By then Miquel could barely work: although he sat in front of
the typewriter for two or three hours a day, weakness and fever prevented
him from coaxing more than a feeble trickle of words out onto the paper.
He had lost several of his regular columns due to missed deadlines. Other
papers were fearful of publishing his articles after receiving anonymous
threats. He had only one daily column left in the *Diario de Barcelona,* which
he signed under the name of Adrián Maltés. The specter of the war could
already be felt in the air. The country stank of fear. With nothing to occupy
him, and too weak to complain, Miquel would go down into the square or
walk up to Avenida de la Catedral, always carrying with him one of Julián's
books as if it were an amulet. The last time the doctor had weighed him, he
was only 125 pounds. We listened to the news of the Morocco uprising on
the radio, and a few hours later a colleague from Miquel's newspaper came
around to tell us that Cansinos, the editor in chief, had been murdered with
a bullet in the neck, opposite the Canaletas Café, two hours earlier. Nobody
dared remove the body, which was still lying there, staining the pavement
with a web of blood.

The brief but intense days of initial terror were not long in coming. General Goded's troops set off along the Diagonal and Paseo de Gracia toward the center, where the shooting began. It was Sunday, and a lot of people had still come out into the streets thinking they were going to spend the day picnicking along the road to Las Planas. The blackest days of the war in Barcelona, however, were still two years away. Shortly after the start of the skirmish, General Goded's troops surrendered, due to a miracle or to poor communication between the commanders. Lluís Companys's government seemed to have regained control, but what really happened would become obvious in the next few weeks.

Barcelona had passed into the hands of the anarchist unions. After days of riots and street fighting, rumors finally circulated that the four rebel generals had been executed in Montjuïc Castle shortly after the surrender. A friend of Miquel's, a British journalist who was present at the execution, said that the firing squad was made up of seven men but that at the last moment dozens of militiamen joined the party. When they opened fire, the bodies were riddled with so many bullets that they collapsed in unrecognizable pieces and had to be put into the coffins in an almost liquid state. There were those who wanted to believe that this was the end of the conflict, that the fascist troops would never reach Barcelona and the rebellion would be extinguished along the way.

We learned that Julián was in Barcelona on the day of Goded's surrender, when we got a letter from Irene Marceau in which she told us that Julián had killed Jorge Aldaya in a duel, in Père Lachaise cemetery. Even before Aldaya expired, an anonymous call had alerted the police to the event. Julián was forced to flee from Paris immediately, pursued by the police, who wanted him for murder. We had no doubts as to who had made that call. We waited anxiously to hear from Julián so that we could warn him of the danger that stalked him and protect him from a worse trap than the one laid out for him by Fumero: the discovery of the truth. Three days later Julián still had not appeared. Miquel did not want to share his anxiety with me, but I knew perfectly well what he was thinking. Julián had come back for Penélope, not for us.

"What will happen when he finds out the truth?" I kept asking.

"We'll make sure he doesn't," Miquel would answer.

The first thing he was going to discover was that the Aldaya family had disappeared. He would not find many places where he could start looking for Penélope. We made a list of such places and began our own expedition. The mansion on Avenida del Tibidabo was just an empty property, closed away behind chains and veils of ivy. A flower vendor, who sold bunches of roses and carnations on the opposite corner, said he only remembered seeing one person approaching the house recently, but this was almost an old man, with a bit of a limp.

"Frankly, he seemed pretty nasty. I tried to sell him a carnation for his lapel, and he told me to piss off, saying there was a war on and it was no time for flowers."

He hadn't seen anyone else. Miquel bought some withered roses from him and, just in case, gave him the phone number of the editorial room at the *Diario de Barcelona*. The man could leave a message there if by chance anyone should turn up looking like the person we'd described. Our next stop was San Gabriel's School, where Miquel met up with Fernando Ramos, his old school companion.

Fernando was now a Latin and Greek teacher and had been ordained a priest. His heart sank when he saw Miquel looking so frail. He told us Julián had not come to see him, but he promised to get in touch with us if he did, and try to hold him back. Fumero had been there before us, he confessed with alarm, and had told him that, in times of war, he'd do well to be watchful.

"He said a lot of people were going to die very soon, and uniforms— soldiers' or priests'—weren't going to stop the bullets. . . ."

Fernando Ramos admitted that it wasn't clear what unit or group Fumero belonged to, and he hadn't wanted to ask him. I find it impossible to describe to you those first days of the war in Barcelona, Daniel. The air seemed poisoned with fear and hatred. People eyed one another suspiciously, and the streets smelled of a silence that knotted your stomach. Every day, every hour, fresh rumors and gossip circulated. I remember one night when Miquel and I were walking home down the Ramblas. They were completely deserted. Miquel looked at the buildings, glimpsing faces that hid behind closed shutters, noticing how they scanned the shadows of the street. He said he could feel the knives being sharpened behind those walls.

The following day we went to the Fortuny hat shop, without much hope of finding Julián there. One of the residents in the building told us that the hatter was terrified by the upheavals of the last few days and had locked himself up in the shop. No matter how much we knocked, he wouldn't open the door. That afternoon there had been a shoot-out only a block away, and the pools of blood were still fresh on Ronda de San Antonio. A dead horse lay on the paving, at the mercy of stray dogs that were tearing open its bullet-ridden stomach, while a group of children watched and threw stones at them. We only managed to see the hatter's frightened face through the grille of the door. We told him we were looking for his son, Julián. The hatter replied that his son was dead and told us to get out of there or he'd call the police. We left the place feeling disheartened.

For days we scoured cafés and shops, asking for Julián. We made inquiries in hotels and *pensiones,* in railway stations, in banks where he might have gone to change money—nobody remembered a man fitting Julián's description. We feared that he might have fallen into Fumero's clutches, and Miquel managed to get one of his colleagues from the newspaper, who had contacts in Police Headquarters, to find out whether Julián had been taken to jail. There was no sign of him. Two weeks went by, and it looked as if Julián had vanished into thin air.

Miquel hardly slept, hoping for news of his friend. One evening he returned from his usual afternoon walk with a bottle of port, of all things. The newspaper staff had presented it to him, he said, because he'd been told by the subeditor that his column was going to have to be canceled.

"They don't want trouble, and I can understand."

"And what are you going to do?"

"Get drunk, for a start."

Miquel drank barely half a glass, but I finished off almost the entire bottle without noticing, on an empty stomach. At around midnight I was overpowered by drowsiness and collapsed on the sofa. I dreamed that Miquel was kissing my forehead and covering me with a shawl. When I woke up, I felt a sharp, stabbing pain in my head, which I recognized as the prelude to a fierce hangover. I went to look for Miquel, to curse the hour when he'd had the bright idea of getting me drunk, but I realized I was alone in the apartment. I went over to the desk and saw that there was a note on the typewriter in which he asked me not to be alarmed and to wait for him there. He'd gone out in search of Julián and would soon bring him home. He ended the note saying that he loved me. The note fell out of my hands. Then I noticed that before leaving, Miquel had removed his things from the desk, as if he wasn't planning to use it anymore. I knew that I would never see him again.

· 8 ·

THAT AFTERNOON THE FLOWER VENDOR HAD CALLED THE OFFICES of the *Diario de Barcelona* and left a message for Miquel saying he'd seen the man we had described to him prowling around the old mansion like a ghost. It was past midnight when Miquel reached number 32, Avenida del Tibidabo, a dark, deserted valley struck by darts of moonlight that filtered through the grove. Although he hadn't seen him for seventeen years, Miquel recognized Julián by his light, almost catlike walk. His silhouette glided through the shadows of the garden, near the fountain. Julián had jumped over the garden wall and lay in wait by the house like a restless animal. Miquel could have called to him, but he preferred not to alert any possible witnesses. He felt that furtive eyes were spying on the avenue from the dark windows of neighboring mansions. He walked around the walls of the estate until he reached the part by the old tennis courts and the coach houses. There he noticed the crevices in the wall that Julián must have used as steps, and the flagstones that had come loose on the top. He lifted himself up, almost out of breath, feeling an acute pain in his chest and experiencing periodic waves of blindness. He lay down on the wall, his hands shaking, and called Julián in a whisper. The silhouette that hovered by the fountain stood still, joining the rest of the statues. Miquel saw two shining eyes fixing on him. He wondered whether Julián would recognize him, after seventeen years and an illness that had taken away his very breath. The silhouette slowly came closer, wielding a long, shiny object in his right hand. A piece of glass.

"Julián . . ." Miquel murmured.

The figure stopped in its tracks. Miquel heard the piece of glass fall on the gravel. Julián's face emerged from the shadows. A two-week stubble covered his features, which were sharper than they used to be.

"Miquel?"

Unable to jump down to the other side, or even climb back to the street, Miquel held out his hand to him. Julián hauled himself onto the wall and, holding his friend's fist tightly with one hand, laid the palm of his other hand on his face. They gazed silently at one another for a long time, each sensing the wounds life had inflicted on the other.

"We must leave this place, Julián. Fumero is looking for you. That business with Aldaya was a trap."

"I know," murmured Carax in a monotone.

"The house is locked. Nobody has lived here for years," Miquel added. "Come, help me get down, and let's get out of here."

Carax climbed down the wall. When he clutched Miquel with both hands, he felt his friend's wasted body under the loose clothes. There seemed to be no flesh or muscle left. Once they were on the other side, Carax supported Miquel by the armpits, so that he was almost carrying him, and they walked off together into the darkness of Calle Román Macaya.

"What is wrong with you?" whispered Carax.

"It's nothing. Some fever. I'm getting better."

Miquel already gave off the smell of illness, and Julián asked no further questions. They went down León XIII until they reached Paseo de San Gervasio, where they saw the lights of a café. They sought refuge at a table in the back of the room, away from the entrance and the windows. A couple of regulars sat at the bar, smoking cigarettes and listening to the radio. The waiter, a man with a waxy pallor and downcast eyes, took their order. Warm brandy, coffee, and whatever food was available.

Miquel didn't eat at all. Carax, obviously starving, ate for the two of them. The two friends looked at each other in the sticky light of the café, spellbound. The last time they had seen each other face-to-face, they were half the age they were now. They had parted as boys, and now life presented one of them with a fugitive and the other with a dying man. Both wondered whether this was due to the cards they'd been dealt or to the way they had played them.

"I've never thanked you for everything you've done for me during these years, Miquel."

"Don't begin now. I did what I had to do and what I wanted to do. There's nothing to thank me for."

"How's Nuria?"

"As you left her."

Carax looked down.

"We got married months ago. I don't know whether she wrote to tell you."

Carax's lips froze, and he shook his head slowly.

"You have no right to reproach her for anything, Julián."

"I know. I have no right to anything."

"Why didn't you come to us for help, Julián?"

"I didn't want to get you into trouble."

"That is out of your hands now. Where have you been all this time? We thought the ground had swallowed you."

"Almost. I've been home. In my father's apartment."

Miquel stared at him in amazement. Julián went on to explain how, when he arrived in Barcelona, unsure where to go, he had set off toward his childhood home, fearing there would be nobody left there. The doors of the hat shop were still open, and an old-looking man, with no hair and no fire in his eyes, languished behind the counter. Julián hadn't wanted to go in, or let him know he'd returned, but Antoni Fortuny had raised his eyes and looked at the stranger on the other side of the window. Their eyes met. Much as Julián wanted to run away, he was paralyzed. He saw tears welling up in the hatter's eyes, saw him drag himself to the door and come out into the street, speechless. Without uttering a word, he led his son into the shop and pulled down the metal grille. Once the outer world had been sealed off, he embraced him, trembling and howling with grief.

Later the hatter explained that the police had been around asking after Julián two days earlier. Someone called Fumero—a man with a bad reputation, of whom it was said that only a month before he'd been in the pay of General Goded's fascist thugs and was now making out to be friends with the anarchists—had told him that Julián Carax was on his way to Barcelona, that he'd cold-bloodedly murdered Jorge Aldaya in Paris, and that he was sought for a number of other crimes, a catalog that the hatter didn't bother to listen to. Fumero trusted that, if by some remote and improbable chance his prodigal son made an appearance there, the hatter would see fit to do his duty as a citizen and report him. Fortuny told him that of course they could count on his help, though secretly it irritated him that a snake like Fumero should assume such baseness in him. No sooner had the sinister cortege left the shop than the hatter set off toward the cathedral chapel where he had first met Sophie. There he prayed to his saint, begging him to guide his son back home before it was too late. Now that Julián had arrived, he warned him of the danger that hung over him.

"Whatever you have come to do in Barcelona, son, let me do it for you while you hide in the apartment. Your room is just as you left it and is yours for however long you may need it."

Julián admitted that he'd returned to look for Penélope Aldaya. The hatter swore he would find her and that, once they had been reunited, he would help them both flee to a safe place, far from Fumero, far from the past, far from everything.

For days Julián hid in the apartment on Ronda de San Antonio while the hatter combed the city looking for some sign of Penélope. He spent the days in his old room, which, as his father had promised, was unchanged, though now everything seemed smaller, as if objects had shrunk with time. Many of his old notebooks were still there, pencils he remembered sharpening the week he left for Paris, books waiting to be read, the boy's clean clothes in the closets. The hatter told Julián that Sophie had left him shortly after his escape, and although for years he didn't hear from her, she wrote to him at last from Bogotá, where she had been living for some time with another man. They corresponded regularly, "always talking about you," the hatter admitted, "because it's the only thing that binds us." When he spoke those words, it seemed to Julián that the hatter had put off falling in love with his wife until after he had lost her.

"One loves truly only once in a lifetime, Julián, even if one isn't aware of it."

The hatter, who seemed caught up in a race against time to disentangle a whole life of misfortunes, had no doubt that Penélope was that love in his son's life. Without realizing it, he thought that if he helped him recover her, perhaps he, too, would recover some part of what he had lost, that void that weighed on his bones like a curse.

Despite his determination, and much to his despair, the hatter soon discovered that there was no trace of Penélope Aldaya, or of her family, in the whole of Barcelona. A man of humble origins, who had had to work all his life to stay solvent, the hatter had never doubted the staying power of money and social station, but fifteen years of ruin and destitution had been sufficient to remove mansions, industries, and the very footprints of a dynasty from the face of the earth. When the name Aldaya was mentioned, there were many who had heard of it but very few who remembered its significance.

The day Miquel Moliner and I went to the hat shop and asked after Julián, the hatter was certain we were two of Fumero's henchmen. But nobody was going to snatch his son from him again. This time God Almighty could descend from the heavens, the same God who had ignored the hatter's prayers all his life, and he would gladly pull out His eyes if He dared push Julián away again.

The hatter was the man whom the flower vendor remembered seeing a few days before, prowling around the Aldaya mansion. What the flower vendor interpreted as "pretty nasty" was only the intensity that comes to those who, better late than never, have found a purpose in life and try to make up for lost time. Unfortunately, the Lord once again disregarded the hatter's pleadings. Having crossed the threshold of despair, the old man was still unable to find what he needed for his son's salvation, for his own salvation: some sign of the girl. How many lost souls do You need, Lord, to satisfy Your hunger? the hatter asked. God, in His infinite silence, looked at him without blinking.

"I can't find her, Julián. . . . I swear that—"

"Don't worry, Father. This is something I must do. You've already helped me as much as you could."

That night Julián at last went out into the streets of Barcelona, determined to find Penélope.

As Miquel listened to his friend's tale, it did not occur to him to be suspicious of the waiter when he went over to the telephone and mumbled something with his back to them or, later, when he surreptitiously kept an eye on the door, wiping glasses too thoroughly for an establishment where dirt was otherwise so at home. It didn't occur to him that Fumero would already have been in that café, and in dozens of cafés like it, a stone's throw away from the Aldaya mansion; that as soon as Carax set foot in any one of them, the call would be placed in a matter of seconds. When the police car stopped in front of the café and the waiter disappeared into the kitchen, Miquel felt the cold and serene stillness of fate. Carax read his eyes, and they both turned at the same time and saw the apparition: three gray raincoats flapping behind the windows, three faces blowing steam onto the windowpane. None of them was Fumero. The vultures preceded him.

"Let's leave this place, Julián. . . ."

"There's nowhere to go," said Carax, with an oddly calm tone of voice that made his friend eye him carefully.

It was only then that Miquel noticed the revolver in Julián's hand. The doorbell sounded above the murmur of the radio. Miquel snatched the gun from Carax's hands and fixed his eyes on him.

"Give me your papers, Julián."

The three policemen pretended to sit at the bar. One of them gave Miguel and Julián a sidelong glance. The other two felt inside their raincoats.

"Your papers, Julián. Now."

Carax silently shook his head.

"I only have a month left, perhaps two, with luck. One of us has to get out of here, Julián. You have more going for you than I do. I don't know whether you'll find Penélope. But Nuria is waiting for you."

"Nuria is your wife."

"Remember the deal we made. The day I die, all that was once mine will be yours . . ."

". . . except your dreams."

They smiled at each other for the last time. Julián handed him his passport. Miquel put it next to the copy of *The Shadow of the Wind* that he had been carrying in his coat pocket since the day he'd received it.

"See you soon," Julián whispered.

"There's no hurry. I'll be waiting."

Just when the three policemen were turning toward them, Miquel rose from the table and went up to them. At first all they saw was a pale, tremulous man who seemed at death's door as he smiled at them with blood showing on the corners of his thin, lifeless lips. By the time they noticed the gun in his right hand, Miquel was barely three yards away from them. One of them was about to scream, but the first shot blew off his lower jaw. The body fell on its knees, lifeless, at Miquel's feet. The other two police officers had already drawn their weapons. The second shot went through the stomach of the one who looked older. The bullet snapped his backbone in two and splattered a handful of guts against the bar. Miquel never had time to fire a third shot. The remaining policeman was already pointing his gun at him. He felt it in his ribs, on his heart, and saw the man's steely eyes, lit up with panic.

"Stand still, you son of a bitch, or I swear I'll tear you apart."

Miquel smiled and slowly raised his gun toward the policeman's face. The man couldn't have been more than twenty-five, and his lips trembled.

"You tell Fumero, from Carax, that I remember his little sailor suit."

He felt no pain, no fire. The impact, like a muffled blow from a hammer, threw him into the window, extinguishing the sound and color of things. As he crashed through the pane, he noticed an intense cold creeping down his throat and the light receding like dust in the wind. Miquel Moliner turned his head for the last time and saw his friend Julián running down the street. Miquel was thirty-six years old, which was longer than he'd hoped to live. Before he collapsed onto a pavement strewn with bloodstained glass, he was already dead.

· *9* ·

THAT NIGHT AN UNIDENTIFIED VAN ARRIVED IN RESPONSE TO THE call from the policeman who had killed Miquel. I never knew his name, nor do I think he realized whom he had murdered. Like all wars, whether private or public, that one was like a stage show. Two men carried off the bodies of the dead policemen and made sure the manager of the bar understood that he must forget what had happened or there would be trouble. Never underestimate the talent for forgetting that wars awaken, Daniel. Miquel Moliner's corpse was abandoned in an alleyway of the Raval quarter twelve hours later, so that his death could not be connected to that of the two police officers. When the body finally arrived at the morgue, Miquel had been dead for two days. He had left his own papers at home before going out. All that the employees at the mortuary could find was a disfigured passport in the name of Julián Carax, and a copy of *The Shadow of the Wind*. The police concluded that the deceased man was Julián Carax. The passport still gave his address as that of the Fortunys' apartment on Ronda de San Antonio.

By then the news had reached Fumero, who went along to the morgue to bid farewell to Julián. There he met the hatter, whom the police had fetched to identify the body. Mr. Fortuny, who hadn't seen Julián for two days, feared the worst. When he recognized the corpse as that of the man who only a week earlier had knocked on his door asking after Julián (and whom he'd taken to be one of Fumero's henchmen), he began to scream and left. The police took this response as an admission of recognition. Fumero, who had witnessed the scene, went up to the body and inspected it silently. He hadn't seen Julián for seventeen years. When he recognized Miquel Moliner, all he did was smile and sign the forensic report confirming that the body in question was Julián Carax. He then ordered its immediate removal to a common grave in Montjuïc.

For a long time, I wondered why Fumero would do something like that. But that was simply Fumero's logic. By dying with Julián's identity Miquel had involuntarily provided him with the perfect alibi. From that moment on, Julián Carax didn't exist. There would be no official link between Fumero and the man who, sooner or later, he hoped to find and murder. It was wartime, and few would ask for explanations concerning the death of someone who didn't even have a name. Julián had lost his identity. He was a shadow. I spent two days in the apartment waiting for Miquel or Julián, thinking I was going mad. On the third day, Monday, I went back to work at the publishing firm. Mr. Cabestany had been hospitalized a few weeks before and would not return to his office. His eldest son, Álvaro, had taken over the business. I didn't say anything to anyone. There was nobody I could turn to.

That same afternoon I received a call from an employee at the morgue, Manuel Gutiérrez Fonseca. He explained that the body of someone called Julián Carax had been brought to the mortuary. Having compared the deceased man's passport with the name of the author of the book that was on the body when it arrived, and suspecting, moreover, if not a breach in the rules, a certain laxity on the part of the police, he had felt it his moral duty to call the publishers and inform them of what had happened. As I listened to him, I almost died. The first thing I thought was that it was a trap set up by Fumero. Mr. Gutiérrez Fonseca expressed himself with the correctness of a conscientious public official, although something else tinged his voice, something that even he would have been unable to explain. I had taken the call in Mr. Cabestany's office. Thank God, Álvaro had gone out for lunch and I was alone; otherwise it would have been difficult for me to explain away the tears and the shaking hands with which I held the telephone. Mr.

Gutiérrez Fonseca told me he had thought it appropriate to let me know what had happened.

I thanked him for his call with that artificiality of coded conversations. As soon as I put down the receiver, I closed the office door and bit my fists so as not to scream. I washed my face and left for home immediately, leaving a message for Álvaro to say I was unwell and would return the following day earlier than usual, to catch up with the correspondence. I had to make an effort not to run in the street, to walk with the anonymous gray calm of people who have no secrets to hide. When I inserted the key in the apartment door, I realized that the lock had been forced. I froze. The doorknob began to turn from within. I wondered whether I was going to die like this, in a dark staircase, and without knowing what had become of Miquel. The door opened, and I encountered the dark eyes of Julián Carax. May God forgive me, but at that moment I felt that life was returning to me, and I thanked the heavens for giving me back Julián instead of Miquel.

We melted in a long embrace, but when I searched for his lips, Julián moved away and lowered his eyes. I closed the door and, taking Julián's hand, led him to the bedroom. We lay together on the bed in silence. Evening was closing in, and the shadows of the apartment were ablaze with purple. As on every night since the start of the war, shots could be heard in the distance. Julián was crying as he lay on my chest, and I felt a tiredness beyond words. Later, once night had fallen, our lips met, and in the shelter of that pressing darkness, we removed our clothes, which smelled of fear and of death. I wanted to remember Miquel, but the fire of those hands on my stomach stole all my shame and my grief. I wanted to lose myself in them, even though I knew that at dawn, exhausted and perhaps overcome by contempt for ourselves, we would be unable to look each other in the eye without wondering what sort of people we had become.

· 10 ·

I WAS WOKEN BY THE PITTER-PATTER OF THE RAIN AT DAYBREAK. THE bed empty, the room bathed in gray light.

I found Julián sitting in front of what had been Miquel's desk, stroking the keys of his typewriter. He looked up and gave me that lukewarm, distant smile that said he would never be mine. I felt like spitting out the truth to him, like hurting him. It would have been so simple. Reveal to him that Penélope was dead. That he was living a lie. That I was now all he had in the world.

"I should never have returned to Barcelona," he murmured, shaking his head.

I knelt beside him. "What you are searching for is not here, Julián. Let's go away. The two of us. Far from here. While there is still time."

Julián looked at me for a long moment, without blinking. "You know something you haven't told me, don't you?" he asked.

I shook my head and swallowed. Julián just nodded.

"Tonight I'm going back there."

"Julián, please . . ."

"I must make sure."

"Then I'll go with you."

"No."

"The last time I stayed here and waited, I lost Miquel. If you go, I go, too."

"This is nothing to do with you, Nuria. It's something that concerns only me."

I wondered whether, in fact, he didn't realize how much his words hurt me, or whether he just didn't care.

"That's what you think," I said.

He tried to stroke my cheek, but I drew his hand away.

"You should despise me, Nuria. It would bring you luck."

"Yes, I know."

We spent the day out, far from the oppressive darkness of the apartment that still smelled of warm sheets and skin. Julián wanted to be by the sea. I went with him to La Barceloneta, and we walked along the almost deserted beach, the shimmering sand seeming to trail off into the summer haze. We sat on the sand, near the shore, the way children or old people do. Julián smiled, saying nothing.

As evening fell, we took a tram near the aquarium and went up Vía Layetana to Paseo de Gracia, then onto Plaza de Lesseps and Avenida de la República Argentina, until we came to the end of the route. Julián gazed silently at the streets, as if he were afraid of losing the city as we traveled through it. Halfway along our journey, he took my hand and kissed it without saying a word. He held it until we got off. An elderly man who accompanied a little girl dressed in white looked at us, smiling, and asked us whether we were engaged. It was dark by the time we walked up Calle Román Macaya toward the Aldayas' old mansion on Avenida del Tibidabo. A fine rain was falling, giving a silver coat to the thick stone walls. We climbed the property wall at the back, near the tennis courts. The large, rambling house rose into view through the rain. I recognized it immediately. I had come across that house in a thousand different guises in Julián's books. In *The Red House,* it was a sinister mansion that was larger inside than out. It slowly changed shape, grew new corridors, galleries, and improbable attics, endless stairs that led nowhere; it illuminated dark rooms that came and went from one day to the next, taking with them the unsuspecting who entered them, never to be seen again. We stopped outside the main door, locked with chains and a padlock the size of a fist. The large windows on the first floor were boarded up with wooden planks that were covered in ivy. The air smelled of weeds and wet earth. The stone, dark and slimy with rain, shone like the skeleton of a huge reptile.

I wanted to ask him how he intended to get past that large oak door, which looked like the door of a basilica or a prison. Julián pulled a jar out of his coat and unscrewed the top. A fetid vapor issued from it, forming a slow, bluish spiral. He held one end of the padlock and poured the acid into the lock. The metal hissed like red-hot iron, enveloped in a cloud of yellow smoke. We waited a few minutes, and then he picked up a cobblestone that lay among the weeds and split the padlock by banging it half a dozen times. Julián then gave the door a kick. It opened slowly, like a tomb, exhaling a thick, damp breath. Beyond the doorway I could sense a velvety darkness. Julián had brought a benzine lighter, which he lit after taking a few steps into the entrance hall. I followed him, leaving the door behind us ajar. Julián walked on a few yards, holding the flame above his head. A carpet of dust lay at our feet, with no footprints but ours. The naked walls took on an amber hue from the flame. There was no furniture, there were no mirrors or lamps. The doors were still on their hinges, but the bronze doorknobs had been pulled out. The mansion was just a skeleton. We stopped at the bottom of the staircase. Julián looked up, his eyes scanning the heights. He turned around for a moment to look at me, and I wanted to smile, but in the half-light we could barely see each other's eyes. I followed him up the stairs, treading the steps on which Julián had first seen Penélope. I knew where we were heading, and I felt a coldness inside me that had nothing to do with the biting, damp air of that place.

We went up to the third floor, where a narrow corridor led to the south wing of the house. Here the ceilings were much lower and the doors smaller. It was the floor for the servants' living quarters. The last room, I knew without Julián's having to tell me, had been Jacinta Coronado's bedroom. Julián approached it slowly, fearfully. That had been the last place where he'd seen Penélope, where he had made love to a girl barely seventeen years old, who, months later, would bleed to death in that same cell. I wanted to stop him, but Julián had reached the doorway and was looking absently inside. I peered into the room with him. It was just a cubicle stripped of all ornamentation. The marks left where a bed had once stood were still visible beneath the flood of dust that covered the floorboards. A tangle of black stains snaked through the middle of the room. Julián stared at that emptiness for almost a minute, disconcerted. I could see from his look that he hardly recognized the place, that the sight of it seemed to him like a cruel trick. I took his arm and led him back to the stairs.

"There's nothing here, Julián," I murmured. "The family sold everything before leaving for Argentina."

Julián nodded weakly. We walked down the stairs again, and when we reached the ground floor, Julián made his way to the library. The shelves were empty, the fireplace choked with rubble. The walls, a deathly pale hue, flickered in the breath of the flame. Creditors and usurers had managed to remove every last bit of the room, most of which must be lost in the twisted heaps of some junkyard by now.

"I've come back for nothing," Julián mumbled.

Better this way, I thought. I was counting the seconds that separated us from the door. If I managed to get him away from there, we might still have a chance. I let Julián absorb the ruin of that place and purge his memories.

"You had to return and see it again," I said. "Now you see there's nothing here. It's just a large, old, uninhabited house, Julián. Let's go home."

He looked at me, pale-faced, and nodded. I took his hand, and we went along the passageway that led to the exit. The chink of outdoor light was only half a dozen yards away. I could smell the weeds and the drizzle in the air. Then I felt I was losing Julián's hand. I stopped and turned to see him standing motionless, his eyes staring into the darkness.

"What is it, Julián?"

He didn't reply. He was gazing, mesmerized, at the mouth of a narrow corridor that led toward the kitchen area. I walked over to him and looked into the shadows that were being pushed aside by the blue flame of the lighter. The door at the end of the corridor was bricked up, a wall of red bricks roughly laid with mortar that bled out of the corners. I couldn't quite understand what it meant, but I felt an icy cold taking my breath away. Julián was slowly getting closer. All the other doors in the corridor—in the whole house—were open, their locks and doorknobs gone.

"Julián, please, let's go. . . ."

The impact of his fist on the brick wall drew a hollow echo on the other side. I thought I saw his hands trembling when he placed the lighter on the floor and gestured for me to move back a few steps.

"Julián . . ."

The first kick brought down a rain of red dust. Julián charged again. I thought I could hear his bones breaking, but Julián was unperturbed. He banged against the wall again and again, with the rage of a prisoner forcing his way out to freedom. His fists and his arms were bleeding when the first brick broke and fell onto the other side. In the dark, with bloodstained fingers, Julián began struggling to enlarge the gap. He panted, exhausted, possessed by a fury of which I would never have thought him capable. One by one the bricks loosened and the wall came down. Julián stopped, covered in a cold sweat, his hands flayed. He picked up the lighter and placed it on the edge of one of the bricks. A wooden door, carved with angel motifs, rose up on the other side. Julián stroked the wood reliefs, as if he were reading a hieroglyphic. The door yielded to the pressure of his hands.

A glutinous darkness came at us from the other side. A little farther back, the form of a staircase could be discerned. Black stone steps descended until they were lost in shadows. Julián turned for a moment, and I met his eyes. I saw fear and despair in them, as if he could sense what lay beyond. I shook my head, begging him without speaking not to go down. He turned back, dejected, and plunged into the gloom. I looked through the brick frame and saw him lurching down the steps. The flame flickered, now just a breath of transparent blue.

"Julián?"

All I got was silence. I could see Julián's shadow, motionless, at the bottom of the stairs. I went through the brick hole and walked down the steps. The room was rectangular, with marble walls. It exuded an intense, penetrating chill. The two tombstones were covered with a veil of cobwebs that fell apart like rotten silk with the flame from the lighter. The white marble was scored with black tears of dampness that looked like blood dripping out of the clefts left by the engraver's chisel. They lay side by side, like chained maledictions.

PENÉLOPE ALDAYA   DAVID ALDAYA
1902—1919   1919

· *11* ·

I HAVE OFTEN PAUSED TO THINK ABOUT THAT MOMENT OF SILENCE AND tried to imagine what Julián must have felt when he discovered that the woman for whom he had been waiting seventeen years was dead, their child gone with her, and that the life he had dreamed about, the very breath of it, had never existed. Most of us have the good or bad fortune of seeing our lives fall apart so slowly we barely notice. In Julián's case that certainty came to him in a matter of seconds. For a moment I thought he was going to rush up the stairs and flee from that accursed place, that I would never see him again. Perhaps it would have been better that way.

I remember that the flame from the lighter slowly went out, and I lost sight of his silhouette. My hands searched for him in the shadows. I found him trembling, speechless. He could barely stand, and he dragged himself into a corner. I hugged him and kissed his forehead. He didn't move. I felt his face with my fingers, but there were no tears. I thought that perhaps, unconsciously, he had known it all those years, that perhaps the encounter was necessary for him to face the truth and set himself free. We had reached the end of the road. Julián would now understand that nothing held him in Barcelona any longer and that we could leave, go far away. I wanted to believe that our luck was about to change and that Penélope had finally forgiven us.

I looked for the lighter on the floor and lit it again. Julián was staring vacantly, indifferent to the blue flame. I held his face in my hands and forced him to look at me. I found lifeless, empty eyes, consumed by anger and loss. I felt the venom of hatred spreading slowly through his veins, and I could read his thoughts. He hated me for having deceived him. He hated Miquel for having wished to give him a life that now felt like an open wound. But above all he hated the man who had caused this calamity, this trail of death and misery: himself. He hated those filthy books to which he had devoted his life and about which nobody cared. He hated every stolen second and every breath.

He looked at me without blinking, the way one looks at a stranger or some unknown object. I kept shaking my head, slowly, my hands searching his hands. Suddenly he moved away roughly and stood up. I tried to grab his arm, but he pushed me against the wall. I saw him go silently up the stairs, a man I no longer knew. Julián Carax was dead. By the time I stepped out into the garden, there was no trace of him. I climbed the wall and jumped down onto the other side. The desolate streets seemed to bleed in the rain. I shouted out his name, walking down the middle of the deserted avenue. Nobody answered my call. It was almost four in the morning when I got home. The apartment was full of smoke and the stench of burned paper. Julián had been there. I ran to open the windows. I found a small case on my desk with the pen I had bought him years ago in Paris, the fountain pen I had paid a fortune for on the pretense it once had belonged to Victor Hugo. The smoke was oozing from the central-heating boiler. I opened the hatch and saw that Julián had thrown into it copies of his novels. I could just about read the titles on the leather spines. The rest had turned to cinders. I looked on my bookshelves: all of his books were gone.

Hours later, when I went to the publishing house in the middle of the morning, Álvaro Cabestany called me into his office. His father hardly ever came by anymore; the doctors said his days were numbered—as was my time at the firm. Cabestany's son informed me that a gentleman called Laín Coubert had turned up, early that morning, saying he was interested in acquiring our entire stock of Julián Carax's novels. The publisher's son told him he had a warehouse full of them in the Pueblo Nuevo district, but as there was such a demand for them, he insisted on a higher price than Coubert was offering. Coubert had not taken the bait and had marched out. Now Álvaro Cabestany wanted me to find this person called Laín Coubert and accept his offer. I told that fool that Laín Coubert didn't exist; he was a character in one of Carax's novels. That he wasn't in the least interested in buying his books; he only wanted to know where we stored them. Old Mr. Cabestany was in the habit of keeping a copy of every book published by his firm in his office library, even the works of Julián Carax: I slipped into the room, unnoticed, and took them.

That evening I visited my father in the Cemetery of Forgotten Books and hid them where nobody, especially Julián, would ever find them. Night had fallen when I left the building. I wandered off down the Ramblas and from there to La Barceloneta, where I made for the beach, looking for the spot where I had gone to gaze at the sea with Julián. The pyre of flames from the Pueblo Nuevo warehouse was visible in the distance, its amber trail spilling over the sea and spirals of smoke rising to the sky like serpents of light. When the firefighters managed to extinguish the flames shortly before daybreak, there was nothing left, just the brick-and-metal skeleton that held up the vault. There I found Lluís Carbó, who had been the night watchman for ten years. He stared in disbelief at the smoldering ruins. His eyebrows and the hairs on his arms were singed, and his skin shone like wet bronze. It was he who told me that the blaze had started shortly after midnight and had devoured tens of thousands of books, until dawn came and he was faced with a river of ashes. Lluís still held a handful of books he had managed to save, some of Verdaguer's collected poems and two volumes of the *History of the French Revolution*. That was all that had survived. Various members of the union had arrived to help the firefighters. One of them told me the firefighters found a burned body in the debris. At first they had assumed that the man was dead, but then one of them noticed he was still breathing, and they had taken him to the nearby Hospital del Mar.

I recognized him by his eyes. The fire had eaten away his skin, his hands, and his hair. The flames had torn off his clothes, and his whole body was a raw wound that oozed beneath his bandages. They had confined him to a room of his own at the end of a corridor, with a view of the beach, and had numbed him with morphine while they waited for him to die. I wanted to hold his hand, but one of the nurses warned me that there was almost no flesh under the bandages. The fire had cut away his eyelids. The nurse who found me, collapsed on the floor crying, asked me whether I knew who he was. I said I did: he was my husband. When a priest appeared to administer the last rites over him, I frightened him off with my screams. Three days later Julián was still alive. The doctors said it was a miracle, that his will to stay alive gave him a strength no medicine could offer. They were wrong. It was not a will to live. It was hatred. A week later, when they saw that this death-bitten body refused to expire, he was officially admitted under the name of Miquel Moliner. He would remain there for eleven months. Always in silence, with burning eyes, without rest.

I went to the hospital every day. Soon the nurses began to treat me less formally and invite me to lunch with them in their hall. They were all women who were on their own, strong women waiting for their men to return from the front. Some did. They taught me how to clean Julián's wounds, how to change his bandages, how to change the sheets and make a bed with an inert body lying on it. They also taught me to lose all hope of ever seeing the man who had once been held by those bones. Three months later we removed his face bandages. Julián was a skull. He had no lips or cheeks. It was a featureless face, the charred remains of a doll. His eye sockets had become larger and now dominated his expression. The nurses would not admit it to me, but they were revolted by his appearance, almost afraid. The doctors had told me that, as the wounds healed, a sort of purplish, reptile-like skin would slowly form. Nobody dared to comment on his mental state. Everyone assumed that Julián—Miquel—had lost his mind in the blaze, and that he had survived thanks to the obsessive care of a wife who stood firm where so many others would have fled in terror. I looked into his eyes and knew that Julián was still in there, alive, tormenting himself, waiting.

He had lost his lips, but the doctors thought that the vocal cords had not suffered permanent damage and that the burns on his tongue and larynx had healed months earlier. They assumed that Julián didn't say anything because his mind was gone. One afternoon, six months after the fire, when he and I were alone in the room, I bent over him and kissed him on the brow.

"I love you," I said.

A bitter, harsh sound emerged from the doglike grimace that was now his mouth. His eyes were red with tears. I wanted to dry them with a handkerchief, but he repeated that sound.

"Leave me," he said.

"Leave me."

Two months after the warehouse fire, the publishing firm had gone bankrupt. Old Cabestany, who died that year, had predicted that his son would manage to ruin the company within six months. An unrepentant optimist to the last. I tried to find work with another publisher, but the war did away with everything. They all said that hostilities would soon cease and things would improve. But there were still two years of war ahead, and worse was yet to come. One year after the fire, the doctors told me that they had done all that could be done in a hospital. The situation was difficult, and they needed the room. They recommended that Julián be taken to a sanatorium like the Hospice of Santa Lucía, but I refused. In October 1937 I took him home. He hadn't uttered a single word since that "Leave me."

EVERY DAY I TOLD HIM THAT I LOVED HIM. I SET HIM UP IN THE armchair by the window, wrapped in blankets. I fed him with fruit juices, toast, and milk—when there was any to be found. Every day I read to him for a couple of hours. Balzac, Zola, Dickens . . . His body was beginning to fill out. Soon after returning home, he began to move his hands and arms. He tilted his neck. Sometimes, when I got back, I found the blankets on the floor, and household objects that had been knocked over. One day I found him crawling on the floor. Then, a year and a half after the fire, I woke up in the middle of a stormy night and found that someone was sitting on the bed stroking my hair. I smiled at him, hiding my tears. He had managed to find one of my mirrors, although I'd hidden them all. In a broken voice, he told me he'd been transformed into one of his fictional monsters, into Laín Coubert. I wanted to kiss him, to show him that his appearance didn't disgust me, but he wouldn't let me. He would hardly allow me to touch him. Day by day he was getting his strength back. He would prowl around the house while I went out in search of something to eat. The savings Miquel had left me kept us afloat, but soon I had to start selling jewels and old possessions. When there was no other alternative, I took the Victor Hugo pen I had bought in Paris and went out to sell it to the highest bidder. I found a shop behind the Military Government buildings where they took in that sort of merchandise. The manager did not seem impressed by my solemn oath that the pen had belonged to Victor Hugo, but he admitted it was a marvelous work of its kind and agreed to pay me as much as he could, bearing in mind these were times of great hardship.

When I told Julián that I'd sold it, I was afraid he would fly into a rage. All he said was that I'd done the right thing, that he'd never deserved it. One day, one of the many when I'd gone out to look for work, I returned to find that Julián wasn't there. He didn't come back until daybreak. When I asked him where he'd been, he just emptied the pockets of his coat (which had belonged to Miquel) and left a fistful of money on the table. From then on he began to go out almost every night. In the dark, concealed under a hat and scarf, with gloves and a raincoat, he was just one more shadow. He never told me where he went, and he almost always brought back money or jewels. He slept in the mornings, sitting upright in his armchair, with his eyes open. Once I found a penknife in one of his pockets. It was a double-edged knife, with an automatic spring. The blade was marked with dark stains.

It was then that I began to hear stories in town about some individual who was going around smashing bookshop windows at night and burning books. Other times the strange vandal would slip into a library or a collector's study. He always took two or three volumes, which he would burn. In February 1938 I went to a secondhand bookshop to ask whether it was possible to find any books by Julián Carax in the market. The manager said it wasn't: someone had been making them disappear. He himself had owned a couple and had sold them to a very strange person, a man who hid his face and whose voice he could barely understand.

"Until recently there were a few copies left in private collections, here and in France, but a lot of collectors are beginning to get rid of them. They're frightened," he said, "and I don't blame them."

More and more, Julián would vanish for whole days at a time. Soon his absences lasted a week. He always left and returned at night, and he always brought money back. He never gave any explanations, and if he did, they were meaningless. He told me he'd been in France: Paris, Lyons, Nice. Occasionally letters arrived from France addressed to Laín Coubert. They were always from secondhand booksellers or from collectors. Someone had located a lost copy of Julián Carax's works. Like a wolf, he would disappear for a few days, then return.

It was during one of those absences that I came across Fortuny, the hatter, wandering about in the cathedral cloister lost in his thoughts. He still remembered me from the day I'd gone with Miquel to inquire after Julián, two years before. He took me to a corner and told me confidentially that he knew that Julián was alive, somewhere, but he suspected that his son wasn't able get in touch with us for some reason he couldn't quite figure out. "Something to do with that cruel man Fumero." I told him that I felt the same. Wartime was turning out to be very profitable for Fumero. His loyalties shifted from month to month, from the anarchists to the communists, and from them to whoever came his way. He was called a spy, a henchman, a hero, a murderer, a conspirator, a schemer, a savior, a devil. Little did it matter. They all feared him. They all wanted him on their side. Perhaps because he was so busy with the intrigues of a wartime Barcelona, Fumero seemed to have forgotten Julián. Probably, like the hatter, he imagined that Julián had already escaped and was out of his reach.

MR. FORTUNY ASKED ME WHETHER I WAS AN OLD FRIEND OF HIS SON'S, and I said I was. He asked me to tell him about Julián, about the man he'd become, because, he sadly admitted, he didn't really know him. "Life separated us, you know?" He told me he'd been to all the bookshops in Barcelona in search of Julián's novels, but they were unobtainable. Someone had told him that a madman was looking for them in every corner of the city and then burning them. Fortuny was convinced that the culprit was Fumero. I didn't contradict him. I lied as best I could, I know not whether through pity or spite. I told him that I thought Julián had returned to Paris, that he was well, that I knew for a fact he was very fond of Fortuny the hatter, that he would come back to see him as soon as circumstances permitted. "It's this war," he complained, "it just rots everything." Before we said good-bye, he insisted on giving me his address and that of his ex-wife, Sophie, with whom he was back in touch after many years of "misunderstandings." Sophie now lived in Bogotá with a prestigious doctor, he said. She ran her own music school and often wrote asking after Julián.

"It's the only thing that brings us together now, you see. Memories. We make so many mistakes in life, young lady, but we only realize this when old age creeps up on us. Tell me, do you have faith?"

I took my leave, promising to keep him and Sophie informed if I ever had news from Julián.

"Nothing would make his mother happier than to hear how he is. You women listen more to your heart and less to all the nonsense," the hatter concluded sadly. "That's why you live longer."

Despite the fact that I'd heard so many appalling stories about him, I couldn't help feeling sorry for the poor old man. He had little else to do in life but wait for the return of his son. He seemed to live in the hope of recovering lost time through some miracle from the saints, whom he visited with great devotion at their chapels in the cathedral. I had become used to picturing him as an ogre, a despicable and resentful being, but all I was able to see before me was a kind man, blind to reality, confused like everybody else. Perhaps because he reminded me of my own father, who hid from everyone, including himself, in that refuge of books and shadows, or because, without his suspecting it, the hatter and I were also linked by the hope of recovering Julián, I felt a growing affection for him and became his only friend. Unbeknownst to Julián, I often called on him in the apartment on Ronda de San Antonio. The hatter no longer worked in his shop downstairs.

"I don't have the hands, or the sight, or the customers . . ." he would say.

He waited for me almost every Thursday and offered me coffee, biscuits, and pastries that he scarcely tasted. He spent hours reminiscing about Julián's childhood, about how they worked together in the hat shop, and he would show me photographs. He would take me to Julián's room, which he kept as immaculate as a museum, and bring out old notebooks, insignificant objects that he adored as relics of a life that had never existed, without ever realizing that he'd already shown them to me before, that he'd told me all those stories on a previous visit. One of those Thursdays, as I walked up the stairs, I ran into a doctor who had just been to see Mr. Fortuny. I asked him how the hatter was, and he looked at me strangely.

"Are you a relative?"

I told him I was the closest the poor man had to one. The doctor then told me that Fortuny was very ill, that it was just a matter of months.

"What's wrong with him?"

"I could tell you it's the heart, but what is really killing him is loneliness. Memories are worse than bullets."

The hatter was pleased to see me and confessed that he didn't trust that doctor. Doctors are just second-rate witches, he said. All his life the hatter had been a man of profound religious beliefs, and old age had only reinforced them. He saw the hand of the devil everywhere. The devil, he said, clouds the mind and ruins mankind.

"Just look at this war, or look at me. Of course, now I'm old and weak, but as a young man I was a swine and a coward."

It was the devil who had taken Julián away from him, he added.

"God gives us life, but the world's landlord is the devil. . . ."

And so we passed the afternoon, nibbling on stale sponge fingers and discussing theology.

I once told Julián that if he wanted to see his father again before he died, he'd better hurry up. It turned out that he, too, had been visiting the hatter, without his knowing: from afar, at dusk, sitting at the other end of a square, watching him grow old. Julián said he would rather the old man took with him the image of the son he had created in his mind during those years than the person he had become.

"You keep that one for me," I said, instantly regretting my words.

He didn't reply, but for a moment it seemed as if he could think clearly again and was fully aware of the hell in which we had become trapped.

The doctor's prognosis did not take long to come true. Mr. Fortuny didn't see the end of the war. He was found sitting in his armchair, looking at old photographs of Sophie and Julián.

The last days of the war were the prelude to an inferno. The city had lived through the combat from afar, like a wound that throbs drowsily, with months of skirmishes and battles, bombardments and hunger. The spectacle of murders, fights, and conspiracies had been corroding the city's heart for years, but even so, many wanted to believe that the war was still something distant, a storm that would pass them by. If anything, the wait made the inevitable worse. When the storm broke, there was no compassion.

Nothing feeds forgetfulness better than war, Daniel. We all keep quiet and they try to convince us that what we've seen, what we've done, what we've learned about ourselves and about others, is an illusion, a passing nightmare. Wars have no memory, and nobody has the courage to understand them until there are no voices left to tell what happened, until the moment comes when we no longer recognize them and they return, with another face and another name, to devour what they left behind.

By then Julián hardly had any books left to burn. His father's death, about which we never spoke, had turned him into an invalid. The anger and hatred that had at first possessed him were spent. We lived on rumors, secluded. We heard that Fumero had betrayed all the people who had helped him advance during the war and was now in the service of the victors. It was said that he was personally executing his main allies and protectors in the cells of Montjuïc Castle—his preferred method a pistol shot in the mouth. The heavy mantle of collective forgetfulness seemed to descend around us the day the weapons went quiet. In those days I learned that nothing is more frightening than a hero who lives to tell his story, to tell what all those who fell at his side will never be able to tell. The weeks that followed the fall of Barcelona were indescribable. More blood was shed during those days than during the combat, but secretly, stealthily. When peace finally came, it smelled of the sort of peace that haunts prisons and cemeteries, a shroud of silence and shame that rots one's soul and never goes away. There were no guiltless hands or innocent looks. Those of us who were there, all without exception, will take the secret with us to our grave.

A faint patina of normality was being restored amid resentments, but by now Julián and I lived in abject poverty. We had spent all the savings and the booty from Laín Coubert's nightly escapades, and there was nothing left in the house to sell. I looked desperately for work as a translator, typist, or cleaner, but it seemed that my past association with Cabestany had marked me out as an undesirable person, a source of unnamed suspicions. A government employee in a shiny new suit, with brilliantined hair and a pencil mustache—one of the hundreds who seemed to crawl out of the woodwork during those months—hinted that an attractive girl like me shouldn't have to resort to such mundane jobs. Our neighbors accepted my story that I was caring for my poor husband, Miquel, who had become an invalid and was disfigured as a result of the war. They would bring us offerings of milk, cheese, or bread, sometimes even salted fish or sausages that had been sent to them by relatives in the country. After months of hardship, convinced that it would take a long time to find a job, I decided on a strategy borrowed from one of Julián's novels.

I wrote to Julián's mother in Bogotá, adopting the name of a fictitious new lawyer whom the deceased Mr. Fortuny had consulted in his last days, when he was trying to put his affairs in order. I informed her that, as the hatter had died without having made a will, his estate, which included the apartment on Ronda de San Antonio and the shop situated in the same building, was now theoretically the property of her son, Julián, who, it was believed, lived in exile in France. Since the death duties had not been satisfied, and since she lived abroad, the lawyer (whom I christened José María Requejo in memory of the first boy who had kissed me in school) asked her for authorization to start the necessary proceedings and carry out the transfer of the properties to the name of her son, whom he intended to contact through the Spanish embassy in Paris. In the meantime he was assuming the transitory and temporary ownership of the said properties, as well as a certain level of financial compensation. He also asked her to get in touch with the building administrator and instruct him to send all the documents, as well as the payment for the property expenses, to Mr. Requejo's office, in whose name I opened a PO box with a fake address—that of an old, disused garage two blocks away from the ruins of the Aldaya mansion. I was hoping that, blinded by the possibility of being able to help Julián and getting back in touch with him, Sophie would not stop to question all that legal gibberish and would agree to help us, taking into account her prosperous situation in far-off Colombia.

A couple of months later, the building administrator began to receive a monthly money order to cover the expenses of the apartment on Ronda de San Antonio and the fees of José María Requejo's law firm, which he proceeded to send as an open check to PO Box 2321 in Barcelona, just as Sophie Carax had requested him to do. The administrator, I noticed, retained an unauthorized percentage every month, but I preferred not to say anything. That way he wetted his beak and did not question such a convenient arrangement. With the rest, Julián and I had enough to survive. Terrible, bleak years went by, during which I had managed to find occasional work as a translator. By then nobody remembered Cabestany, and people began to forgive and forget, putting aside old rivalries and grievances. I lived under the perpetual threat that Fumero might decide to begin rummaging in the past again. Sometimes I convinced myself that it wouldn't happen, that he must have given Julián up for dead by now or forgotten him. Fumero wasn't the thug he was years ago. Now he had graduated into a public figure, a career man in the fascist regime, who couldn't afford the luxury of Julián Carax's ghost. Other times I woke up in the middle of the night with my heart pounding, covered in sweat, thinking that the police were hammering on my door. I feared that some of the neighbors might begin to be suspicious of that ailing husband of mine who never left the house, who sometimes cried or banged the walls like a madman, and that they might report us to the police. I was afraid that Julián might escape again, that he might decide to go out hunting for his books once more. Distracted by so much fear, I forgot that I was growing old, that life was passing me by, that I had sacrificed my youth to love a man who was now almost a phantom.

But the years went by in peace. Time goes faster the more hollow it is. Lives with no meaning go straight past you, like trains that don't stop at your station. Meanwhile, the scars from the war were, of necessity, healing. I found some work in a couple of publishing firms and spent most of the day out of the house. I had lovers with no name, desperate faces I came across in cinemas or in the subway, with whom I would share my loneliness. Then, absurdly, I'd be consumed by guilt, and when I saw Julián again, I always felt like crying and would swear to myself that I would never again betray him, as if I owed him something. On buses or on the street, I caught myself looking at women who were younger than me holding small children by the hand. They seemed happy, or at peace, as if those helpless little beings could fill all the emptiness in the world. Then I would remember the days when, fantasizing, I had imagined myself one of those women, with a child in my arms, a child of Julián's. And then I would think about the war and about the fact that those who waged it were also children once.

I had started to believe that the world had forgotten us when someone turned up one day at our house. He looked young, barely a boy, an apprentice who blushed when he looked me in the eye. He asked after Miquel Moliner, and said he was updating some file at the School of Journalism. He told me that perhaps Mr. Moliner could be the beneficiary of a monthly pension, but if he were to apply for it, he would first have to update a number of details. I told him that Mr. Moliner hadn't been living there since the start of the war, that he'd gone abroad. He said he was very sorry and went away leering. He had the face of a young informer, and I knew that I had to get Julián out of my apartment that night, without fail. By now he had almost shriveled up. He was as docile as a child, and his whole life revolved around the evenings we spent together, listening to music on the radio, as he held my hand and stroked it in silence.

When night fell, I took the keys of the apartment on Ronda de San Antonio, which the building administrator had sent to a nonexistent Mr. Requejo, and accompanied Julián back to the home where he had grown up. I set him up in his room and promised him I'd return on the following day, reminding him to be very careful.

"Fumero is looking for you again," I said.

He made a vague gesture with his head, as if he couldn't remember who Fumero was, or no longer cared. Several weeks passed in that way. I always went to the apartment at night, after midnight. I asked Julián what he'd done during the day, and he looked at me without understanding. We would spend the night together, holding each other, and I left at daybreak, promising to return as soon as I could. When I left, I always locked the door of the apartment. Julián didn't have a copy of the key. I preferred to keep him there like a prisoner rather than risk his life.

Nobody else came around to ask after Miquel, but I made sure it got about in the neighborhood that my husband was in France. I wrote a couple of letters to the Spanish consulate in Paris saying that I knew that the Spanish citizen Julián Carax was in the city and asking for their assistance in finding him. I imagined that sooner or later the letters would reach the right hands. I took all the precautions, but I knew it was only a question of time. People like Fumero never stop hating.

The apartment on Ronda de San Antonio was on the top floor. I discovered that there was a door to the roof terrace at the top of the staircase. The roof terraces of the whole block formed a network of enclosures separated from one another by walls just a yard high, where residents went to hang out their laundry. It didn't take me long to locate a building at the other end of the block, with its front door on Calle Joaquín Costa, to whose roof terrace I could gain access and therefore reach the building of Ronda de San Antonio without anyone seeing me go in or come out of the property. I once got a letter from the building administrator telling me that some neighbors had heard sounds coming from the Fortuny apartment. I answered in Requejo's name stating that occasionally some member of the firm had gone to the apartment to look for papers or documents and there was no cause for alarm, even if the sounds were heard at night. I added a comment implying that among gentlemen—accountants and lawyers—a secret bachelor pad was no small treasure. The administrator, showing professional understanding, answered that I need not worry in the least, that he completely understood the situation.

During those years, playing the role of Mr. Requejo was my only source of entertainment. Once a month I went to visit my father at the Cemetery of Forgotten Books. He never showed any interest in meeting my invisible husband, and I never offered to introduce him. We would skirt around the subject in our conversations like expert mariners dodging reefs near the water's surface. Occasionally he asked me whether I needed any help, whether there was anything he could do.

On Saturdays, at dawn, I sometimes took Julián to look at the sea. We would go up to the roof, cross over to the adjoining building, and then step out into Calle Joaquín Costa. From there we made our way down toward the port through the narrows streets of the Raval quarter. We never encountered anyone. People were afraid of Julián, even from a distance. At times we went as far as the breakwater. Julián liked to sit on the rocks, facing the city. We could spend hours like that, hardly speaking. Some afternoons we'd slip into a cinema, when the show had already started. In the dark nobody noticed Julián. As the months went by, I learned to confuse routine with normality, and in time I came to believe that my arrangement was perfect. Fool that I was.

· 12 ·

Nineteen forty-five, a year of ashes. Only six years had elapsed since the end of the Civil War, and although its bruises were felt at every step, almost nobody spoke about it openly. Now people talked about the other war, the world war, which had polluted the entire globe with a stench of corpses that would never go away. Those were years of want and misery, strangely blessed by the sort of peace that the dumb and the disabled inspire in us—halfway between pity and revulsion. At last, after years of searching in vain for work as a translator, I found a job as a copyeditor in a publishing house run by a businessman of the new breed called Pedro Sanmartí. Sanmartí had built his company with the fortune of his father-in-law, who had then been promptly dispatched to a nursing home on the shores of Lake Bañolas while Sanmartí awaited a letter containing his death certificate. The businessman liked to court young ladies half his age by presenting himself as the self-made man, an image much in vogue at the time. He spoke broken English with a thick accent, convinced that it was the language of the future, and he finished his sentences with "Okay."

Sanmartí's firm (which he had named Endymion because he thought it sounded impressive and was likely to sell books) published catechisms, manuals on etiquette, and various series of moralizing novels whose protagonists were either young nuns in humorous capers, Red Cross workers, or civil servants who were happy and morally sound. We also published a comic-book series about soldiers called *Brave Commando*—a raging success among young boys in need of heroes. I made a good friend in the firm, Sanmartí's secretary, a war widow called Mercedes Pietro, with whom I soon felt a great affinity. Mercedes and I had a lot in common: we were two women adrift, surrounded by men who were either dead or hiding from the world. Mercedes had a seven-year-old son who suffered from muscular dystrophy, for whom she cared as best she could. She was only thirty-two, but the lines on her face spoke of a life of hardship. All those years Mercedes was the only person to whom I felt tempted to tell everything.

It was she who told me that Sanmartí was a great friend of the increasingly renowned and decorated Inspector Javier Fumero. They both belonged to a clique of individuals that had risen from the ruins of the war to spread its tentacles throughout the city, a new power elite.

One day Fumero turned up at the publishing firm. He was coming to visit his friend Sanmartí, with whom he'd arranged to have lunch. Under some pretext or other, I hid in the filing room until they had both left. When I returned to my desk, Mercedes threw me a look; nothing needed to be said. From then on, every time Fumero made an appearance in the offices of the publisher, she would warn me so that I could hide.

Not a day passed without Sanmartí's trying to take me out to dinner, to the theater or the cinema, using any excuse. I always replied that my husband was waiting for me at home and that surely his wife must be anxious, as it was getting late. Mrs. Sanmartí fell well below the Bugatti on the list of her husband's favorite items. Indeed, she was close to losing her role in the marriage charade altogether, now that her father's fortune had passed into Sanmartí's hands. Mercedes had already warned me: Sanmartí, whose powers of concentration were limited, hankered after young, unseen flesh and concentrated his inane womanizing on the new arrivals—which at the moment meant me. He would resort to all manner of ploys.

"They tell me your husband, this Mr. Moliner, is a writer. . . . Perhaps he would be interested in writing a book about my friend Fumero. I have the title: Fumero, the Scourge of Crime. *What do you think, Nurieta?"*

"I'm very grateful, Mr. Sanmartí, but Miquel is caught up with a novel he's writing, and I don't think he would be able to do it at the moment. . . ."

Sanmartí would burst out laughing.

"A novel? Goodness, Nurieta . . . the novel is dead and buried. A friend of mine who has just arrived from New York was telling me only the other day. Americans are inventing something called television, which will be like the cinema, only at home. There'll be no more need for books, or churches, or anything. Tell your husband to forget about novels. If at least he were well known, if he were a football player or a bullfighter . . . Look, how about getting into the Bugatti and going to eat a paella in Castelldefels so we can discuss all this? Come on, woman, you've got to put your back into it . . . You know I'd like to help you. And your nice husband, too. You know only too well that in this country, without the right kind of friends, there's no getting anywhere."

I began to dress like a pious widow or one of those women who seem to confuse sunlight with mortal sin. I went to work with my hair drawn back into a bun and no makeup. Despite my tactics, Sanmartí continued to shower me with lascivious remarks accompanied by his oily, putrid smile. It was a smile full of disdain, typical of self-important jerks who hang like stuffed sausages from the top of all corporate ladders. I had two or three interviews for prospective jobs elsewhere, but sooner or later I would come up against another version of Sanmartí. They grew like a plague of fungi, thriving on the dung on which companies are built. One of them took the trouble to phone Sanmartí and tell him that Nuria Monfort was looking for work behind his back. Sanmartí summoned me to his office, wounded by my ingratitude. He put his hand on my cheek and tried to stroke it. His fingers smelled of tobacco and stale sweat. I went deathly pale.

"Come on, if you're not happy, all you have to do is tell me. What can I do to improve your work conditions? You know how much I appreciate you, and it hurts me to hear from others that you want to leave us. How about going out to dinner, you and me, to make up?"

I removed his hand from my face, unable to go on hiding the repugnance it caused me.

"You disappoint me, Nuria. I have to admit that I don't see a team player in you, that you don't seem to believe in this company's business objectives anymore."

Mercedes had already warned me that sooner or later something like this would happen. A few days afterward, Sanmartí, whose grammar was no better than an ape's, started returning all the manuscripts that I corrected, alleging that they were full of errors. Practically every day I stayed on in the office until ten or eleven at night, endlessly redoing pages and pages with Sanmartí's crossings-out and comments.

"Too many verbs in the past tense. It sounds dead, lifeless. . . . The infinitive should not be used after a semicolon. Everyone knows that. . . ."

Some nights Sanmartí would also stay until late, secluded in his study. Mercedes tried to be there, but more than once he sent her home. Then, when we were left alone in the premises, he would come out of his office and wander up to my desk.

"You work too hard, Nuria. Work isn't everything. One must also enjoy oneself. And you're still young. But youth passes, you know, and we don't always know how to make the most of it."

He would sit on the edge of my table and stare at me. Sometimes he would stand behind me and remain there a couple of minutes. I could feel his foul breath on my hair. Other times he placed his hands on my shoulders.

"You're tense. Relax."

I trembled, I wanted to scream or run away and never return to that office, but I needed the job and its miserly pay. One night Sanmartí started on his routine massage and then he began to fondle me.

"One of these days you're going to make me lose my head," he moaned.

I leaped up, breaking free from his grasp, and ran toward the exit, dragging my coat and bag. Behind me, Sanmartí laughed. At the bottom of the staircase, I ran straight into a dark figure.

"What a pleasant surprise, Mrs. Moliner. . . ."

Inspector Fumero gave me one of his snakelike smiles. *"Don't tell me you're working for my good friend Sanmartí! Lucky girl. Just like me, he's at the top of his game. So tell me, how's your husband?"*

I knew that my time was up. On the following day, a rumor spread around the office that Nuria Monfort was a dyke—since she remained immune to Don Pedro Sanmartí's charms and his garlic breath—and that she was involved with Mercedes Pietro. More than one promising young man in the company swore that on a number of occasions he had seen that "couple of sluts" kissing in the filing room. That afternoon, on her way out, Mercedes asked me whether she could have a quick word with me. She could barely bring herself to look at me. We went to the corner café without exchanging a single word. There Mercedes told me what Sanmartí had told her: that he didn't approve of our friendship, that the police had supplied him with a report on me, detailing my suspected communist past.

"I can't afford to lose this job, Nuria. I need it to take care of my son. . . ."

She broke down crying, burning with shame and humiliation.

"Don't worry, Mercedes. I understand," I said.

"This man, Fumero, he's after you, Nuria. I don't know what he has against you, but it shows in his face. . . ."

"I know."

THE FOLLOWING MONDAY, WHEN I ARRIVED AT WORK, I FOUND A skinny man with greased-back hair sitting at my desk. He introduced himself as Salvador Benades, the new copyeditor.

"And who are you?"

Not a single person in the office dared look at me or speak to me while I collected my things. On my way down the stairs, Mercedes ran after me and handed me an envelope with a wad of banknotes and some coins.

"Nearly everyone has contributed with whatever they could. Take it, please. Not for your sake, for ours."

That night I went to the apartment on Ronda de San Antonio. Julián was waiting for me as usual, sitting in the dark. He'd written a poem for me, he said. It was the first thing he'd written in nine years. I wanted to read it, but I broke down in his arms. I told him everything, because I couldn't hold back any longer. Julián listened to me without speaking, holding me and stroking my hair. It was the first time in years that I felt I could lean on him. I wanted to kiss him because I was sick with loneliness, but Julián had no lips or skin to offer me. I fell asleep in his arms, curled up on the bed in his room, a child's bunk. When I woke up, Julián wasn't there. At dawn I heard his footsteps on the roof terrace and pretended I was still asleep. Later that morning I heard the news on the radio without realizing its significance. A body had been found sitting on a bench on Paseo del Borne. The dead man had his hands crossed over his lap and was staring at the basilica of Santa María del Mar. A flock of pigeons pecking at his eyes caught the attention of a local resident, who alerted the police. The corpse had its neck broken. Mrs. Sanmartí identified it as her husband, Pedro Sanmartí Monegal. When the father-in-law of the deceased heard the news in his Bañolas nursing home, he gave thanks to heaven and told himself he could now die in peace.

· 13 ·

J ULIÁN ONCE WROTE THAT COINCIDENCES ARE THE SCARS OF FATE.
There are no coincidences, Daniel. We are puppets of our subconscious
desires. For years I had wanted to believe that Julián was still the man I had
fallen in love with, or what was left of him. I had wanted to believe that we
would manage to keep going with sporadic bursts of misery and hope. I had
wanted to believe that Laín Coubert had died and returned to the pages of
a book. We humans are willing to believe anything rather than the truth.

Sanmartí's murder opened my eyes. I realized that Laín Coubert was
still alive, residing within Julián's burned body and feeding on his memory.
He had found out how to get in and out of the apartment on Ronda de San
Antonio through a window that gave onto the inner courtyard, without hav-
ing to force open the door I locked every time I left him there. I discovered
that Laín Coubert, impersonating Julián, had been roaming through the city
and visiting the old Aldaya mansion. I discovered that in his madness he had
returned to the crypt and had broken the tombstones, that he had taken out
the coffins of Penélope and his son. What have you done, Julián?

The police were waiting for me when I returned home, to interrogate
me about the death of Sanmartí, the publisher. They took me to their head-
quarters, where, after five hours of waiting in a dark office, Fumero arrived,
dressed in black, and offered me a cigarette.

"You and I could be good friends, Mrs. Moliner. My men tell me your husband isn't home."

"My husband left me. I don't know where he is."

He knocked me off the chair with a brutal slap in the face. I crawled into a corner, seized by fear. I didn't dare look up. Fumero knelt beside me and grabbed me by my hair.

"Try to understand this, you fucking whore: I'm going to find him, and when I do, I'll kill you both. You first, so he can see you with your guts hanging out. And then him, once I've told him that the other tart he sent to the grave was his sister."

"He'll kill you first, you son of a bitch."

Fumero spit in my face and let me go. I thought he was going to beat me up, but I heard his steps as he walked away down the corridor. I rose to my feet, trembling, and wiped the blood off my face. I could smell that man's hand on my skin, but this time I recognized the stench of fear.

They kept me in that room, in the dark and with no water, for six hours. Night had fallen when they let me out. It was raining hard and the streets shimmered with steamy heat. When I got home, I found a sea of debris. Fumero's men had been there. Among the fallen furniture and the drawers and bookshelves thrown on the floor, I saw my clothes all torn to shreds and Miquel's books destroyed. On my bed I found a pile of feces and on the wall, written with excrement, I read the word WHORE.

I ran to the apartment on Ronda de San Antonio, making a thousand detours and ensuring that none of Fumero's henchmen had followed me to the door on Calle Joaquín Costa. I crossed the roof terraces—they were flooded with the rain—and saw that the front door of the apartment was still locked. I went in cautiously, but the echo of my footsteps told me it was empty. Julián was not there. I waited for him, sitting in the dark dining room, listening to the storm, until dawn. When the morning mist licked the balcony shutters, I went up to the roof terrace and gazed at the city, crushed under a leaden sky. I knew that Julián would not return there. I had already lost him forever.

I saw him again two months later. I had gone into a cinema at night, alone, feeling incapable of returning to my cold, empty apartment. Halfway through the film, some stupid romance between a Romanian princess eager for adventure and a handsome American reporter immune to untidy hair, a man sat down next to me. It wasn't the first time. In those days cinemas were crawling with anonymous men who reeked of loneliness, urine, and eau de cologne, wielding their sweaty, trembling hands like tongues of dead flesh. I was about to get up and warn the usher when I recognized Julián's wrinkled profile. He gripped my hand tightly, and we remained like that, looking at the screen without seeing it.

"Did you kill Sanmartí?" I murmured.

"Does anyone miss him?"

We spoke in whispers, under the attentive gaze of the solitary men who were dotted around the orchestra, green with envy at the apparent success of their shadowy rival. I asked him where he'd been hiding, but he didn't reply.

"There's another copy of The Shadow of the Wind," he murmured. "Here, in Barcelona."

"You're wrong, Julián. You destroyed them all."

"All but one. It seems that someone more clever than I am hid it in a place where I would never be able to find it. You."

That's how I first came to hear about you, Daniel. Some bigmouthed bookseller called Gustavo Barceló had been boasting to a group of collectors about having located a copy of The Shadow of the Wind. The world of rare books is like an echo chamber. In less than two months, Barceló was receiving offers for the book from collectors in London, Paris, and Rome. Julián's mysterious flight from Paris after a bloody duel and his rumored death in the Spanish Civil War had conferred on his works an undreamed-of market value. The black legend of a faceless individual who searched for them in every bookshop, library, and private collection and then burned them only added to the interest and the price. "We have the circus in our blood," Barceló would say.

Julián, who continued to pursue the shadow of his own words, soon picked up the rumor. This is how he learned that Gustavo Barceló didn't have the book: apparently the copy belonged to a boy who had discovered it by chance and who, fascinated by the novel and its mysterious author, refused to sell it and guarded it as his most precious possession. That boy was you, Daniel.

"For heaven's sake, Julián, don't say you're going to harm a child . . ." I whispered, not quite sure of his intentions.

Julián then told me that all the books he'd stolen and destroyed had been snatched from people who felt nothing for them, from people who just did business with them or kept them as curiosities. Because you refused to sell the book at any price and tried to rescue Carax from the recesses of the past, you awoke a strange sympathy in him, and even respect. Unbeknownst to you, Julián observed you and studied you.

"Perhaps, if he ever discovers who I am and what I am, he, too, will decide to burn the book."

Julián spoke with the clear, unequivocal lucidity of madmen who have escaped the hypocrisy of having to abide by a reality that makes no sense.

"Who is this boy?"

"His name is Daniel. He's the son of a bookseller whose shop, on Calle Santa Ana, Miquel used to frequent. He lives with his father in an apartment above the shop. He lost his mother when he was very young."

"You sound as if you were speaking about yourself."

"Perhaps. This boy reminds me of myself."

"Leave him alone, Julián. He's only a kid. His only crime has been to admire you."

"That's not a crime, it's a misconception. But he'll get over it. Perhaps then he'll return the book to me. When he stops admiring me and begins to understand me."

A minute before the end of the film, Julián stood up and left. For months we saw each other like that, in the dark, in cinemas or alleyways, at midnight. Julián always found me. I felt his silent presence without seeing him and was always vigilant. Sometimes he mentioned you. Every time I heard him talk about you, I sensed a rare tenderness in his voice that confused him, a tenderness that, for years now, I had thought lost. I found out that he'd returned to the Aldaya mansion and that he now lived there, halfway between a ghost and a beggar, watching over Penélope's remains and those of their son. It was the only place that he still felt was his. There are worse prisons than words.

I went there once a month to make sure he was all right, or at least alive.

I would jump over the tumbled-down wall in the back of the property, which couldn't be seen from the street. Sometimes I'd find him there, other times Julián had disappeared. I left food for him, money, books. . . . I would wait for him for hours, until it got dark. A few times I ventured to explore the rambling old house. That is how I discovered that he'd destroyed the tombstones in the crypt and taken out the coffins. I no longer thought Julián was mad, nor did I view that desecration as a monstrous act, just a tragic one. When I did find him there we spoke for hours, sitting by the fire. Julián confessed that he had tried to write again but was unable to. He vaguely remembered his books as if they were the work of some other person that he'd happened to read. The pain of his attempts to write was visible. I discovered that he burned the pages he had written feverishly while I was not there. Once, taking advantage of his absence, I rescued a pile of them from the ashes. They spoke about you. Julián had once told me that a story is a letter the author writes to himself, to tell himself things that he would be unable to discover otherwise. For some time now, Julián had been wondering whether he'd gone out of his mind. Does the madman know he is mad? Or are the madmen those who insist on convincing him of his unreason in order to safeguard their own idea of reality? Julián observed you, watched you grow, and wondered who you were. He wondered whether your presence was perhaps a miracle, a pardon he had to win by teaching you not to make his own mistakes. More than once I asked myself whether Julián hadn't reached the conclusion that you, in that twisted logic of his universe, had become the son he had lost, a blank page on which to restart a story that he could not invent but could remember.

Those years in the old mansion went by, and Julián became increasingly watchful of you, of your progress. He talked to me about your friends, about a woman called Clara with whom you had fallen in love, about your father, a man he admired and esteemed, about your friend Fermín, and about a girl in whom he wanted to see another Penélope—your Bea. He spoke about you as if you were his son. You were both looking for each other, Daniel. He wanted to believe that your innocence would save him from himself. He had stopped chasing his books, stopped wanting to destroy them. He was learning to see the world again through your eyes, to recover the boy he had once been, in you. The day you came to my apartment for the first time, I felt I already knew you. I feigned distrust so I could hide the fear you inspired in me. I was afraid of you, of what you might discover. I was afraid of listening to Julián and starting to believe, as he did, that we were all bound together in a strange chain of destiny, afraid of recognizing in you the Julián I had lost. I knew that you and your friends were investigating our past, that sooner or later you would discover the truth, but I hoped that it would be in due course, when you were able to understand its meaning. And I knew that sooner or later you and Julián would meet. That was my mistake. Because someone else knew it, someone who sensed that, in time, you would lead him to Julián: Fumero.

I understood what was happening when there was no turning back, but I never lost hope that you would lose the trail, that you would forget about us, or that life, yours and not ours, would take you far away, to safety. Time has taught me not to lose hope, yet not to trust too much in hope either. Hope is cruel, and has no conscience. For a long time, Fumero has been watching me. He knows I'll fall, sooner or later. He's not in a hurry. He lives to avenge himself. On everyone and on himself. Without vengeance, without anger, he would melt away. Fumero knows that you and your friends will take him to Julián. He knows that after almost fifteen years, I have no more strength or resources. He has watched me die for years, and he's only waiting for the moment when he will deal me the last blow. I have never doubted that I will die by his hand. Now I know the moment is drawing near. I will give these pages to my father, asking him to make sure they reach you if anything should happen to me. I pray to that God who never crossed my path that you will never have to read them, but I sense that my fate, despite my wishes and my vain hopes, is to hand you this story. Yours, despite your youth and your innocence, is to set it free.

WHEN YOU READ THESE WORDS, THIS PRISON OF MEMORIES, IT WILL mean that I will no longer be able to say good-bye to you as I would have wished, that I will not be able to ask you to forgive us, especially Julián, and to take care of him when I am no longer there to do so. I know I cannot ask anything of you, but I can ask you to save yourself. Perhaps so many pages have managed to convince me that whatever happens, I will always have a friend in you, that you are my only hope, my only real hope. Of all the things that Julián wrote, the one I have always felt closest to my heart is that so long as we are being remembered, we remain alive. As so often happened to me with Julián, years before meeting him, I feel that I know you and that if I can trust in someone, that someone is you. Remember me, Daniel, even if it's only in a corner and secretly. Don't let me go.

Nuria Monfort

The

Shadow

of the Wind

1955

· 1 ·

DAY WAS BREAKING WHEN I FINISHED READING NURIA MONFORT'S manuscript. That was my story. Our story. In Carax's lost footsteps, I now recognized my own, irretrievable. I stood, devoured by anxiety, and began to pace up and down the room like a caged animal. All my reservations, my suspicions and fears, seemed insignificant; I was overwhelmed by exhaustion, remorse, and dread, but I felt incapable of remaining there, hiding from the trail left by my actions. I slung on my coat, thrust the folded manuscript into the inside pocket, and ran down the stairs. I stepped out of the front door: it had started to snow, and the sky was melting into slow tears of light that seemed to lie on my breath before fading away. I ran up to Plaza de Cataluña. It was almost deserted but in the center of the square stood the lonely figure of an old man with long white hair, clad in a wonderful gray overcoat. King of the dawn, he raised his eyes to heaven and tried in vain to catch the snowflakes with his gloves, laughing to himself. As I walked past him, he looked at me and smiled gravely. His eyes were the color of gold, like magic coins at the bottom of a fountain.

"Good luck," I thought I heard him say.

I tried to cling to that blessing, and I quickened my step, praying that it would not be too late and that Bea, the Bea of my story, was still waiting for me.

My throat was burning with cold when, panting after the run, I reached the building where the Aguilars lived. The snow was beginning to settle. I had the good fortune of finding Don Saturno Molleda stationed at the entrance. Don Saturno was the caretaker of the building and (from what Bea had told me) a secret surrealist poet. He had come out to watch the spectacle of the snow, broom in hand, wrapped in at least three scarves and wearing commando boots.

"It's God's dandruff," he said, marveling, offering the snow a preview of his unpublished verse.

"I'm going up to the Aguilars' apartment," I announced.

"We all know that the early bird catches the worm, but you're trying to catch an elephant, young man."

"It's an emergency. They're expecting me."

"Ego te absolvo," he recited, blessing me.

I ran up the stairs. As I ascended, I weighed up my options with some caution. If I was lucky, one of the maids would open the door, and I was ready to break through her blockade without bothering about the niceties. However, if the fates didn't favor me, perhaps Bea's father would open the door, given the hour. I wanted to think that in the intimacy of his home, he would not be armed, at least not before breakfast. I paused for a few moments to recover my breath before knocking and tried to conjure up words that never came. Little did it matter. I struck the door hard with the knocker three times. Fifteen seconds later I repeated the operation, and went on doing this, ignoring the cold sweat that covered my brow and the beating of my heart. When the door opened, I was still holding the knocker in my hand.

"What do you want?"

The eyes of my old friend Tomás, cold with anger, bored through me.

"I've come to see Bea. You can smash my face in if you feel like it, but I'm not leaving without speaking to her."

Tomás observed me with a fixed stare. I wondered whether he was going to cleave me in two then and there. I swallowed hard.

"My sister isn't here."

"Tomás . . ."

"Bea's gone."

There was despondency and pain in his voice, which he was barely able to disguise as wrath.

"She's gone? Where?"

"I was hoping you would know."

"Me?"

Ignoring Tomás's closed fists and the threatening expression on his face, I slipped into the apartment.

"Bea?" I shouted. "Bea, it's me, Daniel. . . ."

I stopped halfway along the corridor. The apartment threw back the echo of my voice. Neither Mr. Aguilar nor his wife nor the servants appeared in response to my yells.

"There's no one here. I've told you," said Tomás behind me. "Now get out and don't come back. My father has sworn he'll kill you, and I'm not going to be the one to stop him."

"For God's sake, Tomás. Tell me where your sister is."

He looked at me as if he wasn't sure whether to spit at me or ignore me.

"Bea has left home, Daniel. My parents have been looking everywhere for her, desperately, for two days, and so have the police."

"But . . ."

"The other night, when she came back from seeing you, my father was waiting for her. He slapped her so much he made her mouth bleed. But don't worry, she refused to name you. You don't deserve her."

"Tomás . . ."

"Shut up. The following day my parents took her to the doctor."

"What for? Is Bea ill?"

"She's ill from you, you idiot. My sister is pregnant. Don't tell me you didn't know."

I felt my lips quivering. An intense cold spread through my body, my voice stolen, my eyes fixed. I dragged myself toward the front door, but Tomás grabbed me by the arm and threw me against the wall.

"What have you done to her?"

"Tomás, I . . ."

His eyes flashed with impatience. The first blow cut my breath in two. I slid to the floor, my back leaning against the wall, my knees giving way. A powerful grip seized me by the throat and held me up, nailed to the wall.

"What have you done to her, you son of a bitch?"

I tried to get away, but Tomás knocked me down with a punch on the face. I fell into blackness, my head wrapped in a blaze of pain. I collapsed onto the corridor tiles. I tried to crawl away, but Tomás clutched my coat collar and dragged me without ceremony to the landing. He tossed me onto the staircase like a piece of rubbish.

"If anything has happened to Bea, I swear I'll kill you," he said from the doorway.

I got up on my knees, begging for a moment of time, for an opportunity to recover my voice. But the door closed, abandoning me to the darkness. A sharp pain struck me in my left ear, and I put my hand to my head, twisting with agony. I could feel warm blood. I stood up as best I could. My stomach muscles, where Tomás's first blow had landed, were smarting— that was just the beginning. I slid down the stairs. Don Saturno shook his head when he saw me.

"Here, come inside for a minute, until you feel better."

I shook my head, holding my stomach with both hands. The left side of my head throbbed, as if the bones were trying to detach themselves from the flesh.

"You're bleeding," said Don Saturno with a concerned look.

"It's not the first time. . . ."

"Well, then, keep on fooling around and you won't have many chances left to bleed again. Here, come in and I'll call a doctor, please."

I managed to get to the main door and escape the caretaker's kindness. It was now snowing hard; the pavement was covered in veils of white mist. The icy wind made its way between my clothes and licked at the bleeding wound on my face. I don't know whether I cried with pain, anger, or fear. The indifferent snow silenced my cowardly weeping, and I walked away slowly in the dusty dawn, one more shadow leaving his tracks in God's dandruff.

· *2* ·

As I was approaching the crossing with Calle Balmes, I noticed that a car was following me, hugging the pavement. The pain in my head had given way to a feeling of vertigo that made me reel, so that I had to walk holding on to the walls. The car stopped, and two men came out of it. A sharp whistling sound had filled my ears, and I couldn't hear the engine or the calls of the two figures in black who grabbed hold of me, one on either side, and dragged me hurriedly to the car. I fell into the backseat, drunk with nausea. Floods of blinding light came and went inside my brain. I felt the car moving. A pair of hands touched my face, my head, my ribs. Coming upon the manuscript of Nuria Monfort, which was hidden inside my coat, one of the figures snatched it from me. I tried to stop him with jellylike arms. The other silhouette leaned over me. I knew he was talking when I felt his breath on my face. I waited to see Fumero's face light up and feel the blade of his knife on my throat. Two eyes rested on mine, and as the curtain of consciousness fell, I recognized the gap-toothed, welcoming smile of Fermín Romero de Torres.

I woke up in a sweat that stung my skin. Two hands held my shoulders firmly and settled me into a small bed surrounded by candles, as in a wake. Fermín's face appeared on my right. He was smiling, but even in my delirium I could sense his anxiety. Next to him, standing, I recognized Don Federico Flaviá, the watchmaker.

"He seems to be coming around, Fermín," said Don Federico. "Shall I go and prepare some broth, to revive him?"

"It won't do him any harm. While you're at it, you could make me a sandwich of whatever you find. Double-decker, if you please. All these nerves have suddenly revived my appetite."

Federico scurried off, and we were left alone.

"Where are we, Fermín?"

"In a safe place. Technically speaking, we're in a small apartment on the left side of the Ensanche quarter, the property of some friends of Don Federico, to whom we owe our lives and more. Slanderers would describe it as a love nest, but for us it's a sanctuary."

I tried to sit up. The pain in my ear was now a burning throb.

"Will I go deaf?"

"I don't know about that, but a bit more beating and you'd have certainly been left bordering on the vegetative. That troglodyte Mr. Aguilar almost pulped your gray cells."

"It wasn't Mr. Aguilar who beat me. It was Tomás."

"Tomás? Your friend? The inventor?"

I nodded.

"You must have done something to deserve it."

"Bea has left home . . ." I began.

Fermín frowned. "Go on."

"She's pregnant."

Fermín was looking at me openmouthed. For once his expression was impenetrable.

"Don't look at me like that, Fermín, please."

"What do you want me to do? Start handing out cigars?"

I tried to get up, but the pain and Fermín's hands stopped me.

"I've got to find her, Fermín."

"Steady, there. You're not in any fit state to go anywhere. Tell me where the girl is, and I'll go and find her."

"I don't know where she is."

"I'm going to have to ask you to be more specific."

Don Federico appeared around the door carrying a cup of steaming broth. He smiled at me warmly.

"How are you feeling, Daniel?"

"Much better, thanks, Don Federico."

"Take a couple of these pills with the soup."

He glanced briefly at Fermín, who nodded.

"They're painkillers."

I swallowed the pills and sipped the cup of broth, which tasted of sherry. Don Federico, the soul of discretion, left the room and closed the door. It was then I noticed that Fermín had Nuria Monfort's manuscript on his lap. The clock ticking on the bedside table showed one o'clock—in the afternoon, I supposed.

"Is it still snowing?"

"That's an understatement. This is a powdery version of the Flood."

"Have you read it?" I asked.

Fermín simply nodded.

"I must find Bea before it's too late. I think I know where she is."

I sat up in bed, pushing Fermín's arms aside. I looked around me. The walls swayed like weeds at the bottom of a pond. The ceiling seemed to be moving away. I could barely hold myself upright. Fermín effortlessly laid me back on the bed again.

"You're not going anywhere, Daniel."

"What were those pills?"

"Morpheus's liniment. You're going to sleep like a log."

"No, not now, I can't. . . ."

I continued to blabber until my eyelids closed and I dropped into a black, empty sleep, the sleep of the guilty.

IT WAS ALMOST DUSK WHEN THAT TOMBSTONE WAS LIFTED OFF ME. I opened my eyes to a dark room watched over by two tired candles flickering on the bedside table. Fermín, defeated on an armchair in the corner, snored with the fury of a man three times his size. At his feet, scattered like a flood of tears, lay Nuria Monfort's manuscript. The headache had lessened to a slow, tepid throb. I tiptoed over to the bedroom door and went out into a little hall with a balcony and a door that seemed to open onto the staircase. My coat and shoes lay on a chair. A purplish light came in through the window, speckled with iridescence. I walked over to the balcony and saw that it was still snowing. Half the roofs of Barcelona were mottled with white and scarlet. In the distance the towers of the Industrial College looked like needles in the haze, clinging to the last rays of sun. The windowpane was veiled with frost. I put my index finger on the glass and wrote:

Gone to find Bea. Don't follow me. Back soon.

The truth had struck me when I woke up, as if some stranger had whispered it to me in a dream. I stepped out onto the landing and rushed down the stairs and out of the front door. Calle Urgel was like a river of shiny white sand, and the wind blew the snow about in gusts. Streetlamps and trees emerged like masts in a fog. I walked to the nearest subway station, Hospital Clínico, past the stand of afternoon papers carrying the news on the front page, with photographs of the Ramblas covered in snow and the fountain of Canaletas bleeding stalactites. SNOWFALL OF THE CENTURY, the headlines blared. I fell onto a bench on the platform and breathed in that perfume of tunnels and soot that the sound of trains brings with it. On the other side of the tracks, on a poster proclaiming the delights of the Tibidabo amusement park, the blue tram was lit up like a street party, and behind it one could just make out the outline of the Aldaya mansion. I wondered whether Bea had seen the same image and had realized she had nowhere else to go.

· 3 ·

WHEN I CAME OUT OF THE SUBWAY TUNNEL, IT WAS STARTING to get dark. Avenida del Tibidabo lay deserted, stretching out in a long line of cypress trees and mansions. I glimpsed the shape of the blue tram at the stop and heard the conductor's bell piercing the wind. A quick run, and I jumped on just as it was pulling away. The conductor, my old acquaintance, took the coins, mumbling under his breath, and I sat down inside the carriage, a bit more sheltered from the snow and the cold. The somber mansions filed slowly by, behind the tram's icy windows. The conductor watched me with a mixture of suspicion and bemusement, which the cold seemed to have frozen on his face.

"Number thirty-two, young man."

I turned and saw the ghostly silhouette of the Aldaya mansion advancing toward us like the prow of a dark ship in the mist. The tram stopped with a shudder. I got off, fleeing from the conductor's gaze.

"Good luck," he murmured.

I watched the tram disappear up the avenue, leaving behind only the echo of its bell. Darkness fell around me. I hurried along the garden wall, looking for the gap in the back, where it had tumbled down. As I climbed over, I thought I heard footsteps on the snow approaching on the opposite pavement. I stopped for a second and remained motionless on the top of the wall. The sound of footsteps faded in the wind's wake. I jumped down to the other side and entered the garden. The weeds had frozen into stems of crystal. The statues of the fallen angels were covered in shrouds of ice. The water in the fountain had iced over, forming a black, shiny mirror, from which only the stone claw of the sunken angel protruded, like an obsidian sword. Tears of ice hung from the index finger. The accusing hand of the angel pointed straight at the main door, which stood ajar.

I ran up the steps without bothering to muffle the sound of my footsteps. Pushing the door open, I walked into the lobby. A procession of candles lined the way toward the interior. They were Bea's candles, almost burned down to the ground. I followed their trail and stopped at the foot of the grand staircase. The path of candles continued up the steps to the first floor. I ventured up the stairs, following my distorted shadow on the walls. When I reached the first-floor landing, I saw two more candles, set along the corridor. A third one flickered outside the room that had once been Penélope's. I went up to the door and rapped gently with my knuckles.

"Julián?" came a shaky voice.

I grabbed hold of the doorknob and slowly opened the door. Bea gazed at me from a corner of the room, wrapped in a blanket. I ran to her side and held her. I could feel her dissolving into tears.

"I didn't know where to go," she murmured. "I called your home a few times, but there was no answer. I was scared. . . ."

Bea dried her tears with her fists and fixed her eyes on mine. I nodded; there was no need to reply with words.

"Why did you call me Julián?"

Bea cast a glance at the half-open door. "He's here. In this house. He comes and goes. He discovered me the other day, when I was trying to get into the house. Without my saying anything, he knew who I was and what was happening. He set me up in this room, and he brought me a blanket, water, and some food. He told me to wait. He said that everything was going to turn out all right, that you'd come for me. At night we talked for hours. He talked to me about Penélope, about Nuria—above all he spoke about you, about us two. He told me I had to teach you to forget him. . . ."

"Where is he now?"

"Downstairs. In the library. He said he was waiting for someone, and not to move."

"Waiting for who?"

"I don't know. He said it was someone who would come with you, that you'd bring him. . . ."

When I peered into the corridor, I could already hear footsteps below, near the staircase. I recognized the spidery shadow on the walls, the black raincoat, the hat pulled down like a hood, and the gun in his hand shining like a scythe. Fumero. He had always reminded me of someone, or something, but until then I hadn't understood what.

· 4 ·

I SNUFFED OUT THE CANDLES WITH MY FINGERS AND MADE A SIGN TO Bea to keep quiet. She grabbed my hand and looked at me questioningly. Fumero's slow steps could be heard below us. I led Bea back inside the room and signaled to her to stay there, hiding behind the door.

"Don't go out of this room, whatever happens," I whispered.

"Don't leave me now, Daniel. Please."

"I must warn Carax."

Bea gave me an imploring look, but I went out into the corridor. I tip-toed to the top of the main staircase. There was no sign of Fumero. He had stopped at some point of the darkness and stood there, motionless, patient. I stepped back into the corridor and walked down it, past the row of bed-rooms, until I got to the front of the mansion. A large window coated in frost refracted two blue beams of light, cloudy as stagnant water. I moved over to the window and saw a black car stationed in front of the main gate, its lights on. I recognized it as the car of Lieutenant Palacios. The glowing ember of a cigarette in the dark gave away his presence behind the steering wheel. I went slowly back to the staircase and began to descend, step by step, placing my feet with infinite care. Stopping halfway down, I scanned the darkness that had engulfed the ground floor.

Fumero had left the front door open as he came in. The wind had blown out the candles and was spitting whirls of snow and frozen leaves across the hall. I went down four more steps, hugging the wall, and caught a glimpse of the large library windows. There was still no sign of Fumero. I wondered whether he had gone down to the basement or to the crypt. The powdery snow that blew in from outside was fast erasing his footprints. I slipped down to the base of the stairs and peered into the corridor that led to the main door. An icy wind hit me. The claw of the submerged angel was just visible in the dark. I looked in the other direction. The entrance to the library was about ten yards from the foot of the staircase. The anteroom that led to it was sunk in shadows, and I realized that Fumero could be watching me only a few yards from where I was standing. I looked into the darkness, as impenetrable as the waters of a well. Taking a deep breath and almost dragging my feet, I blindly crossed the distance that separated me from the entrance to the library.

The large oval hall was submerged in a dim, vaporous light, speckled with shadows that were cast by the snow falling heavily on the other side of the windows. My eyes skimmed over the empty walls in search of Fumero— could he be standing by the entrance? An object protruded from the wall just a couple of yards on my right. For a moment I thought I saw it move, but it was only the reflection of the moon on the blade. A knife, perhaps a double-bladed penknife, had been sunk into the wood paneling. It pierced a square of paper or cardboard. I stepped closer and recognized the stabbed image. It was an identical copy of the half-burned photograph that a stranger had once left on the bookshop counter. In the picture, Julián and Penélope, still adolescents, smiled in happiness. The knife went through Julián's chest. I understood then that it hadn't been Laín Coubert, or Julián Carax, who had left that photograph like an invitation. It had been Fumero. The photograph had been poisoned bait. I raised my hand to snatch it away from the knife, but the icy touch of Fumero's gun on my neck stopped me.

"An image is worth more than a thousand words, Daniel. If your father hadn't been a shitty bookseller, he would have taught you that by now."

I turned slowly and faced the barrel of the pistol. It stank of fresh gunpowder. Fumero's face was contorted into a dreadful grimace.

"Where's Carax?" he demanded.

"Far from here. He knew you would come for him. He's left."

Fumero observed me without blinking. "I'm going to blow your head into small pieces, kid."

"That's not going to help you much. Carax isn't here."

"Open your mouth," ordered Fumero.

"What for?"

"Open your mouth or I'll open it myself with a bullet."

I parted my lips. Fumero stuck the revolver in my mouth. I felt nausea rising in my throat. Fumero's thumb tensed on the hammer.

"Now, you bastard, think about whether you have any reason to go on living. What do you say?"

I nodded slowly.

"Then tell me where Carax is."

I tried to mumble. Fumero slowly pulled out the gun.

"Where is he?"

"Downstairs. In the crypt."

"You lead the way. I want you to be present when I tell that son of a bitch how Nuria Monfort moaned when I dug the knife into—"

Glancing over Fumero's shoulder, I thought I saw the darkness stirring and a figure without a face, his eyes burning, gliding toward us in absolute silence, as if barely touching the floor. Fumero saw the reflection in my tear-filled eyes, and his face slowly became distorted.

When he turned and shot at the mantle of blackness that surrounded him, two deformed leather claws gripped his throat. They were the hands of Julián Carax, grown out of the flames. Carax pushed me aside and crushed Fumero to the wall. The inspector clutched his revolver and tried to place it under Carax's chin. Before he could pull the trigger, Carax grabbed his wrist and hammered it with great strength against the wall, again and again, but Fumero didn't drop the gun. A second shot burst in the dark and hit the wall, making a hole in the wood paneling. Tears of burning gunpowder and red-hot splinters spattered over the inspector's face. A stench of singed flesh filled the room.

With a violent jerk, Fumero tried to get away from the force that was immobilizing his neck and the hand holding the gun. Carax wouldn't loosen his grip. Fumero roared with anger and tilted his head until he was able to bite Carax's fist. He was possessed by an animal fury. I heard the snap of his teeth as he tore at the dead skin, and saw Fumero's lips dripping with blood. Ignoring the pain, or perhaps unable to feel it, Carax grabbed hold of the dagger on the wall. He pulled it out and, under Fumero's terrified gaze, skewered the inspector's right wrist to the wall with a brutal blow that buried the blade in the wooden panel almost to the hilt. Fumero let out a terrible cry of pain as his hand opened in a spasm, and the gun fell to his feet. Carax kicked it into the shadows.

The horror of that scene passed before my eyes in just a few seconds. I felt paralyzed, incapable of acting or even thinking. Carax turned to me and fixed his eyes on mine. As I looked at him, I was able to reconstruct his lost features, which I had so often imagined from photographs and old stories.

"Take Beatriz away from here, Daniel. She knows what you must do. Don't let her out of your sight. Don't let anyone take her from you. Anyone or anything. Look after her. More than your own life."

I tried to nod, but my eyes turned to Fumero, who was struggling with the knife that pierced his wrist. He yanked it out and collapsed on his knees, holding the wounded arm that was pouring blood onto his side.

"Leave," Carax murmured.

Fumero watched us from the floor, blinded by hatred, holding the bloody knife in his left hand. Carax turned to him. I heard hurried footsteps approaching and realized that Palacios was coming to the aid of his boss, alerted by the shots. Before Carax was able to seize the knife from Fumero, Palacios entered the library holding his gun up high.

"Move back," he warned.

He threw a quick glance at Fumero, who was getting up with some difficulty, and then he looked at us—first at me and then at Carax. I could see horror and doubt in that look.

"I said move back."

Carax paused and withdrew. Palacios observed us coldly, trying to work out what to do. His eyes rested on me.

"You, get out of here. This isn't anything to do with you. Go."

I hesitated for a moment. Carax nodded.

"No one's leaving this place," Fumero cut in. "Palacios, hand me your gun."

Palacios didn't answer.

"Palacios," Fumero repeated, stretching out his blood-drenched hand, demanding the weapon.

"No," mumbled Palacios, gritting his teeth.

Fumero, his maddened eyes filled with disdain and fury, grabbed Palacios's gun and pushed him aside with a swipe of his hand. I glanced at Palacios and knew what was going to happen. Fumero raised the gun slowly. His hand shook, and the revolver shone with blood. Carax drew back a step at a time, in search of shadows, but there was no escape. The revolver's barrel followed him. I felt all the muscles in my body burn with rage. Fumero's deathly grimace, and the way he licked his lips like a madman, woke me up like a slap in the face. Palacios was looking at me, silently shaking his head. I ignored him. Carax had given up by now and stood motionless in the middle of the room, waiting for the bullet.

Fumero never saw me. For him only Carax existed and that bloodstained hand holding the revolver. I leaped upon him. I felt my feet rise from the ground, but I never regained contact with it. The world froze in midair. The blast of the shot reached me from afar, like the echo of a receding storm. There was no pain. The bullet went through my ribs. At first there was a blinding flash, as if a metal bar had hit me with indescribable force and propelled me through the air for a couple of yards, then knocked me down to the floor. I didn't feel the fall, although I thought I saw the walls converging and the ceiling descending at great speed to crush me.

A hand held the back of my head, and I saw Julián Carax's face bending over me. In my vision Carax appeared exactly as I'd imagined him, as if the flames had never torn off his features. I noticed the horror in his eyes, without understanding. I saw how he placed his hand on my chest, and I wondered what that smoking liquid was flowing between his fingers. It was then I felt that terrible fire, like the hot breath of embers, burning my insides. I tried to scream, but nothing surfaced except warm blood. I recognized the face of Palacios next to me, full of remorse, defeated. I raised my eyes and then I saw her. Bea was advancing slowly from the library door, her face suffused with terror and her trembling hands on her lips. She was shaking her head without speaking. I tried to warn her, but a biting cold was coursing up my arms, stabbing its way into my body.

Fumero was hiding behind the door. Bea didn't notice his presence. When Carax leaped up and Bea turned, the inspector's gun was already almost touching her forehead. Palacios rushed to stop him. He was too late. Carax was already there. I heard his faraway scream, which bore Bea's name. The room lit up with the flash of the shot. The bullet went through Carax's right hand. A moment later the man without a face was falling upon Fumero. I leaned over to see Bea running to my side, unhurt. I looked for Carax with eyes that were clouding over, but I couldn't find him. Another figure had taken his place. It was Laín Coubert, just as I'd learned to fear him reading the pages of a book, so many years ago. This time Coubert's claws sank into Fumero's eyes like hooks and pulled him away. I managed to see the inspector's legs as they were hauled out through the library door. I managed to see how his body shook with spasms as Coubert dragged him without pity toward the main door, saw how his knees hit the marble steps and the snow spit on his face, how the man without a face grabbed him by the neck and, lifting him up like a puppet, threw him into the frozen bowl of the fountain; I saw how the hand of the angel pierced his chest, spearing him, how the accursed soul was driven out like black vapor, falling like frozen tears over the mirror of water.

I collapsed then, unable to keep my eyes focused any longer. Darkness became tinted with a white light, and Bea's face receded from me. I closed my eyes and felt her hands on my cheeks and the breath of her voice begging God not to take me, whispering in my ear that she loved me and wouldn't let me go. All I remember is that I let that mirage go and that a strange peace enveloped me and took away the pain of the slow fire that burned inside me. I saw myself and Bea—an elderly couple—walking hand in hand through the streets of Barcelona, that bewitched city. I saw my father and Nuria Monfort placing white roses on my grave. I saw Fermín crying in Bernarda's arms, and my old friend Tomás, who had fallen silent forever. I saw them as one sees strangers from a train that is moving away too fast. It was then, almost without realizing, that I remembered my mother's face, a face I had lost so many years before, as if an old cutting had suddenly fallen out of the pages of a book. Her light was all that came with me as I descended.

Postmortem

November 27, 1955

*T*he room was white, a shimmer of sheets and curtains made of mist and bright sunshine. From my window I could make out a blue sea. One day someone would try to convince me that one cannot view the sea from the Corachán Clinic, that its rooms are not white or ethereal, and that the sea of that November was like a leaden pond, cold and hostile; that it went on snowing every day of that week until all of Barcelona was buried in three feet of snow, and that even Fermín, the eternal optimist, thought I was going to die again.

I had already died before, in the ambulance, in the arms of Bea and Lieutenant Palacios, who ruined his uniform with my blood. The bullet, said the doctors, who spoke about me thinking that I couldn't hear them, had destroyed two ribs, had brushed my heart, had severed an artery, and had come out at full speed through my side, dragging with it everything it had encountered on the way. My heart stopped beating for sixty-four seconds. They told me that when I returned from my excursion to eternity, I opened my eyes and smiled before losing consciousness.

I didn't come around until eight days later. By then the newspapers had already published the news of Francisco Javier Fumero's death during a struggle with an armed gang of criminals, and the authorities were busy trying to find a street or an alleyway they could rename in memory of the distinguished police inspector. His was the only body found in the old mansion of the Aldayas. The bodies of Penélope and her son were never discovered.

I awoke at dawn. I remember the light, like liquid gold, pouring over the sheets. It had stopped snowing, and somebody had exchanged the sea outside my window for a white square from which a few swings could be seen, and little else. My father, sunk in a chair by my bed, looked up and gazed at me in silence. I smiled at him, and he broke into tears. Fermín, who was sleeping like a baby in the corridor, and Bea, who was holding his head on her lap, heard my father's loud, wailing sobs and came into the room. I remember that Fermín was white and thin like the backbone of a fish. They told me that the blood running through my veins was his, that I'd lost all mine, and that my friend had been spending days stuffing himself with meat sandwiches in the hospital's canteen to breed more red blood corpuscles, in case I should need them. Perhaps that explains why I felt wiser and less like Daniel. I remember there was a forest of flowers and that in the afternoon—or perhaps two minutes later, I couldn't say—a whole cast of people filed through the room, from Gustavo Barceló and his niece Clara to Bernarda and my friend Tomás, who didn't dare look me in the eye and who, when I embraced him, ran off to weep in the street. I vaguely remember Don Federico, who came along with Merceditas and Don Anacleto, the high-school teacher. I particularly remember Bea, who looked at me without saying a word while all the others dissolved into cheers and thanks to the heavens, and I remember my father, who had slept on that chair for seven nights, praying to a God in whom he did not believe.

When the doctors ordered the entire committee to vacate the room and leave me to have a rest I did not want, my father came up to me for a moment and told me he'd brought my pen, the Victor Hugo fountain pen, and a notebook, in case I wanted to write. From the doorway Fermín announced that he'd consulted with the whole staff of doctors in the hospital and they had assured him I would not have to do my military service. Bea kissed me on the forehead and took my father with her to get some fresh air, because he hadn't been out of that room for over a week. I was left alone, weighed down by exhaustion, and I gave in to sleep, staring at the pen case on my bedside table.

I was woken up by footsteps at the door. I waited to see my father at the end of the bed, or perhaps Dr. Mendoza, who had never taken his eyes off me, convinced that my recovery was the result of a miracle. The visitor went around the bed and sat on my father's chair. My mouth felt dry. Julián Carax put a glass of water to my lips, holding my head while I moistened them. His eyes spoke of farewell, and looking into them was enough for me to understand that he had never discovered the true identity of Penélope. I can't remember his exact words, or the sound of his voice. I do know that he held my hand and I felt as if he were asking me to live for him, telling me I would never see him again. What I have not forgotten is what I told him. I told him to take that pen, which had always been his, and write again.

When I woke again, Bea was cooling my forehead with a cloth dampened with eau de cologne. Startled, I asked her where Carax was. She looked at me in confusion and told me that Carax had disappeared in the storm eight days before, leaving a trail of blood on the snow, and that everyone had given him up for dead. I said that wasn't true, he'd been right there, with me, only a few seconds ago. Bea smiled at me without saying anything. The nurse who was taking my pulse slowly shook her head and explained that I'd been asleep for six hours, that she'd been sitting at her desk by the door to my room all that time, and that certainly nobody had come into my room.

That night, when I was trying to get to sleep, I turned my head on my pillow and noticed that the pen case was open. The pen was gone.

The

Waters

of March

1956

Bea and I were married in the Church of Santa Ana three months later. Mr. Aguilar, who still spoke to me in monosyllables and would go on doing so until the end of time, had given me his daughter's hand in view of the impossibility of obtaining my head on a platter. Bea's disappearance had done away with his anger, and now he seemed to live in a state of perpetual shock, resigned to the fact that his grandson would soon call me Dad and that life, in the shape of a rascal stitched back together after a bullet wound, should rob him of his girl—a girl who, despite his bifocals, he still saw as the child in her first-communion dress, not a day older.

A week before the ceremony, Bea's father turned up at the bookshop to present me with a gold tiepin that had belonged to his father and to shake hands with me.

"Bea is the only good thing I've ever done in my life," he said. "Take care of her for me."

My father went with him to the door and watched him walk away down Calle Santa Ana, with that sadness that softens men who are aware that they are growing old together.

"He's not a bad person, Daniel," he said. "We all love in our own way."

Dr. Mendoza, who doubted my ability to stay on my feet for more than half an hour, had warned me that the bustle of a wedding and all the preparations were not the best medicine for a man who had been on the point of leaving his heart in the operating room.

"Don't worry," I reassured him. "They're not letting me do anything."

I wasn't lying. Fermín Romero de Torres had set himself up as absolute dictator of the ceremony, the banquet, and all related matters. When the parish priest discovered that the bride was arriving pregnant to the altar, he flatly refused to perform the wedding and threatened to summon the spirits of the Holy Inquisition and make them cancel the event. Fermín flew into a rage and dragged him out of the church, shouting to all and sundry that he was unworthy of his habit and of the parish, and swearing that if the priest as much as raised an eyebrow, he was going to stir up such a scandal in the bishopric that at the very least he would be exiled to the Rock of Gibraltar to evangelize the monkeys. A few passersby clapped, and the flower vendor in the square gave Fermín a white carnation, which he went on to wear in his lapel until the petals turned the same color as his shirt collar. All set up and without a priest, Fermín went to San Gabriel's School, where he recruited the services of Father Fernando Ramos, who had not performed a wedding in his life and whose specialty was Latin, trigonometry, and gymnastics, in that order.

"You see, Your Reverence, the bridegroom is very weak, and I can't upset him again. He sees in you a reincarnation of the great glories of the Mother Church, there, up high, with Saint Thomas, Saint Augustine, and the Virgin of Fátima. He may not seem so, but the boy is, like me, extremely devout. A mystic. If I now tell him that you've failed me, we may well have to celebrate a funeral instead of a wedding."

"If you put it like that."

From what they told me later—because I don't remember it, and weddings always stay more clearly in the memory of others—before the ceremony Bernarda and Gustavo Barceló (following Fermín's detailed instructions) softened up the poor priest with muscatel wine to rid him of his stage fright. When the time came for Father Fernando to officiate, wearing a saintly smile and a pleasantly rosy complexion, he chose, in a breach of protocol, to replace the reading of I don't know which Letter to the Corinthians with a love sonnet, the work of a poet called Pablo Neruda.

Some of Mr. Aguilar's guests identified him as a confirmed communist and a Bolshevik, while others looked in the missal for those verses of intense pagan beauty, wondering whether this was already one of the first effects of the impending Ecumenical Council.

The night before the wedding, Fermín told me he had organized a bachelor party to which only he and I were invited.

"I don't know Fermín. I don't really like these—"

"Trust me."

On the night of the crime, I followed Fermín meekly to a foul hovel on Calle Escudillers, where the stench of humanity coexisted with the most potent odor of refried food on the entire Mediterranean coast. A lineup of ladies with their virtue for rent and a lot of mileage on the clock greeted us with smiles that would only have excited a student of dentistry.

"We've come for Rociíto," Fermín informed a pimp whose sideburns bore a surprising resemblance to Cape Finisterre.

"Fermín," I whispered, terrified. "For heaven's sake . . ."

"Have faith."

Rociíto arrived in all her glory—which I reckoned to amount to around 175 pounds, not counting the feather shawl and a skeleton-tight red viscose dress—and took stock of me from head to toe.

"Hi, sweetheart. I thought you was older, to tell the God's honest truth."

"This is not the client," Fermín clarified.

I then understood the nature of the situation, and my fears subsided. Fermín never forgot a promise, especially if it was I who had made it. The three of us went off in search of a taxi that would take us to the Santa Lucía Hospice. During the journey Fermín, who, in deference to my delicate health and my fiancé status, had offered me the front seat, was sitting in the back with Rociíto, taking in her attributes with obvious relish.

"You're a dish fit for a pope, Rociíto. This egregious ass of yours is the Revelation According to Botticelli."

"Oh, Mr. Fermín, since you got yourself a girlfriend, you've forgotten me, you rogue."

"You're too much of a woman for me, Rociíto, and now I'm monogamous."

"Nah! Good ole Rociíto will cure that for you with some good rubs of penicillin."

We reached Calle Moncada after midnight, escorting Rociíto's heavenly body, and slipped her into the hospice by the back door——the one used for taking out the deceased through an alleyway that looked and smelled like hell's esophagus. Once we had entered the shadows of the Tenebrarium, Fermín proceeded to give Rociíto his final instructions while I tried to find the old granddad to whom I'd promised a last dance with Eros before Thanatos settled accounts with him.

"Remember, Rociíto, the old geezer is probably as deaf as a post, so speak to him in a loud voice, clear and dirty, with sauciness, the way you know how. But don't get too carried away either. We don't want to give him heart failure and send him off to kingdom come before his time."

"No worries, pumpkin. I'm a professional."

I found the recipient of those rented favors in a corner of the first floor, the wise hermit still barricaded behind walls of loneliness. He raised his eyes and stared at me, confused.

"Am I dead?"

"No. You're very much alive. Don't you remember me?"

"I remember you as well as I remember my first pair of shoes, young man, but seeing you like this, looking so pale, I thought it might be a vision from beyond. Don't hold it against me. Here one loses what you outsiders call discernment. So this isn't a vision?"

"No. The vision is waiting for you downstairs, if you'll do the honors."

I led the grandpa to a gloomy cell, which Fermín and Rociíto had decorated festively with some candles and a few puffs of perfume. When his eyes rested on the abundant beauty of our Andalusian Venus, the old man's face lit up with intimations of paradise.

"May God bless you all."

"And may you live to see it," said Fermín, as he signaled to the siren from Calle Escudillers to start displaying her wares.

I saw her take the old man with infinite delicacy and kiss the tears that fell down his cheeks. Fermín and I left the scene to grant them their deserved intimacy. In our winding journey through that gallery of despair, we encountered Sister Emilia, one of the nuns who managed the hospice. She threw us a venomous look.

"Some patients are telling me you've brought in a hooker. Now they also want one."

"Most Illustrious Sister, who do you take us for? Our presence here is strictly ecumenical. This young lad, who tomorrow will be a man in the eyes of the Holy Mother Church, and I, have come to inquire after the patient Jacinta Coronado."

Sister Emilia raised an eyebrow. "Are you related?"

"Spiritually."

"Jacinta died two weeks ago. A gentleman came to visit her the night before. Is he a relative of yours?"

"Do you mean Father Fernando?"

"He wasn't a priest. He said his name was Julián. I can't remember his last name."

Fermín looked at me, dumbstruck.

"Julián is a friend of mine," I said.

Sister Emilia nodded. "He was with her for a few hours. I hadn't heard her laugh for years. When he left, she told me they'd been talking about the old days, when they were young. She said that man had brought news of her daughter, Penélope. I didn't know Jacinta had a daughter. I remember, because that morning Jacinta smiled at me, and when I asked her why she was so happy, she said she was going home, with Penélope. She died at dawn, in her sleep."

Rociíto concluded her love ritual a short while later, leaving the old man merrily exhausted and in the hands of Morpheus. As we were leaving, Fermín paid her double, but Rociíto, who was crying from the sight of those poor, helpless people, forsaken by God and the devil, insisted on handing her fees to Sister Emilia so that they could all be given a meal of hot chocolate and sweet buns, because, she said, that was something that always made her forget the sorrows of life.

"I'm ever so sentimental. Look at that poor old soul, Mr. Fermín. . . . All he wanted was to be hugged and stroked. Breaks your heart, it does. . . ."

We put Rociíto into a taxi with a good tip and walked up Calle Princesa, which was deserted and strewn with mist.

"We ought to get to bed, because of tomorrow," said Fermín.

"I don't think I'll be able to get any sleep."

We set off toward La Barceloneta. Before we knew it, we were walking along the breakwater until the whole city, shining with silence, spread out at our feet like the greatest mirage in the universe, emerging from the pool of the harbor waters. We sat on the edge of the jetty to gaze at the sight.

"This city is a sorceress, you know, Daniel? It gets under your skin and steals your soul without you knowing it."

"You sound like Rociíto, Fermín."

"Don't laugh, it's people like her who make this lousy world a place worth visiting."

"Whores?"

"No. We're all whores, sooner or later. I mean good-hearted people. And don't look at me like that. Weddings turn me to jelly."

We remained there embracing that special silence, gazing at the reflections on the water. After a while dawn tinged the sky with amber, and Barcelona woke up. We heard the distant bells from the basilica of Santa María del Mar, just emerging from the mist on the other side of the harbor.

"Do you think Carax is still there, somewhere in the city?" I asked.

"Ask me another question."

"Do you have the rings?"

Fermín smiled. "Come on, let's go. They're waiting for us, Daniel. Life is waiting for us."

She wore an ivory-white dress and held the world in her eyes. I barely remember the priest's words or the faces of the guests, full of hope, who filled the church on that March morning. All that remains in my memory is the touch of her lips and, when I half opened my eyes, the secret oath I carried with me on my skin and would remember all the days of my life.

Dramatis
Personae

1966

J ULIÁN CARAX CONCLUDES *THE SHADOW OF THE WIND* WITH A
brief coda in which he gathers up the threads of his characters' fates in
years to come. I've read many books since that distant night of 1945, but
Carax's last novel remains my favorite. Today, with three decades behind
me, I can't see myself changing my mind.

As I write these words on the counter of my bookshop, my son, Julián,
who will be ten tomorrow, watches me with a smile and looks with curios-
ity at the pile of sheets that grows and grows, convinced, perhaps, that his
father has also caught the illness of books and words. Julián has his mother's
eyes and intelligence, and I like to think that perhaps he possesses my sense
of wonder. My father, who now has some difficulty reading the book spines,
even though he won't admit it, is at home, upstairs. I sometimes ask myself
whether he's a happy man, a man at peace, whether our company helps him
or whether he lives within his memories and within that sadness that has al-
ways followed him. Bea and I manage the bookshop now. I do the accounts
and the adding up. Bea does the buying and serves the customers, who pre-
fer her to me. I don't blame them.

Time has made her strong and wise. She hardly ever speaks about the
past, although I often catch her marooned in one of her silences, alone with
herself. Julián adores his mother. I watch them together, and I know they

are linked by an invisible bond that I can barely begin to understand. It is enough for me to feel a part of their island and to know how fortunate I am. The bookshop provides us with enough to live modestly, but I can't imagine myself doing anything else. Our sales lessen year by year. I'm an optimist, and I tell myself that what goes up comes down and what comes down must, one day, go up again. Bea says that the art of reading is slowly dying, that it's an intimate ritual, that a book is a mirror that offers us only what we already carry inside us, that when we read, we do it with all our heart and mind, and great readers are becoming more scarce by the day. Every month we receive offers to turn our bookshop into a store selling televisions, girdles, or rope-soled shoes. They won't get us out of here unless it's feetfirst.

Fermín and Bernarda walked down the aisle in 1958, and they already have four children, all boys and all blessed with their father's nose and ears. Fermín and I see each other less than we used to, although sometimes we still repeat that walk to the breakwater at dawn, where we solve the world's problems. Fermín left his job at the bookshop years ago, and when Isaac Monfort died, he took over from him as the keeper of the Cemetery of Forgotten Books. Perhaps one day someone will find all the copies of Julián's books that Nuria hid there. Isaac is buried next to Nuria in Montjuïc. I often visit them. There are always fresh flowers on Nuria's grave.

My old friend Tomás Aguilar went off to Germany, where he works as an engineer for a firm making industrial machinery, inventing wonders I have never been able to understand. Sometimes we get letters from him, always addressed to Bea. He got married a couple of years ago and has a daughter we have never seen. Although he always sends me his regards, I know I lost him forever years ago. I like to think that life snatches away our childhood friends for no reason, but I don't always believe it.

The neighborhood is much the same, and yet there are days when I feel that a certain brightness is tentatively returning to Barcelona, as if between us all we'd driven it out but it had forgiven us in the end. Don Anacleto left his post in the high school, and now he devotes his time exclusively to erotic poetry and to his jacket blurbs, which are more grandiose than ever. Don Federico Flaviá and Merceditas went off to live together when the watchmaker's mother died. They make a splendid couple, although there is no lack of malicious people who maintain that a leopard cannot change his spots and that, every now and then, Don Federico goes out on a binge, dressed up as a Gypsy queen.

Don Gustavo Barceló closed his bookshop and sold us his stock. He said he was fed up to the back teeth with the bookseller's trade and was looking forward to embarking on new challenges. The first and last of these was the creation of a publishing company dedicated to the rerelease of Julián Carax's works. Volume I, which contained his first three novels (recovered from a set of proofs that had ended up in a furniture warehouse of the Cabestany family), sold 342 copies, many tens of thousands behind that year's best-seller, an illustrated hagiography of El Cordobés, the famous bullfighter. Don Gustavo now devotes his time to traveling around Europe accompanied by distinguished ladies and sending postcards of cathedrals.

His niece Clara married the millionaire banker, but their union lasted barely a year. Her list of suitors is still long, though it dwindles year by year, as does her beauty. Now she lives alone in the apartment in Plaza Real, which she leaves less and less often. There was a time when I used to visit her, more because Bea reminded me of her loneliness and her bad luck than from any desire of my own. With the passing years, I have seen a bitterness grow in her, though she tries to disguise it as irony and detachment. Sometimes I think she is still waiting for that fifteen-year-old Daniel to return to adore her from the shadows. Bea's presence, or that of any other woman, poisons her. The last time I saw her, she was feeling her face for wrinkles. I am told that sometimes she still sees her old music teacher, Adrián Neri, whose symphony is still unfinished and who, it seems, has made a career as a gigolo among the ladies of the Liceo circle, where his bedroom acrobatics have earned him the nickname "The Magic Flute."

THE YEARS WERE NOT KIND TO THE MEMORY OF INSPECTOR FUMERO. Not even those who hated and feared him seem to remember him anymore. Years ago, on Paseo de Gracia, I came across Lieutenant Palacios, who left the police force and now teaches gymnastics at a school in the Bonanova quarter. He told me there is still a commemorative plaque in honor of Fumero in the basement of Central Police Headquarters on Vía Layetana, but a new soft-drinks machine covers it entirely.

As for the Aldaya mansion, it is still there, against all predictions. In the end Mr. Aguilar's estate agency managed to sell it. It was completely restored, and the statues of angels were churned down to gravel to cover the parking lot that takes up what was once the Aldayas' garden. Today it houses an advertising agency dedicated to the creation and promotion of that strange poetry singing the glories of cotton socks, skim milk, and sports cars for jet-setting businessmen. I must confess that one day, giving the most unlikely reasons, I turned up there and asked if I could be shown around the house. The old library where I nearly lost my life is now a boardroom decorated with ad posters of deodorants and detergents possessing magical powers. The room where Bea and I conceived Julián is now the bathroom of the chief executive.

That day, when I returned to the bookshop after visiting the old house, I found a parcel bearing a Paris postmark. It contained a book called *The Angel of Mist,* a novel, by a certain Boris Laurent. I leafed through the pages, inhaling the enchanted scent of promise that comes with all new books, and stopped to read the start of a sentence that caught my eye. I knew immediately who had written it, and I wasn't surprised to return to the first page and find, written in the blue strokes of that pen I had so much adored when I was a child, this dedication:

For my friend Daniel, who gave me back my voice and my pen.
And for Beatriz, who gave us both back our lives.

A YOUNG MAN, ALREADY SHOWING A FEW GRAY HAIRS, WALKS through the streets of a Barcelona trapped beneath ashen skies as dawn pours over Rambla de Santa Mónica in a wreath of liquid copper.

He holds the hand of a ten-year-old boy whose eyes are intoxicated with the mystery of the promise his father made him at dawn, the promise of the Cemetery of Forgotten Books.

"Julián, you mustn't tell anyone what you're about to see today. No one."

"Not even Mommy?" asks the boy in whisper.

His father sighs, taking refuge in the sad smile that has followed him through life.

"Of course you can tell her," he answers. "We have no secrets from her. You can tell her anything."

Soon afterward, like figures made of steam, father and son disappear into the crowd of the Ramblas, their steps lost forever in the shadow of the wind.

A walk in the footsteps of

The

SHADOW

of the

WIND

This walk is designed to give a flavour of the setting for *The Shadow of the Wind,* and can be used as a starting point to explore more of the world of the novel, many of its locations and sceneries. We advise that you also use a proper guidebook to find your way about the streets, as this is purely an outline. Of course many of the places described in the novel, such as the Cemetery of Forgotten Books and the rambling Hospice of Santa Lucía, are inventions, but in wandering the streets of the Gothic quarter or strolling down the Ramblas, you might just catch a glimpse of the city in which Daniel and Fermín pursued their mysterious quarry, where Julián Carax first fell in love and Nuría Monfort met her fate, and perhaps hear the hollow laugh of Laín Coubert . . .

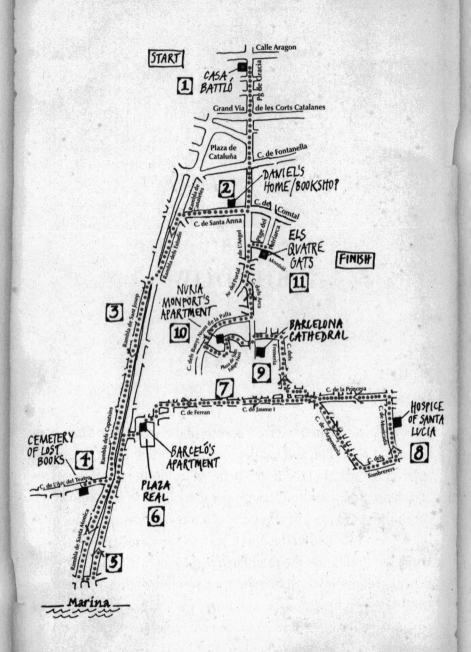

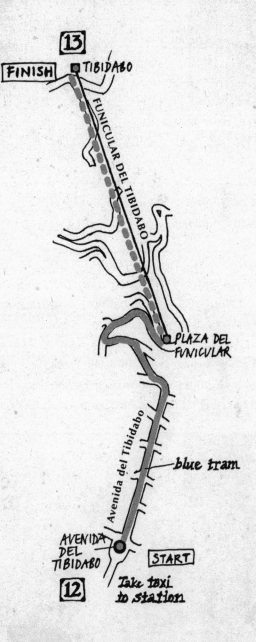

'The skies were electric blue and a crystal breeze carried the cool scent of autumn and the sea.'

1 Beginning on the elegant Paseo de Gràcia, the Casa Batlló is one of the most famous houses designed by Antoni Gaudí i Cornet, and is said to represent the legend of St George, Catalonia's patron saint, and his battle with the dragon.

From here head south and through the Plaza de Cataluña into Puerta del Ángel, where Daniel is first followed by the sinister figure of Laín Coubert.

'The bookshop, a legacy from my grandfather, specialized in rare collectors' editions and secondhand books – an enchanted bazaar, which my father hoped would one day be mine.'

2 Take the first turning right into Calle Santa Ana, the site of the Sempere & Sons bookshop above which Daniel and his father lived. At the end of Calle Santa Ana, turn left into the Ramblas.

'The lamps along the Ramblas marked out an avenue in the early-morning haze as the city awoke, like a watercolour slowly coming to life.'

3 Walk right down the Ramblas – the Rambla dels Estudis with its cages of birds, the Rambla de Sant Josep filled with dozens of flower sellers, La Rambla dels Caputxins, home to the city's Opera House, and finally the Rambla de Santa Mónica at the threshold of the port. Imagine walking here on a misty morning at dawn, as Daniel did on his way to the Cemetery of Forgotten Books.

———◆———

'The brightness of dawn filtered down from balconies and cornices in streaks of slanting light . . . At last my father stopped in front of a large door of carved wood.'

4 On the right, peer in through the archway leading into Calle Arco del Teatro, the narrow alleyway, 'more of a scar than a street', the setting for the mysterious Library, a labyrinth of passageways and crammed bookshelves.

'The stranger turned around and walked off toward the docks, a shape melting into the shadows, cocooned in his hollow laughter.'

5 Back on the Ramblas, walk towards the port and the statue of Columbus, where Daniel is first approached by Laín Coubert as he sits on the steps by the water.

'A golden, dusky light filtered through the glass panes of the gallery, and the languid tones of a piano hovered in the air.'

6 Turning back up Las Ramblas, head towards the Plaza Real, the spectacular square in which Barceló and Clara lived in their palatial apartment. It is also in this square that Daniel first encounters Fermín Romero de Torres, sheltering under the arches.

'A cold, piercing breeze swept the streets, scattering strips of mist in its path. The steely sun snatched copper reflections from the roofs and belfries of the Gothic quarter.'

7 Leave the square by the arch into Calle Ferran, then Jaume I, walking deep into the Gothic quarter with its spectacular old buildings and narrow winding alleyways that lie at the heart of *The Shadow of the Wind.*

———◆———

'A front door of rotted wood let us into a courtyard guarded by gas lamps that flickered above gargoyles and angels, their features disintegrating in the old stone.'

8 The Calle de L'Argenteria takes you to the stunning Iglesia Santa María del Mar. Behind the church is the Calle Moncada, filled with ancient crumbling palaces and secluded courtyards, the inspiration behind the Santa Lucía Hospice where Daniel and Fermín hear the tale of Penélope and Juliàn from Penélope's old nurse, Jacinta Coronada.

9 The Calle de la Princesa leads back to the hub of the Gothic quarter. On the left-hand corner of Calle del Call and Calle Frenería, pause to look in the window of the pen shop – you might find a Montblanc Meisterstück . . . Calle Frenería takes you round the back of Barcelona's towering cathedral on the steps of which the hatter Antoni Fortuny and Sophie Carax first met.

'Plaza de San Felipe Neri is like a small breathing space in the maze of streets that criss-cross the Gothic quarter.'

10 To the side of the cathedral is a tiny alley leading to the Plaza de San Felipe Neri, home of Nuría Monfort.

'Stone dragons guarded a lamplit façade. Inside, voices seemed to echo with shadows of other times. Accountants, dreamers and would-be geniuses shared tables with the spectres of Pablo Picasso, Isaac Albéniz, Federico García Lorca, and Salvador Dalí.'

11 From the square, head back to the front of the cathedral. Off Puerta del Angel you will find Calle Montsió and Els Quatre Gats – Daniel and Fermín's local haunt and an excellent place to stop for lunch.

In the afternoon . . .

'Dawn was breaking, and a purple blade of light cut through the clouds, spraying its hue over the fronts of mansions and the stately homes that bordered Avenida del Tibidabo. A blue tram was crawling lazily uphill in the mist.'

12 Take a taxi to the Avenida del Tibidabo train station, where you can catch the 100-year-old blue tram as it slowly rumbles up Avenida del Tibidabo, 'hugging the shade of trees and peeping over the walls and gardens of castle-like mansions'. Behind one of these rusted wrought-iron gates could be the Angel of the Mist, the haunted Gothic mansion containing the grave of Penélope Aldaya, where Laín Coubert finally confronts his nemesis.

'Recent arrivals complained about noises and banging on the walls at night, sudden putrid smells and freezing draughts that seemed to roam through the house like sentinels. The mansion was a compendium of mysteries.'

13 At the top, take the high-speed funicular railway to the summit of Tibidabo and its spectacular views over the whole of the city.

"The city is a sorceress, you know, Daniel?
It gets under your skin and steals your soul
without you knowing it . . .'

FOR THE BEST IN PAPERBACKS, LOOK FOR THE

In every corner of the world, on every subject under the sun, Penguin represents quality and variety—the very best in publishing today.

For complete information about books available from Penguin—including Penguin Classics and Puffins—and how to order them, write to us at the appropriate address below. Please note that for copyright reasons the selection of books varies from country to country.

In the United States: Please write to *Penguin Group (USA), P.O. Box 12289 Dept. B, Newark, New Jersey 07101-5289* or call 1-800-788-6262.

In the United Kingdom: Please write to *Dept. EP, Penguin Books Ltd, Bath Road, Harmondsworth, West Drayton, Middlesex UB7 0DA.*

In Canada: Please write to *Penguin Books Canada Ltd, 90 Eglinton Avenue East, Suite 700, Toronto, Ontario M4P 2Y3.*

In Australia: Please write to *Penguin Books Australia Ltd, P.O. Box 257, Ringwood, Victoria 3134.*

In New Zealand: Please write to *Penguin Books (NZ) Ltd, Private Bag 102902, North Shore Mail Centre, Auckland 10.*

In India: Please write to *Penguin Books India Pvt Ltd, 11 Panchsheel Shopping Centre, Panchsheel Park, New Delhi 110 017.*

In the Netherlands: Please write to *Penguin Books Netherlands bv, Postbus 3507, NL-1001 AH Amsterdam.*

In Germany: Please write to *Penguin Books Deutschland GmbH, Metzlerstrasse 26, 60594 Frankfurt am Main.*

In Spain: Please write to *Penguin Books S. A., Bravo Murillo 19, 1° B, 28015 Madrid.*

In Italy: Please write to *Penguin Italia s.r.l., Via Benedetto Croce 2, 20094 Corsico, Milano.*

In France: Please write to *Penguin France, Le Carré Wilson, 62 rue Benjamin Baillaud, 31500 Toulouse.*

In Japan: Please write to *Penguin Books Japan Ltd, Kaneko Building, 2-3-25 Koraku, Bunkyo-Ku, Tokyo 112.*

In South Africa: Please write to *Penguin Books South Africa (Pty) Ltd, Private Bag X14, Parkview, 2122 Johannesburg.*